Second Growth

A Novel

Novels by Ruth Moore

The Weir (1943)
Spoonhandle (1946)
The Fire Balloon (1948)
Candlemas Bay (1950)
A Fair Wind Home (1953)
Speak to the Winds (1956)
The Walk Down Main Street (1960)
Second Growth (1962)
The Sea Flower (1965)
The Gold and Silver Hooks (1969)
"Lizzie" and Caroline (1972)
The Dinosaur Bite (1976)
Sarah Walked Over the Mountain (1979)

Collections of Poetry

Cold as a Dog and the Wind Northeast (1958)
Time's Web (1972)
The Tired Apple Tree (1990)

Second Growth

A Novel

RUTH MOORE

ISLANDPORT PRESS

ISLANDPORT PRESS

Islandport Press
P.O. Box 10
Yarmouth, Maine 04096
www.islandportpress.com
info@islandportpress.com

Originally published February 1962 by William Morrow & Co.
Printed 2021

Print ISBN: 978-1-952143-23-6
ebook ISBN: 978-1-952143-32-8
Library of Congress Card Number: 2021935313

The background of this novel is authentic, but I have not described in it any living person, nor would I wish to do so. It would be difficult to write a story about a place so well-known and beloved as the Maine coast without apparent character resemblances; but if anyone feels he recognizes himself or his neighbor in this book, he is mistaken, and such description is only a coincidence.

Dean L. Lunt, Publisher
Teresa Lagrange, Book designer

To any American Town

Table of Contents

Prologue

The old Cooney place was at the edge of town, just off the state highway, a small parcel of seven acres, two of field, five of woodland, enclosed on three sides by a swamp, which had once been the oxbow of a small, clear-running stream. Abandoned in 1907, when the farmhouse burned down, it was of no use to anyone. Charley Cooney's aged outbuildings—backhouse, barn, and shed, left by the fire—were all falling down. Fields and orchard were choked with puckerbrush. The acre or so of old apple trees, unsuckered for generations, bloomed every spring, but brought forth a small and sour crop of pig apples, nothing to compare with the McIntosh and Delicious brought forth by the A and P. Even the farmhouse, by 1907, had not amounted to much, being too old and rotten to be any good. Charles Cooney had lived in it, a lost man, whose wife and children were long dead; and since, without company, and subsisting hand-to-mouth on the odd jobs which sympathetic neighbors award to the poor and the old, he had little use for himself, some might say that the whole establishment might as well end, now that no one remembered or valued what was ending there.

Charley Cooney was too unregarded, the Cornier family too long gone. Family records, of which there had not been many—some old letters, the Bible with its notations in faded handwriting and, in the beginning, in French—had gone up with the house. A few records of land transfers remained in the county courthouse, bearing the name of Cooney; land titles could be cleared there back to 1820 and continued in the archives of Massachusetts to 1761, when Rupert Cornier bought the land—should anyone wish to take the trouble, which no one did. Three generations back was all that was necessary to clear a title if anyone wished to buy. For over half a century, no one wished to buy the few acres left of Rupert Cornier's original eight hundred, from which acre after acre, lot after lot had leaked away like rain water through the hull of a beached ship—as the generations of his family had leaked away, dwindled like the land to near the vanishing point: seven acres, one man. And then did vanish. Were gone.

Rupert Cornier, son of a nobleman's gardener at Crécy, in France, who fought his way to the freedom of a new country; bought a farm there; rid it of Indians as a man rids his land of vermin; set into his new earth by tooth and claw a hold which he must have thought would last forever: Rupert Cornier kept no records. No one knows how he felt about his place, seeing it for the first time, in the new time, after the long journey overland by ox team, or by following the coast north in the small seaworthy ship of his day; whether he came in fog or storm or jingled along down the prevailing southwest wind under a blue and gentle sky. But others took note of what the countryside was like, wrote down and handed on as treasure the tale of sweet rivers and fields of tall marsh grass as gold as wheat, the forests of mighty pines, the growth called virgin, whose ten billion shining needles sang to the sun. Thus Rupert Cornier, unless he was blind in both eyes and horny-hearted, must have taken joy at the end of his journey, when he set down his bales and put foot by the oxbow of the quiet stream.

That he was a worker, a provident and thrifty man, was proved by the cleared land, the fat fields and cattle, the notpretentious but comfortable farmhouse which he handed on to his sons and they to theirs. The dwindling process did not noticeably begin, nor his name become Cooney in his time. The name became Cooney in 1850, when a town clerk in a hurry miswrote it on a land deed; but long before that, the Cornier timberlands were gone. Times change, with economics always imponderable; no man could say where the Cornier dwindling began.

Cynics might say that the shadow of man is a blight over the land; that he is more destructive than the squirrel or the porcupine. After his passage, the trees are gone, the water table down, the streams no longer sweet—a proven fact, they say, by places which flowered once and now do not: the deserts in Egypt; in China, the treeless plain. A man might say that there are many of him, that he has to take or starve; that taking means taking what there is. Yet a mole going through a garden, eating the roots by which the garden lives, could say the same; and no one has ever taught the mole that once the plant dies, there will be no more roots.

The mouse that gnawed the live end of the match in Charley Cooney's woodbox, had a nest, with offspring, in one corner of the box; when the match sparked, the mouse recoiled in horror from the bright rosette of flame, fled headlong into her house, and, with her children, burned. It might be said of her, as of Charley Cooney, that she had behind her a family tree of which no records had been kept, going back to the edge of time; that something ended, too, with her. But a man is more than a mouse; at least, men think so. Both died in the same fire, was all.

Part One
November, 1959

Everard Peterson, on Monday mornings early, made his regular trip to the town dump. Sunday was dump day for most people; setting out for the afternoon's ride to settle dinner, they would shove the week's accumulation of trash into the car trunk and drop it off as they went by, or if a working man had had a clean-up, he had time then to haul his truckload of spoiled hay or old shingles. By Monday morning, the dump would be piled high with everything under the sun. That was the time to find things, before anybody else got around. A couple of others besides Everard made a living, or part of one, junking. So he was always there at the crack of dawn on Monday, poking around, loading his rickety old truck.

Mostly, he salvaged returnable bottles and metal. In the old days, he had done well with bottles, but not now. He complained that the refusal of beer companies to take back their empties had hurt his business. There was only one thing to do with beer bottles now—tip them up and drain the few drops left in them. Sometimes he got to feeling quite good that way.

Besides bottles, there were other things—treasure at times, that people hadn't intended to throw away: a silver spoon in the garbage, money in the mail. Everard could generally tell who had dumped what, where, by names on envelopes and magazines; he informed himself about what was going on in town by what people threw away. He always underran the mail; it was as good as a job in the post office. Nobody cared if you read the letters as well as the postcards, and the whole town worked for you opening envelopes. What was in the letters was sometimes enough to kill a man laughing; and once he had found, in a kind of little pocket stuck to the back of a Christmas card, a crackly new twenty-dollar bill that Ma Paulson's boy, Alfie, had sent home just before he went to Korea. The old gal hadn't noticed it when she'd read the card; so much the better for Everard. That boy, that Alfie, he got killed in Korea. Too bad; he was a nice boy, good to his mother.

Most Monday mornings, when the day's take was totted up, when there were no more piles to pick over and anything that would be of use to him was loaded in his truck, Everard would set the dump on fire. It was against the law; no one was supposed to have outdoor fires without a permit, and the dump was burned officially every so often by the Fire Department; but who cared about that? Everard was always chilly by the time he got through, needed to get warm. He guessed he could take his chances with any law they had a mind to bring up to him; and had, and did, every day of his life. Let them squawk all they wanted to about the dry season, put him in jail if they felt like it. In jail, he got a rest, a good bed, and plenty to eat, which was more than he got at home. Besides, Everard loved to see a big fire. It wasn't often he got a chance to, unless there was a woods fire or somebody's house burned down; then it was great, just to see folks scurry and the pretty flames shooting in to the air. Made him wish, sometimes, that he dared to touch off something big, like the hotel or the Town Hall—that would be worth seeing. The trouble with a man's life was, there wasn't enough excitement to it; you had to make your own.

He certainly would touch her off this morning, he thought, poking around through the heaps; lots of burnable stuff here: spoilt hay, for instance. Nobody kept any stock anymore, cows or horses; in Everard's opinion, too damn lazy to, they'd rather have the milk truck come and get a bill; so the only thing to do with what hay they cut, which wasn't but only around their houses to keep the dead grass down and protect the house in case the field caught afire, was to haul the hay to the town dump. Been a lot of it burnt here this fall; somebody'd been late hauling, though; there were a couple of truckloads left. And those old asphalt shingles, too; they'd burn good, Everard thought; he might as well do it now. He could see, just by glancing around him, that he wasn't going to have any kind of a morning. Nothing here worth lugging off; some days were like that. All he had to show for his trouble was a nice, big, new, white handkerchief, tied like a flag to a stick. Some kid's works. Likely stole one of his pa's good handkerchiefs. Kids, nowadays, never give no thought; steal your pocketbook, like as not, and brag round town about it.

Phew, up to Gertie Warren's they'd certainly had a righteous old week end; must be six gin bottles in that racked-out bushel basket. Well, that wasn't nothing unusual, but if them folks had had any consideration for a man, they'd have stood the bottles right side up, instead of chucking them in all anyhow.

Everard poked the bottles, lifting them out carefully, one by one. Dreened dry, each and all.

Then he stopped, peered, unable to believe his eyes. The one in the bottom was a full bottle, seal unbroken. He lifted it out reverently.

Why, them lushes. Them extravagant lushes. Now, they must've been some old good and howling tight, not to care what they th'owed away. Something ought to be done about them week-end parties up to Gertie's. Gives the town a bad name. If them cops wasn't so busy nosing around my cellar after deer meat, something would be done, too.

Everard broke the seal, unscrewed the metal top, took a cautious sniff.

Hah, that wasn't no bottle of kerosene. Once some joker had rigged a bottle on him and he'd got a mouthful before all to once he'd realized. He threw back his head and upended the bottle.

With his beard whitened by dawn, his shabby long black overcoat buttoned tight against the November chill, Everard looked like a patriarch from a painting—Moses, perhaps, or Joshua standing upon a mound and winding a ram's horn above the sack of a city. The dump itself might well have been the scene of some such human destruction. It had been built in a sightly place where men might once have built a city—a hilltop from which could be seen not-too-distant mountains and a strip of the sea, while back from its foot, almost like a moat, flowed a small, placid stream. The ground for a hundred yards around its base had been bulldozed down to mineral earth, topsoil and trees shoved back to the banks of the stream, a helter-skelter, bristly mass that lay like a fortification or, perhaps, a burial ground, a long barrow, present-day.

If, technically, it was a good place for a medieval city, it was, practically, a good place for a dump. It could be burned without setting the woods on fire, or, if by some mischance it did, there was water in the stream for the Fire Department's pumper; charred remains, bulldozed off at the top, could roll down the hillside and make room for the next batch of end products from the town. In the early morning light, the dump lay like the background of the painting, rich brown in the shadows, with old timbers sticking out, and scattered chunks of weathered wood highlighted at the top, where shards of glass, tin cans, and other assorted metals began to shine, some pinkish, in the rising sun.

From somewhere in the shadow came a sound, and Everard jumped and yanked the bottle away from his mouth.

"Who's that?" he said. "Who hollered at me?"

He glared around.

Why, there wasn't nobody, only an old black crow. Damn thing, setting in that treetop down by the brook. Cawed a couple of times, it was.

You set there a minute, Everard silently told the crow. I got something for you.

Casually whistling, not looking at the crow, he moved toward the truck where he had his rifle.

But the crow was an old hand; he knew well the likes of Everard, who was a great shooter of creatures, large or small. All year round, in season and out, Everard lived on wild meat—deer, ducks, partridge, rabbit; he was a dead shot and liked to keep his hand in, so that anything that swam, flew, crawled, or ran was game for him. The oblivious heron standing on one leg at the water's edge; the beaver swimming about his own business in the marsh; the thrush in the middle of its song: he liked to sneak up and let them have it, a little surprise just from old Everard. He had even been known to blast an aged turtle asleep on the creek bank, to see the giblets fly. At his first movement, the crow dropped, ducking out of sight behind the trees. "Some old smart you think you are," Everard said. "Well, all you got to do is wait."

Four bulgy purple clouds hurried away east; the sun looked like a fried egg that had busted in the pan. The crow had gone, but that cawing noise still seemed to be going on. Maybe it was kids, down in the bushes, mocking old Everard; well, that wouldn't be nothing new. More likely, though, it was noises in his head from the gin. The tide was down some in the bottle. Better save the rest to enjoy when he got his fire going, especially if he was hearing noises this early in the game. He thrust the bottle into his overcoat pocket and set fire to the dump.

The hay smoldered, but crumpled newspapers and cardboard cartons went up with a roar. Asphalt shingles kindled. Bottles began to pop. A nice little breeze, just right to get her going, began to blow fragments, charred and flaming, down into the pulpwood slash across the clearing.

Everard found himself a substantial wooden box, padded it with somebody's old discarded sofa cushion—damp, but not too damp, he concluded, it would warm up. Lowering his stern cautiously onto it, he unbuttoned his overcoat to enjoy the magnificent heat. Felt good, sure was one chilly morning. He set the bottle in an empty gallon fruit-juice can for safekeeping on the ground beside him, and held his rifle across his lap. When she het down into them runs underneath her, the rats was going to start a-going, and he wanted his hands free.

That cawing noise in his head had stopped. He guessed it was all right now to finish the bottle.

He had finished it and had shot two rats before he heard a car grinding in second up the hill. Coming, the way they all did, dammit, right at the peak of the good time. Never got up to the peak in his life, but what some of them norated around. Spoilers they was, one and all. Likely whoever it was would notify the Fire Chief, Jack Riley, and the whole enduring gang of the Fire Department'd come tarryhooting up here. No knowing what they might do, maybe nothing at all, but once, during the dry, it was, they'd taken him down and ducked him in the brook. Lucky for him it *had* been during the dry, not much water there then and he couldn't swim a stroke; but there'd been one or two rains might've raised the level some. He craned his neck, discovered to his surprise that the bulldozed windrow hid the brook from him, and commented aloud, "Land sake, I thought you could always see that crick from here."

Better get over into his truck, get her started. A good thing he'd finished that bottle.

But he couldn't seem to get together, his knees didn't work right. Stiffened up some, setting here.

The car came hustling into the cleared space at the dump top and turned. To Everard, it seemed to spin. Shoot, it was only Doc Garland. He was a nice feller, wouldn't bother nobody; besides he was always in a terrible hurry and he looked to be, now. He yanked a run-over garbage can and some cartons of trash out of the trunk of his car and began heaving their contents on the fire.

"You been saving up," Everard said. "Looks like." A lot of stuff, but nothing ever come out of a doctor's office of interest to a man.

"Yup," Garland said. "Have to, when my wife's a way. No time to go to the dump, and first thing I know my back yard's built up to a public monument. You're at it again, I see," he went on. "Looks real comfortable, too, like you'd set up housekeeping."

Everard grinned. "I seen someone touched her off this morning," he said confidingly. "So I thought I'd just put down here and shoot me some rats."

"Uh huh," the doctor said. "Well, all I can say is, it's a good thing it's rained." He paused, his hand on his car door. "Plastered again, too. Well, you know what I told you last time."

"Why, shoot, Doc," Everard said. "I don't recall ever coming to you for advice, now, did I?"

"You've been lugged into my office a time or two. Or I've had to drop everything and run to you."

"Nope," Everard said. "Don't recall."

"You better recall. I told you. A couple more good binges, the shape you're in, and boom. Curtains."

"Well, now, Doc, you know, I never took serious one word you said. Never had a sick day in m'life. All I got, s'help me, is now'n again a noise in my head. Had it a while ago, cawing noise, kind of. Gone now."

"Well, then, you're lucky. Don't blame me if you pop your string. I'll bet your blood pressure, right now, is up to five hundred." He opened the car door, prepared to get in.

"Now, you know, that makes me kind of mad," Everard said. "Man of my muscles. My hand's as steady's a rock."

Might as well show the fool. Maybe he thought he was a doctor, but no squirt, couldn't be thirty-five if he was a day, was going to tell Ev Peterson his blood pressure was five hundred. A moment ago, he had caught, out of the corner of his eye, a slight movement behind a carton on top of a heap that was just beginning to burn. There was a rat there or his name wasn't Everard Peterson. He snapped up the rifle and let go, and a round hole appeared slap in the middle of the round trademark on the side of the carton.

"Bull's-eye!" Everard said, ejecting the shell.

The only thing was, no rat came from behind the carton, and the noise in his head started up, quite some higher and shriller.

"There, I told ya," he said. "Ain't nothing but a cawing noise in my head. You can hear it yourself."

The effect on the doctor was surprising. He gave a jump as if the bullet had gone into him. He said, "Good God!" and "Hey, cut that out!" and gave Everard a good hard shove. Then he ran, full tilt, right into the fire .

"Godfrey mighty!" Everard said. "Man's gone crazy!"

He had been getting ready to cut down on the carton again, just to show the doc that, drunk or no drunk, he could put another bullet through the same hole, or close to. The shove had knocked the rifle out of his hands, thrown him off balance. He wobbled, and fell off the box.

For a moment he lay there, thinking how comfortable it was to stretch out, before his mind started to work again. He sat up, dimly scrabbling around. Better get his hands on that gun. Take no chances. The doc ever get out of that fire, he was likely as not to come at a man again. Then he saw that the doc had got out already. He was hopping from one foot to the other, slapping at his pants cuffs, which were on fire.

"I got the gun on you," Everard said. "You stay a wagon's length away from me, now." He hadn't, of course. He couldn't even find the gun.

Not that the doc was looking his way. He was kneeling down, slashing with his jackknife at some string around the carton. He'd lugged that thing out of the fire; now he was poking around in it with his bare hands. Damn fool'd get rat-bit. I ain't a-going to be the one to tell him they could be a rat in there.

Everard watched, waiting for the jump and the holler, but none came. All the doc did, he shoved the carton into the front seat of his car and piled in after it, his pants legs still smoking. Everard gazed after the car as it tore down the hill.

Now, them is some old peculiar actions for what is supposed to be an educated man. That's what you get, them new doctors ain't no good; if I'd gone to old Doc Thomas with a noise in my head, he'd of give me a pill for it. I know one thing, I ain't a-going to have him to my blood pressure again, I'll take my business elsewhere.

Dr. Miles Garland was not new in the town, only as newness goes; he had settled down there to practice, with his wife and family, five years ago. In that time, he had thought he'd seen everything; but, back in his office, as he unwrapped the contents of the charred carton, he began to figure that this was probably the payoff, up to now.

The child was a boy, a matter of hours old, a good, strong sturdy one—eight pounds or so, and not a mark on him except for the red bullet burn on his right thigh. Whoever had brought him into the world had known a little something about the process; the job hadn't been professional but it was adequate, and a stout flannel bellyband had been pinned carefully in the proper place. He had been washed, and oiled with something—smelled like cooking oil, the doctor decided, sniffing—and wrapped in a woolen square which looked as though it had been cut from an old blanket. Over this was a new blue baby blanket.

"Blue for a boy," the doctor muttered, through clenched teeth.

He hauled off and gave the carton a solid kick, partly to express his feelings, but mostly to get it out from under his feet; as it upended, a layer of newspapers and two stout red hot-water bottles fell out, still, he discovered, slightly warm.

Well, that's one reason why you aren't a gone coon. Somebody halfway decided to hang onto you and then got cold feet. Or maybe had human feelings enough not to be able to stand the notion of sticking you out with the trash to pass out quick. Thought it would be decenter to prolong it. Ought to have had the courage of his convictions, like the savages. Exposure of infants, that's nothing new. Only we don't have wolves around here, all we got's Everard Peterson. Well, you damn near are a gone coon, or will be unless I can get that smoke out of you.

He worked fast because there was need to, and sweated because he was mad. He was alone in the office, because his wife had taken the kids to Vermont to their grandparents for a vacation; and Lucy Wilkinson, the practical nurse who had helped him, not long ago had had to quit. As he worked, he got madder. This was a helluva fine baby, a fighter, who was working his head off to come back, helping.

"You want to, don't you?" Garland said, watching. "By gum, why? Most people would give up cold, go through what you have. It's too young, it's too damn young to have this happen to you . . . to have to cope with . . ."

The thought choked him; he felt the rage, cold and brassy at the back of his throat.

Human life. You worked your guts out trying to stuff it back into the busted-up bodies it was doing its best to get out of, after you'd spent eight or ten years to learn how. And then along comes some joker who holds it so cheap he chucks it out on a dump like an old can. Well, I won't stand for it; I'll be damned if I . . . Atta boy!

His fingers, dressing the bullet burn, had touched a sore spot. The baby's arms flew up and he kicked Garland's hand; he set up a yell, hoarse and croaky, but surprisingly strong, considering.

"Hopping mad, are you? Well, darned if I wouldn't be in your place. Good. Go ahead, get madder. It's doing us both good."

Fifteen minutes later, he stood back and doubtfully mopped his forehead. The baby was in a basket, warmly covered, with the two hot-water bags, reheated with fresh water. His pulse was stronger. He'd either make it now or he wouldn't. He might; but he'd breathed a lot of smoke. The way it would probably end would be pneumonia.

The place for him, now, was the hospital over in Bishop. But Garland had house calls to make that ought not to wait; somebody would have to take the baby over there, or look after him till Garland was free. Damn it, Min would be gone this week.

Min, his wife, was helping him now in the office when she could. She hadn't wanted to leave, even for a vacation, but what with her own housework and the three kids, she was tired out; he'd persuaded her to go.

Well, better call the District Nurse, Nellie Overholt. She'd have to take over, anyway, if the baby survived. Let her take him to Bishop and telephone the Welfare.

Because if you don't conk out in the next day or so, that's where you're going to end up, young cooky. The Welfare Department. A nice orphanage somewhere, or a foster home. A state boy.

It's a damned shame.

He dialed the District Nurse's number and waited.

People, hundreds of people, be tickled to death to have you, good, strong, healthy kid, if only you were theirs, their own. People the size and shape of human beings, living in a rosy little TV-world, smack 'em once on the chin with reality, half the time what you get's a pack of scared children . . . Damn it to the living hell, where's Nellie?

At the other end of the line, the nurse's number rang and rang.

Finally a child answered it.

"Mama ain't here, she had to go down to Clem's. Mama said to write down whoever it was and she'd come soon 's she could. But she's got to go over to Mertie's when she gets back, one of Mertie's kids swallered a rock . . ."

The earnest falsetto cut off as the doctor hung up.

Now what, blast it? The child that swallowed the rock was probably all right, waiting for a laxative, or Nellie would have been in touch before now. With Clem—Clementina Wilkinson—you never knew. She was old and frail; in the spring, however, she had survived pneumonia, and, according to Nellie, her main trouble now was too much alcohol. Nothing Nellie couldn't handle herself, probably.

But who else? Randall's was working today, which meant that about every able-bodied woman in town was busy packing fish. There was, of course, Lucy Wilkinson, his one-time office nurse; but Lucy's husband, Amos, had forbidden her to have anything further to do with the job. Amos was old Clementina's grandnephew; he seemed to spend a lot of his time forbidding. He forbade Lucy, who was a nurse, to go near or speak to the old lady; his solution to her problem was to commit Clementina to the state asylum.

"Why, good Lord!" Garland had said, astonished, when Amos had requested him to sign committal papers. "That old lady's not crazy, she isn't even senile, though she may be if Nellie can't find out where she's getting her liquor supply. If you wanted to help, you could take her up to your house for a while, let Lucy look after her. Crazy? She's sound as a blueberry."

He had been unprepared for Amos's rage.

"Don't you tell me what I ought to do, you goddam quack! By the god, I'll get another doctor. I'll get Forrest over from Bishop."

"According to law, you need two doctors for a committal," Garland said. "Since she's my patient, they'd very likely consult me, and so would the Town Selectmen. What's the matter with you? You want to kill the old lady? You keep on, I'll begin to wonder who needs treatment."

Since then, Amos had let it be known that he was put out with

Garland; and Lucy had had to give up her job, regretfully, because she had liked it.

So that was that. There was nobody else Garland could think of. This youngster for a while would need somebody who knew what to watch for and what to do. Professional care. Well, I'll have to run him over to the hospital myself. The house calls couldn't wait, but they would have to.

Yup, I will. And I can take those autopsy reports and stuff at the same time.

As County Medical Examiner, Garland had occasionally to perform an autopsy; some of his tests he made in his own small lab, but others, which he wasn't equipped for, he had to have done in the hospital lab at the nearby city of Bishop. The material, wrapped and labeled, was ready to go; he got it from the lab and put it into the back seat of his car.

Better phone the hospital from here, expedite matters, he thought, coming back.

But when he tried to ring through to Bishop, the line was busy. As he lifted the receiver, a querulous female voice said, "I never had nothing else to do this morning, so I washed. And Mama washed, too."

"Well, what did you use?" a second voice said. "Lestoil?"

"Yes, I did, but Mama, you know Mama, she swears by Mr. Clean."

Garland hung up. Fuming, he waited a few moments, then tried again.

"Some say that Handy Andy's awful good—"

Damned old fools, Garland muttered. What'd they think a phone's for?

There was a sudden shocked silence on the line.

"Somebody's listening," the first voice said.

"Somebody wants the line," said the second voice.

"Hnf. Somebody always does. Well, want will be their master. I pay just as big a phone bill as they do. There's a clock ticking, hear it?"

"Hah, I guess I do. I've heard that clock tick over the phone too many times not to know who 'tis, too. The nosy old busybody's going to listen in, she better move her clock away from the phone table—"

Somewhere on the line, a receiver was hung up with an affronted bang.

Garland grinned wryly, shaking his head. Oh, to heck with it, they'd be there now forever, just to show they could, telling how they washed, what with and who for, and how many hours to the half-second it took to hang it out on the line. Better get going.

He checked the baby's pulse again, before leaving, and then stood back, one eyebrow raised, whistling softly between his teeth.

Wouldn't it kill me if you turned out to be okay? If, just this one time, something—

The phone rang.

Blast, it would. What now?

"Dr. Garland speaking," he barked into it. "Who's this? . . . Well, who is it?"

The brief silence contrived to be reproachful, a rebuke, he judged, for his being short over the phone.

"It's me, Doctor," a voice said distantly. "I been trying to get you. Your line's been busy for over an hour."

"Well, I haven't been using it. I haven't had a chance to."

Angie Coons, over at Joe Randall's; he would know that nasal honk anywhere.

"Oh, I know who's been using it. I had to tell them two katydids to get off, I had an emergency."

Oh, Lord, no. Not now. But if it's been going on for over an hour—"What's up? Is it Amy? . . . Well, what is it?"

"I'm sure I don't know, Doctor."

"Is she sick to her stomach? Throwing up?"

"No, she ain't."

"Any pains?"

"She ain't said any."

"Look, Angie, speak up, will you? What is it, then?"

"Well, I ain't a doctor, Dr. Garland."

Oh, blast Angie! He knew well how her mind was working, having had it to deal with before.

If that Dr. Garland can't be civil to folks over the phone, I am not going to tell him one single solitary thing, he can just come over here and see for himself.

He calmed down a little. "Look, Angie, is Amy in bed?"

"Of course she ain't. She's peeling potatoes for dinner."

"I see."

Phew! Garland drew a breath of relief. He had been very concerned about Amy Randall, who, up to now, had had three miscarriages and, with great care and Garland's help, had managed to bring a fourth try up to its seventh month without mishap. It would be a shame if she lost it—it, or them, for he was certain it was going to be twins. Well, Angie was just hollering wolf again; she had been known in the past to lay and light powder trains. She didn't like Amy, and the Lord knew why Joe Randall put up with her, except she was his old cousin and he probably thought he ought to; but it was no wonder his wife had miscarriages.

"Look, Angie—" he began.

"Now you look, Dr. Garland. Amy is not the only one in this house. All this worrying, I've got so's I can't keep my food down, it rises up on me, to the back of my throat."

"What did you eat for breakfast?"

"Nothing to hurt. I had beans. And brown bread with some bacon fat on it and a doughnut and coffee."

"Uh huh. Take some soda."

"That's what *she* said!" Angie's voice rose. "She good and well knows that all sody does is make me burn. It's her fault, anyhow, we have got to go through this mealey again, with all she's had, you'd think she'd be a little mite careful, but all Joe's got to do is hang his pants on the bedpost and she—"

"Okay, Angie," Garland said wearily. "Skip the soda. Sodium bicarbonate is what I mean. I'll drop by sometime today and write you out a prescription for some."

"Oh," Angie said. "Well, when? Do I have to suffer while you—"

"About an hour. On the way back from Bishop."

"Oh. Well, all right, then." She hung up with a mollified click.

Wonderful word, "prescription." Something pretty magic about the sound of that. Well, he only hoped she'd stay smoothed down. Wouldn't hurt, anyway, to drop by Randall's on the way back, have a look at Amy. She'd need it, with Angie on the warpath.

He had better step on it. The baby, now sleeping, had no temperature, but his breathing had a slightly croupy sound. If that was going to amount to anything, it could get worse fast; he might need some oxygen before long.

Garland wrapped a heavy blanket around the basket and ran down the steps to his car. Thank the Lord his old Pontiac had a good heater and that, right now, it was working. As he turned the ignition key, a jet plane broke the sound barrier directly overhead with a bang like the crack of doom, and he snatched his fingers away from the key before he realized that the car hadn't blown up in his face.

Brother! he thought, with irritation. If someone can only make a bigger bang these days, he's happy. A bigger bang that someone can hear, he growled, starting his engine. Because a bang's no good unless someone can hear it, know what a hot-shot you are. Those guys could go south a few miles out over the ocean and bang away to their hearts' content to the fish, but no, they've got to do it over a town.

He grinned suddenly at himself. Hell, do I need a vacation! The older I grow, the worse I get. How do I know, those kids maybe can't help their bangs. Anyway, if I keep on, by the time I'm sixty I'll— and oh, brother! From right now, does sixty look a long ways away!

Weather had warmed up some, he observed, as he rolled down Main Street and took the turn into the state highway leading to town. Going to be a nice, sunny Indian summer day. Like to get out in that sun somewhere and sleep for a week. Somewhere where no one could find me and the phone couldn't ring.

The river, bowling along to the left of the highway, was like a sheet of silk, the current deep and fast now after the rain, not a ripple on it, reflecting bare trees and quiet sky. All summer, a dry season, it had been low, sand and pebble banks out and black rocks, normally underwater, showing. Thank the Lord for that rain. Two weeks ago, old Everard's dump fire, by now, probably would have been well into the trees and slash along the brook, and everybody in town would be wondering how soon to start moving out household goods.

Damned old drunk, Garland muttered. Served him right if I'd chucked that gun into the fire. Wish I had.

Everard was a menace with it. He listened to all the TV shows and half the time wasn't sober enough to make any distinction between himself and Wyatt Earp; as likely to shoot a good guy as a bad guy. Probably, in the end, he would shoot somebody. Still and all, the gun was likely the only link with reality the old sod had, and the only thing he valued in life.

But, God, I hate guns, Garland thought. Any gun.

At this time of year, hunting season, he had reason to; he could count on at least a dozen gunshot wounds to be cleaned up, and one or two violent deaths in the woods, for no reason that any sensible man could see. The autopsy he had just finished had been on a deer hunter, a young fellow of twenty or so, who, stashed in a thicket, had had the misfortune of having to blow his nose, whereupon another hunter, seeing the flick of his white handkerchief through the twigs, had let go at it with a heavy-caliber rifle.

Hell, if you were on the side of keeping blood functioning inside living organisms, you didn't have much use for the blood-must-flow boys. There were so many of them, rooting-tooting-shooting, one and all. How long would you have to go painting civilization on before you got a generation that wasn't preoccupied with the weapons of its time? Not one, yet, that had ever outgrown the clubs, the spears, the bows and arrows, the tanks, the guns, the bombs. King Arthur's knights; the Three Musketeers; Natty Bumppo. Cops and robbers, marshals and outlaws, cowboys and Indians. The smartest guy, the roaring red-eyed hero, the one who could kill the most the fastest, whether it was dragons, ducks, rabbits, deer, or human beings. The whole works of them, cocked back through the ages. Well, you knew what the psychiatrists said about it; but at this stage of progress, it seemed as if a man ought to be able to be a man within himself, without needing a built-on extension . . .

Well, goddammit, *go* by, I'm not hogging the road.

The car behind had been blasting off on its horn for quite a spell, he realized. He glanced up at the rear-view mirror and saw that it was Joe Randall's Cadillac, with Joe at the wheel making frantic gestures to flag him down. As Garland slowed, Joe pulled in ahead of him and stopped so fast that the doctor had to swing out around to keep from plowing into the rear of the Cadillac. As it chanced, no other cars were coming.

"You trying to kill someone?" he demanded as Joe came alongside.

Joe was white-faced and sweating. "What in thunder you doing, Doc, kiting off to Bishop? Angie said she called you."

"She called me about her own bellyache. What's wrong, Joe?"

"All hell's broke loose with Amy. God, Doc, Angie phoned me, I got home, Amy was on the floor and that damn Angie was in the hall closet with a cardboard box over her head. The only sense I could get out of her, she said she'd called you. But then I saw you go by, headed this way and going like a bat out of—Amy's having the baby, Doc, I—" Joe's breath gave out.

"Okay. Don't stand there, move your car, so I can turn around. Look, you hop it down to Clementina's and send Nellie up to the house. Tell her, if the old lady still needs help, to get Lucy Wilkinson. Tell her to step on it."

He made it back to Joe's house in fifteen minutes.

A couple of kids, standing at the foot of the steps, were staring, bug-eyed, at Joe's front door, apparently aware that something of interest was going on. They scattered at Garland's approach and ducked out of sight into the shrubbery. As Garland went in, carrying the blanket-wrapped basket in his arms, he could hear Amy moaning in the downstairs bedroom. The house was faintly chilly—Joe had an oil furnace, but no one had thought to turn it on. Where the hell was the thermostat? He found it beside the living-room door, spun it with his thumb, and thanked God as he heard the gun burner kick on in the basement. He tore through the house to the kitchen, lit all the burners on the gas range, including the oven, and opened the oven door.

"For godsakes, keep pumping," he said under his breath. "I'll be back," and left the basket on a kitchen chair in front of the range, with the blanket draped over the chairback to keep off draughts.

Amy smiled at him gamely as he came through the door.

"It was a jet plane," she said faintly. "It broke the sound barrier right over the house, and Angie let out an awful screech and fell down. I thought for a minute something awful had happened, like the gas blowing up in the kitchen and I ran and stumbled . . . I guess I've killed another one of the poor little mites, haven't I, Doctor?" Slow tears began to trickle down her white face.

"Not on your life!" Garland said. "Just don't forget, you and I are a darned good team. Don't talk, now; concentrate. Atta girl! You're going to be okay. I told you we'd pull it off, and we will."

They did; but it was nip and tuck. For two hours, Garland wasn't sure whether Amy or either of her puny twins would make it. For the worst of the emergency, he was alone with Amy—Angie, if she still wasn't in the closet, was making herself scarce in some other part of the house. It was nearly an hour before Nellie Overholt came stamping in.

"Where in thunder you been?" Garland snapped at her, over his shoulder.

"Where d'*you* think?" Nellie wasn't the sort who took from anyone, even the doctor. "Clem's. And Mert's kid swallowed a rock. And someone said Amos Wilkinson was sick. I was headed over there to see if I could help Lucy out when I heard Joe Randall was hunting me. Poor Joe, I guess he still is. Huh! It *was* twins, wasn't it?"

Nellie knew her business too well to expect comment. She took over her share of the proceedings expertly and in silence.

She had the twins attended to and warmly wrapped in their bassinets—they were tiny, but they were living—and Amy was just beginning to come out of the fog when Nellie had occasion to go to the kitchen. She came back looking flabbergasted.

"My lord, Doc, you didn't tell me it was triplets. And, brother!

Did that one in the kitchen get all the cream!"

"Huh?" the doctor said, coming out of his absorption. "What? Oh, hell! Shut up, will you, Nellie?"

For at that moment, Amy Randall had opened her eyes.

"Oh, thank God!" she said in a raspy whisper. "It's God's blessing . . . it makes up for the three I lost . . . Oh, thank you, God!"

"Good girl, Amy," Garland said. "You did okay. It's all right, now go to sleep."

Cursing silently, he got to his feet. "Take over, Nellie," he said. "She's all right, but I'll be back."

He heard the crooning as he went through the kitchen door.

". . . Auntie's God-lovingest sweet little soul, the boofulest, best, cunningest, 'ittle baby-boo Aunt Angie ever saw—"

In the kitchen, Angie sat in front of the open oven. She had the baby out of the basket and on her lap, and over her hung Joe Randall, his chest out, his hands in his pockets, the proudest, cockiest father that ever begot a son.

"What in thunder do you two think you're doing?" Garland said. He gave a bound, landing at Angie's side, hauling out his stethoscope.

"We're a-looking at Joe's boy," Angie said, eyeing him. "I guess us in the family's got a right to, ain't we?"

Joe said, "By gum, Doc, three times Amy and I's tried, three accidents, and this is the first baby we ever got through, and by the god, if he don't look like me, only where in hell'd he ever get red hair? Ain't he a heller, though! What's that, Doc? He ain't got anything the matter with him, has he?" He stood, anxiously watching the stethoscope, the thermometer.

"Um-m," Garland said.

After a moment, he sat back on his heels. The baby was warm as toast, no croup, no congestion, no fever. No nothing. Whether it had been Garland's emergency treatment, or the heat from the oven acting on a basically healthy organism; or whether it was what the medical profession all over was now saying was the best thing there was for any baby—T. L. C., tender loving care—well, didn't matter.

Right now, this was as healthy a young male as Garland had ever seen.

"No," he said in a dazed voice. "He's okay. Nothing the matter with him."

He got up and walked over to the window, trying to think.

God, he was bushed. His mind wouldn't even begin to tick over.

I said he didn't have any luck, and by God, he didn't, the whole works aimed right at him. And then, events clicking together, balls into sockets, all headed toward reversing the process. It was as if fate, circumstance, the devil with a ring in his tail, whatever you cared to call the force that had started out to raise this particular hell, had changed its mind. Everard Peterson didn't know; nobody here knew. Not Joe, who, obviously, had just come in; not Angie, creeping fearfully out of the closet and swooping down on the basket in the kitchen. Angie's mind had room for only one thing at a time. "Baby," it had said to her, "Amy's having a baby." And here was the baby, what else? Not Amy, who thought it was the hand of God, and not Nellie—she, of all people, should have smelled a rat, and she had swallowed it down, hook, line, and sinker.

Only me. I know.

And in a minute he would have to find the courage to tell them that this wasn't their baby; theirs were a couple of gasping mites that might make it and might not—not this strong fellow, this fighter.

"Whoops!" Angie said. "For heaven's sake! Doctor, this baby's burped up Pablum. Now, how could he burp up Pablum?"

Joe snorted. "Pablum! Angie, you darned old fool! Kid's just been born!"

"I swear it's Pablum," Angie said.

"Well, wipe if off his chin, can't you?" Joe said; and when she did not move fast enough to suit him, he took the cloth away from her and did it himself.

The doctor, his courage found at last, turned to say what he had to say, and saw Joe's hand, the big, blunt, brown fingers clutching the crumpled cloth as if it had been a wad of cotton waste—the small mouth, the chin, some part of an engine, a carburetor, perhaps, from which excess grease had to be wiped away—dabbing, dabbing, the awkward masculine movements ungentle without meaning to be; and the force, the ring-tailed devil, the father of particular hell which had changed its mind because it was sorry or because it had decided that fun was fun, the joke had gone far enough, really showed its hand, reversed the process in Garland and made him compound a felony.

He walked back to the three at the open oven and stood watching for a moment. The vomited stuff was not baby food, he knew, but a potent formula from his medicine cabinet; some of it was what had probably turned the trick, unless you believed in miracles.

"Shoot, Angie," he said. "A woman of your experience ought to know better."

He grinned, felt the strained muscles of his face, his whole body, go limp with relief. If the twins didn't make it, Amy and Joe would have this one; and if they did, why, hell, if anybody in town could afford triplets, it was Joe Randall.

"Why, Angie," he said. "You know yourself that sometimes in childbirth the hyperbole glands get involved with the trichinosis, and that causes a slight spasm of the pandanus vehicle, so the baby throws up a milky substance that looks like Pablum. But isn't. Come on, Joe, his mother wants to see him. And you. You haven't seen the other two yet, have you?"

Joe's mouth opened; or it was more as if the whole lower part of his jaw dropped down with an audible click. He said, "The other . . . *two?*"

"You're a lucky guy, Joe. You've got Amy—for a while, there, I wasn't too sure you would have. And you've got triplets. All boys."

"Jesus Henry Christ!" Joe said. He started toward the bedroom, walking stiffly, like a man in his sleep.

From the bed, Amy said, "Oh, Joe, look what I've done to you!" and Joe said, "You done good, old girl. You done darned good," standing looking, dazed, from her to the baby which Garland had laid beside her, to the two wrapped shapes in the bassinets.

"One, Two, and Three," he murmured blankly. "Noodle, poodle, and sky-doodle. Mince pie, apple pie, and doughnuts. Funny, Money, and Montgomery."

Watching him, Amy giggled. "No, sir!" she said. "Call them anything—One, Two, and Three if you want to, but we are not going to name anybody for my horrible old grandfather!"

"Look like him," Joe said. He had lifted a corner of blanket in one of the bassinets, and hastily dropped it back. "A dead ringer for old Funny-Money when he was eighty-five . . ." He turned back to the bed. "How is it now, you feel okay? Amy . . . old Amy."

Later, getting ready to leave the house, whose invalids, now relaxed or sleeping, he judged Nellie could take care of unless something unforeseen happened, Garland faced up to what he had done and found he was not sorry. Barefaced liar that he was, he had no conscience in the matter now, only concern that he might not have covered his tracks. The baby had belonged to someone, either in this town or some town nearby. Whoever it was had lost title. You might be sorry for someone, if you knew who, if you knew the circumstances—someone so crazed by rage or shame, desperation or despair, that he could bring himself to leave a live baby on a dump, to rats, to cold, to fire.

But I guess the only ones I'm really sorry for now are those other two, Funny and Money, Joe's twins. Because unless I miss my guess, Montgomery's going to take over.

He picked up the basket he had brought the baby in, glanced into it. If anybody noticed two strange hot-water bags, a strange blanket, he'd be up the crick without a paddle. Too late now; he was committed.

I'm the only doctor who ever lived, he told himself with a wry grin, who really did bring the baby in his little black bag; or something.

He shoved the basket under his arm and left the house.

One of the children who had been playing by the steps when he'd arrived was still around, not playing now, though; she was squatting in the hedge, staring out at him with round, unwinking eyes.

One of Nellie's kids, he realized absently, and said, "Hi. Your mother's going to be busy for a long time yet; you better trot home."

To his surprise, she made a face at him, pulling the corners of her mouth down with a thumb and forefinger and running her tongue out as far as she could.

"Hey!" Garland said. "What's that about? You look like a rubber monkey."

"Yah!" the child said. "Yah, yah, yah!" She ducked into the bushes, calling back a name that raised the hair on the back of his neck.

Phew! What's she so put out with me for? Nellie ought to put a tin ear on her for talk like that.

Sometimes before, now that he thought of it, he'd seen this one—what was her name? Becky—hanging around outside houses where he and Nellie had been tending the sick.

Little ghoul, he thought irritably. I'll tell Nellie to put a stop to it; and then, shoot, what's the matter with me, poor kid's probably only waiting around for her mother.

For Becky Overholt, aged ten, that day had begun without anything to recommend it. Sitting up in bed and craning toward the window, she saw that the sunrise was four sloppy purple clouds, like one of Kate's crumby paintings. The pasture pond was flat and shiny, a tin-can lid tinted mauve. Hoping against hope, she thought, at first, it might be frozen, but even as she looked, a muskrat swam across it, making two glassy, darker-mauve rolls of water that fanned out in a V from his small, dark head.

A day like yesterday. A day of broken promises; for last night there had been a cloud bank low down in the sunset and the TV forecast had said it was going to snow.

So be poison, she told the weather. Don't freeze ice and don't snow snow. I have got better things to do than go sliding *or* skating.

But, what was there? Still two days of Thanksgiving vacation to go, so no school. Mama would be gone all day, as usual; that could mean being stuck with the telephone and with Henry, because during vacations Mama didn't pay a babysitter, she figured Kate and Becky could do it.

Well. Today it is not going to be Becky. Becky has got other fish to fry.

But, what fish?

No going to the playhouse in the woods, because the woods back of the house where the playhouse was was full of a mess of men making a gravel pit. They hollered at you the minute they saw you.

"You kids beat it! Gwan, take off, or I'll glom you!"

That old Amos Wilkinson. And Mack Jensen—he had better not let Jody Morelli's mother catch up with him.

At first, when the crew had come with bulldozers and trucks, all the kids had thought it was going to be exciting: something going on every minute. They could go and watch the bulldozers push the big trees down. But the day Becky and Jody Morelli, with Henry trailing, had walked partway up the old woods road, everything had been awful. There were men all over the place, hollering dirty things, and getting madder than hornets when they found that kids were around and had heard them. The playhouse was gone forever, buried under hundreds of trees that had been pushed down right into the brook, roots and all, and shoved together in a great, tangly pile. And Mack Jensen, the foreman, said there was a bear under there waiting to catch kids, and when that didn't scare them off, he called Jody over and gave him a drink out of a bottle, laughing his head off, because Jody ran and ran and turned summersets and then had to throw up. Big joke. Big deal. Sometime soon, old Mister Mack Jensen was going to be awful sorry; all he had to do was wait.

Well, what she would do this morning, she would go over to Jody's and get some breakfast out of old Elena Morelli, Jody's mother, and then watch their TV. They had a great big one, and that program about the man with white gloves on that choked little girls in the park was on today .

From the next bed, Kate said sleepily, "Did it snow?"

Becky froze, still as a mouse, waiting. Old Misslady Kate *would* wake up early, clobber everything. But after a moment, Kate mumbled, "Um-mmm," and went back to sleep.

Um-mmm to you, too. What do you care? If it snows, you'll go sliding. If it freezes, you'll go skating. If it doesn't, you sit down happy and paint another picture. Water-andgulls, sky-and-clouds. Birches-by-the-pond-with-cow. *Be* twelve years old, see if I care.

Downstairs the back door closed; brisk steps clicked away down the walk. Mama, going to work. So that was that.

No good sticking around home all day to be bossed by old Kate, just because she was the biggest. So get cracking.

Becky jumped out of bed, but at the light bump of her feet on the floor, Henry turned over in his crib. She reached stealthily for her clothes, began quietly to dress. Her plans today included no part of Henry, who had no business being in this room, the girls' room, anyway.

Henry was two; except for vacations, when the babysitter didn't come, he always slept in Mama's room; but now that Becky and Kate were the babysitters, and in case he woke up early to find Mama gone, his crib had been moved in here. He snorkled in his sleep, and if he woke up and felt lonesome, he would paddle over into Becky's bed. Oh, not Kate's; never Kate's. Because Kate didn't care, she would just shove over, not even wake up, and make room. But Henry liked people to know he had come. He loved to snuggle. No matter how Becky turned and twisted, Henry's round, warm, stubborn bottom would come searching until it found the place where it fitted, her stomach.

Snaking the comb through her hair, Becky yanked out a snangle wabbed up around a burdock. She was pulling it out of the comb when, from Henry's crib, came a gurgle, then a yell, of laughter. He was standing, one hand pointing at the snangle, the other keeping him from falling backwards in the crib. He said, "Mouse!" and roared, peal after peal, his eyes creased shut in his fat cheeks.

"S-s-shut up!" Becky hissed. "You'll wake up Sister!" With a bound, she was by the cribside, her hand over his mouth. But Henry wriggled free; he hugged both arms around her neck and planted a fat, wet kiss on her cheek.

Downstairs in the hall, the telephone started to ring.

Oh, that was the way it was, always something. That darned old phone, someone always calling, wanting Mama, someone always sick.

And if I don't answer it, it'll wake up Kate and I'll be stuck here all day, because she's bigger . . .

She snatched Henry out of his crib.

"You want to play a game, Henry? Want to have some fun, play a trick on Sister?" she whispered.

"Sure," Henry said. He had waked up feeling like a million; he was ready for anything.

"Well, I have to answer the phone. When you hear me, you go over, creep, creep, like a mouse and grab Sister by the nose and give it a good hard pull—like this, see, only hard, real hard; and you holler, 'Wake up, quick, Sister, the house is afire!' Okay? You got it? You see?"

Henry saw, but he was doubtful, having had the quick getaway played on him before.

"And I'll wait downstairs to hear her holler," Becky said, "and then we'll both laugh—"

She vanished into the hall, leaving him wondering.

"Oh, shut up!" she told the telephone, hurrying to answer it. For a cent she wouldn't even take the receiver off the hook. Begin, and, who knew what, there'd be no end to what people would ask you to do. Run all over town and find Mama was the least of it; they thought they owned your life, just because your mother was the District Nurse. But you had to answer the phone; Mama always found out when you didn't and then there was Hell to Pay; besides, it might be Dr. Garland. She always left a note saying where she was, in case he called.

It was Dr. Garland. He was in a hurry. When she told him that Mama was down to Clem Wilkinson's, he swore, just before he hung up. Hnf, swearing in front of children. A grown man.

Now, what was he in such a hurry for? Who was sick? Maybe old Miss Amy Randall was going to have her baby; or no, it wasn't time yet, Mama had said to Aunt Gert the other night; or maybe something had gone wrong. Mama had said that, too, that something might.

That would be a thing to do today, too, because if you watched Dr. Garland or walked around town until you saw his car stopped outside a house, a lots of times you found that what was going on there was very exciting indeed.

From upstairs came a shrill yawp as Kate got her nose pulled; Becky did not wait for developments. She ducked out of the back door into the bushes.

Jody Morelli was having breakfast with his parents, who did not look pleased to see Becky come in through their door so early in the morning. Jody's father, Tony Morelli, looked up from a plate loaded with pancakes and sausage and rolled his eyes at his wife.

"She don't ever go to bed," he said heavily. "Vacation. Two days more, God."

Elena shook her head at him, making a *shush* movement with her mouth. "Good-a morning, Rebecca," she said. "Your Mama she's-a gone out already? Somebody is sick so early?"

Becky nodded, not taking her eyes off the toppling pile of pancakes on a plate in the warming oven. "That old Clem Wilkinson's drunk again," she said. "Mama always has to go."

"Oh-h," Elena said. "The poor lady! Again, Tony! Is a shame, no?" She meant poor Miss Wilkinson, but Becky took the opening in stride, neatly. "Poor Mama's so tired. We don't scarcely ever see her. She don't even have time to get our breakfast."

"I betcha my life," Tony said. "Well, you are crippled? You cannot cook-a the breakfast? Bigga the girl, like you?"

"Tch, no, Tony!" Elena shook her head at him again. "A child, hungry, in our house? I die of shame!"

Tony sighed. "You live-a the long time already," he said. He burped slightly, pulled out his handkerchief, blew his nose with a prolonged toot and broke into explosive Italian. The tenor of his talk was that this kid was a tough little nut, that she ran wild through the neighborhood battening on handouts and getting respectable kids into trouble; and if she didn't stop running Jody, he, Tony, was going to call the state cops and the Reform School—he broke off, seeing that his wife was merely looking at him, smiling. "Well, bring-a the chair ," he said. "What is keeping you? Put under the table the feet, God. We have enough."

He pushed back his chair, got up, and picked up his hat. "I go. Jody! Once more the scrape. Is all. No bike. You get it?"

"Sure, Pa." Jody lifted innocent round eyes at his father. "Beck and I's just going to play."

"I betcha!" Tony said. He moaned slightly, looking at Becky, who, needing no second invitation, was digging into a stack of pancakes, over which she had dumped lavishly the entire contents of the maple-syrup pitcher. "Eat, God!" he said. "Well, what for supper, Elena? The loaves and the fishes?"

Elena lifted her face for his good-bye kiss. "Haddock in wine sauce, for cross old man," she said. "You bring, I cook. Go now, Tony. I take care these scarum-harums."

He went, still muttering, calling back just before he closed the door, "They get you down, you call me."

"I will. I'm fine today, Tony."

Becky said, through a mouthful, "My, he's ugly, ain't he?"

"No, he is not," Elena said briskly. "He is nice. He's bark worse than bite. If Jody is spanked, I do, not the papa, eh, Jody?"

"Uh huh."

Jody was a skinny little boy, with black eyes and curls and creamy skin like his mother's, three years younger than Beck. He was not inclined toward scrapes and troubles unless he were in her company. This vacation, for some reason known only to her, she had taken him up, and there had been incidents which Jody's parents did not care to have repeated. The windows in Mr. Wickham's chicken house, for example: you might have expected Jody to break one by accident; but to smash out the whole bank of windows, forty of them, along the front of the building, with rocks thrown on purpose—how could you believe this of two small children?

Tony, of course, had paid all since he was a man, the town butcher, and Elena had a job at Randall's—the Morellis more prosperous, of course, than Nellie Overholt, a woman alone, with three children. Elena had had to spank Jody, a thing she seldom did because, left alone, he seldom needed it; but in spite of Tony, she would not forbid

Becky the house. Elena loved children; and this one was untended and rackety; a little mothering might do wonders. But since the day Becky had got Jody mixed up with the gravel-pit crew and he had come home sick from having been given gin, Elena was beginning to wonder. She was concerned; and Tony was beginning to cut up very much, because their new baby was due soon and he did not think she should have this worry on her mind.

"Is better not to eat so much so fast, Rebecca," Elena said. "Makes the stomach-aches, no?"

"She's bet me she can eat twenty-five pancakes," Jody said, turning fascinated eyes on his mother. "I bet her she can't."

"Well, I could," Becky said. "I could if I had some more syrup. I can't be expected to eat twenty-five pancakes *dry*." She turned to Elena an expectant face, smeared halfway to the eyes, and with the mouth hanging open. "You got any more syrup?"

Elena was long over her period of morning sickness, but in the early days of her pregnancy it had been very bad, and sometimes, even now, in mornings, a suggestion would recall how it had been. In Becky's mouth, a wad of half-chewed pancake lay idle on a small, pink tongue.

Elena said, "Oo-oh," and turned pale.

Jody remembered, too. "You sick, Ma? You going to throw up?" He stared, fascinated, at his mother. "She throws up, sometimes in the morning," he went on importantly, by way of enlightenment to Becky. "She used to all the time."

Becky stared, too. She smiled wisely. Not for nothing was she the District Nurse's daughter. "Hah!" she said. "A-hahhah-*hah*!"

"Phooey, Jody, I am not sick, I am all over," Elena said with firmness. "But Becky will be, if she eats so much-a pancake. I am sorry, the syrup is all gone, fff-t, kaput! So you go play now."

"Okay," Becky said. "Sure, if you're all out. That's okay."

She looked around the table, saw that she had cleaned up everything edible except the sugar and the butter, and meditatively took a spoonful of butter, which she dipped into the sugarbowl, turning it around and around. Holding this morsel poised for a moment while she admired the magnificent coating of sugar, she said delicately, "You are going to have a baby, I expect," and popped it into her mouth.

It was to Elena's credit that, confronted with two emergencies, either of which might prove embarrassing in a moment, she was able to manage the matter with a smile. Swallowing hard, she said, "Why, yes, Becky. Jody knows there is to be a baby in this house."

"Uh huh," Jody said, beaming. "The doctor's going to bring me a brother in his little black bag."

"A-hah!" Becky said. "A-hah, ahah!"

"Oh, God is love!" Elena said in a choked voice. "Go and play— the sandpile—the swing. *Anyssing!* Only, go, go, go!"

"Dope," Becky said. "Dopey, dopey, dope, dope. The Seventh Dwarf."

Jody said, "Who's a *dope?*"

Laboring after her as they crossed the swale in back of his father's house, Jody was out of breath. He was worried about his shoes, which were nearly new; he was worried about where they were going, because he had strict orders not to go near the river. But if you wanted to be with Becky, you had to go where she went. And Jody dearly wanted to; something had happened to him this vacation; he did not know what it was. He was not normally bad or a trouble to his parents; he only knew that he had to be where Becky was, do what she did; that without her, life lost its flavor, nothing was any fun. When she didn't answer him, he said again, "Well, who is a dope?"

"You are. Look, can you stand on your hands? I can."

Thrusting her hands into the marsh grass, she upended her skinny, dungareed legs, balanced triumphantly a moment, and then began to wobble as the swale sank under her weight. Just before she flopped sideways into the mud, she jackknifed down and bounced to her feet. "Can you do that?"

Jody looked at the mud. "No," he said. "I can't."

"Chicken!"

They went along.

"Beck, Mama said not to go near the river."

"Who's going to the river?"

"But we are. We're almost there."

"The riverbank," Beck said, "is not the river. She's a dope, too."

"Who is?"

"Little black bag! Oh, merciful go! A-hah, hah, hah!"

"Yeah, well, sure. Mama said—"

"Little black bag! Hoo!"

Jody prepared to be patient. Sometimes she was nice, sometimes she was awful to him. He mumbled, "Well, Mama told me, is all I know. Don't you believe what your mother tells you?"

Becky made no answer. She went along.

Jody was really in no doubt. Mama had said. Kids' talk about babies was foolish; nobody said two things alike. One kid said you found them in the pasture under a rotten stump; and another kid said that a big bird flew over with a baby in a diaper and dropped it down the chimney—he had a picture book to prove it. It all seemed pretty farfetched to Jody. The only birds around like that were cranes and herons and they never had a baby pinned in a diaper.

"Oh, crapiola! Crapiola all day long," Becky sang, to some tune she knew. She spun around suddenly and faced him. "What'd you think they got that tankful of guppies in the fourth-grade room *for*?" she demanded.

"Well, to look at," Jody said. He recoiled a little; you never could be sure what she might do. She might hit you if you argued.

"Yah, to look at! And we saw our cat have kittens, didn't we?"

"Yes, but—"

He didn't often stand up to her, but he had asked his mother and he knew for sure. Doctors brought babies. When you were ready for a baby the doctor came; when he left, the baby was there. He said sturdily, "People is different."

Becky's eyes narrowed. Jody was not supposed to argue; he was supposed to listen. "A baby," she said, "grows inside of its mother."

They had come out on top of the riverbank, and she picked up a stick which she shied down into the silky, fast-running water. "And then pops out of her belly button," she said.

"You're talking nasty," Jody said. Embarrassed, he looked around for a stick of his own, sent it flying into the water. "Hoo! See that old stick go!"

"Your mother," Becky said. "She probably believes in Santa Claus, too."

She did. So did Jody. He saw no reason not to. He said under his breath, "You're mean. You stink."

"What did you say?"

"Nothing."

"You called me a name. Okay."

"No, I didn't. Honest, I didn't."

She either hit you or she went off, if you talked back. Jody closed his eyes and waited, hoping she would hit him and not go; but when he opened them, she was already moving off down the riverbank.

She said, not turning around, "I forgot. I told my Aunt Gert I would come over there this morning. She is going to read to me out of her new *True Romances*."

The light was going out of the day; Jody found another stick, which he threw listlessly into the river. Tears came into his eyes and ran over.

On the highway, across the river, a few cars were going along. He watched without interest. What to do now? With a whole day?

One of the cars suddenly burst into a series of loud honks, then pulled out around the car ahead of it and stopped. That was old Joe Randall's Cadillac, anybody could tell it a mile away. He was chasing somebody. Old Doc Garland. I don't care if he is. Let him chase everybody, all day long, if he wants to. Now I have got to go home and Mama will be mad about these shoes.

Becky came flying back along the riverbank. "C'mon!" she yapped, passing him on a dead run.

"Where to?"

She didn't stop.

He panted after her, running as fast as he could. They didn't cross the swale this time; they went around it. Becky took a shortcut on a path through the woods. She came out in a field, crossed a couple of back yards, jumping the fences, and came to light on Joe Randall's front doorstep. Jody made it a minute later. The best he could do, he had fallen some ways behind.

"Now you'll get told!" she said, breathing hard in his ear as he dropped on the step beside her. "Now you'll see, Mr. Dopey!"

Jody's eyes were bulging from the run. His mouth hung open. He didn't have the breath to ask, "Show me what?" but she went on anyway.

"Something has happened to old Miss Amy Randall and she is going to have her baby. I know. I heard Mama tell Aunt Gert that Something might happen. Now, Mr. Dopeychicken Jody, you'll see with your own two eyes. Dr. Garland is coming, and his little black bag ain't big enough even for a Teddy bear, all is in it is bottles. S-s-so!"

Jody was totally bewildered now. He said in a faint voice that he guessed everything was all screwed up. They waited.

Sure enough, there was the doctor's car. He stopped, got out, and opened the right-hand door.

"Now he's getting his bag. You take one good look, Mister, and you tell me if—" Beck's hiss wheezed into silence; her jaw dropped slightly.

For while Dr. Garland had in one hand his little black bag, which did indeed look too small for anything but a Teddy bear, on his other arm, clasped tightly against his chest, was a basket wrapped in a blanket.

He hustled up the walk, giving them a hard look as he went by, and Beck put for the shrubbery. She knew from previous encounters that he wasn't one to be fooled with.

"He's got it!" Jody said at her heels. "That basket's big enough, Beck, he's got it in a basket. Beck? Did you see?"

Oh, this was great, this was wonderful, the doctor coming, really bringing the baby, and you there to see! This was the way it would be at home, soon, when the new brother, when Mama said . . . Jody took a couple of dance steps, bouncing up and down. "Oh, Beck, isn't it fun, look—" he began all over again; and found himself confronted with a face of fury, two eyes narrowed to slits.

"That was stuff!" Beck said. She shook him, one hand hard and bony as a claw on his arm. "Stuff he needs, medicine and that. You come along with me!"

Still holding his arm, she yanked him around the corner to the shed. At the door Jody hung back. You weren't supposed to go into people's houses unless the people told you to, Mama had said. But Beck was going in through the shed to the kitchen and he couldn't dig his heels in hard enough. She said, "Stop that!" so he went along, and stood shaking in his soggy shoes while she eased the kitchen door open a slit and peered through. Someone was lighting the gas in the kitchen, you could hear the little pops.

"Ssh," she said. "Now. He's gone. You creep in there and take a look in that basket. You'll see *medicine*."

"I don't want to," Jody said. He peeked fearfully under Beck's arm and saw the basket on a chair in front of the range. Somewhere he could hear Dr. Garland talking to old Miss Amy Randall, too close for comfort.

"You going?" Beck said. "I'll cut your ears off, then. And feed them to the rooster. Go *wan*, like I say."

Jody went. He tiptoed across the kitchen floor and looked into the basket. There was a blue blanket, wrapped around. He put out a finger and touched the blanket and felt a warm and a moving, and lifted a loose corner that lay over. And there it was.

A smile of pure pleasure spread across Jody's face. He put both hands on his knees, bending down. Little silky red hair. Little fingernails. He began to chuckle and then to laugh, unable to stop.

"Sss-t!" Beck was across the floor in a couple of jumps. "Get out of here, quick! You want them to—" Her voice died; she, too, stood looking into the basket.

"Like I told you," Jody said. "Didn't I? Ain't he nice, Beck? You think he's a brother?" Entranced, he could not take his eyes off the baby.

"Liars!" Beck said. "A pack of big, fat liars, the whole works of them!"

"And lied to you about Santa Claus, too, I'll bet!" Jody said, in sympathy. "That's awful," and glanced up at her face.

He began uncertainly to back away; halfway across the kitchen, he took to his heels and put for home as fast as his legs could carry him.

Joe Randall, most people would have said without a second thought, was better able than most Hillville men to afford triplets; if the town had a leading citizen, he was it. He and his wife Amy were the sole owners of the Randall Packing Company, an inherited family business begun by their great-grandfathers, who had made money in the days when Hillville had been a boom town. The original J. J. Randall and Paul Montgomery had started out with a modest plant for the processing of dried cod, which was a thriving coast industry then and the only one of all Hillville's industries which had been able to survive by changing its product to meet the demands of changing times.

Hillville had had lumber once, and lumber mills and shipyards, and a river made to order for floating logs down from the back country. But the last log had come down the river outside the memory of any man living; a man now would have to know where to look to find even a foundation stone where the big yards and mills had been. And the only signs of lumbering were those left by the pulpwood crews rummaging through the second- and third-growth stands of trees for a stick big enough to cut down.

Hillville had had granite quarries, but nobody built stone buildings anymore. It had once shipped cut stone, lumber, and ice from its river halfway round the world in its own vessels; it had sent to market schooner loads of salt fish and dried beans. The sandy, gravelly fields where the Ice Age glaciers had dumped raised fine beans; but the market for beans, too, had followed the market for ice and stone into the graveyard of the sailing ships. Modern progress had washed over Hillville like a rising tide over a reef; so far as the townspeople were concerned, it was nearly high tide now.

No one, from the look of it, could have called the area distressed.

It had a "shacktown" of course, but that was "out back," between the town and a swampy area five miles wide, called Cooney's Heath—*Hayth*, according to local pronunciation. But the big houses along Main and Prospect Streets looked much as they had in the prosperous early days, shingled and in repair, and all with neat coats of paint, and the mortgages, of course, didn't show. Even in Shacktown, people had cars and television sets; their kids had bikes. They went all out for Mother's Day and Christmas. But this plenty was almost without exception on credit. A man whose grandfather would have been uneasy at the thought of a bill for five dollars outstanding, would have to use this summer's pay to meet last winter's bills; this year's Christmas might roll around before last year's Christmas presents were paid for. Most families scraped through the winter on unemployment checks; grocery stores carried them until work season. The town's economy merely was hind side to. Instead of being pushed in front to a place where it might have amounted to something, it dragged behind like a bagful of hammers.

Nobody was easy about this state of affairs. The community had behind it a long tradition of use-it-up, wear-it-out, make-it-do; enough of the ironclad thrift of former generations still hung like a whiff of guilt in the corners of old houses to take some of the pleasure out of the new icebox or the new car. About the only consolation a man had was the reassurance that this was the custom; everybody did it. And how long would you have to save, with your-sized family, before you could put by enough for full payment on a deep-freeze? Besides, next summer was coming, when there'd be work again.

For years, until young Joe Randall got his head full of notions, Hillville had no year-round business. Amos Wilkinson dealt in gravel, loam, and fill during seasons when the earth was not too frozen to be moved; in a mild winter, his crews worked most months, but he could hire only a limited number of men. The real jobs were in the tourist trade, July and August, and at Randall's, June through November, if the season produced a good herring run; but this was not always to be depended on. Sometimes the big schools of fish came; sometimes they didn't. The herring were the same as they had always been, even though modern progress had washed over that industry, too.

In the old days, a man built a herring weir out of materials at hand which didn't cost him much—sticks, brush, piling, which he cut himself in his own wood lot. He might invest a couple of hundred dollars in nets and tar, and he was in business. The weir might dream away half a summer in a quiet cove and catch a monkfish, while the man cussed the herring and enjoyed leisure time watching the monkfish—homely damn thing puddling around on the bottom. Sooner or later, he might get a haul, which he cussed if it were small; or if it were big, he cussed that, too, all that work and hurry. Over the years he might get his investment back, with enough cash left to live on. Once in a while somebody—usually somebody else—made a killing, when a decent price for herring, good working weather, and a school of fish all happened at the same time. Meanwhile the man didn't need much to live on and he had fun watching the monkfish.

Nowadays herring was industry. A herring trap was a lethal affair of dressed nylon net costing into thousands; or maybe the man didn't bother with so static a thing. He invested his savings, plus a big wad of borrowed money, in a seiner equipped with a diesel, a radiotelephone, depth recorder, automatic pilot, and loran; trailed by five dories and a tender with outboard motor; carrying a mile of seine and a crew of men to set it; accompanied by a trained pilot and spotter airplane. When he headed out of harbor with the small boats in tow and the plane tailing on behind, he looked like a mother duck with ducklings; fifty thousand dollars wouldn't pay for his investment and every turn of the propeller cost him a cent.

Investment was tied up ashore, too. The packing companies waited, working crews on tap, machinery oiled, ready to roll. The sardine carriers—big, load-hauling boats—had not only electronic devices, but other complicated machinery such as fish pumps and scalers—no more back-breaking work bailing fish with a hand dip net these days. The carrier would range alongside weir or seine, lower a pump nozzle, and suck up a hundred bushels to a lick. On the way to the hold, the herring went whizzing through a contraption which neatly removed all their scales, so that herring scales, once a nuisance, sticking to everything, and as like as not flying into a man's eye, were salvaged now, sold at a whacking price to the costume-jewelry trade. Everything was salvaged down to the last dab of waste, which went through a dehydrator at the plant and came out as fish meal. A practical, well-organized industry which cost a lot of money and, like all man's hope, was based on chance—the migration of a fish which had changed no habits since the coast drowned and the sea rolled up to form coves and inlets, and some prehistoric skin-clad fisherman prayerfully watched the night tide for the mysterious firing of the waters.

The cussed things might come, and they might not.

They might come by the million-million in sizes too large or too small for the plants' machinery to handle—big females nearly a foot long, fat with spawn; or brit no bigger than a sail needle. Well, if you had expensive equipment, it was a foregone conclusion: sooner or later you had to use it or go broke. So that year the plants would meet expenses by putting everything—females, spawn, brit—by the hundreds of tons through the dehydrator to make fish meal, thus leaving nothing to be born or to grow up. And then, to everyone's honest astonishment, the next year nothing would come; there wouldn't be a herring the length and breadth of the coast.

When this happened, everything shut down. Seiners and carriers tied up; the coast died. The weir men, standing on the rails of their herring traps, looked down into water where nothing moved except a monkfish, totting up in their minds the payments still due on the expensive nylon net. And in Hillville Town Meeting that year when the school budget article came up, with a raise in teachers' salaries suggested, some would bitterly ask, "Why?" Because in March, in Hillville, the schoolteachers were the only ones who had any money, anyway.

On a June morning when the wind was east, Hillville smelled like any other coast town, of salt wind blended with clam flats and spring. When the wind was west, if the herring run was on, the smell was the sardine factory.

It was not fundamentally a disagreeable smell—merely a hearty combination of hot oil, coal smoke, and cooked fish; but it was all-pervasive, hanging over the town like a film on the wind. People told themselves they disliked it and were apologetic to outsiders. Hillville, they mourned, would never amount to anything as a summer resort; that smell would always make it a factory town. The tourists had nice noses; they would take their dollars elsewhere. Hillville people went on repeating this tradition, even after all the shore property was sold, with summer cottages blossoming like the rose, and with hundreds of fascinated tourists being shown through the factory every season.

Actually the smell was so much a part of the town that nobody noticed it unless there was a reason. A woman sniffing out the back door would put off washing until the wind changed, because the soft coal smoke blowing over her lines would smudge the clean clothes; at the same time, she could tell herself comfortably that Randall's was working, and if Randall's was, so was nearly everybody else in town. If you smelled Randall's, you smelled prosperity. The hot oil cooked out shoes and clothes for kids; down payments on cars and deep-freezes and television sets; breakfasts and Santa Claus. Times Randall's didn't work, it wasn't only the smell you missed; and actually it wasn't anything, compared to what it used to be.

The first J. J. Randall and Paul Montgomery had always dumped all their fish waste off the head of the wharf, where the tide floated it around the harbor and the waterfront. By the time of the second J. J. and old "FunnyMoney" Montgomery, Amy's grandfather, the summer air had got so nourishing that a man, old-timers said, could go down there and hack out chunks of it with a shovel; spread it on his field and it would grow potatoes. Only, of course you had to do it when Funny-Money wasn't looking, or he would charge you for it. His nickname indicated merely that he was "funny" about money; some said that he'd been in business for the smell of it, anyway.

Early summer people complained to no effect of this treatment of the waterfront; the big change came in the time of the present Joe

Randall's father, when a Navy destroyer lay over in the harbor for a night. Her captain landed to stretch his legs ashore; he got the pants of his dress uniform covered with slime, climbing the ladder of Randall's wharf; and, people said, the government got into it. The factory had to invest in a lighter with which to haul its waste out to sea: an awkward process compared to the compact, modern dehydrator which cooked everything into a profitable by-product, shipped away and sold, of all things, for fertilizer.

J. J. and Funny-Money and young Joe's father as well had run the business more or less along the same lines. As soon as the herring run was over, they laid off everyone; there'd be no more work till spring. Sure, there were other fish besides herring in the sea and the plant could can them; but to do it meant a certain amount of reconversion and expense. Randall and Montgomery were doing all right as they were; it wasn't up to them who went broke. A good summer's work, they had it made for the rest of the year; a man wasn't in business for shoe buttons. So get-in, get what-there-was, get-out. What else? Why risk a loss?

Young Joe might have carried on the same tradition if he hadn't spent the impressionable years of his boyhood growing up through the Big Depression, when nothing moved but grass blades in the wind. He had been a bright young fellow with nothing to do but watch grass blades; and he had got to figuring. After his father died, he racked his brains trying to find a way to keep the plant running the year round and still stay solvent.

Looking back now, he supposed he had simplified his economics; the system was like a Chinese box: you worked through one problem to find another just inside it. But at the time the matter seemed simple enough. If people had jobs, they could buy; if they could buy, he could sell; if he could sell, he could pay wages. What was the sense in closing down eight months out of the year, throw the whole town on its uppers, if there was something else you could do?

"So, goddammit," he told his stunned workmen—stunned at the idea that the factory was going to try to run the year around—who ever heard of such a thing? "If worse comes to worst, and we go broke, we can always eat our own codfish cakes."

Codfish cakes, Year in, year out, Joe fought the battle of the codfish cakes. It got so the sight of a can with its bright-colored label, *Randall's Codfish Cakes*, made him want to throw up. He had had to dig into reserves to install separate machinery. Times in a bad spell of winter weather, there wouldn't be a codfish obtainable the length and breadth of the coast; the only way to get his raw material would be to have it shipped by truck from Boston at a whacking price. The necessity for this always enraged him; it was coals to Newcastle. Dealers with the market tied up would buy from the fishermen, ship by refrigerated truck to city middlemen; the same fish might be re-priced and promptly shipped back where it came from to the retail trade, so that the fisherman's wife, if she were fool enough to buy at a fish market, might pay forty cents a pound for the same beat-up haddock which her husband had sold fresh, a week ago, for three.

Joe finally surmounted this problem by making a deal with Walt Sheridan, the skipper of a big trawler out of New Bedford, who had once been a Bishop man and whom Joe knew, to call by the factory with a load of ground fish periodically; but it cost more than it was worth. Walt had commitments in his home port, Hillville harbor was out of his way; he had to charge extra for the service.

Joe did his best to figure things out. He added more machinery and equipped to can clam chowder. Clams you could always dig; even in the winter, when the tide went out there was some part of the flats bare of ice. It was rugged work, but work-hungry men would do it. But what with the summer trade's capacity for fried clams, it got so that a digger had to travel miles before he could find flats hadn't petered out. Then a series of mild winters brought north another type of summer visitor, a host of green crabs from the Carolina coast. They like clams, too; and they cleaned out the flats. The price of clams went sky-high, and that finished the chowder business.

Joe switched to fish chowder, using the same machinery. He canned crab meat. He went back to codfish cakes. He puzzled his brains and lay awake nights. An oceanful of food on his doorstep, a plant to process it, plenty of workmen—there must be some way, some gimmick. But one year there'd be a scare in the cities about canned fish products; the next, people would decide they plain didn't like fish, or the supermarket shelves would be jammed with stuff that sold retail for less than Joe could sell it wholesale. In a good herring season, he could make enough to keep the factory running all winter, using his summer's profits.

He kept the facts to himself—that he just about broke even, with, some years, a little profit. The winter's pack, whatever it was, generally turned out to be a headache; he might as well, he told himself glumly, take it out and dump it off the wharf. But the thing that was really stopping him now was the frozen-foods industry. He couldn't figure out a way to bypass that competition.

Thus Joe Randall might be known as the town's leading solvent citizen; but hunched in the back of his mind as he handed out three cigars to each of his workmen to celebrate the birth of his triplets and let everyone know what a lucky guy he was, was the same worry about bills that nagged at everyone else. His nice, modern, ranch-type house was mortgaged; the monthly payments on his car came around as regularly as anyone's, the only difference being that the payments on a Cadillac were bigger.

Not that anyone worried too much about credit. A man might die before the loan company got tired of waiting and repossessed, and then his insurance would take care of everything. The loan companies were as lenient as they could be; they didn't want a lot of secondhand goods on their hands, either. The Cadillac and the ranch-type house were as much for appearances as for anything; as long as Joe Randall at least looked solvent, the town felt secure. And, Joe supposed, in a way so did he. The looks of it were there, anyhow.

He knew well enough, though, that two years' short herring runs would finish him. And then the town's comment would be: "Well, he ought to have known where all them newfangled notions would land him. If he'd stuck to the way his father run things, we'd have had jobs in the summer, anyhow. The way it is, we ain't got nothing."

Gaily Joe handed out his cigars.

"Amy's seeing stars, I guess," he commented. "Movie stars. Wants to call the two little ones Cary and Gary. Well, I guess I don't object, they're nice names enough. But the big guy, I put my foot down. He's going to be named after the old man, John Jay Randall. And we can call him Jay."

So they called him Jay.

Amy Randall said she didn't mind, adding weakly that it was a small price to pay if Joe forgot about nicknaming either of the others Montgomery.

But Amy did not live long enough to have much say in the matter. She rallied at first; then, two nights later, what Dr. Garland had feared all along happened in the night. Her overburdened heart gave out and she died. Joe found her when he woke up in the morning.

Garland had a busy week. A car accident near town scattered portions of three people around the highway, leaving little basic material for a surgeon to work on. The open season on deer was ending with a grand total of eleven hunters killed and one innocent bystander, who got a bullet through the windshield of his car and his lungs while driving along a wooded highway. The doctor divided his time between the hospital and the Randall twins, who, in spite of all he and Nellie Overholt could do, produced crisis after crisis. He judged, at the end of the week, that he had got them around the corner. They were shaky, but functioning. The third baby was fine; and Joe Randall, moving about his house stunned, in a coma of grief, turned to him as a man turns to salvation.

The baby, from the beginning, was a sunny little thing; he would smile at a touch or the sound of a voice, but more at Joe's than at anyone's, or so it seemed to Joe. He would hang onto Joe's forefinger and grin; and this, in the first days after Amy's death, was the only thing that would get an answering smile from Joe.

"My God, Doc," Joe said. "Look at that grip he's got on him! Strong as a horse. Knows me, too. You think he sees me?"

"I doubt it," Garland said. "Babies are pretty blind at that age."

"Huh?" Joe said, affronted. "You mean to tell me he don't see me? Look at that grin!"

"Well, he's quite a boy. Maybe he does."

He didn't; but if it eased Joe to think so, that was fine. Joe wasn't a man to talk about feelings. He stayed bottled up. But what needed to come out, Garland judged, might be coming through Joe's silence as he sat by the crib. It was a full-sized crib, too, not like the twins' bassinets, which Joe had brought home from downtown on the first afternoon.

"Old J. J.," Joe said under his breath. "My God, Doc, I'd be off my rocker without him." Which was quite a lot for Joe to say.

J. J.

John Jay Randall.

Oh, brother! Garland thought.

If you had time, if you weren't out straight twenty-four hours a day, you might feel compunction; if you were superstitious, you might wake up nights, wonder about a guy who had the gall to play God; who was certainly outside the law and in for a hard time if he got found out.

But Garland wasn't superstitious, or so he told himself. Every time he stopped at Joe's, the only thing he could feel was satisfaction. If the twins didn't make it, Joe wouldn't be alone; he would have J. J. Checking, Garland found he was pretty proud himself of J. J. Randall.

"Hi, J. J.," he would say. "Get a load of you today," and once, under his breath, "One in the eye for your ring-tailed devil."

Nellie Overholt, nearby, heard him, or thought she did. "Ring-tailed devil is right!" she snapped. "Kicked a bar of soap out of my hand this morning halfway across the room." Nellie was overworked most days—there were other sick people in town who needed the

District Nurse—but she was on duty nights as well, here at Joe's, until Joe could find somebody. Neighbor women were as helpful as they could be; they would come in daytimes and stay with the babies when Nellie had to go elsewhere. But most of them worked in the factory and had families of their own, and the way Angie was acting, not many would stay very long.

Angie had announced that she herself was perfectly capable of keeping house for Joe. Any other woman he got in there, she said, had better look out. Dr. Garland and Nellie Overholt were fools for fussing so over them little babies; all they needed was a little toughening up, which she could do as well as anybody. She wasn't going to stand by, she said, and see them reared up as a couple of sissies; and when Nellie's back was turned, Angie tried. The sad fact was, Angie took pride in her likes and dislikes; she took pride in having taken a dislike to the twins; she only liked J. J. She had to be watched and coped with. If anybody had the stamina to do that, Nellie had; but even she was ready to fly.

Nellie was short-tempered when she was tired, and outspoken; the glare she turned now on J. J. Randall was one of pure frustration.

"Give you a hard time, does he?" Garland grinned.

"Hnf! Nothing I can't handle. If only I could get Joe and that blasted Angie out of my hair. I tell you one thing, Doc, this lad's going to run this house unless somebody comes down on him hard and soon."

"Can't you?"

"I try. But the minute I do, he bawls, Joe and Angie come running, so I'm killing the baby. I thought yesterday Angie was going to lay me out with the poker. Honest, Doc, something's got to be done about that damned old kook. You know what she was doing when I got back from Clem's yesterday? I had my sister Gert in here babysitting whilst I was gone, but Gert got her nose stuck into *True Romances* and died to the world. I could've wrung her neck and almost did, but what's the good, she'd never have known it. She gets reading them sex situations and looking at the pictures, and, what I mean, she really gets into it, it's her, herself, you can't do nothing, her arse runs away with her head. So I come in, there was Gert, living it up, and Angie had a bowl of clam chowder all ready to feed them two sick babies."

"Good God!" Garland said. "Did they get any of it?"

"No, they did not, but they would have if I'd been two minutes later. And don't think," Nellie said grimly, "that I didn't put her on the run, too. I told her Joe was going to send her to an old folks' home if she didn't stop her cussed actions. She'll be okay for a while, till she forgets I said it. But I tell you, Doc, Joe has got to find some good strong woman for a housekeeper, somebody ain't got any nerves. Because I've got some, and I'm a-getting more."

"I hate to push Joe," Garland said. "The way he feels. He was going to list the job with the employment agency in Bishop, the last I knew. Wonder if he has?"

"Poor old Joe," Nellie said. "Maybe, but I doubt it. He don't know whether he's going or coming."

"It's a darn shame Lucy Wilkinson can't help us out."

"Lucy handle Angie? Angie could come it over her in five minutes. Anybody can talk Lucy into anything, and you know it."

"Well, yes. But Lucy could take over some of the other sick, so you could stay here full time for a while."

"Oh, great! Well, she couldn't take over Clementina. Not with Amos acting like the god's full-time fool. What's the matter with him, anyway?"

"I don't know. But from the way he acted in my office when I wouldn't go along with his notion of sending the old lady to an asylum, I'd guess he had some paranoid tendencies stashed away there, somewhere."

He regretted at once that he had said this in Nellie's hearing. Nellie was a good nurse; in an emergency he wouldn't ask for better; but she was a talker. In her job she had unparalleled opportunities to pick up gossip, which she passed on with details added and enriched. It would not be too much to expect that sooner or later an incautious remark made by him would be flying around town on wings of gospel truth: in this case, a first-run tidbit—that Doc Garland had said Amos

Wilkinson was crazy.

"I wouldn't want you to mention that, Nellie," he said. "That's only a guess, in passing. I don't have any medical evidence to—"

"Certainly not!" Nellie said, shocked. "And I'd like to know what makes you think I ever do pass on a word you say, Dr. Garland. I would not think of it!"

The hell you wouldn't, Garland thought, with a grin.

Not that he blamed her, if she could get some pleasure out of her life. Her day's work, carried on year in and year out, was a grinder. She had three children to support at home and a wandering husband. She could not, like her sister Gert, get any vicarious pleasure out of *True Romances* or anything else concerning sex; her own romance had been true enough to last a lifetime. Her husband had fled her bed and board three years ago as a result of trifling with waitresses at motels; the story was that Nellie had spanked him with a board and thrown him out of the house. This might not have been true—Nellie herself was a town institution which gossip tended to exaggerate—but the fact remained that she could have done it, and Billy Overholt hadn't been seen around town in quite some time.

She was a big, rawboned woman, tough, weather-beaten, and homely; her eyes, deep-set beside a craggy beak of nose, could at need produce a gray-green, baleful stare which could scare a sick man well or a malingerer into lasting activity. Garland had seen her in a below-zero blizzard at a shack in the back country, with a rag and a basin of soapsuds, scrubbing a woods hermit who had gone on a New Year's celebration, all by himself; a man who had not washed in months, if ever, all over; who, on the edge of D.T.'s from a prolonged drunk, had tried to fight her off with his fists, dribbling a stream of filthy talk. Nellie had put up with him for a while; then, out of patience, she had grabbed him by the bush of his hair and crammed her soapy rag into his mouth, swabbing it out thoroughly, and remarking, "Now, shut up. That's enough."

That she was heavy-handed, Garland knew, cross-grained and at times bad-tempered; of this the more thin-skinned of her patients were likely to complain, not that it helped them any. Nellie had no patience with human foolishness—she had seen too much of it—and weakness was something you were a fool if you did not get over. She herself was toughly righteous up to a point, and honest unless she saw good reason not to be—undeniably, items of Welfare Department clothing intended for the poor sometimes appeared on Nellie's children's backs, which meant merely that Nellie had asked herself who were the poor and had decided that, on her wages, *she* was. Yet her judgment of right and wrong, as she saw it in other people, was of the hardness of a stone; wrong was black, right was white, with nothing in between.

Oh, she was rough on people, all right, including her own children—Garland sometimes wondered what the poor little buggers would turn out to be when they grew up; he couldn't help but see that Nellie enjoyed the almost unlimited power she had over the sick and the helpless. But at the same time he made all the excuses he could for her. If she was ugly-tempered, it meant that she was tired to death, and with reason; she was afraid of nothing, would go anywhere, do anything; and if you had help like that, he told himself, you couldn't grudge a few by-products. He had had patients who had got up off the bed and walked and been well the next day, rather than put up any longer with Nellie Overholt.

"I ought to get along to the hospital," he said, picking up his bag. "Unless you've got something around town for me."

"Well, drop by Clem's if you got time. She's better, but it wouldn't hurt to check. I'd give a pocketful," Nellie said with venom, "to know where she's getting that *liquor*."

Nellie, in her job, heard plenty of ugly talk, which she took in her stride and even used herself if an occasion warranted; but if there was one word in the language that was obscene to her, that word was *liquor*. As District Nurse, she had been on the receiving end of conviviality too many times, had had to clean up, patch up, sober up, or get ready for the undertaker too many drunks to have any patience in the matter. Whiskey, gin, rum, beer were all words in her vocabulary; she was knowledgeable, too, about the drinking mores of the area—white port or muscatel for a cheap binge, vodka if you were going to drive a car, because the superstition among the experts was that the cops couldn't smell it on your breath. She did not give to these abominations the dignity of names; she lumped them all into one contemptuous word, *liquor*, and spat it forth like a malediction.

"The only one who goes there regular," she went on, "is Everard Peterson. Clem pays him to bring meat scraps for her cats."

"You think they have wild parties together when nobody's around?"

This was nonsense, as he knew; and Nellie let him know what she thought of it.

"Well!" she said. "For heaven's sake! Clem's a lady, after all! She never touched a drop till Connie went away, and the Lord knows, it's lonesome down there with nothing but that cussed old ewe sheep and them cats. When I think what she used to be in this town . . . Somebody ought to slap some sense into Amos Wilkinson, leaving her down there all soul alone!"

"You like to be the one to try?"

"No, sir, I wouldn't! I wouldn't want to fool with Amos Wilkinson in any way whatsoever. Nor would you if you knew what I know about him, or maybe you do."

"Mm-hm, I heard," Garland said hastily. If she got started on the Wilkinsons, he'd never get away. She was put out over having to tend out on the old lady when Lucy was a nurse and could have done it, and when the Wilkinsons could have afforded a full-time hospital nurse, only Amos was too stingy.

"According to the statues, he ain't legally responsible, being only but her grandnephew," Nellie said. "And the cussed tightwad knows it." From long experience she could quote chapter and verse from what she called the "statues," the section of the state code of law dealing with the aged, the helpless, or the needy poor. "But if the rickety old thing dies down there alone some night, he's the only heir. That's when you'll see him slap on the hair oil and a black suit and step right in, Johnny-on-the-spot, in case she's left a quarter."

"Mm, I guess so. Look, Nellie, I've got to—"

"Of course she may not have a quarter, what she's got is between her and God. She buys cat food in cans, and she pays Everard for scraps from the market, and hay for that sheep. She must pay somebody for that *liquor*."

"Well, I'll stop by there. Look, I'm puzzled a little," Garland said. "She had a hard time with pneumonia this spring, but she's over that, and maybe some hardening of the arteries; she would have, at eighty-two; but whenever I go there, she's chipper as a sparrow. I've never seen any signs of her drinking, and even if she did, a little, well, she's pretty old; might do her good—"

Nellie bristled. "If you went down there as often as I do, and had to take the remnants of a fifth, half-, three-quarters gone, out and smash it on the stone wall, and found the whole place *reeking*—"

"Oh, sure, sure—" Garland began, hastily backing down.

"I guess I would know if anybody would. I am not entirely a damned fool. I—"

Nellie's voice, when raised, had a resonant clang guaranteed to wake any sleeper; it had waked up all three babies. Cary and Gary were still too weak to do anything but stir languidly in their bassinets, but J. J. Randall's eyes popped open. His face creased in a wide, engaging smile, then puckered; he let out a bawl like a bull.

"Now look what you've done," Nellie said, giving Garland an indignant glare. "You've woke up the baby."

"Uh—guess I did at that." Garland thought, with some amusement, that Nellie, too, showed signs of believing that there was only one baby in the house.

"Gas!" Nellie said. She scooped up J. J., held him to her shoulder and let him have a brisk wallop on the back.

J. J's burp resounded through the kitchen.

"Brother!" Garland said.

"Good grief, yes, he gets rid of as much wind and as loud as a man. Hnf, I tell his father that grin is nothing but gas, but you try tell Joe anything about this feller! How poor Amy ever produced any such power plant as this is beyond my imagination when those two other poor little sods . . . Oh, well, maybe you did bring him in a basket. He's one of Paul's, for my money."

Garland felt for a moment as if his tongue had swelled up in his mouth.

The practical joker, he thought. The ring-tailed devil's old kick-in-the-pants. He isn't through yet, and now he's after me. So think fast. Nellie's no fool.

"That's the orthodox way a baby comes," he said, keeping it light. "Little black bag usually, isn't it? Paul who?"

"Paul Bunyan, natch," Nellie said.

"Oh." Garland grinned with relief. "Maybe it's the original old J. J. coming out. He was said to be quite a boy, in his day."

"Must be, I guess. *Did* you bring a big market basket in here that day, Doc? I've been meaning to ask you."

"Basket?" Garland said. He picked up his bag again, hoping she hadn't seen him twitch.

Nellie laughed. "My kid Beck's got me going round and round," she said. "The Lord knows, I try to bring my girls up nice, but too much goes on around my house and they both take phone calls. So I give up long ago on the bees and the flowers and told 'em what the score was. Seems Beck was snooping around here that day, and don't think I didn't give her a good one for it, she's supposed to stay to home, but she saw something that's made a liar out of me and I can't talk her out of it. She swears to the god you brought one of Amy's triplets in a basket."

"Oh. Oh, yes, sure," Garland said. "Come to think of it, I did have a basket, some tests I was taking to the lab to check, which was where I was headed when Joe caught up with me. Stuff I didn't want to get chilled, so I hauled it in here and stuck it by the stove. I saw those kids, Beck and a boy, wasn't it? I expect that's what they saw."

"Mm, yes, but—"

Nellie had seen J. J. in the basket. Garland nailed it down, lying with ease and fluency.

"Hell, you know what happened. Amy took her time between

triplets, and when you didn't get here, out gallivanting around town," he said, desperately flinging down a red herring, "I cleaned up the first one myself and chucked him into the warmest place I could find. And don't ask me what's with the goddam tests, for all I know they're still in the back of my car. I haven't had time to—have to do them over—"

Nellie promptly fielded the red herring. "You good and well know where I was," she said. "I was *not* gallivanting around town. If I had the time to, which I do not, I would lay up in bed for a day and rest my feet. Well, there! When Beck stuck to it that she'd sneaked in here and took a peek and saw a baby in that basket, why, loving godfrey, I knew she'd seen something!"

Loving godfrey, she did, Garland thought.

Outside, in his car, Garland closed his eyes and drew a long breath. Brother! That kid! Well, I made a good try, but the timing's off. Nellie could put two and two together on that if she really set her mind to it.

All right, he said, to the air in front of his face. That round's to me, you hear me? Why don't you lay off? Go fool with somebody else for a while?

J. J. Randall's ring-tailed devil made no comment, if, even, he heard at all, and Garland started his engine and drove down the road toward Clementina's.

But he didn't make it, not that day. As he passed the front gate of Amos Wilkinson's house, Lucy flagged him down.

"I guess," she said, to Garland's astonishment, "I've got to have you to Amos."

It was true that Amos Wilkinson could have taken care of his old great-aunt if he had wanted to; he did not need anybody's money, having enough of his own. He was a contractor, dealing in sand, gravel, and loam, earth-moving jobs of all kinds. His wealth could be counted in machines and in the marks he left everywhere on the countryside. His bulldozers, loaders, backhoes, power shovels, and trucks were busy three seasons of the year, beginning when frost came out of the ground in the spring. He ranged the countryside, looking for unused land which might have on it enough loam, surfacing gravel, or fill to make it worth his buying. If it were farmland, so much the better— the price of screened loam for lawns and greenhouses was high.

Throughout the area, abandoned farm stands coming up to briers and puckerbrush could be bought for a song, provided they were not shore property or with a view of the sea, when they could be considered real estate. Inland were only cut-over wood lots and fields, hopeful once when early settlers cleared and farmed the land and planted apple trees, but worth nothing much now except to look at when their orchards were in bloom. Usually their heirs thought themselves lucky when Amos Wilkinson turned up with an offer of a hundred or so for the "old place," which by now had little left on it—a falling-down house, maybe, or a cellar foundation; some old fruit trees, an outbuilding or two; and who'd want that?

Amos Wilkinson would. He would buy it, often not even bothering to record the land title, and move in with his machines. His bulldozers took care of the obstacles to a good clean operation, tumbling buildings, apple trees, puckerbrush, boulders into a windrow and pushing the jackstrawy mess back out of the way. Heavy equipment loosened up the loam, scraped it into piles, tossed it into a mechanical gravel screen, which freed it of roots, sticks, and stones and left it stacked in heaps half as high as a house for the trucks to haul away. It was lovely stuff, silky and dark, resilient in the hand: the life of the land, ready to go and grow somewhere else; and Amos got a lot of money for it.

His mechanical gravel screen ran for days on end, separating loam from gravel, gravel from fill. Rocks clanged along its forty-foot length and dumped off its end into trucks, with a sound like brick buildings successively collapsing. People whose property abutted on one of Amos's operations were likely to complain—ladies whose babies couldn't sleep, chicken farmers whose hens went crazy, or some bewildered summer man who found his vacation quiet blasted. It never did any good. If you were against what Amos was doing, you were against progress; that was that.

As for the mess he left, he wasn't, he said, a landscape gardener. He was a businessman with the monkey of practical economics riding on his back. If you wanted to see a real mess, you ought to go north, where, in years gone by, whole townships had been left covered with slash from the lumbering operations. Amos had been brought up on them; in his young manhood he had been a timber cruiser: a woodsman. He still had that reputation—one of the best woodsmen in the state. Sportsmen from all over the country wrote him for advice on fishing and hunting still, and he took pride in his reputation. He got a hunting or a fishing trip out of it, sometimes, in the company of rich sports from away, who treated him like one of themselves—not that he cared a damn about that, but when they left, they slipped him a pocketful of folding money for tracking down a deer or two or showing them a good fishpond. He liked to hunt and fish all right, but they could have their woods.

For himself, he'd never seen a tree in his life without wanting to cut it down. A tree was a nuisance, something to be got out of the way; cost a man money. And there was something else, too, not that he thought of it often, only once in a while, maybe, looking over a bunch of woods that would have to be bulldozed down to make way for a gravel pit. There they were, a part of the known and visible world that ought to be a servant to a man; that ought to be a good place, a safe place, for him to live in, and wasn't. A man owned it, by God, it was his. He was top dog; it ought to bow under his foot, work along with him; cooperate. And it didn't. Some part, or the whole of it, was always weaseling out to one side, getting ahead of him, snapping back in his face.

Well, he could cope with it, and had, all his life. A man hadn't ought to have to. If you wanted authority on what his worth was and his right to be top dog, you could go straight to the Bible, where it said a man was somebody God had taken the trouble to die for; which set the rest of the world right back where it belonged, didn't it?

As for trees, they made him mad. The look they had of belonging to themselves; that secret, you-be-damned, this is-ours-not-yours look, and no matter what you do it won't make a dent, this'll be here when you're dead and rotten.

So Amos stood by while the boys bulldozed them down, shoved them into a windrow of jackstraws, got them out of the way of a good, clean operation. Apple, cherry, spruce, birch—whatever there was; it didn't make any difference. There was nothing in the world he hated so much as a goddam tree.

He was thorough; when he finished with a piece of land he was down to bedrock or the big useless boulders of glacial drift too big for his rock crusher. Nothing would be left of the "old place" but a hole in the ground like a bomb crater, surrounded by a windrow of assorted debris which would take generations to rot down. No seed would ever take root there again, no stock feed on grassland, no apples grow, because the loam was stockpiled behind a greenhouse somewhere or under turf on someone's lawn; the gravel which might in a hundred years or so have broken down into loam, was packed down under hardtop on a highway. After a while, spring rains might make stagnant puddles covered with green slime or, if the hole went deep enough, a pond for frogs.

And why not? The land was worthless for anything else. "A. Wilkinson, Contractor" had jobs to bestow, wages to pay. If the countryside was beginning to look like an old battlefield, why that was too bad, but you couldn't blame a man for making a living, and there was no doubt of it, Amos made a good one. He was all right, people said. Oh, you had to look out for him in a deal, he would cheat the eyeteeth out of you, but that was your lookout. A respectable man, a hard worker, against liquor and against sin; kept his family fed, clothed, and comfortable; went to church Sundays and to lodge meeting on Thursday nights; a man of forethought, who owned a plot in the cemetery with a monument already up, his and his wife's names and half of their dates carved, so that when the time came, nothing would have to be done but dig the graves and fill in the dates. It was a nice monument, too, of local red stone polished to gloss; must have cost

Amos a pocketful of money. Not many could afford a stone like that.

Amos's great-aunt, Clementina Wilkinson, had had a word to say about the monument when it was first put up, which was repeated around town and even got back to Amos; but then, of course, she was crazy.

"Monument!" she said. "What's he need a monument in the cemetery for? This whole countryside is a monument to him that'll last longer than any chunk of granite will."

They had never been on good terms, Amos and his Great-Aunt Clementina; but the final row, which dated back for some years, concerned who should justly inherit the family money. The Wilkinsons had made money from the days when the pines in the region were tall enough to carry the King's Broad Arrow; a Wilkinson back along, when the land could still produce high-grade lumber, had even made a fortune. This, of course, had been picked away at, divided among heirs, lost in this or that speculation—an earlier Amos, in the 'Eighties, had sunk a good deal of it in a silverfox farm project, as a good many had in his day, only to have the venture turn out to be a scheme promoted by some fast-working slickers from away, who handed the entire region a brick and made off with the savings of a generation.

But the present Amos's grandfather—Clementina's brother—had pulled things together again, had made money and invested it in good sound stocks and bonds; then he had had a stroke and, after a long illness, died, leaving everything to Clementina.

This was a body blow to Amos, who had counted on getting the money for his business. He could not at first believe that an astute old businessman like Gerald Wilkinson could have left all that money to a woman. True, Clementina had sold her house in the city and had come home to look after her brother throughout his illness; probably she should have had a little something. But to get everything, even the fine, old Wilkinson house—Amos couldn't see it. So far as he was concerned, that money was legally his; he would have tried litigation, but his lawyer advised him not to. The will had been drawn years before Gerald Wilkinson's illness; it was unbreakable. Amos, after all, was not a son, but a grandson; his parents were dead.

He settled down to play a waiting game—Clementina was old; at eighty-two, she couldn't last forever, though at times it seemed she might. Nobody knew how much she had left now; whatever the sum had been in the beginning, she had been living on it for years and in her day had been a handsome spender. From time to time Amos had tried to find out, with no luck; even the local bank, of which Amos was a trustee, didn't know where Gerald Wilkinson had invested his money. Clementina's checks came monthly from a law firm in Boston; but when Amos wrote them, on grounds that the old lady was getting pretty senile and that he was the responsible one in the family, they were noncommittal.

The final break came on the day, some years ago now, when Clementina came home one afternoon from Bishop and caught Amos red-handed, rummaging through her desk. The old lady, who was peppery, had told him off in no uncertain terms.

"You get out of here," she'd said, "or I'll have you arrested. I'd just as soon see you in jail as any other sneak thief."

Amos went. He was not particularly angry or even embarrassed; he felt perfectly justified: no one could blame a man for trying to get together a little information about his own money. Which that old crow, and he knew it, was spending hand over fist. It cost to go to New York on trips twice a year; theatres and concerts, she told his daughter, Constance, she went for; but God knew what else she did while she was down there. Hotels and all. It would be expensive.

After the row he didn't go near her again, but he did not forbid his womenfolks—his wife, Lucy, and Constance to visit, at least not then. He didn't want to be completely out of touch; it was just as well to keep a foot in the door, and now and then he got quite a little information about Clementina's doings from Constance. From childhood Constance had always spent a lot of time down there; she loved the old lady, and she loved Clementina's rackety establishment, which was always fun to go to and overrunning with pets—every stray or homeless animal in town sooner or later ended up there.

At the time of the open quarrel Constance was twenty; she had been out of high school for two years and, after graduation, had found herself exactly the job she wanted in the veterinary department of a big research laboratory in Bishop which bred thousands of animals for study in the investigation of human diseases through genetics. It was as close as she could come for now to being a veterinarian herself, which someday she hoped she might, though it would not be, she knew, with any of Amos's cooperation.

Amos approved, all right, of his womenfolks working, pulling their weight in the boat—his wife, of course, was Dr. Garland's office nurse—but beyond their earning their board at home, he wasn't interested. He had other plans for Connie anyway; his foreman, Mack Jensen, was an up-and-coming young fellow who, as a son-in-law, might make a partner in his business. She could get as interested as she wanted to over at that mouse factory in Bishop, but that was only for the time being. He guessed he could leave the rest of it to Mack.

The Bishop Laboratory was world-famous. Scientists from many countries worked there; and from its various projects had come some of the most exciting discoveries of the century. While its investigations included research in the genetics of cats, dogs, and other animals, it bred, principally, hundreds of strains of mice. A mouse has cancer as humans do; through these small generations, Bishop Laboratory scientists for years had traced and recorded the action on tissue of the terrible cells, of many kinds, on the trail of an ultimate discovery which was not yet. You might try to explain to Amos Wilkinson what was being done there: Constance tried.

He couldn't get past the mice. A mouse to him was something to set a trap for. A damned nuisance; one of the multitudinous tribes of the useless, put into the world for no reason except to hinder serious business. Half a man's lifetime, he said, was spent coping with damned inhabitants, which all they wanted was for him to shove over and make room or get out of the world altogether so they could have it— flies, bats, mosquitoes, mice, rats, ants, birds—well, he didn't have any quarrel with the scientists; thanks to them we had DDT and

2-4D, and he only hoped he'd be able to stay alive long enough to see someone invent something that would wipe out all the rest of the damned trash for good.

Amos's temper, always uncertain, was particularly ruffled at the time because of a cave-in in one of his gravel pits, which he blamed on the holes of a colony of bank swallows. In a pleasanter mood he would simply have stirred Connie up by making a few cracks about "the mouse factory." Both he and Mack Jensen occasionally did this, knowing it would start fireworks. Connie was a girl of considerable spirit.

"Well, all I can say is," she said now, "I hope you never have cancer."

Lucy, her mother, gasped. "Connie, darling! Don't *ever* mention that awful word in this house!"

Constance liked her job; she was pretty, bright, and popular in the town and, apparently, happy enough at home: yet, suddenly, to everyone's surprise, she picked up and went away somewhere without warning. A better job, her mother told everyone, at a laboratory in Boston.

The town speculated. Some said that Connie and Amos had had a terrible fight. Over Clementina, wasn't it, when he finally forbade her even to go down there? Or maybe she wanted to get married to somebody besides Mack Jensen; she'd been seen a couple of times out with a stranger, quite a good-looking boy, too, and the story was that Amos wouldn't let her see him at home, so she'd been seeing him at Clementina's. If that were so, and Amos had found it out, it would have been plenty of reason for a battle. Everyone knew how Amos was, didn't they?

After a while Constance wrote to a friend in town. She *was* married. Her name was Grindle now, and she was living in Massachusetts.

Funny, wasn't it, her folks never said anything; and Lucy, of all people, never peeped a word. Well, Amos was an odd man; had an awful temper. Some recalled how he'd got mad once on the job and beaten up one of his workmen, a Polish fellow, and had nearly killed him, and how the man's wife had taken Amos to court and got a judgment, too, and Amos had had to pay. He'd never opened his yip about that, either, and anyone would know better than to mention it to him, too. Once he got mad with you, that was it. Look at the way he treated poor old Clementina, wouldn't go near himself, nor let Lucy.

He would, though, talk about Clementina. In the spring of the present year, when she had had pneumonia and Nellie Overholt had gone down to nurse her and everybody was wondering why on earth the District Nurse had to be called in, for goodness' sake—Clementina was supposed to be rolling, wasn't she? —word began to get around town that the old lady had taken to drink. It was one of those stories you heard, didn't really believe but wondered about, passed on and half-forgot till somebody else brought it up. Besides, you knew Nellie, didn't you? Divide what she said by two, you might get somewhere within the region of the truth. But one day somebody asked Amos. Why, he said laconically, he wouldn't be surprised; not many knew about it, but years ago Clementina had had to take a cure. Once a lush always a lush, it wasn't anything anybody ever got over.

Well, the old lady was being looked after, she wasn't a public responsibility. At least nobody thought so until Lura Blandish addressed the Ladies' Club about her at regular meeting and sparked off the Clementina Campaign, on a day when Lucy Wilkinson wasn't there. You wouldn't, of course, want to offend the Wilkinsons.

Lura was the wife of Jones Blandish, who was head of the Building and Loan; she was very active in civic affairs, and a business woman, too. She ran—not that she needed to, it was a hobby on the side—a little antique shop.

Sympathy, Lura said, was not in itself enough. She went from past glories to present troubles, appealing to the conscience of the town. That nice, old house that Will Wilkinson built in 1802, a showplace then, where, within the memory of some older citizens present, the Wilkinson ladies of an earlier day had been accustomed to entertain with tea and fruitcake on Thursday afternoons. What fruitcake that had been—the Wilkinson recipe, which most of the ladies' grandmothers had had and passed on . . .

At least one of the older citizens present, listening with closed eyes, was reminded at this point that the Wilkinson recipe was one which she herself now refused out of delicacy to use, because Clementina drank; it was all a scandal and a howling, and you had to take a stand somewhere. And Lura went on.

That house ought to be restored, set up as a museum, a monument to the early days of the town; and the lovely old furniture . . . the linen . . . the quilts. . . . Why, when they thought of what a moth could do in a single summer in an unguarded closet; and neglect, and mildew, and dampness . . . and we do not have left too many mementos of the honorable tradition of our town. And, as she had said, sympathy was not in itself enough.

Over tea and cupcakes, the ladies discussed the problem, now become, it seemed, an emergency. There was no doubt that the house was full of old and valuable things; someone recalled the antique dealer who, passing through town, had called on Clem and had finally got in. He had come out with tears in his eyes because she wouldn't sell him anything.

Somebody ought at least to go in and clean house for her. Yet how could you clean that house? they asked each other. A house in which upwards of twenty cats lived all the time, plus a cosset lamb grown into a sheep, and who knew what all? You could only clean it with a shovel or a fire hose. Still, the Ladies' Club could try.

It was their custom to have weekly study groups in arts and crafts. Lura gave a course in antiques—furniture, pewter, and glass—and they got in outside speakers on weaving, tray design, or painting in oils; but if a community duty needed to be done, they would forego their arts and, all together, go do it. In this way they accomplished much useful and necessary work, such as cleaning the parish house, cutting its lawn and caring for its flowerbeds; or holding food and rummage sales for the benefit of the church or some needy family. After discussion they decided to announce a Clean-Up-Clementina Day, and fourteen of them went down and cleaned her house from top to bottom. It was not a success.

Clementina could not seem to get it through her head what they were there for. She was not in the least cooperative; she seemed to look upon it as an intrusion.

No, she said, they could *not* houseclean; they could *not* go upstairs.

In the goodness of their hearts, they told each other that the poor, addled soul didn't mean anything by it; they would go ahead anyway. But, Lura suggested, perhaps they had better begin upstairs, out of her sight, until she got used to them. It was a conundrum, anyway, where to begin; and certainly the need justified everything.

They found the upstairs rooms dusty and uncared-for, heavy with the smell of must. Many of the ladies had never been upstairs in the fine, old house; there were so many things to see that no one at first could do much but look around. Wilkinsons, in their day, had traveled; they had brought home Things. In Bide Wilkinson's room, for instance— and you couldn't mistake whose room had been whose because the names were hand-carved on pine panels set into the lintels above the doors: BIDE'S ROOM, JOSEPH'S ROOM, WILL'S ROOM, surrounded by a design of roses and wheat—in Bide's room, three of the walls were lined with cases and glass-fronted shelves with nothing in them but bugs and butterflies, mounted and labeled; and the fourth wall, from floor to ceiling, was books.

Bide Wilkinson. Died young. Somebody remembered hearing her grandfather tell how he got killed in the Andes Mountains in South America. In the 'Eighties, was it? Well, anyway, a long time ago. Bug hunting. That was what he did with *his* life. Seemed a footless way to spend time, and on something that ended up that serious, too. Well, when you thought back, some of the Wilkinsons had been pretty footless. With all that money, they could afford to be.

Lura Blandish said what a lesson this room was on the fruitlessness of piling up treasure on earth, which struck a sour note, because everyone knew what Jones Blandish had piled up; and Mert Wasgatt said, yes, specially when you knew that after you were gone somebody was going to have to do an almighty job of housecleaning, which she got out of, smooth as a smelt, when Lura began to swell up, by adding,

"With all them glass fronts and picture frames. And books! One more mess of stuff to dust. I get my stories out of the TV, thank God, and I can dust that in ten seconds flat."

Someone said, "Skip the bugs and books, girls, cast your eyes around at the furniture," and for a while nobody did anything but look.

The canopy beds. The hoop-back Windsor chairs. The Chippendale desk with the oxbow front. The mahogany secretary full of pewter and old silver. The Sandwich glass. The old whale-oil lamps. The hand-carved seventeenth-century armchair. And the fireplaces and original Franklin stove! And the wainscots in butternut-colored pine.

Lura, of course, was an authority on dates and makers; nearly all the ladies knew, from her, what dealers and antique hunters were likely to buy. In this house was a fortune . . . a fortune . . . a fortune.

Bemused, they went from room to room. They opened all the chests, closets, drawers—to air and clean out, of course, for no other reason. Lovely, old patchwork quilts in complicated and subtle patterns, hand-sewn, their colors blended by time—faded just right for the antique market for nowadays, when quilts were in style. Bedspreads, crocheted, appliquéd, quilted, in tiny, spidery stitches. A tall closet packed from floor to ceiling with fine, musty linens.

"Wouldn't you think," Lura said in sympathy, "that the poor old dear would rather go to an old ladies' home?"

Sun and air would do a lot, they said; but most of this stuff ought to be washed. They divided it all into equal piles, assigned each lady a share to take home and put through her washing machine, and began carrying loads of linen, quilts, and bedspreads out to their automobiles. To do this, they had to pass Clementina, who was sitting in her rocking chair in the kitchen, not saying anything, merely watching, but with an odd expression that made some of the ladies feel nervous. After all, there'd been talk; she might, just possibly, be a little, well, *off*. Or drunk? She looked as if she might be something, with a tight-twisted pug of white hair and the bright, gold-yellow eyes that didn't miss a move anybody made.

She said after a while, "Are you ladies having a bonfire?"

"Why, no, dear, of course not!" Lura said. "Whatever made you think—We'll bring every bit back all nice and clean. You wait. You'll see."

"I see you've got Grandmother Wilkinson's Star of Bethlehem quilt there. It took her two years to make."

"Don't you worry, dear. It'll come back in a little while."

It was the cheerful, chirpy tone sometimes used to a child, and Clementina's eyes took on a gleam.

"Poor Grandmother!" she said. "She never had anything to do with her spare time except to sew together scraps and pieces. She and I were always at swords' points in the matter, belonged to different schools of thought, as you might say. She liked to sew, I liked to read books. It was her opinion that reading books would addle a girl's brains, they not being strong enough to stand it. You think there might have been something in what she said, Mrs. Blandish?"

"Of course not, dear. What a horrid way to think!"

"Well, I wondered what was your opinion, it's nice to know. Have you read Dickens, Mrs. Blandish?"

Lura said brightly, "Oh, yes, dear. Of course."

"Such nice *fat* books. Aren't they?"

"There, dear, you rest now. Before we go, we'll have time to chat a little, I know."

"That will be nice. I always enjoy intelligent conversation. About the quilts, I'd better tell you, there're more in the attic, upwards of ten million stitches in tired thread. Poor Grandmother. I always felt that most women might be somebody you'd care to have around your house if they were let to use brains instead of needles. I was sick to death of quilts before I was as old as you are, so your bonfire's no trial to me. Where are you having it? I'll move my chair so I can watch it."

There was, of course, no answer for this foolishness; you might talk all day and not convince her, though it was embarrassing to have her not appreciate, to think you were looting the house.

Lura said, outside the door, "They always talk your ear off when they're, uh, in that condition."

Someone said, shocked, "Oh, my, Lu! You think she's tight? Now? This early in the day?"

"Ss-h. Keep your voice down. What d'you think?"

They got on with their cleaning and did a magnificent job. When they finished, the old house shone from top to bottom; it might be said that few, if any, movable objects had not been turned over at least once. Worn out, but in a glow of accomplishment, the ladies gathered in the kitchen, ready to go home.

"There, dear," Lura said. "Your house is spick-and-span as can be, and—" she went on, speaking clearly and loudly, spacing the words so that the old lady could understand—"and we'll—wash those things—and—bring—them—*right back!*"

Clementina sat rocking slightly back and forth, looking Lura over with her tawny-yellow eyes.

"That box of buttons you've got in your pocket," she said. "Some of them are pretty old. I expect they could do with a wash."

Lura turned red as a brick. She had found the box of buttons upstairs, but she had not shown them to anybody. She grabbed them, now, out of her sweater pocket.

"You c'llect buttons, I guess," Clementina said.

"Why, nonsense, honey, I just brought them downstairs to show the girls. I'll put them right back—"

"Oh, take them along," Clementina said. "Everybody has problems. I suppose you have to furnish your store with something."

"Why, honey, of course I don't want your buttons!" Lura said. She looked around at the girls, smiling brightly, shaking her head a little to indicate what foolishness this was, and changed the subject. "Now you keep those nasty animals out of the house, dear, you'll stay clean longer."

"My animals?" Clementina said. "But animals are so restful. I am sure if you knew Mame, my sheep, you would rather have her in your kitchen than many people you could mention."

Lura was, finally, put out. After all, you could take only so much. From the wise way some of the girls looked, you'd think they thought she actually meant to steal those buttons. "Well, nuh-nanny plums on the floor!" she sputtered. "Disgusting! After the way we've worked all day, I should think—"

Clementina's voice cut in over the sputter. "Mame was a cosset," she said. "And she doesn't know she still isn't one. Like some people, you know . . . once a cosset, always a cosset. I got her from Tony Morelli, twelve years ago this spring. He had a whole truckload of lambs, taking them down to the slaughterhouse, and Mame didn't like what she saw, so she jumped off the truck when it went by the house. I gave Tony ten dollars for her, and I've never regretted the investment. If in her old age she is unattractive, I don't see that she can be blamed for it."

"Well, it's your house. If you want a mess like that in—"

"Certainly. And Mame lives here. It's her house, too."

"So I could see, when we first came in. You could at least say thank you, I'm sure, not let us feel that we've had our trouble for our pains. Come on, girls—"

She flung open the door to depart and drew back in consternation. Ranged outside were Clementina's animals waiting to come in.

Mame, the sheep, stood there, head down, nose to the crack of the door; beside her was a small black poodle standing on three legs, which were all the legs he had; behind him was an army of cats in all sizes and colors, mostly yellow. They had been waiting there, in patience, and the moment Lura turned the knob, they all walked in. Mame shoved the door wider for herself to come through, gently nudging Lura out of the way. Under her, between her legs, flowed a river of cats.

Lura made a grab for the broom, but too late; the last cat in, a disreputable tom with slit ears and battle-scarred head—why, he was as big as a dog!—walled a baleful green eye at her, spat so viciously that she recoiled in horror, and went past the broom as if it weren't there at all.

"Oh, my!" said Clementina.

The cats made a beeline for her, streaking around and between the ladies; a considerable competition developed as to which ones were going to make it into her lap. The poodle, seeing the congregation in the kitchen, did not come in. He limped along the porch and sat down, back to. Mame the sheep paused in the middle of the clean kitchen floor, glancing around with a pleasant expression, as if to say, "Why, isn't this nice!" Then she, too, marched over and thrust her head against Clementina's hand.

"Oh, my!" Clementina said again. She spoke as if from under a varicolored fur coverlet spread across her lap, and the diamond on her finger sparkled as she patted Mame's grizzled head. "Dear me, I *am* sorry. I meant to tell you not to open the door."

Starting out for Clementina's house that morning, after his conversation with Nellie, Dr. Miles Garland found he was looking forward to a visit there. So far as he was concerned, he always found the old lady as bright as a button nowadays; but he didn't go often, there being only one of him to cope with many whose needs were greater than hers.

Up to now his feeling had been that a little alcohol, at Clementina's age, would do more good than harm; and like the rest of the town, he was inclined to divide most of Nellie's reports by two.

But if it's getting that bad, he thought, recalling her story of the smashed fifths, maybe I ought to take time out and help locate the source of supply.

Everard, without a doubt, but how could you check? The old son was slippery as an eel, nocturnal as an owl. Clementina was probably paying him. You couldn't reason with her about it, either; Garland recalled, with a wry grin, the time he'd tried.

"I'm sure I don't understand modern medicine," she'd said. "You and Nellie Overholt going around people's houses asking for liquor. I've told Nellie that if she wants a drink, she will have to buy her own; my funds are limited these days."

Garland had raised an eyebrow. "You know what I'm talking about—" he began.

"Certainly. I'd suggest you wait till your day's work is over, and come in for a cocktail before dinner, the civilized time. It's not yet ten o'clock."

"All right. Be glad to. Look, you're being a responsibility. What if you fell, here alone, hurt yourself? A number of people have mentioned it, including Amos—"

"I know. Amos wants to commit me."

"How do you know that?" Garland had asked, a little flabbergasted. He hadn't planned to tell her that.

"Oh, Nellie doesn't mince words. She's been waving insane asylums and rest homes at me all summer."

"Well, how about a nice rest home, till you feel better?"

"That would be tiresome. What would I do there?"

"You'd find friends in no time, if I know you."

"And all old people. Why, my cats are more company, any day. Even Herbert," Clementina said, "even old Herbert, there, is interested in a mouse once in a while."

Herbert was the ancient yellow tomcat, king of the varied breed which shared her house and outbuildings. Through his consistent practice of incest over the years, his offspring were mostly in his image. True, there were cats of many colors, due to strays—Clementina's establishment was always increased in the fall when some summer visitor went off, leaving the season's kitten to fend for itself; but to pass the lawn of uncut grass in front of Clementina's house on a bright afternoon when Herbert's get were out sunning themselves, was like passing a field of orange chrysanthemums. It was a sight which the doctor enjoyed when he had time to, and one which never failed to put out Nellie, who considered all unnecessary animals around a house a nuisance.

Driving along this morning, thinking about this, and considering what might have been Nellie's reaction to the suggestion that she buy her own liquor, Garland came near not seeing Lucy Wilkinson, frantically waving by her front gate.

"Sure," he said, listening to her. He remembered, now, that Nellie, earlier on in the week, had mentioned Amos's being sick. "What's the matter with him? Are you sure he wants me?"

"Oh. He fell," Lucy said breathlessly. "Into the track of the bulldozer."

"Good Lord! Was it running?"

"Oh. Yes. He says . . . oh, yes, it was."

And you've had one hell of a rough time with him, Garland thought, glancing at her as they went up the walk together. She sounded half-hysterical, which was surprising for Lucy. In a crisis he had always found her level-headed and sensible; her main characteristic was optimism, invaluable around a sickroom, though Garland had, at times, in the office found it a little wearing for everyday fare, and Nellie Overholt's opinion was that, if you asked her, Lucy was apt to brighten the corner a little too bright.

Lucy was not, however, brightening any corner today. Her usually neat hair was in straggles, her housedress mussed, and her eyes were bloodshot in a face pinched and haggard, as if she had not slept.

"I think he must have plowed his face right into the moving track," she said, ushering Garland through the door.

Brother, he certainly plowed into something, Garland thought, looking Amos over where he lay, fully dressed, on the couch in the kitchen.

The thing you usually noticed first about Amos whenever you saw him with his hat off, or about any of the direct-line Wilkinsons, was their flaming red hair. Clementina had once had it, though now hers was white; and Constance, Amos's daughter, was remarkable for hers, though hers was a little darker than the general run, being a lively reddish-gold. Ordinarily Amos wore his slicked down, crushed flat by his hat; but now, in sickness and pain, combing his hair was the least of his worries. His orange bush stood straight up in a thick, disordered mass above his blackened eyes and mashed nose, his face swollen almost out of recognition.

"Phew! When did this happen?" Garland said in awe.

The man had been terribly pounded and the injuries were surely several days old.

Well, it seemed, on Sunday. He had let it go for a few days, hoping it would get better and he wouldn't have to call the doctor, Lucy said.

"Sunday! Good Lord, Lucy, you know better. What'd you do that for, you thundering fool?" he demanded of Amos.

Amos grunted. He glared, if the sudden spark behind his puffed and slitted lids could be identified as a glare, and made no comment.

"He said I could take care of him." In spite of herself, Lucy clasped her hands together, twisted them. "But, oh my goodness, I couldn't! I didn't know what—His right hand. I think a bone's broken . . ."

"Shut up, Lucy!" Amos's voice was a croak, as if he had been using it a good deal, which, from the shape Lucy was in, Garland didn't doubt he had. "Well, get to it, will you, Doc? Fix me up. I've got work to do."

"You won't do it today. Let's have a look. Your hands get into the bulldozer track, too? Phew!"

Amos's hands, black, puffy, with fingers double their normal size, looked as if he had used them to batter down a stone wall. He said nothing, staring at Garland in silence.

"Okay," Garland said. Funny there wasn't more laceration. He concentrated on filling his hypodermic. "I'll have to have X-rays," he began. "The hospital—"

"Oh, no, you don't! By God, you don't! That's just about what I'd have reason to expect," Amos said.

"What's the matter with you? You want a crippled right hand for the rest of your life?"

"I've got other use for my dough than to buy Cadillacs for them Bishop doctors. If my hand's busted, set it. Or don't you know how?"

"Nope, I don't. Not now. I might have if you'd brought this to me when you did it, but now you're swelled up like a poisoned pig. What d'you think I can do now? Feel of it and give you a pink pill? Here." He pinched up a fold of skin on Amos's arm, deftly pressed home the plunger.

Amos turned greenish. "Don't you shoot none of your goddam dope in to me," he said.

"Hell, that's only a sedative," Garland said. "Acts like aspirin."

"You new doctors are all shot-happy. All you can think about is X-rays and dope. Old Doc Thomas, you broke anything, he fixed it, he didn't frig around." Amos's long, big-shouldered body, for five days braced against pain, suddenly slumped on the couch. "X-rays, for the godsakes," he mumbled. "Old Doc Thomas never heard of them."

"Yup. I wouldn't doubt it," Garland said, watching him. The poor devil without a doubt was half out of his mind with pain. That right hand was broken, one bone at least, and his nose certainly was; but under the circumstances, Garland didn't know that he felt particularly sympathetic, his sympathy being mostly with Lucy, who looked as if she could use some.

Hell of a way to treat a woman, particularly a nice one. She looked as if she'd been sick for weeks.

If he says he fell off a bulldozer, I suppose he did, but he looks more to me as if he'd been in one old bowser of a fistfight. Maybe somebody's finally had the guts to take him apart. If that's so, it couldn't have happened to a nicer guy. Well. Bulldozer or somebody with a good one-two, it's none of my business what story he wants to put out around.

"Took you . . . on the kitchen table," Amos muttered. "Used your own . . . broomstick . . . for a splint. Not a lot of . . . stuff . . . he could charge you a year's income for. Old Doc Thomas . . ." His hoarse voice faded and he slid peacefully into unconsciousness.

"So you can take old Doc Thomas," Garland said, "and shove him. Lucy, where's your phone?"

"Oh, Doctor, you can't take him to the hospital! Not . . . not now! He can't go now! He'll sue you, I know he will, he—"

"Let him sue. I've got your consent. Haven't I?"

"Oh, I don't know. I just don't know—" Her underjaw started to jerk and she put up a shaking hand to hold it still.

"For godsakes!" Garland said, staring at her. "How long since you had any sleep?"

"Well, Sunday. Sunday night. When it happened." She made an effort and finally controlled her chattering teeth.

"Well, the hospital's the place for him; you can't take care of him, the shape you're in. I'll call the ambulance and get him out of here, and then I'll give you a pill. You can go to bed and sleep as long as you like—What's the matter now?"

"No, no, I mustn't, I—" She stopped. "Amos is death on dope. He wouldn't like it if I took dope," she said primly.

"Dope!" Garland snorted. He fished in his bag, came up with a box of capsules, fetched a glass of water from the sink. "Well, come on, take it. You know it's only a mild barbiturate. Take it, dammit!"

Lucy put the capsule in her mouth. She sat for a moment fearfully, with both hands on her stomach.

"All right!" Garland said. "And stop acting as if you're going to blow up, because you aren't." He went on, more gently, "What is it, Lucy? You know better than this, don't you?"

Lucy nodded. She had closed her lips tightly over the pill, and didn't speak.

Garland spun on his heel and went to the phone, which he found in the downstairs hall. As he dialed the hospital number, he heard, over the clicking sound of the dial, somewhere in the house, a sneeze. He glanced, puzzled, up the staircase. If Lucy wasn't alone here with Amos, funny she hadn't mentioned it. Then he saw that the parlor door was open. These old houses, where the stairwell went straight up from the middle of the house, nearly always had odd acoustics. That must've been Lucy sneezing. It wouldn't be anything to wonder at, if after all this she came down with a cold.

As he reentered the kitchen, he saw Lucy sitting where he had left her, motionless in her chair. Her lips suddenly puckered into a wry, involuntary grimace, quickly controlled, and her eyes watered. She stared bleakly at Garland with an expression that could only be reproach.

"Oh, blast!" Garland said. Irascibly he handed her the glass of water. "If you didn't want to swallow it, why didn't you spit it out?"

he demanded. "You knew if you held it in your mouth, the gelatin would melt and you'd get one hell of a bitter dose . . ." He stopped, seeing the tears come into her eyes.

"Oh," she said wanly. "I know . . . I guess I forgot. I've . . . never been able to swallow those big capsules very well . . ."

Garland picked up his bag. "You get some rest. The ambulance'll be along, and I'll see Amos at the hospital. The way he feels, he won't stay very long, and he's going to be just as tough to take care of when he gets home as—"

From somewhere, upstairs certainly this time, somebody sneezed again. Twice.

Lucy jumped. For a moment she looked remote, withdrawn, as if in all the world there were no such thing as a sneeze and, if there were, she hadn't heard it. Then she said carefully, "Oh, dear, Dr. Garland, you must think I'm really to pieces, but Amos has been so . . . and I've been up nights. Imagine my forgetting to tell you that Connie's home. She had the flu down in the city, h-had to give up her job."

"Flu, eh? Oh, that's too bad. No joke, either, I guess. I hear they're having an epidemic, down in the cities. She all right, or do you want me to look at her?"

"Oh, no, no, no need to bother. She was o-over it before she got home, only I'm keeping her in bed for a day."

"Good idea. Nice you're not here alone, takes a load off my mind. But look, if you need help, Lucy, I'll get Nellie to come over, put you to bed—"

"Nellie? Oh, mercy, no! Oh my goodness, we don't need Nellie, we're fine, Connie is over it and all I need is sleep, so . . ." Exhaustedly Lucy ran down, took a breath, and started over. "And she's so busy, and she does talk *so* much—"

"Okay, okay, don't push the panic button. Get some sleep. I'll be in touch."

Back in his car, he started up the engine and swung out into the highway.

That cross-grained hog has sure yanked his wife apart, he thought.

Somebody ought to—well, maybe somebody did. Still, she's put up with him well for years; a few days of him sick shouldn't put her on the edge. And why fly into the air winged-out over having poor old Nellie in to help? I'm darned if I know what goes on there.

Something nudged at his mind, and he shrugged it impatiently away.

Uh huh. I know you. I'm beginning to know you well. You're starting to add the fancy touches and you're still trying to suck me in. Go on. Beat it. I got no time for you. That pretty kid, Connie. Besides, she got married, or didn't you know?

Wasn't much said about her getting married, at the time, said the ring-tailed devil. That was kind of odd if you ask me. The wedding of the only Wilkinson daughter ought to have made quite a splurge in this town; and didn't. Suppose she didn't get married at all? Isn't this what you've been keeping an eye peeled for, in a quiet way—a town girl, come home from away, on the q. t., and just a little sick, maybe? Maybe the flu?

You shut up. The Wilkinsons stick a live baby out on the trash heap? Lucy have any part of that?

Amos is a man of fundamentalist proportions. Paranoid fundamentalist proportions, you said so yourself. Men faced with that particular dilemma, at times have been known to do terrible and unpredictable things.

Sure. So Amos is stingy and cantankerous, but he wouldn't—

How do you know he wouldn't? You think yourself he's crazy.

Now, look. Hold on. Amos got hurt on Sunday. So how could he be around the town dump on Sunday night? If you recall, it was early Monday morning when I snatched J. J. Randall out of old Everard's bonfire. You take off. If I was to speculate on more likely things, I'd pay some attention to the establishment up at Gertie Warren's.

Okay, said the ring-tailed devil, preparing to fly out the window. But Gertie or no Gertie, if you recall, J. J. Randall, for a little baby, has quite a spectacular lot of red hair.

Gertie Warren, Nellie Overholt's younger sister, was twenty and soft. That is, Nellie said she was soft. Whereas Nellie had yanked herself out of Shacktown by main strength, Gertie was content to stay there. She lived, with another girl, in the old Warren house, which she had got after the old folks died, and she worked summers on the packing tables at Randall's. She was fast with her fingers, one of Randall's best packers; she could do three cases of sardines an hour. In a good season she could earn from a thousand to twelve hundred dollars, which made her more than eligible for unemployment checks through the winter, if the winter happened to be workless. She did all right. But to Nellie's eternal fury, she wouldn't spend any of her money to better herself; she spent it all on clothes and hair-dos and things; and she had turned the old Warren house into an Establishment, she and this other girl, which managed, to all intents and purposes, to stay Respectable Daytimes, though God only knew what Went On There Nights.

Gertie had gone for two years to high school, until she was sixteen and could get legal working papers. She had not liked high school. Most of the things they talked about there and tried to teach her seemed unreal to her. Algebra was very boring; she could make neither head nor tail of x and y. Shakespeare shocked her; he was a dirty-minded man. You found that out if you looked up the words; sometimes you didn't have to, he came right out and said, in print. From *Silas Marner* Gertie remembered only one thing: the little piece of poetry on the beginning page before you started the story; if you could call it a story; it was awful boring. The poetry was:

> *A child, more than all other gifts*
> *That earth can offer to declining man*
> *Brings hope with it and forward-looking thoughts.*

That was what she remembered; and it was a lie. Gertie guessed she knew. At seventeen she had had a child. The man she had had it by was "declining," all right. He had declined to have anything to do with it or her; when he'd found out she was going to, zip, he was gone, leaving her with such hope and forward-looking thoughts as she could scrape out of what Nellie and her father and mother had to say about her having a baby and not being married. The three of them had carried on something awful, night and day. Her father had even died of it, at least Nellie and her mother said so, killed by the shame of it all, though everybody knew he had had a weak heart for years and might have gone at any time.

In Home Economics class, they had taught Gertie to sew, but she couldn't sew for the baby, she couldn't keep her mind on it. She would go wandering off, reading or looking out the window, leaving the little garment kicking around on the floor for old Mrs. Warren, who went around the house in bedroom slippers because of her bunions, to step on the needle in it. Old Mrs. Warren refused to do any sewing for a woods colt. Let it come, she said, into the world naked; indecent it was, and indecent, for all of her, it would remain. Nellie finally brought home some diapers and stuff from the Welfare, which, she pointed out, were the same thing as stolen.

"I'm not supposed, for my own or my family's use. I hope you realize if I got found out I'd lose my job."

Well, it wasn't as if the baby clothes were the first things from the Welfare that had ridden into the house inside Nellie's cape. Old Mrs. Warren, right now, had on a pair of shoes and a flannel petticoat from the Welfare. Nellie kept an eye peeled; times this or that of the right size wouldn't even be missed. Nobody had ever thought anything of it before; it was the usual thing. You had a job, you toted from the job. Who ever called that stealing? Gertie guessed she knew what was being done; it was all a part of Pay The Piper and Let It Be A Lesson. Even the old man, it looked like, had died on purpose. She didn't even try to argue the point; what was the use to?

But coming to, after the baby was born, Gertie had had to tell herself that it didn't have much of a trousseau. Other girls, married girls, having babies had showers given; they got lovely things—pink blankets and booties. It just showed to go you. And having had the baby jammed down her craw for months before it was born, she found that when it was, she could hardly bring herself to touch it. She did; she forced herself; but she couldn't help it, she did the minimum and thanked God it had to be a bottle baby.

Experience with life *so* far had taught Gertie two things she could count on: In high school, she had learned to read; Rudy, her first boyfriend, had let her know she was Good In Bed.

"My God," he'd said to her, "but you're Good In Bed. The best I ever seen."

You couldn't, she told herself, have everything, but you could make use of what you did have.

She read, that winter, all winter long: *True Romances, True Love Stories*, never missing a number, sometimes bothering the people at the drugstore until the magazines came. She kept a file of them in her room; when she finished the new one, she went back and read over. She put herself and Rudy in the places of the lovers in the stories; at least, she put Rudy. It wasn't hard to put him instead of one of those men, there. In the pictures, they were all good-looking, and so had Rudy been, with perfect hair for a man, curls and silky. It was hard to put herself for the girls because they were all dolls, and she was ash-blonde with freckles—the mousy type, Nellie and Mama always said—and all out of shape with the baby, and there wasn't any money for hair-dos; she looked awful.

Gertie learned a great deal from her Reading: even a homely girl could get married if she learned how to make the most of herself, with nice clothes and soap and perfume and deodorant. If, added to that, she was Good In Bed, which Gertie cherished that she was, there was no reason why she couldn't get with it, have it made. All she'd ever wanted anyway was to get married, have a home with nice things, and a husband who was nice, too, and had a good job. She learned, with surprise and a great feeling of comradeship, that that was what the girls who got in trouble in the magazines had wanted, too; they were not so much bad as misled. One story said love was all-powerful; and another that there was not enough love in the world. Remembering Rudy, she guessed that this was so; not enough, anyway, to go around, some for everybody. Something, she guessed, was out of line somewhere; else how could anything so beautiful, like with Rudy, be bad? In the magazines, though, it was frowned upon; you had to pay, first, but you came out all right in the end. After the baby was born, Gertie paid for three months; then, according to Nellie, she started all over again.

Nellie came in one night around eleven o'clock, on her way home from a case, to check up on old Mrs. Warren, who hadn't been feeling well, and with reason; she had arthritis, and kidneys, which, Nellie felt, were sooner or later going to kill her. She found her mother still up, huddled in front of the stove with her feet in the oven.

"Hello, Ma," Nellie said. "How you feeling?"

The old lady didn't move or look around. She said, "Pretty good," with the accent on the "pretty," which meant more to come and which Nellie, laying off her nurse's cape, braced herself to hear patiently. She was tired to death; it had been a rotten, cold spring, with a lot of flu in Shacktown.

"An Epsom-salts bath for them aching feet," she said, and went to fix one; bringing it back, she broke into her mother's detailed list of symptoms with, "How's that baby?"

"That baby's sick," Mrs. Warren said. She lowered her feet with a moan of relief into the hot water.

"What's the matter with it now?" Nellie said.

The old lady had kept harping, and Nellie herself was about convinced that Gertie was neglecting the baby; it stayed puny and thin, didn't seem to put on weight the way it ought to. Nellie checked when she could, but she was busy.

"How would I know what ails it?" Mrs. Warren said. "I don't have no part in *that*. It's her'n. Her works. It ain't no part of *me*."

"Well, you knew it was sick," Nellie said.

"It cried all day, was all. If I had had any way of shutting off my ears I wouldn't know. If you ask me, it's starving to death. The bottle's up there in the warming oven, sour, a solid curd. I ain't seen her fix nothing for it today."

"Well, it ain't crying now," Nellie said. "Must have gone to sleep. I'll take a look at it before I go."

They had cake and coffee and a good long gossip. It always did Mrs. Warren good to see Nellie. Nellie was in touch; she knew what went on around town. Before she left, she had the old lady roaring laughing.

"Time you got to bed, Ma," she said at last. "Feet's better, you ought to be able to sleep. And I'm bushed, I got to get home."

"Well, you better take a look at that baby. Feed it for a change, maybe. I don't know what's in *her* mind, and I ain't asking."

Nellie had had her cape on, ready to go; she was bushed. Checking on Gertie's baby had slipped her mind. She reached down the bottle in the warming oven, found it three-quarters full of a sour curd that didn't even slide when she turned the bottle bottom up.

"For heaven's *sake!*" she said. "She didn't try to feed it that, did she?"

"I'm sure I don't know, I don't take no notice what she does."

With hardening lips, Nellie started for the stairs.

When she walked anywhere, she could be heard; going upstairs when she was tired, she could rattle windowpanes. She wished afterwards she'd thought to be a little more quiet. Gertie's door was shut, and apparently the room was dark, but as Nellie rounded the landing, she wondered if she hadn't seen the light just come on, shine through the keyhole and the crack under the door. She didn't think about it at the time, and afterwards she couldn't be sure.

Gertie was lying in bed reading a magazine, which wasn't anything new. But her face wasn't creamed and her hair was down around her shoulders. She had it cut in a long bob which she always put up on curlers at night. Well, tonight, she hadn't. And the window onto the porch roof was wide open, curtains blowing in; and the bed was rumpled, out at the foot.

Nellie didn't say anything. She just looked around the room.

"Hi," Gertie said. "Out kind of late, ain't you?"

"Later than you think, I guess," Nellie said. She fixed Gertie with a cold stare. "Ma says that baby's sick."

"Well, she cried a lot today. And she wouldn't take her milk."

Nellie snorted. "Well, for godsakes, you never thought she would, did you, that stuff? I looked at it. Sourer than swill!"

"It was all right this morning. I tasted it."

"So it would stay that way all day in the warming oven. How come your bed's so tore up, or don't I need to ask? And what's that window doing open, cold air blowing in? That ought to help, if that baby's sick."

"Well, the room was hot. I only opened it a minute ago. I was just going to—"

"Opened it when you heard me coming. Or maybe it wasn't you opened it, hah?"

Gertie went right on with what she'd been going to say. "—going to close it as soon as the room aired out."

Hnf, try to get to that one, Nellie thought. She just looked at you, wide-open, round eyes, didn't even get mad. Most girls would at least get mad, but not Gert. She just looked, as if what you'd said was it's a nice day. And that made you so put out that you didn't have no sympathy whatsoever.

Nellie marched across the room and banged the window down. She took a good look first, out and around the porch roof. It was dark; she couldn't see a sign of anybody there. She spun around in time to catch, well, not a smile, not so much as one, on Gert's face; just a tick of change in expression as if she could have smiled, but had not wanted to let herself.

"You," Nellie said, "Are starting all over again."

Gertie said, "I told you what it was. I only wanted to air out the room."

"Well, *I* would, in your place!"

The baby was in its bed, made out of a pillow on two chairs pushed against the wall. Nellie went over, turned down a corner of blanket.

"Maybe you can tell what's wrong with her," Gertie said. "Or maybe she's better. She went to sleep, all right."

The baby lay there. Nellie put a couple of fingers against its cheek to test if it had a fever. The silky skin, under her fingers, was as cold as a stone.

"Oh, my God!" Nellie said. She put her head down to the small chest and listened. "She ain't breathing," she said. "Gert, for godsakes, that baby's dead!"

That got to Gert, all right. She flung herself out of bed and came tearing across the room to look, and stood looking.

"Oh, what was it?" she said. "She wasn't that sick, not sick enough to—I know she wasn't! Oh, what could it have been?"

"If you ask me," Nellie said grimly, "malurition."

"I tried! I tried all day to make her eat!"

"I know what Ma says. She says you ain't bothered to feed it."

"She's a liar! I did so try!"

"Well, I don't know who 'tis this time," Nellie said. "And I don't care who he is. But I can tell you this, Miss Lady, your arse has run away with your head."

"Oh, I didn't know she was that sick," Gertie said. "How could she have been? She just cried and wouldn't eat. I just thought she'd eat when she got ready to. I didn't know. I never knew nothing about babies anyway, and nobody told me anything. You never told me . . . you never told me nothing! And you could of . . . you could have told me something. You're a nurse, you could of even told me how to get rid of it so I wouldn't have to have it, you could of told me, and you didn't. You knew, and you wouldn't tell me nothing!"

"Don't try to put it off on me. This is one thing you can't blame on nobody—" Nellie began, but she stopped in the middle. If Gert felt bad—and she did, all right, you could see she did, bad enough to show it—that was different. Nellie gave her a good strong sedative and saw she was asleep, before leaving the house.

That had been three years ago, and Gert had lived it down; at least, partly down. It could be mentioned in times of stress, but was brought up less and less as time went on. Old Mrs. Warren had died the second winter; Gertie had got the house. Nellie had Billy Overholt's house on Prospect Street, and she had his children whom she didn't want to bring up in Shacktown, even if she would have been caught dead, now, living there herself. Gert had lived there alone for a while; then she got another girl to come in with her, share the expenses. The other girl was no better than she should be, but Nellie washed her hands of it. She was on speaking terms with Gert, live and let live; she even threw work Gert's way when she could, babysitting for patients and such, when Gert wasn't working at the factory; blood was thicker than water. The only thing Nellie did that showed she remembered was, she wouldn't let her girls go near. She didn't care if Gert did have a new deepfreeze full of ice cream, or a twenty-four-inch TV screen, or a Hi-Fi with lots of records—it was a caution the stuff they'd crowded into that house and the way they'd fixed it up, and you guessed you knew where most of it came from; no matter what there was, Becky and Kate could stay away. On that, Nellie put her big flat foot down.

Thus, if Dr. Garland mused about Gertie Warren's Establishment in connection with J. J. Randall, it was not wholly to be wondered at; and the next thought followed as the night the day: What man around town, outside of Amos Wilkinson, had red hair?

Part Two
November, 1959

T he *Potluck* was a ninety-foot trawler out of New Bedford. She
was brand-new, in the water less than a year; her equipment
was modern and the best that money could buy. Walt Sheridan, her
owner and skipper, had worked and saved for a long time to be able
to have her built. He was a slow and cautious man who knew his
business; when he shopped, he shopped around. He tested and niggled
and asked questions and took things apart, and he hung around the
boatyard where his equipment was being installed until the pestered
workmen bestowed on his boat and on him the nicknames of "Pot"
and "Fusspot."

Walt did not know this, nor would he have cared if he had known.
He had a methodical mind; when he had a project, he concentrated.
Equipping a boat or choosing a wife, he had found that a little care
and attention to detail paid off; at least, for him. He had married late,
having shopped around, picked out, and rejected in that area also;
but now, at forty-four, he had a nice wife whom he loved and who
loved him, and three children of satisfactory ages spaced two years
apart and in the process of growing up into well-disciplined young
people. They had better.

As for his boat, what he wanted and got was a good one that would
carry heavy loads and stay afloat in any weather; he was determined to
have aboard her no jerry-built, or rotten, or second-rate or neglected
gear to play out on him in a gale out in the middle of the Gulf of Maine
or the Bay of Fundy. Finished, the *Potluck* was among the best of her
kind, with the latest in electronic devices. Her nets were of nylon.
She was Diesel-powered and carried a crew of six men, whose cabin
quarters were clean and comfortable and who considered themselves
lucky in their jobs. From the first the *Potluck* made money; the crew's

shares were bountiful. She was not always, but more often than not, a high-liner—to no surprise of Walt's. Let it be said, care and attention to detail were bound to pay off. With his know-how and a good boat alone, he could have found fish; but with all this electronic stuff, he didn't even have to depend on luck. It was riding a gravy train.

Today, the Friday before Amos Wilkinson got hurt, the *Potluck* was headed down the coast home with thirty thousand redfish, riding the tail end of a November blow. Walt was alone in the pilot shelter, or thought he was. The boat was on marine pilot; he hadn't much to do except keep an eye on her just in case, and he was thinking about getting in tonight, seeing the wife and kids. He hoped Marge hadn't forgotten that she'd promised him corn dumplings for supper; and, as he did often when no one was around, he was singing. It was an old tune from Down East, where Walt had been brought up, with a monotonous melody that made a good drone through a man's nose.

"God, Walt!" said a voice behind him. "You sound like the wind in the ballpark fence."

Walt jumped. He wasn't nervous, but he hadn't heard anybody. He sure-God hated to be sneaked up on. This fellow, Anzio Jones, had a trick of doing that. Look around and there he'd be. Of all his crew members, this was the one that Walt liked the least; he wished now he'd never signed him on; he'd about half made up his mind to tell him to haul his freight. Still, maybe it wasn't right to fire a hand just because he was tiresome and a blowhard. Anzio was a good enough man aboard a boat and he knew a little something about Diesels.

But, oh, blast! Walt thought, glancing around with irritation. Now I'll have to listen to what *he* thinks about things in general.

Anzio lounged up beside him, peering out through the streaming windscreen. "Cheese, these old slop buckets!" he said. "Fat woman on a roller coaster. Sometimes I wonder how we ever make it in."

Walt was not sentimental about the *Potluck*. He did not endow her with female temperament or disposition, as many skippers did their boats, and it was only for convenience that he ever referred to her as "she." To him, her design was one of the most efficient that ever came off a drawing board; if she acted like a fat woman on a roller coaster just now, well, she had a load, didn't she? Anzio's comments, therefore, were foolishness; about what you had a right to expect. Walt leaned a little to one side so he could see past Anzio through the windscreen. "What's the trouble?" he asked. "Seems to be handling it all right. You see something out of line?"

"Hell, you want to see craft that can handle it," Anzio said, "you ought to see them outrigger canoes in Tahiti. I ever tell you about them?"

"Uh huh."

And about Ward liners and Chesapeake oyster sloops and tankers in the Merchant Marine; anything from a rowboat to an LST. According to Anzio's tell, he knew them all. To hear him, you'd think he'd been top cock on ships and had saved lives, situations, and women around the world. It was enough to kill you, that glab of his, and a chore to listen to, since most of it was a mess of lies which nobody could be fool enough to swallow. Walt wondered how Anzio, who seemed to be a bright enough kid in other ways, could expect anybody to believe half of the preposterous stuff he put out about himself.

For instance, when Walt had hired him, he'd said he'd just come out of the Navy, and, "Been in the Navy a long time," he had said, with that honest, clear-eyed, you-and-I-are-buddies smile he had. It would sure take you in, that smile would. "I got my nickname, Anzio, in the South Pacific, in World War Two."

"Eh?" Walt said, startled. "Anzio's in Italy."

God, he ought to know. He himself had been with a Commando unit all through that filthy, bloody fighting.

"Oh, I mean the other one," Anzio said. "The one on Paloo-Paloo."

"Pa-what? Where's that?"

"Well, you got to know them South Pacific Islands to recognize the names, they don't sound the way they look written out. Me, I was born in Tahiti, speak the language. They was fighting on Paloo-Paloo would make Iwo and the rest of them look like a rumble in a kindergarten."

"There was?"

"So the fellows nicknamed it, when they come over from Anzio, Italy, after VE Day. I was through the whole of it. I was there."

"So was Kilroy. Godsake, how old are you?"

"Uh? Oh. I'm thirty-five."

"H'm," Walt said.

A warning bell had rung in his head at the time, and he wished now he'd heeded it. This kid didn't look twenty-five. If he'd committed all the hellfire-hero stuff in World War II he told about, be must've done it at the ripe age of from seven to twelve years old. He might, just possibly, have done a hitch in the Navy, the way he said he had; that might be where he'd learned diesels. As for being born in Tahiti, he had a fine old unmistakable Down East accent exactly like Walt's own. But he'd seemed like a strong, able fellow, and Walt had signed him on. Walt could have run his own diesels if he had had to and he had Perley Stokes for regular engineer; it wasn't a bad idea, though, to have a second along, just in case, and you didn't run into a diesel man every day. He was a troublemaker all right, it turned out. Walt didn't doubt the boys would be pleased any time he got rid of him.

They had got onto Anzio fast. In the beginning they'd ribbed him a lot, but not so much now. He had a way of getting his own back, lacing into you in the place where it hurt most, like with Perley Stokes the other day.

Ordinarily Perley would have taken care of himself, but for a week or so he'd had a miserable stiff neck and he was walking on an egg with every step he took. Personally Walt felt that Perley'd been a boob to needle Anzio at any such time; not that it made any difference now, with Perley laid up for the entire trip.

"How old was you, Anzy," Perley'd said with a straight face, "when the French th'owed you off of Tahiti Island for fooling with their wimmen?"

"Hell," Anzio said. "Them wimmen was fooling with me, if you want to know. I never been a place in my life yet, Perley, old socks, old boy, the wimmen didn't want to fool with me."

Walt didn't doubt that, not the way Anzio looked—six-foot-three of lazy length, big limber muscles in all the right places, shoulders nearly a yard across, and that nice, smooth suntan that made his teeth show up white as a colored man's. You couldn't blame the women.

"Oh, sure," Perley said. He felt pretty secure, knowing that nobody would be mean enough to claw up a man with a neck as sore as his was. "Oh, sure, we all know that, Anzy, womenfolks likes pretty playthings, sure, sure. But how old was you then? Some of us was speculating."

"Uh. Let's see." Anzio made a quick show of counting on his fingers, grinning, moving up on Perley slow and easy, and Perley not even noticing. "I was twelve years old then."

"God, got your growth young, didn't you?"

"Why, when I was eight years old, I was six foot tall, and I had more on the ball than you've got now, Perley, old buddy, old son. See?"

He hauled back his fist and let go straight at Perley's nose, stopping the blow before it landed, so that Perley, seeing the big fist coming, jumped and jerked back his head. Anzio hadn't touched him, but he ended up sitting on the deck swearing, holding on to his neck; and he had spent his time, since, in and out of his bunk.

Oh, you had to hand it to Anzio. He could manage.

But if you didn't needle him—and Walt didn't bother to, it was too much trouble and tiresome—then Anzio needled you, as if he had some idea you might be a little timid of him, maybe. A big ox like that, a fighter, he had to let you know he was around. Right now he knew that the boat was coming up New Bedford harbor, would soon swing in for the dock, and that his job was on deck lending a hand; but he wasn't moving.

"Buh-rother, that Diesel stinks," he said. "I had to come up here for some air. Where'd you get that old Civil War monument, anyway, Walt? Smells like something off of Abe Lincoln's funeral train."

Walt said nothing. He took the boat off marine pilot, which ought to have been hint enough; but Anzio merely craned past the wheel to get closer to the windscreen. He stood looking at the New Bedford waterfront, not now very far away. His head came full in Walt's line of vision. "Wonder if that little old gal'll be on the dock this time," he said. "Brother! They don't give up easy, do they?"

Walt said, "Get your damned head out of my way and haul arse!"

Anzio started around in mock surprise. "Well, if I didn't forget we had to stop the old Laundromat!" he said. "Trouble with me is, I'm too used to being the one to tell the coolie when to throw the switches."

"Well, you go tell the coolie, if that's how it is."

"Sure, sure, ole Cap'n, ole Marse. Gol rime it, we're a-going t' split the wharf and land the hull power plant up on Main Street!"

He had reproduced an overdone imitation of Walt's nasal tones, and he grinned. "How's that for a Boston brogue?" he said. "From a Tahitian?"

He went, sliding the pilot-shelter door behind him.

Times, Walt thought, I could kick him off the boat, be shed of him and be happy. And any more of that stuff, by God, I will.

The girl was there, Walt couldn't help but notice, as he left the trawler and walked up the wharf. She was standing by a corner of the wharf shed, in the place where she always waited for Anzio. She had on the same dark red tam o'shanter and the brown cloth coat with the beat-up fur collar, which didn't look too warm for any fall day, let alone a cold, windy one like this. If it was any of a man's business, he might be sorry for her. Pretty little thing, didn't look like a tramp, either; and about as pregnant as a girl could be. The waterfront street was no place for a woman, let alone one who was in the shape she was, and she'd probably been waiting around here, off and on, for a day or so, because nobody could have told her just when the *Potluck* would get back. Walt was near enough to hear what was said when Anzio went by her, walking with a couple of the boys, laughing and carrying on, poking this one and that one in the ribs. The girl stepped out to meet him, but he didn't turn his head until she laid a hand on his arm.

"Hello, Ernie," she said.

Anzio stopped. He raised one eyebrow. He winked at the boys. Big deal. He said, "Who're you?"

The girl pulled back as if she'd burnt her fingers on his sleeve.

"Because you're mistaken, remember?" Anzio said. "My name's Anzio Jones. You'll have to hunt elsewhere for Ernie."

He went on by, and she stood looking after him.

Somebody ought to take that cooky out and drown him, Walt told himself. He couldn't help it, he spoke to her.

"Why don't you call a taxi and get on out of here?" he said.

Somewhere downwharf, some bright joker let off a longdrawn wolf whistle.

"See?" Walt said. "This ain't no place for you."

The blind look she turned on him nearly made the sweat start under his cap; she looked as if she didn't see anything, much less understand what he'd said. Then, all at once, her eyes focused on him.

"Oh," she said. "I guess you mean to be kind, don't you? Would you lend me taxi fare? I came off without any change in my purse."

"Uh—" Walt began. He might have known.

The girl said, "My husband'll pay you back. I guess."

"Is he your husband? Anzio?"

"Why, yes. At least, he was. I don't know who he thinks he is now."

Well, no sense being surprised at anything that joker turned up with. But after the way he'd talked—never let 'em marry you, don't let 'em catch you with anything but your pants down—a couple of times aboard the boat, Walt had had to tell him to cut out the filthy talk, it didn't sound good.

He fumbled with his billfold. The first thing that came to hand was a five-dollar bill which slipped halfway out by accident; with inbred caution, Walt shoved it back. She wouldn't need that much; a dollar ought to do it. Anzio, blast him, had plenty to take care of his wife. If he'd gone through what he'd made in the last eight months, his share of this trip alone would set him up for a while. That was a hell of a thing. Walk off and leave a woman on the wharf broke, and she so far along she could hardly stand, much less walk home. It wasn't Walt's business; but the more he thought about it, the more indignant he got.

Thumbing through his wallet in search of a dollar bill, he happened to glance up and saw that the girl was staring at the wallet with its fat sheaf of bills as if it had been manna from Heaven and she starving in the desert. She had even turned white.

"Hey, what's the matter?" Walt said uneasily. "You feel sick or something?"

"I'm hungry," she said. It was as if the words had said themselves before she could hold them back.

"For the godsakes!" Walt burst out. "Don't that jitterbug give you enough to eat on?"

"He doesn't give me anything."

"Why, blast him, he can be made to help you," Walt said. "You're his wife, he's legally responsible. There's places you can go," he went on, growing more and more uneasy as he realized that somebody certainly ought to take a little responsibility here. "Why, all you got to do is . . . is step into the nearest police station, have the bugger arrested for"—his mind searched for the legal term, found it, with relief—"for nonsupport."

"Yes. I know. But the thing is, he says the baby isn't his."

For a moment Walt thought she was going to cry, but she bit down hard and stopped her chin from trembling.

"He hasn't any reason to think so," she said. "He only wants to be rid of . . . of it, and of me. He even says we're not married now, the wedding was a fake."

My gorry, not married, Walt thought. His mind, conditioned for years in the matter, picked out the two significant words in what she'd said. I better not get mixed up in this. Who's to say what's the right of it? It's Anzio's business, anyway. Not mine.

The girl interpreted his look of embarrassed constraint correctly. She said carefully, "I've tried to get a job, but the way I am . . . you can't blame people. I'm ashamed to talk like this to a stranger, but I'm desperate, I haven't any money and no place to go. I feel like a ghost on the street here, I haven't spoken to anyone for so long."

"Well, for godsakes, where's your folks live? Where's your father and mother?"

She stared at him, and he could see her upper lip stiffen before his eyes. "Ernie, uh, Anzio said . . . your boat goes right by the place where I live, where my folks are. Couldn't you take me, next trip, drop me off there? I wouldn't be any trouble, and—"

Walt grunted as if someone had poked him in the stomach. His reaction, at first incredulous disbelief, passed quickly into indignation. Take a woman? On the boat? Good God, what was she thinking of? And the shape she was in!

"Look, Miss, uh, Mrs. Jones," he said. "You can't do nothing like that; that's crazy. Now, you go to the police, the Travelers' Aid, they'll see you get home."

He started to hand her a dollar bill, then changed his mind and added a second one.

"Here's two dollars, you take it and . . . My gorry, I couldn't . . . It's out of the . . ."

He was talking, he realized, to thin air. The girl had headed off down the street, walking with the awkward, spraddle-footed gait a pregnant woman has. She had not taken the money; left him standing there, foolish, with his two dollars in his hand.

What could a man do?

Maybe he ought to go after her, make her take it. I could hold it back out of Anzio's pay. But that ain't legal, he'd have a kick coming, and him, the way he is, no knowing what he'd say or let on to people, he suspects her anyway, no telling what he'd lay onto me, and me a family man . . .

Realizing what the possibilities, under the circumstances, might be, Walt put his money back in his wallet. He took off his cap and wiped the sweat off his forehead.

Right now, his business was to get home to supper, see his wife and kids what little time he had, which was only the rest of today and tomorrow. Have to get the *Potluck* back to the salt mines, as the boys would say, whilst there was still some fish out there. He settled himself into his peacoat with a hunch of his big shoulders and went off home.

The *Potluck* started back on her next trip early Sunday morning. It was ten that night when Walt found out that the girl was on board. He had just finished his late mug-up and was on deck congratulating himself on the weather. Since the last big blow, the ocean had settled down. Big, glassy swells heaved up out of the darkness, sliding slick and silent under the keel as the trawler pounded north. Away to the west, at sunset, over the distant low line of the coast, the sky had been colored up pink and cold green—the kind of November sunset that usually meant frost ashore, white rime on trees and alders and skating for the kids. Out in the Gulf of Maine, aboard the *Potluck*, it meant a still night and a good chance to drag fish. With luck, if he timed it right, it meant a full hold in jig time, and that the next layover, home, would be Thanksgiving Day.

Good weather, unless that cloud bank, which had lain low down below the green, developed into something. Meditating on it, Walt decided it wouldn't—a few rain or snow squalls, maybe, depending on temperature, and then clearing. He was thinking that in a few hours they'd be on the grounds and could get the drag over, when Giles Green came up from aft, popping like a percolator. Giles, under stress, stuttered. For a moment Walt couldn't make head nor tail of what he was trying to say.

"For the godsakes, take it easy, Giles," he said. "Start over. If we've sprung a leak, we'd be sunk by now," and then, as he realized, his stomach turned over with a flop he could hear.

"Oh, no! Oh, goddammit, no!" he groaned. "Where is she?"

"She's suh-suh-suh-suh-suh—" Giles said. "I heard, I heard her puh-puh-puh—"

"All right, she's sick and you heard her puking. Where is she?"

He made out that the girl had stowed away in the hold on the trawler's salt supply, and he spun on his heel and climbed the ladder down there.

The girl had made herself a hollow, a kind of nest in the salt bags. She was sitting up in it with her knees hugged under her chin and her head bowed on them. When Walt put the beam of his flashlight on her, she lifted her head and stared at him. Her face was sickly green all over, except for the black hollows in which her eyes sent back two fiercely sparking pinpoints of light.

For a moment Walt was reminded of a weasel that he had cornered, years ago, in a brushpile in his grandfather's woodlot—the small, three-cornered, fighting face, desperate, ready to use what it had, which wasn't much compared to Walt's .22, to bite, to tear, to defend itself; and he remembered, the flash of memory gone as quickly as it had come, how there hadn't been any of his cronies around to rib him for being a sissy, so he'd let the weasel go.

He began furiously, "What in the devil do you think you're—"

And then he saw what she had, wrapped in the old brown cloth coat with the beat-up fur collar and laid on the salt beside her; and the words "doing here" came out as if they had popped in his throat like a balloon.

She said hoarsely, "It's dead. I didn't know what to do, so it's dead."

Christ, who did know what to do? He didn't. Somewhere he'd heard that if the right thing wasn't done, and quick, baby and mother both died.

He thought when he put out his hand to touch her that she was going to snap like the weasel, the way she looked at him.

"All right," he said. "Take it easy. Nobody's going to hurt you, now take it easy, this is a hell of a place to . . . Take it easy, we're just going to lug you out of here, get you warm. . . ." He stopped his babbling, realizing that she had slumped in his arms. She was limp as he passed her up the ladder to Giles.

"Juh-Juh-Juh-Jeezus!" Giles said. "What'll I, what'll I do with her?"

"Put her in Anzio's bunk," Walt said grimly.

He scooped up the brown cloth bundle, thinking that if what was in it was dead, he himself was partly to blame and, in his state of shock and horror, that if he could just heave the thing over the side it would save everybody concerned a lot of trouble. And then, as he lifted it to his shoulder and ran up the ladder, it let out, directly into his ear, a strong, muffled yell that scared him so he almost dropped it.

Godfrey mighty, it was alive. Poor little tyke. . . . That blasted Anzio, damn him!

Word had passed. Most of the crew were cluttered around the cabin companionway, gawping, mouths wide-open. Oatey Oatman was standing his trick in the pilot shelter—he kept hollering back, wanting to know what was up—and Anzio wasn't anywhere in sight. But the rest crowded down into the cabin after Walt and his burden.

"Look," Walt said. Distraught, he dumped the baby down on the cabin table, looking desperately from one to another of the men. "Who knows how to—who knows anything about this, what to do? I could call the Coast Guard, head inshore and have them meet us with a doctor, but by that time . . . I heard you got to do whatever it is fast or the whole rig bleeds to—"

For a moment nobody said anything. Finney Brown apparently was trying to; his Adam's apple was moving up and down, but nothing was coming out.

Someone said, "You could get the operator to put a doctor on the radiotelephone, couldn't you, Walt?"

"Yeah, yeah, sure. I guess that's what—"

Finney Brown finally made it. "Oatey knows," he said hollowly. "I think. Heard him tell how he delivered one of his own kids one time, him and his wife got caught short for a doctor in a blizzard, roads was blocked—"

"Well, go get Oatey, don't stand there!" Walt bawled.

Please God, he thought, that Oatey, the old fool, hadn't been bragging his head off.

Oatey, it seemed, hadn't been. He came down the deck on the double. So all scram to hell out of here, he'd take over. He wasn't no expert, but he guessed he could do the necessary. He'd have to have help. Walt could help him.

It was a caution what you could come up with in an emergency, when you had reason to, Walt thought later.

The baby was asleep in an old cardboard carton that had once held tins of coffee. Finney Brown had gone poking around in the salt hold, just on the chance, and he had come up with the girl's suitcase. Among some things of her own were diapers, some flannel bands, a new blue baby blanket. And someone, Walt wasn't going to inquire who, because whoever it was was going to come in for a lot of ribbing, had produced out of his bunk two stout, red hot-water bottles, which were now in the carton with the baby.

The girl herself at first had worried Oatey. She kept on being deathly sick to her stomach, for no reason at all that he could see. She hadn't had a hard time with the baby; not comparable to some, Oatey said; it had been what they called a natural birth. Oatey knew quite a lot; his wife had had nine children.

"Course, Mealie's kids always come easy, like this one must've," he told Walt. "And it's goddam lucky they did, because it was in Depression times when we couldn't no more afford a doctor than we could gold biscuit dough. But I can't figger out why she keeps on puking," he went on, his forehead puckered with concern. "It ain't right."

The crew, who had been chucked out of the cabin, were in the cook's galley except for Perley Stokes, who had relieved Oatey in the pilothouse, and Anzio, who hadn't been seen all evening. Nobody had a thought of going to bed—the bunks were mostly in the cabin, anyway. They were keeping warm in the galley, and quiet. A discreet clinking of pots and pans meant, Walt judged, that everybody was having a late mug-up while they waited.

Angelo Rocco put his head out the galley door. "I betcha my life she's-a seasick," he said. "You try a couple my pills on her, Oatey, why not?" Angelo was an expert on seasickness; he himself was useless aboard a boat without his pills. "By gum!" Oatey said. "Never thought of it! You know, Walt, he may be right. These goddam old oily sea swells'd rise the guts on a hippopotamus, if he wasn't used to it. Where's your pills, Angelo? Le's try a couple."

Angelo produced his pill bottle, remarking cheerfully that without them right now he would be having the bambino himself, only with a holy miracle—it would be coming up instead of down.

The pills worked. The girl, after a while, went quietly to sleep. The greenish look left her face and she got a little normal color back. She was warm under extra blankets, and Oatey had surrounded her with many glass bottles filled with hot water.

"Where to hell did all them come from?" Walt wanted to know, when Oatey began bringing the bottles in from the galley.

"Fifths," Oatey said. He was out of breath and in a hurry, not in a mood for explanations. "You got eyes. Don't you know a fifth when you see one?"

"Well, by the god—" Walt began.

The boys had their orders not to bring any liquor aboard the *Potluck*. That was one thing Walt wouldn't stand for.

"Don't bother me now," Oatey said. "I got enough on my hands for a fat man." He stood back, watching, mopping his head, which was as bald as a button. "Take what the Lord sends. You never can sometimes tell what He'll come up with, happen He's on your side at the time."

"If they've been lugging booze aboard, there'll be some changes made. Dammit, we've got a night's work to do. I'll go call the Coast Guard, get this rig off the boat, and then—"

"You crazy?" Oatey said. He was bushed, and he had plans of his own, which didn't include, he told himself, being a mother to Walt's otter-drag for the rest of the night. "She's just gone to sleep. If you roust her and that baby out into the cold tonight, what they've gone through, you're liable to kill the both of them. What we ought to do is take her in to Bishop, to the hospital. We could be there by five in the morning."

"Lose my whole night's work? I'll be damned if I will!"

"Okay," Oatey said. "Up to you. You take the responsibility, *I* won't have no part of it. Haul them two poor sick things out on a stretcher, jerk their liver and lights out getting them into one of the Coast Guard boats in this old sea swell. Besides," he went on, delicately, rolling his eyes toward the galley, "you won't do much dragging tonight, I guess. The boys ain't in shape."

"What d'you mean, they ain't in shape?"

"Had to get these fifths empty," Oatey said. "Some, o' course, they poured out into the cook's pans. But you know good gin, it loses stren'th when exposed to air." Craftily Oatey produced the needle for Walt's soft spot, jabbed it in. "Why, that passel of drunks, you let them handle gear tonight, the bottom from here to Cashe's Ledge will be strown with nylon net."

His round face bland, he watched Walt stride across, take a look in at the galley.

"Hah, Walt!" he heard Angelo say. "You want some? We have-a the christening party—"

Oatey expected a bellow, but none came. Walt turned around, started for the deck. Old Fusspot. Even his stern, going out of sight up the companionway ladder, looked mad.

Oatey wasn't surprised when the *Potluck* changed course, headed inshore. He permitted himself a mild, triumphant grin. Hum, none of that solid-silk equipment was going to be lost tonight.

Somebody will pay in the morning, he told himself. Somebody will surely pay. Be too bad to have to listen to it sober.

He busied himself, adding a few last touches to what, he felt, was a very good job of work.

He took the carton with the baby in it off the cabin table and set it well back in his bunk, barricaded with bedding so that it couldn't upset.

Just in case she rolls some, he told the baby, when we hit them tide rips between the islands, and I ain't around to keep an eye on you every blessed minute.

The girl was sleeping like a kitten. Oatey touched her cheek, found it pleasantly warm, no fever, and listened to her breathing.

That's a good girl. I've made sure of a night's rest for you, so you make the most of it. I'll be around, if needed, but times a man's accomplishments make him wish to celebrate. So sleep after toil, rest after stormy seas.

He stepped into the galley, into the festivity. Triumph had come aboard the boat, now that they were through with it, now that everything was all right. Of course, a christening party! Who to hell felt like working?

"Can't blame you boys," he said. "You gone to pieces from anxiety. Here, le'me have a little soop of that."

Perley Stokes, in the pilot shelter, was good and put out. No one had been near him for hours and his stiff neck was raging.

"Well, what am I, the forgotten man?" he demanded as Walt came through the doorway. "Seems as though some of you jokers might've thought what this old sea swell could do to a man with a sore neck. I—"

"You shut up your yap," Walt snapped, "or you'll have something besides a sore neck to brag about. Set the course for Bishop Harbor, and stay here! You touch one drop, you so much as whet your cussed whistle, you and I's going to part company along with some others on the Bishop dock!"

He took no notice at all of Perley's aggrieved, astounded face and stamped off down the deck. The furious thump of his rubber boots died away, aft.

Well, godfrey mighty, what was eating him? Found out about the boys' little private stock, Perley would bet himself.

All at once Perley was madder. Some of them down there lifting their elbows, and here was he, a sick roan, the only one aboard that needed to, stuck here in the pilot shelter.

Well, he would set the goddam course for Bishop Harbor; but she could go on marine pilot for a few minutes while he sneaked below and found out what was up, had a little of whatever it was, himself.

The reason Anzio hadn't been around, Walt found, was he had made himself comfortable in the engineer's compartment. He was stretched out in the bunk there, rolled in a blanket. He had had his share of the gin, though, probably from a bottle of his own, since that seemed to be the style aboard the boat tonight; and, by thunder, there'd be some changes made if Walt had to fire the whole works on the Bishop dock in the morning and take the boat back to New Bedford alone. Boats and liquor didn't mix, at least that was the way he had been brought up, and this whole craft smelt like a saloon. The smell of gin in his nice, clean engine room made Walt madder. He gave Anzio a nudge, not gentle, with the toe of his boot.

"Hey, what the—" Anzio demanded. He sat up, rubbing himself. "Who done that?"

"I did. We're taking your wife in to Bishop—"

"My wife, eh?" In the semidarkness Walt could see Anzio's grin, the slow stretch of lips, the glint of teeth. "So that's what she put out, is it? So that's her story. Well, she ain't my wife, Walt, old buddy, old boy, and that kid could belong to a coupla other guys. So bust off. I'm sleepy."

"Look, you get lippy with me, I'll dump you here and now. I don't care what she is, it's your rig, it ain't mine. You take her to the hospital, notify her folks, whichever, only you get her off the boat when we hit dock in the morning."

"You better not dump me anywheres near Hillville," Anzio said laconically. "Her old man's a heller, lives on brimstone. You want a murder on your hands?"

"I don't care if he tears your head off, serve you right," Walt said. He stopped. "So it's Hillville where she lives, is it?"

Hillville was thirty miles nearer than Bishop, easier to get to. Being a former Bishop man, Walt knew Hillville well; and besides he had from time to time done business with Joe Randall. The trawler could be tied up at the Hillville dock by three in the morning, approximately, and headed out again before daylight. If the girl's folks lived there, this loon could take her back to them.

"Sure, she lives in Hillville," Anzio said. "Name's, uh, Fanny. Fanny Wilson. Fanny. Buh-rother! You can call her that again." He stretched and yawned, his hands behind his head.

"All right, you can cut out the filthy talk," Walt snapped.

"Why, Walt, old socks! Derned if you ain't madder'n a hornet! You don't want to put the blame for this on me. This was just a girl I laid somewhere, she wasn't my lifework. I met her in Boston and we did make a real New Year's party of it, but that's all. And what happens, she turns up outside my rooming house in New Bedford, song and dance about this and that, kid's coming, she's run out of dough. All that crapiola. You can't believe a word she says. What she done, she figured out a cheap way to get home, said if she stowed away aboard the boat and didn't show until you got offshore here, you couldn't do nothing else but take her in. Misjudged the time on it a little, was all; made it kind of inconvenient for you—" Anzio was suddenly overcome by the humor of this; he began to chuckle and then to laugh. "Oh, baby!" he said when he could. "Poor old Walt! It couldn't happen to a nicer guy."

Walt's teeth came together with a snap. "So you knew it!" he grated out. "You knew all the time she was there."

"Sure. I helped her get there."

"You knew we'd lose our night's work, and you let the poor little devil pretty nigh die down there amongst the salt. By the god, you ain't human!"

"Only too," Anzio said. "Only too, Walt, old buddy, old boy."

"All right. I've had it. I'm through. In the morning, when we dock, you be first man over the side. You ever show aboard this boat again, I'll break your neck!"

"Oh, Walt, sweetheart! That's *violent*." Lazily Anzio began unrolling the blanket, started to get out of the bunk. "You're so set on it. Let's give her a try. Let's see whose neck gives first."

Why, Walt thought in astonishment and shock, this punk is fixing to tackle *me*!

Being a peaceable man, he had not been in a fight since his days with the Commandos, but he found he remembered some training, the idea having been, as he recalled, to win and not to bother about how. The toe of his boot caught Anzio under the chin just as the boy bent his head to clear the roof of the bunk. The rubber boot was soft-toed, but it had considerable force behind it. Anzio's teeth clacked together. He flopped backwards; his head hit the bunk frame with a punkiny sound, and he slid limply to the deck.

Heb'm sake, Walt thought. I hope I ain't killed the bugger.

He leaned forward, his hands clasping his knees, to look.

No. Wasn't dead. But he was good and well out.

Walt shoved him back into the bunk, covered him with the blanket.

Well, godalmighty, will I be some glad to see the last of him!

On Sunday nights, at Hillville, things closed down. They were still closed down on Monday morning before daylight, when Walt steered the *Potluck* up the silent harbor. It was later than he had thought it would be, but still thick dark. In the starlight he could make out the waterfront, black roofs of wharf sheds and storage buildings, the long dock of the Randall Packing Company, where he planned to tie up, a tall watertank high against the sky. At the wharf head, a single electric bulb burnt coldly yellow and, back in the town, street lamps were spotted here and there; but no one was around.

"What kind of change do you think you're going to get out of this?" Perley asked Walt.

Perley, by now, was feeling no pain either from his neck or from his sense of injustice. He felt noble. He, a sick man, suffering, had been up all night while the able men slept, drunk as coots, every one; but he, slipping down to the cabin now and again—and right under Walt's nose, he told himself with glee—had taken only enough to sweeten his lonely vigil. He felt like a father, taking care of all, and, compassionately, had not even tried to rouse anyone to help make fast while the *Potluck* nudged in to the dock. Tend engine, hustle out on deck to handle lines, tearing around, jumping from deck to dock and back—he could do it, he was a great man.

"So what do we do now?" he asked, gazing dreamily at the dark town.

"We ain't called on to do anything," Walt said. "It's up to Anzio from here on in. Go shake him up, will you?"

"Why, I think it'd be better if we all turned in. These folks here all to bed. Nothing we can do till daylight."

"Turn in? What to hell's the matter with you? We've got to land this traveling nursery, get to hell out of here. Get Anzio up. Well, go on, Perley. You think I'm going to hang around here all day?"

Well, heb'm sake, that was no way to speak to a man. A man been working as hard and willing as Perley had. Come to think of it, all this racing around hadn't done his neck any good. Afar off, he could feel it beginning again, short, sharp jerks. I let this wear off, he said to himself, it will be more than I can bear. I have reached my limit, by God, with this neck.

He glanced out at the dark deck. "Nossir, Walt!" he said. "I ain't going to do it. I ain't in no shape. You want fooling done with Anzio, you do it yourself. Chrissake," he howled suddenly, "it ain't nothing but a woman and a baby aboard. What you think you got here, anyway? A crate of wild African tigers?"

He stared uneasily after Walt's square back as Walt stamped off down the deck. Well, heb'm sake, the bugger could have said something. Let him fire me. All I care. He dumps me, I'll go somewhere and sleep for a week.

Favoring his neck, he eased gingerly down the companionway ladder into the cabin, glanced, without much hope, into the cook's galley. Them fellows was all in their bunks, snoring to beat two of a kind. Likely they hadn't left anything, wouldn't quit if they had.

Well, 'fore God, how could that be? Half a tinnikinful, enough maybe to ease a man's agony. Perley had it, in a couple of long soops.

Anzio was out cold. He would gobble, but he wouldn't wake up. After a while Walt left him and came back on deck, his jaw set. He was into this, he wasn't going to give up. The girl's folks lived here; their name was Wilson. If her old man was a heller, so much the better. He could come down here and tend. Tend to Anzio, too, if he wanted to. He called down the companionway as he passed, "Keep an eye on things, Perley, I'm going to find a phone."

His boots rang hollow on the planking as he jumped to the wharf, walked up past the dark, deserted sheds. Frost sparkled on the walkway and on the long, sloping bank of asphalt shingles covering the roof of the Randall Packing Company. As he remembered, Randall's had a night watchman; and they would have a phone.

The watchman was there, or somebody was. A black Plymouth sedan was parked outside the boiler-room entrance and a light was on inside; but the door was locked. Nobody answered to Walt's pounding. He waited, impatiently pounded again, then let his fist fall and turned away. The watchman was probably asleep somewhere, cuddled down behind the nice, warm machinery, wouldn't come out even if he did hear. Well, the main street of Hillville was just up the slope. Somewhere there'd be a phone booth. Furiously Walt stamped up the hill, his boots leaving a trail of black footprints on the frosty hardtop.

In some stores, night lights were on; street lamps cast down a motionless, cold illumination; but nobody was around. Not even a car parked, the length of the street. But there, in front of a grocery, was a lighted phone booth.

Walt ducked inside with a grunt of relief, and at once felt like a goldfish in a bowl. Anybody looking out of a window could see him, or anybody passing by could. People in a town like this, they remembered anything out of line, like a man seen phoning from a public booth before daylight. Besides, there were some in town who knew Walt; Joe Randall, for instance.

If anything comes of this, this girl and a baby, I could be connected with it. . . .

The sweat started up under Walt's cap. The phone book listed several nearby small towns, but he thumbed through it twice before he could even find Hillville.

Wilkinson, Williams, Wilson. Thank Christ, there was only one Wilson. He dialed the number.

The phone rang and rang. Walt waited. Then the receiver clicked in his ear.

"Hello?" he said. "Wilson's?"

Nobody there. A broken connection. Somebody on the party line had got sore because the phone kept ringing so long and had lifted the receiver.

Damn dial system. At least when you had an operator on the job, she could keep ringing for you, keep some irresponsible cluck from breaking the connection just because the phone bell woke him up.

Walt dialed again. After three rings, the same thing happened.

The third time, whoever it was had apparently left the receiver off, because the dial tone didn't come back on. Enraged, Walt bawled into the phone at the top of his lungs, "I want Wilson's! It's an emergency, dammit!"

A laconic voice spoke. "You're sure pooping down a posthole, bud, if you got an emergency," it said. "Old Het Wilson's deefer'n a crab, you might as well ring the Rock of Gibberaltar. All you do's keep me awake. If you got an emergency, I'll go over and—"

"Look," Walt said desperately. "Has she got a girl named Fanny?"

"Hell, no, she's an old maid."

"Well, are there any other Wilsons in town, somebody might not have a phone? You know any Fanny Wilson?"

"Nope. Het's the only one. What's trouble? Lost your date?"

Walt hung up.

That blasted Anzio. Lied again. Probably lied just for the fun of it, to make somebody some trouble. Wilson wasn't the girl's name at all; ten to one, she didn't even live in this town. Now what?

By the god, this time I *will* kill him. . . .

A car swung around the corner into Main Street. Its lights, as it turned, swept over the phone booth and along the full length of the empty asphalt. It was all Walt could do not to duck. He did grab at the peak of his cap, hauled it down over his eyes. The car, he saw, glancing furtively sideways, looked like the Plymouth sedan that had been parked outside Randall's boiler room. The watchman, probably, going off duty. Whoever it was, he'd sure got a good look at Walt.

Walt waited, back to, till the car had gone out of sight; then he yanked open the folding door and got out of the booth as if it had suddenly burst into flames. He headed back down the hill at a good, fast clip.

Serve me right for mixing into this. They'll sure as shooting think I got something to do with that kid.

You could be sorry for someone, want to help, but in a case of this kind there were limits beyond which a respectable man had better not go. A woman could lie anything onto any man, and be believed; and after all, I've got my wife and kids to think about. . . .

Walt's feet landed on the *Potluck*'s deck with a muffled *thunk*.

It was warm in the engineer's compartment, and Anzio had thrown off his blanket. At some time or other, he had certainly come to, for he had undressed himself and now lay peacefully sleeping. In the beam of Walt's flashlight, his long, slick limbs glistened rosy-brown; his black curls drooped, tousled with sleep, over his forehead, on which shone three clear drops of sweat. The only blemish was a purplish lump, just under the point of his chin.

He looked like somebody's decent son, a nice boy a man ought to be proud of. Thinking of this, Walt said. "Tch, tch."

He grabbed a smooth shoulder and shook. "C'mon, you! Wake up."

Anzio mumbled, driving his head into his pillow. Okay, young sprout, Walt said grimly.

On deck he found a bucket, tied a string to its bale, and scooped up a bucketful of icy water from the harbor. He let it go with a sloosh over Anzio's head and shoulders, and Anzio sat up with a yell.

"You haul yourself together and go phone this girl's folks," Walt told him. "Whatever her name is, damn you, or whether she lives here or not. Call the hospital ambulance, I don't care what you do, but you get the both of you to hell off of this boat! And you get cracking, or I'll hitch a rope to you and slosh you up and down in the harbor!"

He thought, for a moment, that Anzio was going to show fight again; Walt could see him weigh the opportunities and then decide against it.

"Okay," he said. "Let me get dressed."

"All right! But you make time!"

Walt went back along the deck, down the ladder to the cabin. As he turned from the companionway, he ground to a stop and stared, his jaw slowly dropping.

Slumped with his arms on the table, Perley Stokes slept the sleep of the just, by his peaceful head an empty doubleboiler top which had once held gin. In their bunks the crew, variously disposed in lumps, mounds, or rolls of blankets, snored out of time with each other and in different keys. The carton holding the baby was gone . . . No. It was not gone. He could make out the top of it, banked with bedding, in the bunk behind Oatey. But the bunk where the girl had been was empty. The rough gray covers had been flung back in a heap; her clothes, which Walt himself had folded and laid on the foot of the bunk, were gone; and she was gone.

Oh, no! It ain't possible. Sick as she'd been, she couldn't have.

But she had.

Walt drew in his breath to yell. Rouse up Perley, tear him limb from limb for not staying awake to tend; rouse up everybody, get them all moving, doing something. Somebody would have to say what to do. But Walt was conditioned; he had lifted his voice too many times in a room where there was a sleeping baby not to know what happened. The baby woke up; bawled.

And, oh God, that's all I need. That's all I need to finish me.

The breath left his lungs in a wheezing groan.

Behind him he heard a sound: quiet steps along the deck.

So that's where she is, on deck! Sneaking around, getting set to take off!

He lunged out of the companionway just in time to see Anzio, on tiptoe, headed for the rail.

Anzio, seeing him, stopped. "You in too much of a hurry to let a man take a leak?" he asked. "I wouldn't walk out on you, Walt, old buddy, old boy."

"Damn right you wouldn't!" Walt said. He closed in behind Anzio, herded him down the companionway into the cabin.

"Well, hey-hey!" Anzio said. His eyes flicked around, taking in the slumbering Perley, the carton, the empty bunk. "She's gone!" he said. "Oh, brother! What d'ya know!" He burst into a roar of laughter, slapping his leg, dropped helplessly into a seat by the table. "Oh God, if I could only have made it off the boat, too," he gasped. "You tried to leave me holding the bag, and I could've left you holding the baby! Oh, poor old Walt, everybody in the world would have thought it was yours. Dear, dear, dear. How I miss my opportunities!"

Don't hit him, Walt told himself. If you hit him now, you'll kill him.

His fists, doubled rigidly in his pockets, ached to pound at the guffawing face, slam it into the deck, stamp on it. "All right," he said between his teeth. "You know where she's gone. You take the baby to her."

"Oh, I will," Anzio said. "Don't fret, dear. I'd almost settle down with her for this, to a nice sober dull married life, darned if she ain't got it coming! What a woman! Poor old Walt . . . Hey, take it easy. Take it ea-a-sy, now. I'm going, I'm gone."

He got up, with a shrug of his big shoulders settling himself into his clothes, which, Walt now noticed, were very fine. His shore-going outfit. Anzio had on a short jacket of soft brown leather, a wool shirt in dark-blue and green plaid, gray flannel slacks; his tan boots were of the expensive, tooled-leather variety affected by cowboys and, at times, by members of the Air Force. From behind the neat lapel of his jacket, a snowy handkerchief peeped, folded in the pocket of his shirt.

"By God!" For a moment, Walt thought his voice was going to choke him. "All the fast dough you make, you couldn't spare that poor scairt devil of a girl enough for her fare home. Oh, go on, get to hell off the boat before I puke!"

Anzio said nothing. He stepped over to Oatey's bunk, pulled the carton out over Oatey's sleeping form, and came back with it to the table.

"Heavy little bugger," he said, hefting it as he set it down. "Bet she wouldn't have left him if she could have carried him. After all, she thinks quite a lot of me. Where's some string, Walt? I got to have something to lug this by."

Wordlessly Walt rummaged some lengths of cod line out of a locker. He watched while Anzio lashed it around the carton, and all at once Walt's heart misgave him.

What am I doing, sending him off with that? That's a live baby in there. The crazy, irresponsible . . . he's capable of anything.

"Watch out how you handle that!" he burst out. "You tie it up so tight, you'll smother him!"

"Him? Oh, it's a boy, is it? Well, keep your shirt on. There's a nice hole, see? Even you could breathe through it."

Anzio tested his lashings. He picked up the carton by the string, stood for a moment dangling it in his hand. His eyes, still slitted with amusement, looked Walt up and down.

The sweat, starting again under Walt's cap, rolled down his cheek. He pulled out his handkerchief, mopped it away. "Anzio, for godsake . . . she does live here in town, don't she? Who is she? What's her name?"

"Now, don't you worry your little heart. It's all over. You're out from under, remember? Next time, watch it, you might not get off so easy."

He pushed past Walt, went up the ladder. Walt could hear his footsteps along the deck, the light, hollow thump his boots made as he jumped to the dock.

Walt's concern grew; it swelled in his chest, a lump. It drew him on deck, but only as far as the rail. He stood there, peering anxiously after Anzio, but the darkness was thick. The single electric bulb burnt, cast shadows, in which nothing moved at all.

God, what was I thinking of? But how could I get dragged into a rotten thing like that; that punk, he'd say anything, and how could I prove . . . no man ever has proof against it, and me . . . my wife, my kids . . . a family man . . .

From somewhere, out of the wharf shadows, came a heavy splash.

For an instant Walt stood frozen. Then he was over the rail in two jumps, tearing along the wharf, frantically looking this way and that . . . Oh, that bastard, where had he heaved it in, that carton; for a minute or two it ought to float . . .

Then, up beyond the walkway, standing against the lighted boiler-room window so that Walt could surely see him, he saw Anzio; and Anzio waved at him jauntily with one hand, held up the carton with the other. He called, "Only a chunk of old iron, Walt, old buddy, old boy. Made a nice splash, didn't it? That's for the nice, cold shower bath.

With thanks." He vanished into the shadows, and the rest of it floated back to Walt out of darkness. "You oily, sanctimonious son of a bitch!"

The *Potluck* cast off, moved down the quiet harbor, gathering speed. That he had intended to dump his entire drunken crew on the Hillville dock was not in Walt's mind now, but only to get out of there, get clean away from another man's business, now, for him, over and done with. The twin wave of the boat's wake widened as she went, troubled the glassy water, discreetly rippled against the black shores of silent islands, not yet beginning to whiten with morning.

In the early-morning darkness Anzio went trotting up the hill from the dock. The stars, bright before daybreak, cast shadows; the long-legged, blurred shape of a man carrying a square box danced along the road in front of him. Anzio followed the shadow. He saw two sets of footprints on the frosty hardtop, one going, one coming, and a car had been along here not long ago. Showed someone was up, might be around, might see him.

To heck with it, let them see him.

He guessed he could run as fast as anybody in this hick burg, which, brother! hadn't changed any since he'd seen it last.

Oh, he knew this town well enough, knew where he was going. He had been in and around it before, visiting his grandparents, who lived down a back road, in a shabby, unpainted farm house, a couple of miles from here. In Shacktown. He had not seen them for a long time now, since the summer he'd spent running the girl who lived in the big house in the middle of town. He was never going to see them again. He had thrown off that connection. He was Anzio Jones now, born in Tahiti of a Frenchwoman and a Polynesian. Who spoke the lingo and looked the part; whose place was far away, not here, nor in a half-baked hick town twelve miles down the coast, where the son of a woolen-mill worker had been christened Ernest Enoch Grindle.

Ernest E. Grindle. E. E. Grindle. E. Enoch Grindle. A hell of a name. Ernie Grindle in school, till you wanted to vomit. Named for my father, named for my grandfather. Ernie Grindle the Third. Well, Ernie the First had one foot in the grave now and Ernie the Second was dead. Tired or dead. It was the end of the line. Anzio Jones was the name now; good for a double-take, a second glance anywhere; a conversation piece of a name, chosen with care for the contrast between the unusual and the common. A genius of a name. Whoever so much as looked up if you said your name was Ernie Grindle?

Build a life of your own, that was it. Some life when nobody turned around on the street, just because they knew your name. Well, they would hear the name of Anzio Jones, sometime, when he got around to it; but not for doing any of the small-time crab-walking that they thought was important. Work. A job. Pull-yourself-up-by-your-bootstraps. Achievement. Get captain of the ball team, get lieutenant in the Navy. Get a gold star on your Sunday School lesson, for godsake. When all you had to do was look around you at their crumby lives and their slob-faced fat wives and snotnosed kids. And look a little longer, take a good long look, at where the achievement they gobbled about had got them, and where the dead weight of all those good, achieving people, with their noses in each other's placket holes, was taking the world they lived in.

Not for Anzio Jones; not any part of it. And not let them have any part of him, either. Someone was always asking, wherever you went: Where are you from, what are you doing, who are you? So Anzio told them. He told them anything that came into his head, just to see the look on their crumby faces, they could believe it or not, it was all one to him. The more ignorant and mediocre they were, the madder they got when they found you weren't, that you were different; so they figured they had a kind of holy right to whittle you down to size. No part of it; not any part of it; not for him. He used them, places and people, until they wore out on him, and then he went elsewhere; shook off their dust. So what? So he was ready now to go again.

A car rounded the curve in the road ahead, coming fast. The lights, full in Anzio's face, blinded him. He had barely time to jump for the gutter. A black sedan, Plymouth, looked like, traveling sixty on this narrow road.

Staring after it enraged, Anzio yelled at the top of his lungs, "Look where you're going, you goddam crazy fool!" But the car did not slacken speed. It went out of sight down the hill, headed for the dock.

Cluck could've killed me. Easy. Phew! For a cent I'd go back there and wipe him down. A good going-over, what he needs.

For a moment he considered it. But from the carton, shaken up, came a sound. Anzio suddenly recalled the carton; he looked down at it in his hand. It was the first time he'd realized—that is, enough to give his mind to it—that what was there was actually alive.

Ernest Enoch Grindle the Fourth. Well, dog my cats. There he was.

Come on, fella, we got fish to fry. And we know where to fry them, don't we?

He started on up the road.

Anzio had had it figured from the beginning what to do if he got stuck with this. Most guys would've thought he was pretty dumb to let on the girl lived in Hillville; or to take the risk of going wandering around the streets there, where someone might remember him, where once he had been known. The girl's old man, for instance. He wouldn't know Anzio Jones; but he sure-God ought to remember Ernie Grindle. Ernie Grindle worked for him, one summer, on a gravel-pit job; got fed up one day with his yak, and socked him square on the nose. What a day that had been! Oh, he'd had to get out of there fast; no point in getting yourself any more messed up than you had to, and anyway you'd had your fun; so by the time the old man had got the seat of his pants unstuck from the mud puddle he'd sat down in, Anzio was half a mile down the road. Going.

So he knew well enough where to take this little bundle of joy, this gimmick they all figured was the last almighty nail to hold a man down. It appealed to his sense of humor and his sense of justice, added to which it would be kind of fun to sneak in to the big house in the center of town, see whether or not you'd get caught: the house with the tall gables and the glassed-in porches front and back, and the wide stretch of neat, frosty lawn. Dump this on the doorstep, and then make a run for it to the highway.

Anzio squared his shoulders and walked on.

Traffic would start on the highway soon; somebody in a car or a truck would be going to work. He could hitchhike to Bishop, catch him a train. On the train, he would hire a compartment—no, a stateroom, what the hell, he had the money. His roll was in his pants, no thanks to *her*. A lot she'd ever cared that a guy was sick to death of everything he had to look at, till he had to get away, had to go. Chased me all summer, threatened me with the cops. Chrise, some women got no self-respect at all.

A stateroom, then, and sleep the day away while the train hauled to Boston; and then a good, bang-up meal somewhere, a good eating place. And after that, another train to—where? Oh, some sunny place, California. The West. Some place where he was not known; where he could say "Tahiti" if he wanted to and not get called a liar to his face, not that he cared. Where the look would be interested, curious, friendly; with some respect for a romantic, dark-haired guy from faraway places; a guy who had been through a war—only, better say Korea this time—with medals to show for it if he had bothered to hang onto them, only they got lost in the shuffle somewhere, I was moving around, to hell with them.

What was real, after all, was what people believed about a man. If you gave a damn what people believed.

Oh, the sun and the beaches; the new faces. New girls, new friends. The tall, dark guy on the beach there, sunning; he pays no mind to the glances, he doesn't give them a second thought. He's getting a suntan. Who is he? Who could he be? Oh, a Tahitian, a half-Polynesian, brother, get a load of him!

Hold up, though. In California, didn't they look down on Orientals? Sure. Read it in the *Reader's Digest*. They treat Orientals the way the Southerners treat jigs. Better change plan, Anzio, old buddy, old boy; you wouldn't want to be used like a jig is. Better say born in Anzio, Italy, of an American colonel and an Italian, oh, countess. Because if you say Korea, that'd throw out Anzio anyway; and I sure like that name, and wasn't I the damn numby not to know Anzio was in Italy?

A sound in the road behind him jerked him back to here and now. A stumble? Sure sounded like one. Somebody?

But the road stretched white behind him; he could see the glimmer all the way down the hill. Nothing on it. Not a shadow.

Relieved, Anzio trotted on. For a moment, there, he'd thought it might be that goddam Walt chasing him.

I sure got my own back, with him. The sight of the century, Old Fusspot's face, when he thought I'd chucked Ernie, here, into the drink.

He rounded the curve in the road ahead of him and heard the sound again—a stumble, certainly; and a crackling, like somebody sneaking through the brush. He spun around, his heartbeat quickening, but he was past the bend now, he couldn't see very far back behind him. The woods were thick here on either side of the road, with a couple of black rooftops showing; not a sound except that soft stirring in the underbrush, which, while he listened, stopped.

Spooky along here, he thought; and a faint, cold ripple started at the back of his collar.

All right. That was enough of that! He wasn't scared.

If that was Walt trailing him, he'd fix him. He still owed Walt one, anyway, damn him, kick a guy in the chin. What'd you expect, a goon like that; what would he know about a fair fight, the rules of the game? If it was him, well, here was a side road. Duck in to it, wait, jump him from behind. Fix his wagon.

Anzio set the carton down behind a thick bush, squatted and waited.

Nobody passed. The bushes sparkled with frost, catching faint light from the stars. He waited. Not a sound, except somewhere, far off, a dog barked. This side road, he saw, was the road to the dump. A neatly painted sign nearby facing him so that it caught the light, said HILLVILLE TOWN DUMP.

Well, bust my barrel. Civilization at last, caught up with this town. A painted sign to say where the dump is, that's progress. Or maybe they had to stick up something to mark which was the dump and which was the town.

Whatever that sound had been, it wasn't there. Some animal, maybe.

Oh, for gosh sake, a deer, most likely, of course it was! I been a city man too long to remember what a deer in the bushes sounds like.

Disgustedly Anzio jumped to his feet, and stopped in his tracks. Somebody in one of the dark houses had just turned on a light.

Anzio stared at the light; and then he saw, beyond it, in the east, the pale streak in the sky. The light by which he had read the sign was the light of morning.

Hell, of all the lousy luck!

Putting on the pressure. If it wasn't someone, it was something. All together now. You got something special, gang up to clobber it, gun it down. Even above-average brains that the lousy world could have used, was pearls before swine.

Pearls before swine. That's rich.

And suddenly Anzio had a clear picture before his eyes of Ernie the First, his grandfather. With his finger on the verse on the page in the Bible.

Oh, the gimmicks they had, the traps they set. Mother, a good woman's love. The old man. The Bible. This, that he was lugging along here right now. The gimmick to spring the trap.

Okay. It was too late now to get up through the town unseen. Somebody would be around. Because one thing they all did in this place, they got up early. Like it was a part of their religion. One did, they all did, monkey see, monkey do.

Well, they'd stacked the cards on him, let them take over. There might be a dozen people coming to the dump this morning. Let them find their gimmick right where it belonged, on the town dump. Give it back to them right where they lived.

The road was full of potholes, deeply rutted, uphill. Thick woods shut out the wavering early light. He couldn't hurry, couldn't see where to put his feet, had to slow down. A couple of times he heard again the deer in the bushes; the soft, creeping sound seemed almost to be paralleling him up the hill. Twice he stopped, listening.

A deer, sure enough. Or could it be somebody sneaking along in there?

A partridge took off from a roadside bush with a thunder of wings that sent his heart into his throat, where it stayed, beating so that he could hardly get his breath. Once he stumbled and fell, jarring the carton so that from inside it came a whimper.

What if it starts yelling before I can get away? What if there's somebody around to hear it?

But there was nobody. The cleared space on top of the dump was deserted, the light over it growing. Not a sound. Not a movement.

Piles of debris lay deep in shadow; on the highest of these Anzio set the carton. He eased himself down from the top of the heap, stepping fastidiously, with his good leather boots in mind; but a sudden scurrying almost under one foot made him jump. He cleared the rest of the space in a couple of frantic leaps and stood quivering.

Cheese, look at my boots, what a mess! I'll have to get a shine in town . . . A rat. That thing was a rat.

He hadn't thought about rats. This place used to be alive with them, probably still was.

Anzio stared at the carton. What if the rats got in there, got at it, before anybody came?

Hell, I wouldn't want to kill the poor little . . . After all, he's my son. God, I never even looked to see if he looks like me. What if he does?

The thought of the rats gnawing on a face that looked like his, set him to shaking.

Pull yourself together, Ernie, old buddy, old socks. This is the trap. All you got to do is say that word *son* and in go the hooks.

So what? So maybe it meant something. But the something was built in before you were born, you didn't ask to have it. This is the time to run like hell.

Cheese, though. I better stash in the bushes, make sure somebody finds him, before he . . . before the rats. . . .

He realized suddenly that the carton looked exactly like any other carton; there was nothing to distinguish it from many others, thrown away, lying empty, scattered all over the dump.

Hell, there's a little million of them. How would anybody know there's anything in it?

He looked around for something to mark it with; how could you mark it? Write on a piece of paper, *"There's a baby in here"*? Maybe, but no pencil.

At last, desperately, he pulled the snowy linen handkerchief out of his shirt pocket, tied it by two corners to a stick, and climbed to the top of the dump again. His fingers shook, but he managed to stand the stick upright in the carton . . . poking it down carefully so as not to hit the kid in the face.

That ought to mark it, all right. He stood back to look.

Too bad to have to throw away that handkerchief. Those were good linen jobs, cost three dollars apiece. But anybody could see the big white square up there; they'd come up. Anybody'd want a nice handkerchief, new, like that.

A mild morning breeze took hold of the handkerchief, flapped it out from the stick.

Like a flag, hey? Hey, get a load of Ernie the Fourth, he's got up the white flag.

Oh, bud. Better you than me.

I could sneak one look, wouldn't make no difference, except I'd know does he look like me.

He stooped, bending back one corner of the carton cover; and from the highway at the base of the hill he heard the sound of a truck engine—rickety, old, changing into second, then into low as it bucked the slope. Somebody coming. Thank Christ.

Anzio took off down the back side of the dump into the woods. He felt the scrunch of broken glass, the squelch of filth under his feet; his boot sole rolled on an old bottle, throwing him sideways, so that he nearly took a header. Crossing the brook, he did fall down, driving his arms up to the elbows into soft mud. He ran for what seemed a long time.

Out of sight at last, in the shelter of trees, he stopped, pulled out his second handkerchief and cleaned himself off, his face puckered with disgust.

Pu, that was awful, that muck stink. His clothes were a mess. Make it hard to thumb a ride, looking this way.

Well, he could stand in front of a car, stop it, tell the guy a hard-luck story. Some yarn. Let's see. It was hunting season. A hunter could've got lost. Anybody around here'd swallow that.

"Been in the woods two nights, finally came out here. Need help. . . . Where is this, anyway? I'm a city man, don't know this part of the country. . . ."

Rehearsing, Anzio smiled his wide, innocent, white-toothed smile. The one he would use on the guy who was going to be privileged to give him a ride into town.

Or the woman; any woman would stop for that smile. Maybe better pick a car with a woman driving.

"Got to get to Bishop—okay?"

To Bishop; to the nearest decent men's furnishing store, because he'd have to buy new clothes now. Too bad about this jacket; he'd liked this jacket. It cost a lot. Give it to the clerk in the store. Clerk in a hick-town store be bug-eyed. Probably never saw a jacket like this, except on a summer man.

"Got to catch a train. What time's the next train out to Boston? You know? Oh, I can catch up sleep in the stateroom on the Pullman. . . ."

Anzio smiled again at the mythical driver of the car. The guy, or the woman, who knew now that here was a city man used to the best, like staterooms, like Pullmans. The guy who was going to start him on the first leg of a long journey. To the West. To California.

He wadded up the soiled handkerchief, tossed it carelessly into the branches of a leafless alder—plenty more where that came from, what the hell!

And turned to go; and the man who had been following him, who was going to start him on his long journey, stepped out from behind a tree.

Connie Wilkinson had slept, but not for long; when she woke, the sickness had stopped, the nightmare was still going on. She woke remembering that she had been down a deep well where the water moved and her body was thrown from side to side, up and down. The water thumped and hissed, splashed past her face without wetting it. From somewhere a man's voice kept saying, "Take it easy, take it e-e-asy, it's all right, all right now," until she was sure that nothing was all right, that she was lost for good in the dark well with the strange humming sounds and the water moving.

And then the sounds stopped all at once, which was what had waked her up. She lay in the bunk, wondering where, of all the unfamiliar and God-forsaken places she had been in the past months, she was now. Whichever of them it was, it wasn't worth opening her eyes to see the dirty wallpaper, the musty bed, the lavatory nobody ever cleaned. The landladies, so eager at first to rent the rooms, wanted you out when they got wind of the way you were.

Oh, yes. What I was doing. I said I would wait one more day for Clementina's answer to my letter. If it didn't come, I'd get home any way I could.

So I was going to the Welfare place for help, because I was afraid I'd have the baby on the street, and Ernie said . . .

Ernie. It was hard to remember all the things he had said. Connie's thoughts blurred a little, then ran clear again.

He said they'd put me in jail for whoring on the streets. He said we weren't married; that that Justice of the Peace was only an old buddy of his dressed up for a joke. He said I was a fool to think he'd ever marry anybody. Well, I was. I loved him, and I was. The fool of the world.

Oh, I don't know. I don't know.

I didn't want him to have any part in it any longer, or in me. I just wanted never to see him again, only he was the only one I knew to go to. Stow away on the boat, he said . . . The boat. She opened her eyes and looked out of the bunk into the cabin. For a moment everything was blurred; then she saw the bright, naked bulb shining, a foggy halo round it; a man asleep, slumped by the table, his head down on his arms. Ernie? No. This man was smaller. Someone was strangling. No . . . snoring. A lot of people snoring.

I'm still on the boat. Of course—the humming sound was the engine, the water sound was water going past the planking next to my head. The boat has stopped. Where has it stopped?

Connie sat up. The light with its halo went dim, the cabin tilted, swung slowly, righted itself. Then she could see. A round, grayish circle next to her head was a porthole; she clung to its rim, pressing her nose hard against the glass.

Low wharf sheds, black, long outlines of roofs, shadowy walls. A white sign, black letters, obscured by the darkness . . . where?

Don't look right at the letters, look a little above them. R-A-N-D-A-L-L. The Randall Packing Company. They had brought her home.

There it was. After all this long time of not knowing what to do, now I know. What I have to do now is get ashore, up the hill to the house, in at the door. I'll have to say I'm sorry, I didn't mean to bring you trouble, I tried everything else I could. My father . . . he'll never let me alone again about this, but . . .

The baby. What happened? I thought I had it, down in that place. Did I? Or was that another part of the nightmare.

She closed her eyes, trying to remember.

The salt hold. Ernie, sneaking her down there in the dark, early morning just before the boat left the dock, tossing her suitcase down after her, not bothering to be careful, so that if she hadn't dodged, it would have hit her on the head.

She remembered how cold it was, and digging a hole in the salt, trying to get warm. Fighting off seasickness.

I was always deathly seasick in any boat, even on a calm day. I don't know why I thought I could . . . but I wanted to go so much, I made up my mind I wouldn't be, this time. And the boat heaved and yawed, up and down, side to side; and I was sick . . . and sick . . . and sick.

I did have it. It was dead.

Connie leaned her forehead against the rim of the porthole, feeling the ice-cold metal pressed not as if against her skin, but against the fuzzy blankness, like a fog, that lay just behind her eyes.

When it clears, I am going to have to remember. I wish it wouldn't clear. If it could only stay as it is . . . a smoke screen my head is making; that maybe I am making to let myself down easy. . . .

But even as she wished, the fog moved and shifted, becoming not blankness but blackness—the blackness of the salt hold, frozen-cold, with the open square of the hatch over her head showing dim stars reeling dizzily in a dark-blue sky.

Ernie had said they wouldn't close the hatch; some nonsense he had about the salt having to breathe; what foolishness was that? But he would have said anything, told any lie, to keep me quiet. Dear God, *I* had to breathe, didn't I? Anyone has to.

It breathed. It cried once after it was born. I tied the cord and cut it, and then it lay there and cried once, and I wrapped it in my coat because it needed to be warm. But then it choked and I couldn't hear it breathing, and that was when it must have died. Because if it were alive it would be here with me. It isn't here. They have put it somewhere out of sight. Overboard, maybe; the quickest way, if Ernie had anything to do with it. In the sea. Before I even saw it; before I knew whether it was a boy or a girl.

The air coming in around the not quite dogged-shut porthole was the sea—the wild salt smell, bitter, unutterably lonely; saying lost and not to be found, no matter if you walked the cold beaches, searched the gull-haunted places where the tide set close to shore. Lost, because I have been a fool. An irresponsible fool.

What was I thinking of, no matter how scared I was? I should have gone to whatever charity place would take me in, where the baby could have had what it needed to live, because people will give you that, they will always give you that, and all I thought of was me, what would happen to me. I ought to have planned ahead, made preparations in case this happened. Any fool would have known that it might happen. But my preparations were what I read in a book, one afternoon when

I didn't even go in to the library to read the book, but only because I needed a place to sit down. So what I had was a pair of scissors and a ball of string and, by hook or crook, a new blue baby blanket; and that was what I took life into my hands with.

I'm worse than Ernie. I can blame him for a lot, but not for that.

The fog had cleared, all right. Connie lay back on the pillow, and hindsight did not help at all. It didn't help, either, to say "fool" or "irresponsible" or "ignorant," or to wish you had died, too, when you'd had the chance. Maybe I am going to. Maybe I could if I tried. The way I feel, it wouldn't take much.

Across the cabin one of the crew turned over in his bunk with a sigh, long-drawn as if the man were tired. It came at a moment when other noises had briefly fallen silent: a sound of sleep and human warmth and comfort, a sound of living, which jerked Connie out of the stupor and flicked at despair.

I am living; I couldn't stop breathing if I wanted to. There are other people in the world; for a while, it seemed as if there was nobody. These men have been kind; they've helped me when it wasn't up to them, not their fault. I could lie here sniveling and let them take over in the morning; I'm not going to. From now on out, it's up to me. First, to find my clothes and dress and go before they wake up; if I can.

Her clothes were folded on the foot of the bunk.

I can put the dress and coat over whatever it is I have on, this warm stuff.

The warm stuff, she realized, was a suit of men's insulated long-johns, quilted and thick. She thought at first her dress would not go on over it, but it did, though she couldn't close the zipper. She thrust her arms into her coat sleeves and stood up, clinging to the frame of the bunk until her head cleared and the cabin stopped spinning.

I'm strong enough. I've been calling strength from somewhere all these months, and I can now. My shoes. Where? If I bend down to look for them I'll go flat on my face.

She would have to go without them. But at the foot of the bunk was a pair of rubber boots, across which lay two heavy wool socks. By leaning over, she could reach the socks; she pulled them on.

The boots are too heavy, I can go better if I go light. I can't make the hill in those boots. Even if I can make the hill at all. . . .

She took a step, feeling the give and tremor in her knees. I can. I have got to. I have got to go while it is still dark and nobody sees me. That is the least I can do for my father and mother; let nobody see me coming off a fishing boat in the night like this because of what people would think, and that is what would bother him most, what people would think. But if anyone saw me now, anyone who knew me before, I look so strange, no one would know me. . . .

Now she could move. She could creep wavering up the ladder, along the deck, scrubbed white, deserted, with starlight on the frosty planks. Nobody there.

A crevasse of black water between the boat and the wharf . . .

I can't jump that, I'll have to wait till the boat swings in.

She waited, clinging hunched to the rail, feeling the cold bite into her hands, crawl damply through the soles of the wool socks.

The stars threw a queer light on the wharf, black where the buildings threw shadow; into that shadow, go; keep to shadows, to bushes, to trees. Let nobody see.

The boat, idly moving in a current, aimless, idiotic, inhuman, swung in to the wharf.

Remember that it's not far. Remember the times you have run up this hill, feet, body, as if with no weight at all.

Head down, plodding, she brought up with a thump against a car, parked outside the Packing Company boiler room. She clung for a moment to the slippery metal, seeing her hands, sliding down, leave marks like claw marks across the crystals of the frost.

This is Jack Malden's car, the watchman at the plant. He won't need it until morning. He won't care if I take it, my father can bring it back, maybe Jack won't even know it's been gone.

I've got to take it because . . . I can't walk up the hill.

The car started smoothly, backed and turned; its track, wavering, steadied and straightened. Something was wrong with it, it moved in slow motion, the engine only roared when she stepped on the gas. It wouldn't pick up speed. Then, turning the corner into Main Street, she saw a man in the telephone booth in front of the grocery store. Her heart jumped.

There's someone. He mustn't see me.

Her hand flew automatically to the gearshift.

Why, I'm in low. I've been in low all the way up the hill. She shifted—second; high—and flashed past the booth. The man was a figure of a man only, in halflight and shadow, Walt Sheridan, for all she knew, nobody she had ever seen before.

If Amos Wilkinson had not been awake, thinking it was only an hour until time to get up, he would not have heard the car stop outside or the slurred, muffled thumping at the back door. It was not a loud sound.

Amos got up and opened the door . For a moment he stared at the figure which limped past him into the kitchen, dragged itself to a chair. Then he said, "Arrived, have you?"

When she did not speak or lift her head, he let out a roar that brought Lucy out of bed and staggering, half asleep, into the kitchen.

"What? What is it?" Lucy said, and then, jerking awake, she came swiftly across the floor. "Connie! Oh, honey, what's happened? What is it? Oh, Amos, call the doctor!"

Amos stood where he was. "We'll just let her say what's the trouble with her," he said. "Maybe she's got something to say."

"She needs a doctor, for heaven's sake!" Lucy said. "Amos, what's the matter with you?"

"I'm all right," Connie said. "It's these clothes. I need to rest . . ."

"Let her talk," Amos said. "She was so damn set on chasing away to get married in spite of all I said, maybe she's got her reasons for coming home like this. I told her at the time that feller was no damn good. Maybe she thinks I was right. Let her talk."

He was exactly the same as he had been on the day she had left home; ready to pick up the flaming row where she had dropped it and fled from the house. He hadn't forgotten or forgiven anything.

"Yes," Connie said. "You were right. He was no damn good." She stopped, looking at him. It was almost as if he didn't need to wait to hear her out, as if he knew already what she had to say.

"I had to give up," she said. "I'm sorry I had to, but it was too much . . . more than . . . I'll tell you why, I guess you'll have to know."

She told them. It seemed to take a long time. Lucy couldn't seem to realize, couldn't get what had happened through her head. Then, all at once, she moved, unbuttoning Connie's coat, helping her to pull her arms out of the sleeves.

Amos said, "This boat's in the harbor now, you say? And this Grindle's aboard of her. Well, I know him, damn him. I know him well."

It was a quiet statement, quietly made; but Lucy straightened up, looking at him, her hands making little movements at the V of her collar.

"Yes," Connie said, and stopped, realizing suddenly that Amos was not the same, that something was happening now which she had never seen before and had never expected to see. He stood, his head slightly down, his eyebrows pinched together under his bush of flaming hair, tousled from sleep; the face which had been the same since she could remember—lean, reddened by weather, the untanned forehead with the sharp line between white and bronze made by his hat, the stubborn jutting jaw; but on his cheeks the difference—two tears, slowly running down past the hard, tightly closed mouth.

She thought, he's crying. I thought he would be ready to kill me and he's crying.

The room tilted, lifted, and swelled. Colored light moved up and down, through which she heard his flat, expressionless voice.

"Dammit, of course you can't call the doctor. Under the circumstances—what in hell are you thinking about? Fix her up yourself, you're supposed to be a nurse."

Lucy saying something, pleading; the flat voice answering; the words dropping like stones.

"Of course I'm going down there. I've got to take Jack's car back before he misses it."

The voices far away, fading. Somebody lifting her.

A bed. Oh God, a bed. Warmth. Quiet.

Part Three
December, 1959

I t was getting so, Everard Peterson told himself, that a man couldn't find nothing to shoot. He had walked around through the woods outside of town, followed the brook back into the marsh; he had even gone down to the shore, without a sight of a thing, not even a rabbit.

Unless you could count that old black crow been dogging him lately. Cussed thing. It would come close enough to caw a couple times, then drop out of sight amongst the trees. Everard figured it was the same crow each time. Sometimes you run acrost one got fresh like that.

"You norate around sometime when I ain't low on ca'tridges," Everard told it today. "Or when I ain't got a use for them I got. Clem Wilkinson ain't going to pay me for you, even if I do bring you in."

If there was anything liable to make a man good and put out, it was being low on ammunition; that Everard was, wasn't his fault. He had a routine he followed, and the routine had broken down. Each week he did a little job of work for Amos Wilkinson, got paid, took the money and bought, along with this and that, some shells for his gun. Then he would go hunting. Any game he shot that was any good and that he didn't want himself he would take down to Clementina for her cats. She always paid him. Scraps from the meat market was what she thought she paid him for, but what the head didn't know the heart wouldn't cry for. Meat scraps cost money now that the summer people had spoilt Tony Morelli—time was, he'd give them away. But wild meat didn't cost nothing but a ca'tridge or two. Everard could make extra on it. All in all, he guessed he was making a pretty good thing out of the Wilkinsons—which was something, by gumpty, that nobody else in town had ever done, out of Amos, anyway.

But this morning, when Everard had stopped by the post office to pick up his letter—Amos always sent him his pay in cash in a plain white envelope and Everard guessed anybody would know why—the letter wasn't there. He'd heard later, downtown, that Amos had got hurt and was in the hospital.

Everard had done the little job of work anyway. Amos, of course, would pay him later. But it had taken about all the cash he'd had in his pocket and here he was with only three lousy shells. Not that it had made much difference. There wasn't a sight of a thing moving, the length and breadth of the woods.

These woods was spoilt now, anyway. If it wasn't summer cottages, it was pulpwood slash. Along the shore, every hundred yards or so, was a cottage. Damn things. Sometimes he wondered if them people that come from away wasn't all foolish. They couldn't leave the shoreline alone or let the woods grow; they had to have a gangway and float so's they could get into their boats without getting their feet wet, and a nice green lawn in front of their house. You'd think if they was coming on a vacation, they'd want something a little different from what they had to home. But no. They couldn't rest till they got the whole shoreline in a hairnet, and then they had to stick up *No Trespassing* signs, most likely because they didn't want anyone to walk by and see how incompetent everything looked. Why, one old crone, up along, had bought a whole point—Perkins's Point, it was, one of the sightliest places here around—and what she'd done, her offering, was to cover it all over with concrete. Had steps coming down to little railed-in platforms and things, looked like something out of the catalog.

Now, what would anyone want to do a thing like that for? Either she had too much money or too much concrete. If 'twas money, she could of give some to me, I could make a use of it that was some good, if 'twas only to buy shells and fill some more of them goddam *No Trespassing* signs with Number-Five shot.

"Yah, yah, yah!" said the crow.

He was close, but Everard didn't even look up.

Let him fly around, think I don't give a cuss. The time'll come when he'll surely miscalculate. It'd be today, if Clem's cats would eat crow meat.

He stepped around a thicket and was brought up short against a breast-high tangle of lopped-off branches, treetops and whole trees laid flat, an impenetrable mass of decay scattered in all directions. Everard stared at it balefully.

Might as well turn around right here. A moose might get through there, or a snake. Not a man. This here was once old Marm Crawford's five acres of oak trees that she'd sold stumpage on because she'd needed the money; what them spoilers'd done to it you wouldn't believe unless you saw it. If a bunch of fifteen-year-old kids had carried on this way, you might understand it, but for grown men to . . . why, them trees, some of them, had been three foot through the butt; wouldn't of hurt none to thin out the big ones, give the others a chance to grow. But no. Them fellers couldn't be bothered; they'd lit in there with chain saws and dumped the whole works, partly for the fun of it, looked like, and partly because it was easier to cut down a tree than to haul out around it. And then they'd just taken the ones that was easy to get. Any tree that fell to a disadvantage or looked hard to cut up, they'd left to rot. Why, they was enough oak in there rotting to start a lumber yard.

Them fellers, by gumpty, was having one old helmonious good time smashing up the country. If they kept on, they wouldn't be a tree left standing in the whole damn county.

And, blast 'em, this oak grove had been the best place anywhere around for woodcock.

Well, you'd take one helluva long ramble now before you found a place a woodcock could set down on. That hummock in the middle of Cooney's Heath would be about the nearest place, and that was to hellangone the other side of the swamp. If he was as young as he used to be, when the miles didn't mean nothing, he'd take the trip over there. Never went down into that Heath in his life and didn't come out with some kind of game. It was a great place for pa'tridges, ducks, and them; the foolish things had it all figured out: that Heath was such a muddy bog, no humans would come into it, so in the spring they built nests there by the hundred and then set down to hatch out aigs. A lot of people might think them nests was hard to find and maybe they would be, for some. But not for old Everard. He could go down there any time in the spring and get a mess of birds just by shooting their heads off where they sat on their nests.

By the gumpty, he could see it now. There they'd set, all sprod out and comfortable, not knowing there was anybody within a mile, and all of a sudden, *snip,* their head would come off. A little surprise, just from Everard Peterson.

Gorry, if only his legs was like they ust to be, he'd go over there right now. Take it easy, take two-three days for it, he *could* go. Stay in his old camp on the hummock for a week, have himself a time. For a whole week he needn't see no summer cottages and no slash piles. Them spoilers hadn't figured out a way yet to get in there over the boiling springs and shaking bogs and get at the big trees on the high ground in the middle of the Heath. Probably in time they would. Bulldoze the hill down, shove it over into the mud to run the trucks and tractors on . . .

Why, sure, didn't hustle, he could make it over there all right.

But, hell, he couldn't go today. So he couldn't. He'd need a good lot of shells for a week's stay in the Heath; and besides, that pack of wild dogs that the wardens was always trying to round up and shoot because they chased deer, he guessed that if Everard Peterson was willing ever to do a low-down object like a warden a good turn, he could tell them where them wild dogs hung out. In a cave, over on the hummock in Cooney's Heath. But all hands could rot and blow down before he'd tell them. Anyway, you camp out anywheres near where them dogs was, you'd need more than three shells for your gun. Be better, anyway, to wait till spring, till bird-nesting time.

"Yah, yah, yah," said the crow.

He wasn't mocking old Everard this time; he had something on his mind.

"Now, you old bayster, what is it you see that I don't?" Everard muttered.

He stepped silently to the shelter of a spruce thicket and peered down the edge of the slash. Not twenty yards away a doe was standing.

She hadn't taken fright yet, but her ears were up; she'd heard that damned old crow. He slid back the bolt of his rifle and let her have it just as her tail went up at the sound of the click. One movement, one shot. Slick and clean. Then he sauntered over to her, pulling out his knife.

There was one deer, by the gumpty, that the dang out-of-state hunters wouldn' t haul off down the Turnpike.

She was lying sprawled in the moss with her eyes open and surprised-looking. Hadn't had any time to appreciate the surprise, though, got her slap through the heart. She wasn't even twitching.

Looked like a good doe. Nice, fat, young one. Too bad he was just shooting for cat meat today, she would've made nice eating. But he'd already tagged his deer for the season, and them wardens hung around as though catching Everard Peterson and stashing him away in jail was their lifework and the only way they hung onto their jobs. When they might better take a peek or two into some of them out-of-state trailers being hauled off down the Turnpike, with green firs for their Christmas trees stuck up on top to remind the officers of the law that the fellers in the car all had children, was good, respectable family men.

Well, he'd just whack off some chunks for Clem's cats and take along the liver for himself. A fry of deer liver'd go good, and he was out, et the last of his yesterday. Some hunters busted a gut lugging a whole deer out of the woods, but Everard never took more than a hind quarter and the liver. What was the sense? You keep meat around to spoil before you got a chance to use it up, them wardens would smell it. And, anyway, right now, he had three hind quarters hanging in the cool stone pit under the barn that they'd never yet been able to nose out.

An hour or so later, he sauntered up the path to Clementina Wilkinson's back shed door, carrying the chunks of meat in a sack. He stepped inside, emptied the sack into a pan which had been set out on a bench, and then fumbled around in a covered tin can on the shelf, which was where the old lady always put his money.

He counted the bills and stood wagging his head, with a sensible man's wonder at all the foolishness he ran across from time to time in the world. Somebody willing to pay five dollars a week—and he bet he could get more any day he wanted to put the pry to the old lady—five dollars a week for meat to feed a glist of useless cats. Which, by the gumpty, if they was his, cluttered around his house that way, he'd have ten minutes' target practice some afternoon. But that old gal, she was nuts in the belfry and lushed-up three-quarters of the time.

Oh, yes, better not forget Amos's little present. The one Amos was going to be reminded to pay him for when he got out of the hospital.

He reached into the wide game pocket of his hunting coat and produced a fifth of gin which he put carefully among some other bottles in a basket on the shelf, chuckling as he did so. Hee, Nellie Overholt must go by that basket two or three times a day, hunting out the old lady's liquor supply, never thinking that there would be, in plain sight amongst them Mr. Clean and ammonia bottles.

Some old good to his aunt, Amos was. Made sure she got a fresh bottle of gin every so often. Got Everard to buy it at the liquor store, bring it down here and leave it, unbeknownst. Put the cash in an unmarked envelope each week.

He winked at the bottle.

"They's enough of you coming along so's I can have one of you, ever' so often," he told it. "He ain't got no way of checking up on me."

Amos was good, oh, in a pig's eye. The quicker the old gal drunk herself into a pine box, the better off he'd be. Everard guessed a man could tell it was a trout when it stuck its head out of the milk.

Joe Randall, sitting in his office on the dark December afternoon ten days after his wife's death, finished checking over the cash in the pay envelopes which Sarah Jerdan, his bookkeeper, had got ready, and sat back wearily, glad the job was done. Sarah might be remarkable with figures—in fact, she was a mathematical genius who had invented her own system for keeping the plant books, a system with elaborations that Joe himself couldn't even follow; but Sarah couldn't count cash and get the right sum in the proper envelope to save her life.

It was a dark December, dark for the plant and for Joe; darkest of all for Amy, he thought, trying to put the raw, wet earth of the cemetery out of his mind. Maybe he would be able to, sometime; people, well-meaning as all hell, kept telling him that in time things would get better, it was what a man had to hold to, could count on. Well, dammit, if that was all, it wasn't much. Right now, it looked to Joe, nothing would ever be better. Turn and twist as he would, plunge in to work—and he was working now harder than he ever had to keep the plant from going under—he couldn't stop from thinking. The moment he finished a job, like now, sat back, off his guard, it was as if a spotlight snapped on and focused on the spongy earth and gravel that the drenched flowers hadn't hid, not that it would have made any difference if they had. That was Amy, there. Let them try to cover it up with carnations and a pearl-gray casket with a white nylon frill for her head to lay against; it was still Amy.

Joe had known the frill was nylon because that had been one of the selling points the undertaker had used: "Now, this one, just a little more expensive, of course, but this is nylon, an improvement, we feel, over the old style—"

Jerked out of numbness, Joe had stared at the man. He said, "It makes a difference?"

"Well, for looks, we feel it does." He went on with it, about how people felt—the last thing they would be able to do, so most of them did the best they could; of course, he always kept on hand "this one" for those who couldn't afford—and he flicked his hand at a flat, rhomboid-shaped box, obviously cheap, in dull black; something out of a TV horror show, obscenely symbolic of what it was and what it would contain. "That's only one-seventy-nine, of course . . ." And Joe, choking, wanting to vomit, said, "Bring what you want to, I don't care," and went plunging out of the place.

At the funeral Amy did look nice in her wedding dress and against her white nylon frill. Joe supposed it was all right; it was what people did and expected you to do; he couldn't look. He had wanted the casket closed, but Amy's folks wouldn't hear of it; they wanted it open, so everybody could have a "last look"; also, he found out, people would think it peculiar—as if there was something to hide, as if Amy had died of something her family didn't want anyone to know about and wasn't fit for public view. Amy's mother felt strongly about this, so that Joe didn't argue. She was Amy's mother; she probably felt as bad as he did. But death had turned out to be a touchy subject, something you didn't try to buck public opinion on. He had sat through the funeral, trying to get back his first feeling of numbness, knowing now that it was going to wear off and that, when it did, he was probably going to go crazy and almost hoping he would.

The minister had a smarmy voice that Joe couldn't stand anyway in church on an ordinary Sunday. He didn't listen. If he raised his eyes, he could see the lace on the skirt of Amy's dress. He didn't raise his eyes.

At the cemetery the rain had fallen in a downpour, and the undertaker had touched Joe's elbow respectfully and said it was raining. He regretted it was such a bad day for a funeral.

As if some days were good days for funerals; as if any day was. Sure, the guy regretted; he regretted the rain that was spoiling the show; you could see he'd had it in mind to put on a good show, that he liked to.

Suddenly Joe had been furious. He felt the fury, red-hot, flaming, all over him. All this was for Amy, and Amy was dead; she would have hated being looked at when she couldn't look back, or take her own part, just lie there. He hated having her looked at. It was damnable that she was dead; he couldn't spare her, he couldn't stand it; and he couldn't stand this mumbo-jumbo that was nailing it down, that was turning her into a corpse before his eyes, before he was able to stand it. He had shoved the astonished man out of his way and had got away from the cemetery, not even waiting for the "graveside service."

"Poor Joe," people had said. "He felt so awful, he couldn't stand it. But wouldn't you think he'd have waited for the graveside service?"

He had come down to the plant, as being the one place where

everything his eyes fell on wouldn't remind him of Amy, and had found that it was worse, because everything there did remind him of her. The plant had been closed and locked because all hands had been up at the funeral. Joe went in and sat down at his desk.

The whole place had been a reminder of his folks and hers; generations of them, ending and going on: Funny Money Montgomery's desk, where she worked when she helped him to understand Sarah's bookkeeping system; the dog-eared batch of file cards they'd laughed over together because Montgomery and Randall had put down some pretty drastic comments on the state of things in general. Seems they had had their business troubles, too.

Joe certainly had. Now, ten days after, he knew that somehow or other he had to get his mind working, quit huddling here like a sick bird.

God, that old hen hawk Pa and I found with the busted wing and chained up by the leg in the barn. I know just how he felt. Damned if I wouldn't like to do just what he did, sit scrouched down with my eyes shut till I died.

He jerked his mind away from the memory of that sorry sight and was stacking the pay envelopes, getting them in order to hand out, when Marvin Coles came through the door.

Marvin Coles had been foreman at the Randall Packing Company for a long time. He had been foreman under Joe's father, whose junior he had been by something like ten years; he had seen the old man die (or, as Marvin called it, "pass on"); had seen Joe grow up, take over, and make changes. Marvin was in town politics off and on; every so often he took a turn as First Selectman; but the factory was his life. While he liked Joe, he could not abide Joe's changes. Any one of Joe's innovations, no matter what, had had to go out around Marvin, who was against it with his feet dug in. He was convinced that the old men who had started the factory had known how to run it and how to make money. Clam chowder, fish chowder, codfish cakes, trying to make the plant pay running it all winter—to Marvin's mind were all a mess of foolishness.

The old boys had known how. Get-in, get-what-there-was, get-out. It only made sense. You had a good method that worked out, why, for godsakes, change it? He had told Joe this many times in the past and would again. Why was it any man's business whether people in town worked winters or whether they didn't? Let 'em go somewhere where there was work if they wanted to. It wasn't up to Joe, and he was a damn simple fool if he thought so.

Marvin was a stout man up to his neck, but his head was shaped like a peanut, pointed at the top. He had a long, thin neck, dewlap cheeks which gave him a sad expression, and a cast in one eye which made him look as if he could see in two directions at once. Dressed in his Sunday suit, giving his report at town meetings, Marvin was a model of a fine, conservative town official and might have sat for the portrait of one. The suit, a thick, dark-brown woolen one, stiff as a board, made him hot and uncomfortable even on a cold day. His tie was always pulled into a knot the size of a dime and pushed so tightly against his Adam's apple that it stood out in an arc from the V of his vest. In the middle of an argument on town affairs, as Marvin warmed up, his tie would ride higher and higher while everybody waited, fascinated, for the moment when he would suddenly grind to a stop, roll one eye down at his shirt front while the other remained implacably fixed on his opponent, and poke the tie down. It was an excellent attention-diverter, particularly when Marvin was losing, as no one knew better than he. But being a stubborn man who could wear almost anybody down by sheer weight of words, Marvin had no need of such tricks; he only kept a bagful of them handy just in case. He wouldn't lose; but he didn't intend to, either.

Except at lodge and town meetings and church, Marvin was never seen dressed up; he wore his coveralls, with RANDALL'S in dingy letters across his back and FOREMAN stitched on his left breast pocket. These were usually stiff with sardine oil and engine grease; they were more than usually so today because he had been overseeing the plant's usual fall conversion. A piece of damn foolishness and against his better judgment, as he had let everyone know. Joe, in the office, had heard

Marvin roaring around the plant all day. He did not, however, roar at Joe. He said in a hushed voice as he came through the door, "I'll hand them pay envelopes around, Joe. You don't need to bother."

Joe twitched. If people would only act themselves, not treat you like a sickness, remind you all the time. He started to say this, pulled himself up. No sense shocking Marvin. He'd been brought up to show respect for bereavement; one way was to talk soft and easy. That was the custom and he wouldn't be one to change it. Joe said instead, "Better tell the boys to frame this lot. I don't know how many more there'll be."

Marvin looked at Joe or, at least, in Joe's direction, though his divided stare seemed to fall on either end of the ancient roll-top desk. "Short run," he pronounced lugubriously. "Pack's way down."

Under different circumstances this would have been a fine chance to have rasped home the point that if all the money J. J. Randall and Funny Money Montgomery had made and passed along was gone, he knew the reason why. This unuttered thought passed across his face plainly. To hold back any opinion whatsoever gave Marvin actual pain; and Joe, seeing it, couldn't help grinning a little.

"You know, Marvin," he said, "if the ghosts that haunt this office could take shape, the first thing they'd do would be to call me a fool, wouldn't they?"

After his first shock—that anyone whose wife had just been buried could mention a ghost out loud—Marvin couldn't keep still any longer. Bereavement or no bereavement, he was going to have a say. "If them old men could come back," he snorted, "the first thing they'd do is take you out in the coal shed and lay on with a paddle."

That was better. "You think so?" Joe said.

"Hell, I know so! All that money, thrun away on damned newfangled notions that don't work out and never will, not if you hack away a hundred years. Old Funny Money, God, he'd bust wide-open and die dead." Marvin choked and stopped. After all, it wasn't a time to mention death. He looked away and turned red.

Joe, it seemed, hadn't noticed. "A damned fool," he said. "Well,

maybe they were right. Get-in, get-what-there-is, getout. They sure
knew how. The town called them the piggy boys for years. So long
as they had it made, what did they care? Well, God blast it, I care! I
don't know as I'm in the business for the fun of it, either, but there's
some way, goddammit. If I could just dope out how to—what to do."

"I know good and well what you *will* do," Marvin said. "You'll
try to run all winter on a shoestring. Come spring, you'll have a whole
shedful of fishballs, or some other useless commodity, that you can't
sell a can of because some outfits bigger'n you are's got the market
tied up. Don't tell me nothing about it," he went on, warming up.
"I seen this same damn thing happen as long ago as when I was ten
years old and my grandfather lost his shirt raising beans. This land
hereabouts—you'd never know it now the way the fields has all come
up to puckerbrush—will raise beans to patch hell a mile. Grampop
made a good living for years out of beans, but the last shipment he
made he got around ten cents a ton. So he, by the god, didn't need a
hammer'n chisel to pound the facts of life through his thick head—"

"Like me," Joe said. "Well, I can't see as what he did made a hell of
a lot of sense, either. Instead of trying to find out what else there was,
he let his fields come up to puckerbrush. As long as there was plenty
there for the taking, he took, but the minute something came up to
hinder him, he sat down on his can. Don't talk your old grandfather
to me, Marvin. I remember him. Lived to be ninety-nine years old
and set on his arse for forty, thinking up all the chestnuts to tell to
the summer people. I can see him now, dear old Captain Coles, and
all the ladies getting a terrible boot out of how he'd et so many clams
that his guts went up and down with the tide. Why, the first man that
ever said that was likely Adam on the Garden of Eden clam flats, but
I got to hand it to your grampop, he got the full credit."

"That ain't in the Bible," Marvin said. He was mortally offended.

"Well, it might as well be, and for all I can see, the same thing's
still going on, people looking back toward the past and saying what
a fine, lovely, wealthy time that was, nobody ever had it so good, and
taking full credit for what a lot of old men did that have been dead

so long you can't read their names on their tombstones. When all the credit now, my God, is what the finance company is going to catch up on next year or, if not next year, the year after. You can shove your old grandfather and his beans, I ain't interested. What I'm interested in right now is what to do with what there is. Here I sit, a whole oceanful of food on my doorstep, a canning plant ready to roll, the cost of living at an all-time high, and I can't make peanuts."

"Ain't that what I been telling you!"

"I'll say it is. If I had the dough, I'd put in deep-freeze equipment, buy a flock of refrigerator trucks. I been reading up on it—"

"It's what's put you out of business. Ain't it?"

"Well, that and some other things. Only I ain't out of business. Not yet. By the god, I'll find something if I have to can air and sea water."

Marvin got up and stumped toward the door. He was good and mad with Joe. Old Captain Coles, who had lived for ninety-nine years, had been a character, with a reputation for it among people a lot bigger than Joe Randall was or ever would be; and never in Marvin's life had he ever heard one word said against the old man. At the door he said stiffly, without turning, "I s'pose Monday we go onto fishballs. I s'pose."

"I s'pose we do."

"Why not try something good, like, say, brook water and brouse?" He went off. Suddenly remembering the bereavement, he grabbed the door which he had started to slam, catching it in mid-motion. "You never know what them city folks'll go for," he said, and closed the door quietly behind him.

"I might, at that," Joe said aloud to the closed door.

Trust Marvin to fire a good parting shot; he had a fine sense of timing.

Brook water and brouse, the poverty drink of the old times—water sweetened with molasses. If somebody said you lived on that, he meant you were stink-poor. It could contain, however, almost anything a man wanted to put into it and still be brook water and brouse. Old J. J. Randall, who hadn't been so poor, had sometimes laced it with Jamaica ginger or Demerara rum. Joe didn't doubt that if he could can old J. J's recipe and ship it, city folks would like it fine.

But stink-poor was what Marvin had meant.

And poor's what I am, Joe thought wearily, closing his desk. I'm poor without Amy. Without her, I'm the poorest man in the world.

For a while, fighting with Marvin—which wasn't really a fight, only bordering on one and typical of most of their discussions—Joe's trouble had gone to the back of his mind. It had been there, settled in like a blackness, and now, alone, Joe had to look at the blackness.

If I could have taken her myself and put her somewhere, made the place myself, not turned her over to strangers. Seemed like the last thing I could have done for her, made a place on a hill somewhere in the sunshine, a place for her to sleep. But they don't let you be private, they have to make a goddam parade over sticking her in a wet hole with a lot of other dead people around—and most of it because some guy after a fast buck wants to send me a bill for twelve hundred dollars.

Nylon, for chrissake! If you ever saw it, touched it, had to handle it again, you'd feel as if you'd touched a snake.

The old-fashioned clock over the desk struck five, a considered, well-spaced-out *bong, bong, bong, bong, bong,* as conservative and deliberate as the thoughts that went through the mind of Marvin Coles or anybody like him. When it stopped, some tumblers, or something, fell into place with a final click, like a period to substantial thinking. I have said it. It's five o'clock.

Better get home. Supper'll be ready and Angie raging. Poor old Angie, dammit all, if she'd only keep her cover on, but I've got to do something about her. Whoever I get to take care of the kids, she drives them nuts.

Always interfering with the babies now; she had taken a dislike to the two little ones and showed it. She might as likely as not creep up to a bassinet and pinch one of them; her favorite was J. J., and she said so. Her latest was that those two little ones didn't belong to Joe at all. Dr. Garland had fetched them in a basket.

The hospital kept Amos Wilkinson for ten days. To everyone's surprise, he did not object. Lucy had expected him home as soon as he had had his X-rays. The first day, she went to see him braced for a row—after all, she had sent him to a hospital without his consent. She was more frightened than ever when she found he had little or nothing to say.

"He's all right," Garland reassured her. "He stood that pain for a good many hours without any help; now he's had some and he's still dopey. After all, he's got lumps. I'm still puzzled as to how he tangled with a bulldozer track and didn't get more cuts. But I haven't heard of anyone around complaining of assault and battery. Have you?" He grinned, making a joke of it.

"No," Lucy said. She managed to smile back at him, but she got out of there in a hurry. She couldn't trust herself to talk to him.

She had been half out of her mind with worry; she couldn't reason herself out of it. She would, she knew, in time; with the help of hope and prayer, things always came right in the end. Even with bad things you just had to have faith and be strong.

She had known ever since Monday night after dark, when Amos had finally staggered out of the wood lot back of the house, that whatever he had tangled with, it had not been a bulldozer. He had told her to say bulldozer and she had said it. And she had known when he'd left the house that morning that he'd had something in his mind besides returning Jack Malden's car.

Not often, but more than once in her life, she had seen Amos in a murderous rage. Oh, he got mad two or three times a day and roared around the house, but she was used to that, it didn't amount to anything. There was a bottled-up thing, though, that ripped out of him sometimes, and always frightened her terribly. She had always been careful herself not to make that happen with Amos; but when it did happen, she knew. She could tell. It started with two slow tears that gathered in his eyes and rolled down, moving as if they were cold. It always seemed to her that they were forming as they moved two drops of ice. Poor Connie, she had never seen it until the other night;

Lucy had always managed to whisk her at such times out of her father's sight. Such anger was not a good thing for a child, a young girl, to see. And so Connie now thought he had been crying because he felt bad about her trouble, which was just as well. This was the way a girl ought to feel about her father. To see that she did, didn't feel hateful toward him ever, was part of a mother's bounden duty.

Lucy recalled well the last two occasions on which Amos had shed those two cold tears. One was when his grandfather's will had been read, leaving him not a penny; and the other was after the terrible quarrel he had had with Connie, after she had left the house, the time she had gone away. Poor Amos, he never could bear anybody to stand up to him.

The sight of those tears never failed to turn Lucy's own blood cold. You never could be sure what he would do. He might do nothing at all, let it wear itself out without harm to anyone. But on the other hand. . . . Years ago, she had put resolutely out of her mind and she refused to think about it now; but there *was* that workman . . . and the man had been so terribly . . . and when he had got well, he had taken Amos to court . . . and Amos had lost the case. She must not, she told herself, let that incident come knocking at her door now.

But knock it did.

Amos had known who Connie had run away with. A Grindle boy from Shacktown, or his grandparents were; a bad boy, Amos said, with an awful bad name. Oh, how had Connie ever, ever managed to see enough of him to—met him at Clementina's, Amos said. Clementina had allowed him to see her there. Oh, no wonder Amos hated Clementina! Lucy would herself, except of course it was wicked to hate anyone.

That boy. That Grindle boy, Amos had known where to find him—on a boat in the harbor. Had he found him? He had certainly found somebody.

Ever since that Monday night when he had dragged himself out of the woods barely able to walk, Lucy had been terrified, waiting to hear that somebody had been found hurt. She could not bring herself to utter the *word* killed. After all, you put the best light you could on matters.

Perhaps he had gone down and got aboard the boat, ready to fight, and the crew had tackled him; he had looked as if he'd been beaten by three or four men. Of course. That was probably just what . . . but no. He had come out of the woods, from the direction of the big swamp, Cooney's Heath, his clothes covered with swamp muck, as if he had half-drowned, rolled in it; and Cooney's Heath was two miles from the harbor and in the opposite direction. And he had been gone so long, too. Even if he had sneaked into the woods to keep anyone from seeing him, so dirty and bloody—and, oh, surely, that would have been the thought uppermost in his mind, not let the neighbors see!—he could have come home in ten minutes through woods along back roads and stayed all out of sight all the way.

Lucy asked herself over and over, and got no answers. She certainly had got no answers from Amos. In the days before he had gone to the hospital, he'd not said a word about it, except to tell her what to say, and she hadn't dared to press.

The day after he went to the hospital, Lucy got out the car and drove down to the waterfront, looking fearfully at the boats in the harbor to see if a strange one might be there. But she did not know boats well enough to tell, or to say whether one was a trawler or what it might be. Such things were not a part of women's knowledge: boats, trawlers, were men's things. She had no way of knowing whether the boat had gone unless she asked somebody, which of course was out of the question. If it had not gone . . . if it were still there with one of its men . . . maimed; just waiting, ready to pounce . . . all those men, a whole boatload of men who knew about Connie, too, and that awful boy, and who might be talking and talking until the whole town, all the neighbors, would know. . . .

Lucy had taken a course in practical nursing, but she had not been trained or equipped to handle problems outside a household. Brought up by two good women resolute for the right, her mother and her grandmother, she had been early indoctrinated in euphemism and the pleasant maxims to be found in copybooks, which through use had become her laws immutable. Lucy had brightened the corner and looked on the good side for so many years that when the corner was dark and the good side indubitably bad, she could not think what to do except apply the maxims, hope for the best in the best of all possible worlds, and wait for time to pass. Other people were worse off than you were; this made you feel better. War was wicked; so was sin: men's things, about which a good woman not strong to battle could only fold bandages and pray. For frailty, thy name was woman; and frailty goes not forth, it humbly stands and waits (also serving) for someone to come and do something, sop the *lacrimae* out of the *rerum*.

She was a great reader, but she would not open a book unless someone whose judgment she trusted had read it first and assured her that it was a happy one, with nothing "nasty" in it. There was enough evil in the world without reading about it in books. She read the Bible instead. Virtue would conquer; the wicked could not prevail. Whatever army went forth with banners, your side, the side of right, won: as in the war, when Hitler got his come-uppance for being so awful to all those Jews, Lucy had known beforehand that he would get it; it only proved the point. She would only have been confused if anyone had asked her what might have been the opinion of the innocent dead.

A formidable enemy of "trashy" reading, she was made deeply uncomfortable by the new paperbacks, remembering only too well how her mother and her grandmother had fought with cudgels over Nick Carter and the pennydreadfuls of her youth. The similarity, Lucy said, was too much the same. She had once taken away from Connie a paperback copy of *War and Peace*, recommended reading in high-school English, and, because of the picture on the cover, had burned it in the stove. Amos had gone to the teacher about it. Things were getting pretty unbearable, he told the astonished woman, when some damn Communist Russian novels were being taught in the schools. Hereafter he and Connie's mother would supervise her reading; any more such trash would be taken straight to the School Board.

Lucy recommended nice stories from the women's magazines, on which she could depend. Good people wrote them, saw that nothing evil crept in: she could rest easy. Everything would come out all right, everyone be happy in the end, though she wished sometimes it could be said in so many words, not be left for the reader to form his own conclusion. If good were to triumph, as who should doubt, what was wrong with saying so? She did so miss the little paragraph which always had been at the end, years ago, when she was a girl. But then, times changed.

How they changed! And in her own lifetime, too. She took pride in belonging to a century in which there had been so much progress. The vapor trails of jet planes across the sky sometimes caught the upward-reflected rays of the set sun and looked as if a magnificent worm of pure and sparkling gold were headed in from space. "Why," Lucy would say, "if our grandmothers had seen that, they would have thought for sure it was the Second Coming!"

She said this once to Clementina, in the days, of course, when Amos had let her speak to Clementina, and she had been deeply shocked at Clementina's reply.

"Second Coming, my foot!" Clementina had said, staring at the lovely contrail. "What we'd all better do is start figuring fringe benefits from the first one."

Poor Clementina, she was so old and so bitter; she often refused to see the loveliness in things, and how awful that must be!

Oh, the wonders of the times! Lucy marveled at the new inventions, which showed how great is the mind of man, and she took a modest credit to herself. In her own life span, this had taken place! Movies; and movies that talked; and now, in the living room, a box of plebeian metal and glass out of which came wonderment: pictures and sounds, stories and news. She quickly selected the programs she liked best: family stories, plays about little children. She was deeply hurt when Connie called the cute little girls and boys "organization moppets," or when Connie refused to enjoy the programs Lucy liked. Of course, Lucy found it difficult to enjoy the programs Amos liked; but "It takes all kinds," she told herself, sighing; and she did listen to Amos's programs, the men's things, the prize fights and the Westerns.

The prize fights she hated; as often as not the old, ugly, and wicked-looking fighter would hurt, would knock down, the young and handsome boy. But Westerns she found she could get something out of. If you hated to watch shooting and killing and were shocked to see a dead body flung irreverently across the back of a horse, still you could be sure it was only the bad men that this happened to, only what they deserved to be carted away to some evil and moss-grown Boot Hill.

Lucy was not constitutionally adapted to the operation of all the lovely modern things; the properties of electricity, to her, were a mystery. Her vacuum cleaner, a round cylinder which rolled softly on rubber-lined ends, was a masterpiece of up-to-date design. She loved it for its looks; it was blue, with a long, gray, plastic tube and a cord which would reach into any of the downstairs rooms from any floor plug. Everybody had one, and so had she.

Yet week after week, she fought the battle of the "vac." Following after her across rugs, like a faithful puppy on a leash, it would at times and unaccountably develop a will of its own, would slyly go sideways into the leg of a table or some corner of furniture that stuck out. Crash would go movables, and nice vases get broke n. Or there were certain times of day when, for her, the vac refused to suck; she had proved this to herself beyond the shadow of a doubt. Sometimes she had to go over and over a rug; she said this was the fault of the electrical company. In vain Connie would point out that the dust bag inside was full and should be changed; to Lucy, once the dust had vanished up the tube, it was gone forever, as if the vac had eaten it. No, she said, they weren't sending so much power over the wires right now, or one of her neighbors had left something *on*, wasting current. She was convinced that the best time to vac was late at night after everybody had gone to bed and couldn't be using up power. She could do the living room in half the time, she said; and she did, thereby causing Amos in his first sleep to rise up screaming.

She would lose a handkerchief into the cake mixer; of its own volition, it would fall out of the pocket of her blouse and wind up in the beaters, which were then bent and would have to be replaced or repaired. She performed miracles with the heavy items of her laundry in the washing machine. Once it took a service man half a day to extricate a scatter rug; and another time she caught the front of her dress in the wringer, receiving a painful pinch before Connie, who fortunately had been nearby, had yanked out the plug. For days afterwards, Lucy watched herself with concern—a bruise *there* sometimes caused cancer, everyone knew; but nothing happened.

With an automobile on the highway, she was a hazard, avoided at all times by all her neighbors when possible. She loved a car and to drive, but after a while sitting still at the wheel would become a tax on patience; her mind would wander. So many things to look at and admire as she went along; and sometimes, as had been her lifelong habit when sitting with nothing to do such as reading or sewing, she would take advantage of the leisure to say her prayers. Since it had also been her lifelong habit, when praying, to close her eyes, sometimes, in spite of telling herself that she mustn't, not at the wheel of the car, she found she had; it was so absorbing talking to God; she always had so much to tell Him. Once or twice she had had narrow escapes, such as the time she ran the car up on the sidewalk, to the outrage of a summer gentleman in shorts, who had been walking quietly along minding his own business.

"But," Lucy said, indignant at his reaction, "I wasn't going *fast!*"

She was as nice a woman as anyone could hope to meet: agreeable to talk to, tidy in her dress, her hair always neatly and becomingly arranged. In sickness or trouble, she was pleasantly steadfast, often leaned on by friends and neighbors. "Lucy," they said, "is a rock to lean on." Living with Amos had never been easy; but whose life was not a cross to bear? Where a lesser woman might have left him or killed him, or flattened out in a flood of self-pity, Lucy took sustenance. She throve in the assurance that she was doing her duty—her "bounden" duty; she would not have been able to use one word without the other. She guessed she knew what the marriage vow meant to a good woman.

You promised to cleave and you clove, till death did you part; but before *that* happened, you never forgot that you had promised to obey.

For the first few days after Connie's return home, Lucy was not far from a state of shock. The signposts were down, Amos was in the hospital, there was nothing to point which way to turn. But time went on and nothing happened, and presently the built-in mechanism which ordered her life began to take over.

Good people must expect the unpleasant at times. Bad luck, bankruptcy, falling down stairs: a part of life, they happened all the time. You met them with fortitude, as best you could.

Connie had had a baby when she wasn't married, but the baby was dead and disposed of. Nobody knew. What Connie needed now was forgiveness.

Disreputable or criminal things were for newspapers; they could not, and did not, take place in the nice families of the people who *tried*. It was not right to think evil thoughts; but Lucy had lived long enough to know that euphemism was a double swivel in a small town—it worked both ways.

She called up the neighbors, soberly discussed Amos's narrow escape from the bulldozer, then announced gaily that there was no great loss without some small gain, the Lord always saw to it that you were compensated, Connie was home. She had had the flu, said Lucy, and was still in bed; she would be feeling better in a day or so, and, later, they must all call around.

The next morning the mailbox was stuffed with "get well" cards, which Lucy brought upstairs and left in a neat stack on the bedside table.

"Why, you haven't opened your mail, dearest," she said with astonishment when she came up with Connie's lunch tray.

"No," Connie said.

"Don't you feel well enough to? I thought you felt better."

"Oh, I do. Much better. I just, m'm . . . I'm afraid I went to sleep."

"Oh, that's good! Just what you need. Of course." Lucy's face cleared at once.

Connie was better; she had been up and around in the afternoons, even downstairs; but Lucy insisted that she rest mornings.

"Well, you certainly look better," Lucy said briskly. "You've even got some color in your cheeks, like my Connie again. Now, you eat every bit of this nice lunch while I open your cards for you."

Lucy dearly wished to know which of the neighbors had sent cards; it was so nice to get cards. She always sent them herself when people were sick. She opened all of Connie's, read each one aloud, including the "message," and, when she had finished, felt better than she had for days. All that lovely poetry!

"My, now, isn't that nice of people! I guess it shows what this town thinks of you, Connie."

"Mm. What did you tell them was the matter with me?"

Lucy brought up short. She flushed and bit her lip. For a moment the sentiments, good wishes, roses, forget-me-nots, all in pretty colors, had lulled her mind; she had been, herself, believing in Connie's flu. Nobody knew, outside the family; all these cards had come; it could just as well have been the flu . . .

"Well, for goodness' sake, Connie!" she said with a little burst of annoyance. "I said you had the flu. Lots of people down in the cities have had it; Dr. Garland says there's been a real epidemic. So it could be, you know."

"Yes. It could be."

"Now, Connie, it's not a bit of use to feel that way. We have got to look on the bright side. And you have got to pull yourself up by your bootstraps. Time cures all things."

"All right, Ma, I've had the flu. Just don't say those things to me. Don't ask me too soon."

"Now, dear. Those 'things' were all written down years ago, by people who knew a great deal more than we do."

"I'm sure."

"Connie, what's got into you? You don't sound like my girl at all. Oh, dear, I don't see where this misfortune could have come from, we have always been such a nice family. I know I can blame myself for letting you spend so much time with Clementina, wicked is what she is, all those ideas she got from living in the city. No knowing what she's told you—"

"Oh, Ma, that's not fair. She never told me anything I didn't know."

"She let you meet that boy at her house. That was where—"

"For heaven's sake, where did you hear that story? I never met him at Clementina's! I did take him there once to introduce him to her, just before we went away. She liked him."

"There! You see, she hasn't any judgment of people."

"Well, neither did I. Look, Ma, I keep asking you. How is Clementina?"

"Well, your father—"

"I know. He's still mad at her. But surely you could tell me how she is. You remember I asked you in my letters, and you never would say."

"Well, I had my reasons, dear, not to. Unpleasant things—I really don't think your father would want me to talk about it—" She glanced up and, seeing the look on Connie's face, said hastily, "Clementina's not herself, dear. She's taken to drink."

"*Clementina*? Ma, what on earth are you talking about?"

"Well, dear. She always had something of the kind *in* her, we all knew that. Or perhaps you don't, of course we never would tell you such things. She was once an alcoholic."

"She wasn't!"

"Oh, yes, your father knows all about it. When she lived in the city, she had to take a cure. Of course, she hasn't, for years, but she's gone back to it. Your father's thinking about having her committed."

"To an asylum? Clementina?"

"Yes, dear. You can see why I wouldn't write you about it."

"When did it start? How long—"

"Sometime after you left. We found out."

"Oh, no," Connie said under her breath.

It didn't make sense. Clementina had always been so—so *civilized*. Yet maybe it did. Maybe that was why she didn't ever write me, didn't answer any of my letters. And my last letter was desperate; if she'd known, she'd have answered it, I'll always believe. Maybe it figures. Yes, it does.

"Couldn't you and Pa have helped her?" Connie said aloud. "Couldn't you have done *anything*?"

"Oh, your father won't go near, dear, you know how he feels about liquor. He says to wait; when she gets bad enough, Dr. Garland'll have to sign papers, it's the only way to take care of—Now, Connie. If she's really crazy . . . I know it's sad, dear, old age is bad for people, but we have to look on the—"

"Don't tell me," Connie said savagely. "Let me guess. The bright side. So she's been down there alone all this time, and nobody's gone near her. Nobody gave a damn, is that right?"

"Oh, Connie, please don't swear." Lucy began mildly to cry; the tears ran down and she mopped them with her handkerchief. "Lots of people try. Nellie Overholt goes there and the doctor, and they can't find out how she gets liquor, she just sneaks it in on the sly."

Clementina. Well, she had outwitted a good many in her day. Thinking of some of the times when the opposition had had to run to catch up, Connie couldn't help smiling.

"Connie!" Lucy gasped, horrified. "It isn't funny!"

"No, Ma. I know it isn't."

Poor Ma. I ought to know by this time that she can't see out over her maxims. And if you try to make her, it only makes her lose her wits. I'll have to comfort her or she'll spend days trying to crawl back behind her fortress walls, and she's going to need all the wits she's got, because Pa'll be coming home.

Trying to think of something that would comfort Lucy, she seized on the thing at hand. "You know, I'm hungry, Ma. Talking with you has done me good."

Lucy's tears ceased. "Well, there, I knew it! I knew all you needed was to talk with your old Ma!"

She got up, fussed with the tray, then stood back, anxiously watching to see if Connie was going to notice anything. "Oh, dear, I hope things haven't got cold."

"Mm, it looks nice, Ma."

The sight of food, any food, nauseated Connie, but she managed to chew and swallow, at least to make motions. "It *is* nice, Ma."

"Well, I did try to get together a few things I know you like."

"I see you did. And with all you've got to do, too. Now, I'll be all right. I know you've got a lot to tend to."

"Well, I have, with your father coming, and I do want the house to be nice."

But on the edge of going, Lucy teetered, looking coy, obviously expecting something more.

What? Connie glanced at the tray. There must be something on it she ought to mention. The food was tastefully arranged, with dainty touches of lace-cut pink doilies and paper napkin to match.

"It looks so pretty," Connie said faintly.

"I put the little flower on, I thought you might see—" Smiling, expectant, Lucy waited.

Oh, yes. In a tiny bud vase, the little pink flower picked off a house plant. A bloom of Patient Lucy.

Lucy *fecit*. Lucy did this. For you.

"Why, Ma," Connie said, smiling. "You signed your name to it."

"Yes, I did. And I thought you were going to be forever getting the point." Pleased, Lucy went off to her household chores.

Oh, Ma. I would know this was one of your trays if I found it floating on a cloud in the sky.

Clam broth. Soda biscuits. Macaroni and cheese. String beans. Rice pudding.

All solid, nourishing items, turned out by Lucy, by the kettle-, pot-, and plateful, in tonnage, through the years. Because it is good for you.

Thinking back, recalling—"Now, what are all the things that Connie likes?"—Lucy had come up with what she thought Connie ought to like, and you could not have changed her mind about it if you had hit her over the head with her tray.

Oh, Ma. What tells you, what makes you sure that things aren't the way they are, but the way you want them to be? Even me. You're convinced that what I've done is the worst in the book, yet even me you've turned bright side out with a flock of pink and purple get-well cards. The little spot of nastiness you were brought up to have in the back of your mind; your grandmother had it about your mother and your mother about you, and maybe I would have it, too, if I had a daughter, it's made plain enough and pounded into every female child—now it's grown into a glaring, bright red fact, a maxim that wasn't in the copybook. What every mother fears has come to pass. So you're way out there, forgiving a sinful daughter, and I couldn't yell loud enough to make you hear that all I did was what you brought me up and trained me to do—to catch a man. And the worst I did was to be a fool, to let myself get taken in.

Ernie Grindle, the way he was at first: how could I, how could anyone have known? What were the signposts to say? Pa, ranting around, saying he was wild? But Ernie wasn't wild with me. And, besides, Pa got mad if I went out with anyone who wasn't Mack Jensen.

Sitting up, with the almost untouched tray across her knees, Connie took a long look back.

Mack Jensen. Her father's foreman; a lodge brother of Amos's. A "nice, local boy." "Somebody who would make somebody a good husband, someday." Somebody who'd make Amos a nice partner in the business.

Who smelled of beer and sen-sen and an unaired clothes closet. Whose idea of a good time was a double date, a double wrassle going on at the same time in the back and front seats of a car; who thought it was funny, afterwards, to compare notes. Who, to call attention to himself, leaned heavily on his reputation as a practical joker, so that with him you were likely to get an ice cube down your back, if nothing worse. He would creep up behind you and jab you in the ribs, with a juicy, spit sound, "Tschlh!" and guffaw when you jumped. Who had a filthy tongue . . .

Ernie Grindle, who was a first-class mimic, sometimes did Mack Jensen—a caricature to the life, and very funny.

"So, go on, marry him," Ernie had said. "Why not? And in a couple of years, you'll look as though you'd spent your life with King Kong."

Oh, Ernie. I loved you so much before you were Anzio.

It was better with you than I thought it ever could be with a man. Because all I had to go on was what Ma had with Pa, and looking around at one or two girls I knew who did marry "nice, local boys." And the older women, sometimes they do look as if they'd spent their lives with King Kong. How could it start in the way it did, and end with you throwing my suitcase after me down the boat's hold, not caring whether it knocked me flat? Was it something I did, something about the way I was? But how could I ever have known?

I suppose the first signpost was that screwball wedding, the way we were married at that ratty apartment in Boston, with the cardboard sign on the door, *Justice of the Peace*, scratched in ink; and the wild party afterwards, when the Justice got as high as anybody. I should have suspected when the marriage certificate was only that odd-looking blue paper that Ernie got me to sign and then stuck in his pocket. I ought to have asked to read it. But why, when I loved him and trusted him? Do you let the people you love and trust think you don't?

I had no reason not to trust him. Up until the time the baby was coming; he said one more trip on the trawler and we'd be set, we could have the apartment in New Bedford and I could have the baby there. And then he didn't come back. And the nightmare began. When I found him, which was just by asking at the wharves where the *Potluck* came in, he was Anzio Jones and he said he didn't know me.

Oh, I said good-bye to him long before he threw the suitcase down the hatch. He didn't need to do that to make his point, not when he had just shown me the "marriage certificate," a fake stock certificate he said he'd picked out of somebody's second-class mail. I never knew you could turn off love like a faucet, but you can. Somewhere in there everything stopped for good, so that I never want to see him or hear about him again.

The bed felt uncomfortable and hot. Connie shifted a little so that the forgotten tray tilted and she barely rescued it from flopping upside down on the coverlet.

Poor Ma, she went to a lot of trouble. Who am I to be picky? Time was, this meal would've looked like manna from Heaven. It isn't fair to criticize her for something she can't help. If she wants to have herself a fine old romantic time forgiving me, I expect I had better play along. But, dammit, I don't feel that sinful. I can't afford to. Somehow I have got to pick up the pieces of my life. I don't know how, but lying here with weak knees isn't going to help. I had better eat.

She stared at the tray.

The baby was dead. What had they done with it? The skipper of the *Potluck*—Walt; she didn't know his last name; Ernie had never called him anything else but Walt. That cautious man, afraid Anzio's tramp was going to nick him for money, sliding his two dollars out slow and careful, looking around to make sure nobody saw; surely a man like that would know what to do with a baby's small body, which was no practical use that anyone could see aboard a boat. The boat must have gone, slipped away that same night without anyone's coming ashore, because if her crew had done any talking down around the waterfront, Lucy would know by now. Poor Ma, she had antennae out all over town.

No, they were just relieved to be rid of us, the baby and me. The baby took care of his part of it by dying. And I got out as soon as I could, not to cause them any more trouble. Was it his part, or hers? I'm its mother, and I don't know whether it was a boy or a girl. And I won't know. Because it is probably drifting around in the ocean somewhere now, or weighted and sunk where it won't ever cause anybody any trouble again. Did they wrap it in its new blue blanket, I wonder, the one I bought when I hoped so much it would be a boy? Like its father. Or did they just throw it overboard with the trash?

Connie pulled herself up. She was shaking, she realized—the carefully polished silver on Lucy's tray was making a tinkling sound, the knife vibrating gaily against the spoon.

I suppose none of them would tell me what they did. They don't know who I am, unless Ernie told them, and he would have his reasons not to. He is aboard the *Potluck*, and I could write a letter to Anzio Jones, asking; but he wouldn't answer, he would tear it up, the way he is now. Ernie wouldn't have; but *he* would. I could write to Walt, care of the *Potluck*, New Bedford Dock; but there might be more than one Walt on board; besides, him, a man like that, he'd be caught dead before he ever put anything down in writing. The little bald man, who helped me, might. I don't know his name.

Maybe it would be better just to do nothing, forget it, let the shadow close down like a lid, let the nightmare be gone for good.

But no. I can't. I have to live my life in decency, and I couldn't do that, not knowing.

I wanted you, she told the small shade, which had never been much more than that: a brown, cloth-wrapped bundle in the dark, a single cry. Nobody else did, much; you were only a scandal, a guilty disgrace, not to be looked at by nice people. But I loved you and I wanted you. I'll have to do what I can.

When I am stronger. When my knees stop shaking. I have to get a job, and some money. I have to do something about Clementina. I won't do it lying here sorry for myself.

Connie ate, grimly choking the mouthfuls down. The macaroni took away the taste of the clam broth; the rice pudding wiped out the macaroni. There was a big pot of lukewarm tea, thank God, which with plenty of sugar took away the taste of everything.

Amos got home a few nights later, at suppertime. Connie and her mother were halfway through the meal when he walked in, closing the door behind him, turning, not saying a word of greeting to anybody.

"Oh, Amos, dear!" Lucy came fluttering to her feet. "Why didn't you tell me—I was coming for you in the car when—How did you get home?"

"Mack brought me," Amos said. "In the truck." He walked across the room to his armchair, turned on the light beside it, and sat down, opening the newspaper which he carried under his arm. "I've et," he said from behind the paper.

Connie had dreaded the meeting with him. It wasn't the seeing him—she would be glad to see him. He had never been one to show tenderness or affection, and she did not expect him to now. But he had cried the night she got home. A good many things about that night she couldn't remember; but one thing she had only to close her eyes to see—the two tears creeping down his leathery cheeks. He cared about her more than he showed; she held to that. What she dreaded was his talk, his yelling, because, if things were as they had been in the past, now everything would have to be brought out again, paraded, and blame assigned. She got up, crossed the room and stood beside his chair, braced to get it over. He still showed the effects of his accident; the discolorations had faded somewhat from his face, but his nose and right hand were bandaged. Enough remained to show how bad his injuries had been.

"Hello, Pa," Connie said. "How are you, now? Are you better? Oh, my, you had a bad one, didn't you?"

Amos did not turn his head or look at her; he did not speak. He sat silent; his silence grew in the room like a thunderclap.

Neighbors came to call as soon as they were sure Connie was up and around. They brought fruit and jelly and little gifts, told her she certainly looked as if she'd had some old bout of it with the flu, said how tough it must be on Lucy to have her and Amos both down at the same time. But that was the way of things for you, wasn't it? They passed the time of day and went away. Nobody so much as mentioned Connie's marriage.

"What gives?" Connie finally asked Lucy. She was puzzled. Everybody must know she'd gone away to be married. It was only natural that some of them should ask after her husband. Unless they had a reason not to.

"Oh, yes, dear," Lucy said delicately. "I've warned people that it would be tactful not to mention him to you. Your father thinks it best to let it be known that you and your husband have separated."

"Well, thank him for me, will you?" Connie said. "It's nice to know he knows I'm here."

"Now, honey. He'll come around. He always does, you know."

"I know, all right. But it's a strain, waiting."

It was hard to keep her temper about it, Connie found. Though he would not speak to her or acknowledge her presence in the house when the family was alone, Amos was his usual self when outsiders were there, talking with everyone, discussing his accident, making a joke out of it.

Didn't know how he could have done such a darn-fool freak of a thing, he said. He'd remembered how the boys had left the bulldozer pretty near the slant of the hill, and when it'd looked as if it might rain Sunday night, he'd got to thinking about the doggone barn swallows, or whatever, that had undermined the other side of the bank, wondering about another landslide. He'd only gone up to check. Fool thing to do, alone. Oh, sure, he was okay now; this busted bone in his hand was the joker. He'd be back at work pretty soon, he was going nuts sitting around the house. Of course his beauty was spoilt—he'd probably always have a crook in his nose, but he sure-God hadn't lost anything he'd miss.

One of the first to come was Mack Jensen, after supper one evening—to talk business with Amos, he said. To hear the two of them talking shop and guffawing, you wouldn't have known Amos for the same man—the one he would be as soon as the company left.

Connie had intended to go upstairs early; she had been out walking and was tired; with Amos acting as if she did not exist, except when guests were in the house, she tried to keep out of his way as much as possible. But when she and her mother were finishing up the supper dishes, Lucy said with a disingenuous air, as if this were something she'd thought of at the last moment, "Oh, honey, Mack's coming over. Your father's asked me to fix lemonade and cake, and I've got so much to do upstairs—would you do it for me?" She turned with a glance which, to Connie's horror, was unmistakably coy. "And do put on something besides that old dress. It looks so tacky, dear."

"What would you suggest?" Connie said. She had not, of course, brought anything home with her; and, in fact, there had been very little to bring because any of her dresses that would sell, she had had to pawn in New Bedford. She had been wearing some cast-offs, left at home when she had gone away, which were now a little small for her and which, she didn't doubt, looked tacky as all get-out, but they were all there were. Nothing had been said, as yet, about new clothes because, Connie knew, her mother didn't think the time was ripe to ask Amos for money for any.

"Oh, I'm sure there must be something nicer than that," Lucy said. She wrung out the dishcloth, flapped it smartly, and hung it on the rack over the sink. "There, that's done. Now, you mustn't let yourself go, dear, it isn't—Well, I'll depend on you to fix the refreshments, shall I?" And she was gone, up the backstairs, to whatever she had dreamed up to do there so that Connie would have to stay down, be there when Mack came.

Oh, Ma. You and your clever little schemes, Connie thought. And oblivious to all, except what you've got cooking. Mack's coming, so dress up for him. Never mind if there isn't anything to dress up in.

Well, I've got plans, too, and you'd be surprised. Mack isn't included.

The thing with Mack, then, would be starting up all over again. It didn't seem possible that it could, so soon. How can they—they might at least give me a chance to get well. But this little strange interlude of mine, of course, doesn't really exist; it's going to be dropped out, forgotten, as soon as it possibly can be, because it isn't anything a nice girl ought to—so it's as if I'd never really left home at all, and it's going to be Mack, Mack, Mack, from now on out and I can't stand it. And I won't.

She was in the pantry fixing lemonade and cake when Mack came. There was no mistaking his arrival. He always came in with a slam of doors and a gust of loud, roaring talk. "Well, hello-lo!" he said, seeing Amos, apparently alone, in the kitchen. "How's the roaring old heller tonight? You having sober second thoughts about tangling with a bulldozer, hah?"

Amos said something in a low voice which Connie couldn't hear, evidently not making it strong enough, for Mack went on.

"Ah, come off it, Ame, you can't fool old Mack. Neither one of them dozers was moved any, and we never left them on the slope Sunday night anyway. Come on, give! Which one of Gertie Warren's fellers did you have the scrap with?"

Amos, it seemed, had finally succeeded in making himself heard. Mack said, "Whoops! Talking dirty in front of a lady, am I? Tch, tch, excuse me."

It was not, Connie knew from experience, any inherent delicacy about the feelings of ladies that ever held Mack back. He had been brought up on Sunday School precepts, had it dinned into him in grade school and, later, at the Y.M.C.A. that a gentleman did not swear or carry on obscene conversation in the presence of the weaker sex; so Mack sincerely believed he never did. Oh, an occasional dirty joke didn't count—the gals liked that as much as he did, and once in a while he forgot and ripped out something, but that was only funny, good for a yak.

"Jeezus Kuh-riced!" he had said once to Connie when, on the way home from a dance in his car, she had protested at his foul language. "What's the matter with you—I never swore in front of a woman in my life."

Connie put the pitcher of lemonade, with two glasses and two napkins and two slices of cake, on a tray and carried it into the kitchen.

Get it over with, she told herself doggedly. And get away, upstairs, out of the sound of him.

"Well, hello-lo!" Mack greeted her. "How's the little city girl? How's it feel to be home here amongst us slobs again?"

Connie said, "Fine, thanks, Mack," and set the tray down.

Amos took a look at the tray and let out a snort. "What size piece of cake is that to offer a man?" he demanded. "Take it back and bring us something ain't sliced so thin it'll cut my throat."

Mack grinned. "Come back a little mite fancy, has she?" he wanted to know. "Well, I guess! Look at this!" He picked a napkin from the tray, held it delicately between a thumb and forefinger. "Nose whifflers, yet!"

"Oh, I'm sorry, Mack," Connie said with composure. "I ought to have known better than to offer you a napkin."

Amos stared at her. "Good thing she had the flu and had to come home," he said. "Or none of us be able to touch the hem of her garment."

Mack guffawed. "Caught something besides the flu, I guess, didn't you, Connie?" he said.

Connie picked up the cake plates and took them back to the pantry, turning her back quickly to hide the red that flooded into her face. Amos couldn't have told him. Or could he? They were hand-in-glove in everything else. Of course, double-barreled remarks were a part of Mack's reputation for being a wit—he might have been merely referring to the crack-up of her marriage; but there was no way of telling. She waited a minute in the pantry before she could go back; then she slashed the remaining three-quarters of the loaf of cake into two pieces and took the plates into the kitchen. Mack took a look at the two enormous hunks of cake and roared. "Haw! I guess that's telling you, Ame."

Amos said nothing. From the flick of his eyes in her direction, she judged she might hear something later; that is, if he decided to speak to her at all when somebody else wasn't around.

She turned and walked, straight-backed, out of the room, hearing the amiable conversation start up again behind her.

"Ain't come back feeling any too sociable, has she?" Mack said. "What's this slop in the pitcher; why don't you ever give a guy some beer?"

And Amos: "You want beer, you'll have to buy it and drink it off the premises."

"Well, look, Ame, honest to God now, what really happened? Who'd you have the fight with, Sunday?"

Upstairs in her room, Connie lay on the bed staring into the darkness.

What did they mean, Sunday afternoon? Amos couldn't have got hurt on Sunday. It had been early Sunday morning when Ernie had sneaked her aboard the Potluck; Monday morning, before daylight, when she'd got home. He must have hurt himself on Monday; but on Monday the crew would have been working at the gravel pit; other men would have been around, and according to the story Amos had been there alone. Oh, well, something funny there; but who cared? She felt too dispirited to bother thinking about it.

With Mack, as Lucy would say, the handwriting was on the wall. Amos didn't give up easily, ever.

Of course, I'm living in his house; he's feeding me. He'll have to clothe me, too, because I had to hock everything I had to keep alive, before I came home. So long as I take from him, it's only fair to do what he wants . . . where I can. But Mack? Put up with that again? If Ma could only see what he is, but she's brainwashed, she only sees that he's somebody Pa likes, so he's wonderful.

I wonder how long I can stand it, she thought, and knew at once that it couldn't be for long. I thought I might stay here till I got myself together, but now I've got to start figuring out how to get away again. I've come full circle. Where could I go? What could I do, till I'm strong again? They would take me back at the laboratory, I know; but that's in Bishop. I'd have to have money to get there and money for a room; and I haven't got any, not a red cent. But somehow I have got to plan how to go, because there's nobody here I can trust; nobody to depend on. . . . "Who's that?"

It was only Lucy fumbling in through the door in the darkness. She had brought her sewing for a little bedtime chat.

"In the dark, dear, getting broody!" she said, snapping on the light. "Now, honey—"

"I'm just resting," Connie said.

"You didn't feel strong enough to stay down and visit a little while with Mack," Lucy said. She just barely kept a slight tone of accusation out of her voice; it was more commiserating, implying, Connie knew

"Well, that's too bad, dear, but of course you will, later on."

"No," Connie said, between her teeth. "I did not."

"Now, don't be cross, dear." Lucy settled herself and began to sew. The thread, following her needle through the fabric, made a slight hissing sound. "You mustn't mind your father's ways," she said. "Oh, he's coming around. I can see the signs. You know he always does."

"That's great," Connie said. And then, seeing Lucy's glance of gentle reproach, "Oh, never mind it, skip it, Ma. I'm sorry, I don't mean to take it out on you."

"Well, you have to remember, dear—" Lucy paused, bit off her thread with a snap. "It's only, you know, because your father's red-headed. Red-headed people are always hot-tempered."

"Yes," Connie said.

And that's all we've got to cope with now? He isn't a caveman, and he doesn't want to get me married off to one? Oh, no, it's just that he's red-headed. Ma's got herself back on the side of the angels at last; she's tucked in all the seams, with only the shine showing. Things will come right all by themselves now, she knows they will.

Connie felt her cheek muscles grow rigid; she put her palms against them to reinforce an effort not to scream . . . to yell the house down.

Come to think of it, if that's all it is, I'm red-headed myself. . . .

It followed as the night does the day—a few nights later Mack came to call again, and not on Amos. He was all dressed up, in a suit and overcoat, with a brown felt hat. His suit was a hairy tweed mixture, thick and heavy, with threads of orange, red, and green woven in; he wore a pale-blue shirt and a dark-red tie on which white fox terriers leaped in gay abandon. He smelled of whiskey, hair oil, and sen-sen, and since it was raining outside, of wet wool, like old mittens.

Amos, who had just finished supper, was in his armchair by the stove, with his newspaper opened wide before his face; since this visit of Mack's had nothing to do with him, and he obviously knew it, he grunted a greeting and went on reading without lowering the paper.

"Hi-hi, ho-ho," Mack said. "Here's old Yogi Bear, headed for the movies." He stood just inside the door, not taking off his hat, from whose brim rain dripped, and addressed Lucy. "I thought old Con might come out of her shell, go with me. You think she might?"

Lucy turned around with a bright smile at him, swiveled the smile expectantly to Connie. "Why, Mack, how nice! I'm sure she would, wouldn't you, dear?"

"Why, no, thank you," Connie said. "I wouldn't."

Lucy's smile faded; her lips took on the slight pout of reproach, just this side of petulance, which they assumed when she was beginning—just beginning, of course—to be disappointed in somebody. "Why, of course you'll go, dear." Nothing else was remotely possible. "It'll do you good. Talk to her, Mack, I'm sure she just needs a little coaxing."

"Sure. What's the matter, Connie? You feel well enough, you been out rambling the woods. All by your lonesome, I heard. At least, that's what I *heard*." He put his head on one side, roguish, waiting for the snappy comeback. After all woods were for bushes, and bushes were for what Mack called "puckerbrushing" with somebody.

"I was out for a walk today, yes," Connie said. She had been out for a while in the wooded pasture back of the house. Among the leafless trees, the woods getting ready for winter, she had found no solution to problems; but it had been a chance to be alone. And all the time, it seemed, she had been under someone's eye—Lucy's, probably—who had told Amos, and Amos had called up Mack. She's out walking in the pasture, I guess she feels well enough for you to start coming around again. Carefully, holding her temper, Connie said, "So I'm too tired to go out tonight. I'm sorry."

"Ah-h, come on. You can rest, setting in the movies, nice comfortable seats. You got to start sometime, can't set in the house forever like a stone statchoo."

"No. But no, thanks."

Amos's newspaper rustled, and Connie found his glance leveled at her like a pistol barrel.

All right, she thought, setting her teeth. It may as well be now as later.

"It's raining," she said to Lucy. "And you can't be too careful, you know, after the flu."

This was one of Lucy's own gambits. She looked a little flustered, but before she could say anything, Mack went on. "Sure, and you can coddle yourself too long, too. Ya got to make an effort, ain't that right, Lucy?"

"Well, you know, dear, you are pretty well over it," Lucy began. "And—"

"Look, Ma, I've told him I'm too tired. Later, maybe. When I'm strong enough to wrassle in the front seat of Mack's car."

"Connie! You know Mack isn't like that!"

But Mack cut in on Lucy's horrified gasp.

"Where'd we get this 'later' stuff?" he wanted to know. He pushed his hat to the back of his head, stood regarding her. "We gonna poop around once again till 'later' while another peanut-head beats my time? Nn-nn, sister. Not for me. Better be tonight. How about it?"

"Put your coat on," Amos said, "and go with him. What are you, dead from the neck up?"

Connie said nothing. Just in time she caught Mack's wink at Amos. She started for the door.

"Atta girl," Mack said. "I'd figured you to have sense enough to come around. Look, kid, I know you got stuck once, rough as a cob, get took to the cleaners like that, but you can forget it, I'm willing to—"

Connie stopped in the doorway, one hand braced against the jamb. "You're willing to what?"

"Why, forget it, what else? I ain't a man to hold it against ya, baby. It's all water over the mill, far's I'm concerned. What's a woods colt or two, you ain't the first one ever—"

So Amos had told him.

"You're a card, aren't you, Mack?" Connie said. "The real, honest-to-goodness original card. Speaking of the cleaners, why don't you send your clothes there once in a while, and while you're at it, send your mind along, it needs it. I don't like you and I never have. I don't like the way you look or the way you smell, and that's the most horrible tie I ever saw in my life."

She watched, with satisfaction, his grin fade and his face turn from weathered red to purple, thinking, That got the snappy dresser where he lives. And I'm blowing up at last, and it's wonderful.

"By—by God!" Mack said. "Amos, I ain't taking this—what about this?" Mack choked, and stopped.

Amos balled up his newspaper with a crushing rattle, threw the ball on the floor. "That's about enough out of you, you slut!" he said.

"I'm not a slut. I've never been one."

"Well, I don't know what you call it—"

"If that's what you've told Mack, in this deal to get me off your hands, somebody's going to get cheated. Big-hearted Mack is who."

"That's a hell of a way to talk to Mack when he's—what other decent man would—"

"Look, Pa, I was brought up to be decent. At home. They taught me in school to treat people decently, to expect decent treatment from them. A man is decent who'll marry a slut in trade for a partnership in a business? Because that's obviously what Mack thinks I am. Thanks to you."

"By God, that does it . . . that's it. I ain't going through with it, Ame, it wouldn't be worth it." Mack, still red-faced, started to go through the motions of putting on his hat, discovered he still had it on, and started for the door.

"Good," Connie said. "That goes for me, too."

The house echoed with the slam of his departure.

Amos sat for a moment perfectly still; then his left hand, nearly healed now, but still welted and swollen, clenched on the dangling fringe of the cloth of the kitchen table, near his chair. It was a pretty cloth, the one Lucy always spread over the table to neaten up the kitchen between meals; on it were a pair of glass bookends, with the current magazines and books from the library sandwiched between; a sugar bowl; salt and pepper shakers; a spoon holder full of spoons. Amos's movement seemed more methodical than angry. He did not yank; he pulled; and the objects crashed, one by one, to the floor.

Lucy spun around from the sink. She had not been doing anything there—just standing with her hands over her ears, waiting until the argument—the men's argument, one of the men's things, nothing to do with her—was over. But she heard the crash.

"Oh, Amos! My bookends," she said, and burst into tears.

"Let him," Connie said. "Let him smash things, that's all he knows how to do. Sixteen-year-olds do it. Kids kick the table."

"Connie, don't talk to him like that—"

"Then let him be decent to me. I haven't done anything to be ashamed of. For heaven's sake, what's the matter with him, is he crazy? That's a terrible thing he tried to do to me."

"It's no worse," Amos said suddenly, "nor half so bad as what you've done to me." His voice was not violent, but dreary, as if he were sick and tired to death. "I've heard you talk to your mother. 'Pick up the pieces,' you say. You're all ready, ain't you, to forget everything, go back, be the way you was. Well, maybe you can. I can't. There ain't far enough back I could go so as to change anything."

It was far worse than his yelling. Lucy stared at him, her jaw dropping; it was so far different from anything she had been led to expect. Connie felt her anger going, and missed it, for it had been sustaining. She said uncertainly, "But why? What have I done to you? I've told you what happened to me. I haven't lied. Why are things so bad? I made a mistake, yes, but—"

"Yeah," Amos said. "You made a mistake, all right."

He got up, walked over to the window, stood looking out into the rainy darkness. The stillness was heavy in the room, but it did not last long, as the change in him, whatever it had been, had not lasted long.

"You ain't going to make it again. I thought I had a good man all set up to keep tabs on you, but it seems my choice don't suit." The familiar grate was back in his voice. In a moment, Connie knew, he would be yelling. He was.

"You won't get the car, from now on you'll never get it, parade around town, start in all over again. When you go out, your mother'll go with you, and the first time you step over the line, by God, I'll put a man on the payroll full time to—"

"Amos!" Lucy gasped, scandalized. "Oh, no, dear, you can't do that. *What* will people think!"

"You shut up and keep out of it. I'm going to tell this—this—"

"I'm sorry, Pa," Connie said. "I won't stand for any more."

She walked out of the door and up the stairs to her room. It's come sooner than I thought it would. It was bound to come sometime. I wish I'd never come here, I'd have been better off if I'd stayed, gone to the New Bedford police. At least they'd have sent me to a hospital and I might have kept my baby. I'm the fool of the world. What does that kind of a fool do now?

Lock the door, she told herself drearily. Because he's insane. Something awful is the matter with him.

Something awful was the matter with Amos; he was beginning to wonder himself if there wasn't. It was all in his head, he knew that; in his dreams. A nightmare. But the first time it had happened, it had been so real that he was sure the thing was in the room with him. At first it had only bothered him because it kept reminding him; the thing was over and done with, and the quicker it was forgotten, the better. And there was no reason to remember it; not now; not that he could see.

So far as killing that damned jitterbug was concerned, he wasn't sorry; he was glad he'd done it. It was no more to him, he kept telling himself, than stamping on a rat. Feller'd had it coming; and, anyway, by the time he'd caught up with him, it had been self-defense, nothing a man could be blamed for.

Amos hadn't meant to kill him; not in the beginning. He'd only meant to slap him around, get some of his own back. After all, the feller'd knocked him down once, hadn't he? And Amos had been going to show him, too, that no Shacktown culch was going to fool around with the Wilkinson women, get away with it, laugh in Amos's face, which was what it amounted to, when he got Connie to go away with him, treated her like dirt. It wasn't Connie he'd been after, anyway. It was to get ahead of Amos Wilkinson, like all those bums down in Shacktown wanted to. A lot of them had worked for him; they knew what he thought of them—shiftless, lazy, damn trash, soldiering through any job be put them on till he got sick of it and fired them, one after another. Had to. A man working for him, worked or else.

Oh, Amos guessed he knew what all this had been aimed at—him. Long ago he'd promised himself that if he ever ran across that Grindle again, he'd beat the living tar out of him. And that was what he'd meant to do that night. And all he had meant to do.

Hell, I guess if I'd wanted to kill him, I had a good chance to when I was taking Jack's car back to the wharf. I passed him in the road, lugging his damned clothes or whatever it was he had in that carton, headed for my house likely, the bastard, I'll betcha to get after me to support him. I could've run over him right then and there and called it an accident, only the Bible says Thou Shalt Not Kill, and I would have had it to blame myself for. Besides, what I wanted was the satisfaction of getting my hands on him, or maybe with a good club.

Well, Amos had got just that, picked it up outside the dock building—the business end of a broken oar handle. He had sneaked back up the road, keeping to bushes, hoping to God the feller hadn't got too far ahead of him to catch up with; and he hadn't. His luck was sure out that night; Amos had almost lost him twice—once when he'd ducked into the dump road and took off up the hill for whatever crazy reason he had in his head—he might've heard Amos coming and got scared; he sure acted scared enough of anything he heard in the bushes after that; and the second time was when Amos was going through the thickets, following up the hill. By that time it was pretty obvious that the fellow was good and scared, so give him a good scare, let him think something was after him in the undergrowth. Those thickets, though, had been rugged to get through; Amos would have lost the trail entirely if he hadn't heard the tin cans clanking, down the back side of the dump.

He would have caught up with Ernie Grindle then and there; only Ernie ran. He had turned tail and run like a rabbit into the woods, all-anyhow; seemed he didn't care which way he went, just so he got away. Ran like a fool, right down into Cooney's Heath. Scared to death at the sight of an oar handle.

It had been easy enough to trail him. A man didn't need to be a woodsman. He made tracks—jumps, at first, seven feet long, and a noise like a running buck; then, after a while, he got tired and plodded. Plunk, suck; plunk, suck; Amos could hear his feet in the mud. Easy enough to follow. Amos had trailed him until near noon. And then, suddenly, the noises stopped and the tracks stopped; Amos was standing looking, trying to figure where the jasper'd holed up to, when Ernie dropped on him out of a tree. About what you'd expect—drop on a man's back, knock him down, try to choke him.

God, it was self-defense, wasn't it? Either me or him. He would have killed me if I hadn't managed to get my hands on that oar handle he'd knocked out of my hands.

Beyond that, how long the fight lasted, Amos couldn't remember, because he himself had passed out. What brought him to was the sound of a squirrel chittering somewhere nearby in a tree. The oar handle was broken in two, and no one would have known that Ernie Grindle had ever had a face. Amos had barely been able to make it out of the swamp; it had been a long way home.

Self-defense; and the no-good rat had got what was coming to him. Amos had nothing to blame himself for; and he did not blame himself. Only, the first night in the hospital, he had had that dream. It had been nothing much, but it had waked him up in a cold sweat.

After that, from time to time, the same nightmare. It got so he dreaded going to sleep, and so lay awake; and lying awake, thinking: scraps and pictures; the long chase; the scared kid running through the swamp; the bare trees; the piles of dead leaves that rustled, saying where to follow.

Follow? It had been nothing to follow that trail. Not for a woodsman; an expert; an authority; the known best in his field in the state, he told himself with pride. That goon hadn't had a chance. Self-def—

And nothing to blame yourself for. Then why to hell have a

nightmare that kept coming back, reminding of something that could be put away for good, forgotten?

Nobody could possibly know; Cooney's Heath was a place of boiling springs and shaking bogs, dangerous, some of them deep enough to drown a man. There was one main path across it, a deer trail, which hunters sometimes crossed to get to the hummock of dry ground in the middle of the swamp; and there were some passable branch paths, small animal tracks, where nobody within the time of man had ever gone. So far as Amos could remember, the fight had been out at the end of one of these, nowhere near the main trail. He'd left Ernie Grindle near a fallen tree, deep in the Heath; he could lie there, unfound, forever, and nobody be the wiser. It wasn't getting found out, Amos told himself, that was worrying him.

Then why this nightmare, night after night; and not enough anyway to wake a man, shaking and shivering; the sound of a squirrel chittering like mad; an insane clatter in his head, like a small, tinny drill?

Joe Randall was astonished.

"You sure you want to, Connie?" be asked. "We're putting up fishballs this time of year—them jobs is kind of greasy work for someone ain't used to it."

"If you've got a job, Joe. Any job. I'll take it."

"Well, okay, sure. About ten days be all right? Things are pretty slow while we're converting. But there's a little Morelli due, and Elena'll be leaving for a while. You can have her place on the cans. That is, if you want it."

He spoke doubtfully and his glance lingered, puzzled, on the old brown cloth coat, jerked away.

He's wondering, Connie thought, as everyone else will, what Amos Wilkinson's girl is doing around town in those beat-up old clothes, hunting a job in the packing plant.

The coat had been to the cleaner's, but more because Lucy thought the material was good enough for rug rags than that it could be salvaged for further wear. She had said vaguely at the time that of course she would have to buy Connie a new one, as if, Connie told herself, I were still ten years old. Lucy would, too; she would pick it out herself and come triumphantly bringing it home for Connie to wear—that is, as soon as Amos handed over some money.

Well, now he wouldn't have to. I'm not taking anything more from him.

When Connie had left the house this morning, she had taken nothing but her own things—not even the nightgown of Lucy's which she'd had to borrow. This old coat was what there was, so she had worn it.

She said, looking Joe in the eye, "I do want the job, Joe, and thanks a million. Ten days—that'll be a week from Wednesday."

"Okay," Joe said.

She thought for a moment he was going to say something more— "What's your father think about this?" or something of the kind—but all he said was, "Yeah. I'll see you then."

Poor Joe, he was still feeling dreadful about Amy, you could see it. Connie had known him ever since she could remember; he had been one of the big boys in high school when she had been in the grades; she had gone to his and Amy's wedding six years ago. She remembered a vigorous, tanned young man, always gay, always laughing, whom people were always glad to see coming because he was fun to have around; at his wedding people kept circling near him, wanting, it seemed, to get as close as possible to someone who looked so happy.

Now, though, he was thinner, and pale under his tan, with an expression around his eyes of strain, as if he had not slept. He was thirty and looked older; even his black hair, which Connie remembered as a thatch of wiry curls, looked limp and dusty. But what you noticed most was his indifference. He had been pleasant enough, greeted her cordially as an old friend whom he hadn't seen for some time; but there did not seem to be much now that Joe Randall cared deeply about.

I haven't said a word to him about Amy, Connie thought, and I suppose I ought to.

Glancing up, she saw that Joe had guessed what was in her mind and had braced himself. At least he had braced himself for something, perhaps to say the proper thing in return.

So many have, he probably recognizes the look.

She said instead, "How are your triplets, Joe? I hear they're the talk of the town."

Joe's face brightened; for the first time he showed a little animation. "Pretty good now," he said. "It was nip and tuck with two of them for a while; but I guess now they're going to be okay, Dr. Garland thinks so. But old J. J.—my gorry, Connie, you ought to go around and see him. He's a wowser."

"So I've heard."

"Yup, he is. And no more like the other two than chalk is like cheese. The two little ones are twins, all right, you can't tell them apart, and they're Montgomerys, the old Funny-Money sticks out all over them. Why, when they first came, they looked so much like that old duck, the picture of him, I mean, that I—"

Talking about his kids, Joe had temporarily forgotten his trouble; he had started to tell how in the beginning he'd called one baby "Funny" and the other one "Money," only it had touched Amy up so he'd had to stop it. He had been about to mention Amy as if she were still with him. As he realized, his voice cut off, and he fell silent, looking heavily down at the blotter on his desk.

Poor old Joe, as if he'd all at once run head on into a stone wall, Connie thought. It's wonderful, though, that he's got those babies. That must help.

She got up to go.

"You could wait, on that job, till maybe you feel better," Joe said. "You look more to me as if you ought to sit around and soak up a lot of milk and eggs for a while. That work on the cans is no cinch. It's too darn bad you ain't a bookkeeper."

"But I am," Connie said, puzzled. "And a stenographer, too. I took courses in Boston. I'm pretty good as a matter of fact."

"You are? I'll be darned. I knew you worked in a lab, but—"

"Oh, I did. I was secretary to a chemist who was working on a new liquid pet food at the time, and I liked the chemistry part of it best; what I wanted to be was a laboratory technician, but he needed records kept and correspondence done, so I took some night business courses. My husband was away a lot and I really needed something to do, I collected quite a lot of experience. I kept the job until—" Connie came to a dead stop, appalled at what she had been about, casually, to say, which was that she had started a baby. Joe was a beguiling listener; he was as comfortable as an old shoe to talk to; and, once, to talk of the baby had been a natural and casual thing. In spite of herself, she felt the red coming into her face until it showed, and she finished faintly, "I expect you've heard that my husband and I have separated."

Joe nodded. "Yes, I'm sorry, Connie."

"Well, I don't need to sit here and regale you with my whole life history. I'm a bookkeeper, and a good one; but you've got Sarah Jerdan, haven't you?"

"Well, Sarah—" Joe glanced cautiously over his shoulder. Sarah was somewhere in the outer office, nearby, of course; she was a great one for knowing what went on. "The thing is," he began.

The thing was, he couldn't make head nor tail of Sarah's books, and, right now, the plant was in a hard way, and he needed to. Amy had always done the translating for him. Oh, he could, he supposed, get somewhere with it if he took time, but time, right now, was what he didn't have. He had had a couple of goes at it, with Sarah, and he guessed he didn't have too much patience. They had both got mad and Sarah's feelings were still hurt. She was proud of her bookkeeping system she'd invented. "But, darn it, Amy was the only one could—" Joe looked harassed. "I can't fire her, she's worked here a long time, and she won't leave me in the lurch."

"Well, if I could help, I'd be glad to."

"She's got to the point now," Joe said, "where she's holding over me that it's considerable of a sacrifice for her to stay here, she'd like to get married." He grinned. "She's been shuddering on the brink of it for years, but her boyfriend's been in the Marines, and from what I can make out, he doesn't like the idea any better than she does, but they neither one know how to get out of it. He's finishing his hitch pretty soon, and if I could say to Sarah, go with my blessing, I've got somebody to take your place, she might—" He looked at Connie hopefully. "It'd be a lot better than working on the cans."

"It certainly would. But I need a job right away, Joe."

"Well, I'll tell Sarah. You can go on the payroll next Wednesday and get paid while she breaks you in. And then, when—"

From outside the office, somewhere in the plant, came sounds of a rumpus—a man yelling with authority and emphasis, followed by a series of shrill squawks which drowned out the man's voice and went on increasing in tempo and intensity.

Joe jumped. "What to hell's with Marvin?" he said, starting to get up. "Sounds like he's tangled with a flock of guinea hens. Hey"—as Marvin Coles came through the office door—"what? . . . Where did them come from?"

Marvin was lugging along two kids as a man carries suitcases by the handles, only in this case the handles were the backs of the kids' dungarees. One, a small boy, hung limp and unresisting, scared pithless; from his face of shock and horror issued an open-mouthed, soundless yell. The other was a tornado of whirling arms and legs difficult to identify; but from glimpses of flying, be-stringed ponytail and the timbre of the sustained shrill shrieks, Connie judged this one to be a girl. Marvin made heavy weather through the office door; he was boiling mad, but he was trying, you could see, not to bump anybody's head on the door frame.

The boy was no problem, but the girl was trying with singleness of purpose to get at Marvin's leg and he was holding her off; coming through the door he had to narrow his field. She got her chance, latched onto his coveralls with two small clawlike hands, and sank her teeth into his leg.

Marvin yowled, "Ow! Jeezus!," let go of both kids, and clapped his hand to his thigh. The boy landed on all fours, where he remained, slowly collapsing into a heap. The girl landed on her feet and running. She had nearly made it to the other door before Marvin came to with a roar. "No, you don't, by the gumpty!"

He leaped, managed to hook a forefinger at the end of a long, muscular arm in the belt of her jeans. The fabric gave; there was a sound of popping buttons. The jeans, old and faded, of a many-times-washed blue, came down, showing bony legs and thighs and an abbreviated pair of pink rayon panties.

The girl spun around. She turned on Marvin a pair of slitted eyes; her head seemed to flatten.

"You let me go, you old hoo-er," she said. "You wait till I tell my mother you knocked me down and dragged me into the factory and tore my pants off!"

Marvin turned as red as a brick. "Why, I never!" he said, outraged. "I never done no such a thing!"

"You did! They see you!" She scrabbled, pulling up the jeans, and swung around, confronting Connie and Joe. "Did'n you see him? He tore my pants off, did'n he?"

Joe, almost as red as Marvin from holding back laughter, said, "Yes, we sure see him. You done it, Marvin, no use to try to lie out of it."

" 'n there!" the girl said. "You're a nasty old man. I bet you choke little girls in the park with white gloves on. 'n my mother's going to call the state troopers to take you off to jail. We got the witnesses for it, see?"

"Well, by—" Marvin's mouth opened and closed, opened again. "I never heard—be durn if I ever—"

"Now, wait," Joe said when he could. "Everybody hold everything down. What's it all about, anyway?" He got up from his desk, went over, and scooped the boy off the floor, who, at his approach, scrabbled feebly in terror, then buried his face in Joe's shirtfront with a prolonged, hoarse bawl. "Here, quit it, feller," Joe said. "Cut it out now, and take a breath, you'll lose your wind permanent. Beck, you come off it. What's all this about little girls killed in the park? You making up a yarn?"

"They kill little girls all the time on the TV," the girl said. "Hnf."

She gave a prolonged, efficient sniff and a small yellow leg of mucus disappeared, now-you-see-it-now-you-don't, up her nose. "And he"—she glared at Marvin—"he was going to—"

"What was you and Jody doing, hanging around the factory? You know kids ain't supposed to be down in there."

"What was they doing?" Marvin's bass howl cut in, drowning everybody else out. "I'll tell you what they was doing. The darned little hellions was feeding copper cents into the big cogwheel on the—that's what they was doing, and it's going to take me three days to disassemble that machinery and make sure they ain't no metal left in there to frig up and kill somebody!"

"I was not," Beck said. "Jody was. And they was not *copper cents*." She regarded Marvin disdainfully. "They was *Lincoln pennies*."

"Oh, my God," Joe said. "It makes a difference which?" He groaned slightly as he contemplated what any small piece of metal would do in that particular part of the machinery. "Now, what in thunder did you do that for? Didn't you know any better?"

Beck stared back. "I told you it wasn't me. It was Jody."

"That's right, lay it onto the boy," Marvin said. "He's littler'n you are. No use to lie, either. I see you do it, remember."

"Well, he bet me. It was his idea. He thought of it."

Jody lifted his head out of Joe's shirtfront. He spoke, his voice thick with tears and sorrow at the betrayal. "Why, no, I didn't, Beck. You said Abe Lincoln on the penny looked awful glum. You said the pennies'd come out of the other end of the big thing and we could go pick 'em up and it would've squat a smile out of him. You said so. I guess you forgot."

He looked at her hopefully; but she only smiled a superior smile which passed over Jody, indicating him to the grown-ups. "He talks a lot," she said. "Everybody knows he's an awful liar. His mother says she hopes he'll grow out of it."

Joe looked from one kid to the other. "What you was doing, you was trying to change the look on Abe Lincoln's face, that it?" he said. He took hold of his shirtfront, where Jody's tears had stuck it damply to his breastbone, and flapped it in and out a few times, turning his face aside to hide, Connie saw, a grin. But it was no use; he lost. The grin grew to a chuckle; Joe put back his head and let out a whoop of delighted laughter. "Well," he said after a moment. "That makes me some old red-eyed mad, you know it?"

"You can durn well laugh!" Marvin said. Furious, he stared at Joe. "Foreign bodies in the machinery, well, I'd hate to tell ya what a few cents' worth of kids' fun is going to cost, unless I can find out for sure how many they put in there. Somebody's going to have to pay for it, or I'll take it out of some hides—"

"That's right," Joe said, sobering. He pulled out his handkerchief, mopped his eyes. "How many pennies did you put in, remember?"

"Two," Jody said promptly. "And Becky had—"

"You shut up," Becky said. "I said I never put in any." She stared evilly at Jody. "If I did, I can't remember. That nasty old man scared me so, it's gone right out of my head. I can't remember nothing, unless I get paid a dollar."

"Oh, come now, that's pretty cheap," Joe said, his grin starting again. "Small time, I'd call that. A dollar all you want?"

He was kidding, Beck could see that. Making fun. Her eyes slitted again. "And he," she said, swiveling to Marvin, "he is going to have to pay me five dollars for scaring me, so's I won't tell my mother and she'll call the state troopers. And have a court trial and you'll go to jail for the rest of your natural life. We got witnesses. You said you'd be witnesses to it," she finished, triumphantly looking from Joe to Connie. "So that's all we need to rock you back, Mr. old Marvin Coles!"

This is a pretty wise child, Connie thought. The little horror's listened to every court trial program on the TV, you can even recognize the phrases. Why, for goodness' sake, what chumps men are. There's only one thing to do . . .

But before she could do anything, Marvin burst out in a roar.

"Now, you look-a here! If they come after anybody, it'll be after you, take you to the Reform School! Joe, gi'me a holt of that phone, I'm going to call the cops!"

"You don't dare to," Beck said with composure. "Or I will tell them how I see you over at my Aunt Gertie Warren's."

If Marvin had turned red in the beginning, he turned purple now. You could see that this was getting pretty close to home. While a certain proportion of the town's gentlemen visited Gertie Warren's Establishment from time to time, in private, and, in private, it was generally known who did, to mention it out loud was unheard of, and was considered to brand a man. Marvin, appalled, was speechless.

"Look," Joe said in the voice of authority. "Cut this out, right now! You kids have damaged some machinery, but it'll help if you tell us how many cents you put in the cogwheel. If you don't, I'll call up your mothers."

Beck looked at him with the air of one who holds something in reserve. "You want me to tell everyone what ole Doc Garland brought to your house in a basket?" she asked, with delicacy.

"Sure," Joe said. "Only some other time. Right now, I—"

"A baby. So there."

"Uh huh. Three babies. I heard about them. Look, if you say how many pennies, we won't have to take the machinery apart—"

"Ole Doc Garland brought the red-headed one in a basket. Jody and me see him."

"Well, you ask your mother about that. She was there, too," Joe said. He had flushed a little, and his voice, reasonable and patient, suddenly sounded dreary. He was being reminded of the morning his babies had been born, and in a way that was not pleasant.

He's not going, Connie thought, to have to put up with this any longer.

The child's ponytail, at the moment being defiantly flirted, was within reach, and Connie reached it. The process was simple and quick. Beck upended across Connie's knees as neatly as if both of them had previously made a habit of it. The five or six smart slaps resounded through the office.

At first too astonished to resist, Beck was next horrified by the fact that she was being spanked by a perfect stranger, somebody whose looks she had been secretly admiring, and finally preoccupied by the licking, which hurt. She bawled, like any spanked child, with abandon and pain.

"Now," Connie said. "How many pennies?"

Beck said, "Fuf-four."

"Why didn't you say so in the first place? Saved everybody all this trouble." She tilted Beck back onto her feet, took a safety pin from her purse, with which she pinned together the top of the flapping dungarees. She found a clean white handkerchief, mopped away tears, and said, "For goodness' sakes, blow!"

"Now, you two run along," she finished. "Nobody's going to call any cops or hurt you, but you're going to get your tails tanned, both of you, if I catch you around this factory again."

The two went, in silence, out of the office; but Jody, as he went past Connie, gave her a wide, silent smile. Jody's shoulders were squared and his chest was out; his smile said, "This is great. This is fine." Because Beck, the mighty Beck, like anybody else, could have a downfall, and it was balm to his sting.

Connie's stock, it seemed, was high with all the males present. Marvin said, "By the god, that was the prettiest thing I ever see in my life, it's made my day," and stumped off to fix his machinery.

Joe said, "Judast! It looks to me as if I'd got me one asset, anyway, around this place. You couldn't start work tomorrow, could you?"

He began to chuckle again, his eyes brimmed. "My gorry, the look on old Marvin! I thought he was going to blow up. You know, I can't help liking that little devil. I guess I like any kid, but one with spunk'll get to me the most."

"Spunk!" Connie said. "She's dreadful! She probably will end up in the Reform School."

"Yup, most likely. Tony Morelli's been breathing out brimstone all summer. If he hears about this, I don't know what—but I'd sure hate to see—Well, he sure won't hear about it from me. What I'd like to know, what's all this tripe about Doc Garland and a basket, anyway? Old Angie, of course she's a kook, but she's got it into her head that he fetched the two little ones in a basket, and now, this kid—where'd she pick up that yarn? Must be there's talk around, about how he don't look like the rest of us, old J. J., I mean."

"Well, that isn't unheard of, is it, with triplets? I seem to have heard somewhere that they don't always match," Connie said.

"Well, granted, he don't. And he's got red hair, which sure never came from any of Amy's folks or mine. Come to think of it, Connie, now that I see one of you Wilkinsons close to again, old J. J. looks more like your folks than he does like ours. His hair's almost exactly the shade of yours, little lighter, maybe. Why, darn it—" Joe stopped, did a double take, and grinned. "Darned if he ain't a dead ringer for you, now I notice it. Hey, what'd you bet the Randalls and the Wilkinsons didn't get together somehow, back in Colonial times? But I never heard our families was at all related, did you? Oh, well. Some joker must've made a crack about the doctor must've brought him in a basket, and this kid picked it up—Hey, what's the matter, Connie? You're white's a sheet."

"Am I?" Connie said. She managed to get to her feet and to force a smile, but that was all.

"Look," Joe said. "You walking? I'd better ride you home in the truck."

"It's just a hangover from the flu," Connie said. "I'm all right, really." Words, now that they had started, came freely. "Oh, you know you always look like something that's crawled out from under a stump when you've lived a while in the city. No—no fresh vegetables, no—" I'm babbling. Please God, let me stop it and get out of here. "I have to go, Joe. Thanks; and I'll see you Wednesday."

She turned and walked, as briskly as might be, out of the office.

The passageway to the plant's loading ramp was dark, and she turned that way. No one was in sight at either end of it, and she stopped in the middle, leaning shakily against the wall.

It's impossible. I'm crazy even to think . . . this is coincidence; cruel; but coincidence, all the same.

My baby was dead. And afterwards it wasn't anywhere, so the men on the boat must have . . . or Ernie did, it would be like him to take the easiest way out, put it overboard, or . . .

I was so sick that night, half out of my mind; it's so hard to remember. How can I be sure what really happened?

If it had been alive, the men on the boat would have had to do something with it. Walt knew Ernie was its father. What if he had let Ernie take it away somewhere? What would Ernie have done?

Oh, she knew well enough the primitive, direct journey between-two-points that Ernie's mind would have made. That mind, to itself a hero's, able to cope with any emergency, backed up by a hero's big limber muscles and a hero's good looks: Siegfried and chicken-beatnik, all in one, confronted by a real emergency, ran like a rabbit. Leave us to see the easiest way out, like. What would it have been?

He could have paid the doctor; he could have left it on the doctor's doorstep. The big, adolescent, oh, so overgrown boy, brainwashed, nurtured in convention by the movie and TV show, whose hero he was, knew the good, good, good from the bad, bad, bad, but with the connective logic of intelligent self-interest. It followed that the good, good, good was what was good for Ernie. A wife and a child were not good for Ernie: they dimmed the sparkle of the movie-star's star. So, stuck with the child, anyway, what would he have done? Confronted in a free-association test with the word baby, the fifteen-year-old mind might react with mother; but in the stories, in the shows, baby produces doctor. Run, quick, for the doctor.

I could ask the doctor. Dr. Garland. I hardly know him. No, I couldn't. Because then, he would know . . . But would I mind, would I care? Just so long as I could find out? No, I wouldn't care if everybody knew.

That awful child—did she see something? Gossip goes around the town like fire in a thicket. You did not need to listen to hear the voices: "He ain't no more like Joe Randall's folks than if the doctor had brought him in a basket." Or a little black bag. And the child, the little pitcher, listening with the big ears . . .

Stop it. It is over and done with and has to be forgotten. This crazy, impossible notion, it's the kind of notion sick people get. I'm hysterical, I'm not sick. I can't afford to be. Connie straightened up and walked on. She smiled a mechanical greeting to Jack Malden, who lifted a hand to her from his watchman's cubicle inside the door.

It was his car I used that night, but he doesn't know. Nobody knows.

She went down the steps which led to the plant parking lot. Where next to go was Clementina's, and she could take a shortcut across the lot, lessen a little the long walk down to the old Wilkinson house on the Shore Road.

But she did not turn that way. She turned in the opposite direction toward Joe Randall's house, which was not far away.

Because I have got to see him. He looks like the Wilkinsons. Joe said so. He looks like me.

I would be a fool, and sentimental, to believe that I could tell if he belonged to me. That old wives' tale about mother love, reacting by instinct, reaching out and claiming its own—even in hospitals they have to footprint babies so as not to get them mixed up. Why don't I stay away, why do I go there?

But even thinking this, she went up Joe's front steps and rang the bell.

There was no answer for a while; then tentative steps sounded inside, but did not come to the door. Connie had a feeling of being looked at; sure enough, the white curtain on one of the windows was stirring, whisking back into place as she looked at it.

"Angie?" she called. "It's Connie Wilkinson. Joe told me to stop by and see the triplets."

Angie came at once to the door. "Oh," she said. "Connie Wilkinson, is it? Well, you'll have to excuse me for not opening the door. They's been a whole mess of them twippets from Bishop strodding through here, thinking they're going to git in here and keep house for Joe. I ain't a-going to let another damn one of them int' the house, you hear me?"

"I hear you," Connie said, smiling. "How are you, Angie?"

"Well, I'm all right, considering all I been through. We've had a turrible loss." Angie remembered, not quite in time, to pull down the corners of her mouth, making a face of gloom, out of which, however, her small, beady black eyes beamed with unmistakable satisfaction. "I am wore down to the bone," she said. "It is awful hard on me, at my age. Run through this big house, take care of three babies all to once. Joe knows it, o' course, he is a good boy, don't want to make it hard on me, so he was bound 'n determined to put that ad in the Bishop paper, only, manlike, he don't realize how much of my time it takes telling all them flipflaps to git to hell back to Bishop, they ain't no housekeeper needed here. It is bad enough to put up with Nellie Overholt by day, and that nurse from the hospital ain't no better than she should be, by night, and . . ."

Her voice, preceding Connie into the house, suddenly rose to a squawk, and she vanished, hotfoot, into the kitchen, from which, Connie realized, was coming a black smell of burning.

"My shell beans," she called back. "Boiling over, smell 'em, can't you? Come out, Connie, I'll just set 'em back and . . . Goddam gas stove!" she went on, reappearing. "First thing I do, I'm making Joe git me something besides them hot burners to cook on, a nice old black wood-burning range, them gas, you leave them a minute and . . . Yesterday I had a blueberry pie in the oven, some of them froze berries out of Amy's contraption she thought was so lovely, them deep-froze stuff ain't no good, give you a bellyache every time, but they was all the blueberries they was, and I had a turrible hankering. I never took my notice off of it for one minute, but that damn gas oven burnt black in the twinkling. I was so mad I turned it bottom up on the floor for that hospital nurse, Burke her name is, lace-curtain Irish you're born, lace-curtain Irish you die, to clean up when she come, blueberry stain is some old hard to scrape out of that linoleum. But she never come. She ain't coming back," Angie said, "I hear. No loss. If you come to see Joe's triplets, what she calls the nurs'ry's the back bedroom off'n the kitchen. You go right in. Don't make no noise to wake up Jej-jy. I'll be there, soon's I—" She vanished, this time through the outer back door, leaving Connie, unscrambling, in the middle of the kitchen floor.

Surely, Connie thought, Joe can't leave her alone to take care of three helpless babies, poor pixillated old thing. . . .

In the sudden silence, she remained standing where she was.

What on earth am I doing here?

Here in Joe's house, surrounded by his things and by the things that had been Amy's, what she had come for suddenly seemed preposterous. Sunlight lay over Amy's kitchen, touched corners on her white-enameled deep-freeze, her gas stove; flooded across the pretty linoleum, which she must have chosen, and with taste. Joe's battered pipe lay on the windowsill; his slippers, comfortable, old, had been chucked under a deep-seated chair. Evidence of the triplets was everywhere: a small, white-iron bathtub in front of the oven, still full of bath water—they must have just been bathed and put to bed, and no one had had time yet to clear away—the sterilizer full of bottles steaming on the stove, the rackful of beautifully made small clothes, freshly ironed and airing.

What is the matter with me? I am sick. Coming into a man's home, with nothing to go on but a child's made-up story and a chance remark, to check, to see if one of his children, dearly beloved, and all he has to love now that Amy's dead, is actually his own. Even if it does have hair like mine, looks like me, what would that prove—that I'd have a right to say to Joe, this isn't yours, this is mine? When I know how he feels about his kids and that to lose one, after what he's lost, would nearly kill him? I never saw mine in daylight, only touched it in the dark. What would I do with it now, even if I had it, how could I take care of it? I'm a fool. I had better pull myself together and get out of here.

She would have gone; but Angie at that moment saw fit to reappear in the kitchen. At least the rear end of Angie appeared, backing cautiously through the door, which she pulled to as she came until a space was left only large enough for her head. Her head remained thrust out, craning this way and that for a moment before she withdrew it and triumphantly locked the door.

She said to the air in front of her: "She's out there, and out there she'll stay, and now's my chance."

"What?" Connie said. At first, only half-aware of Angie, she realized that at the moment Angie was not at all aware of her. Puffing, for she had apparently come fast from where she had been, Angie got down a cup from the cupboard and began spooning beans into it from the blackened kettle on the stove.

" 'n there!" she said. The cup full, she glanced up and saw Connie. "Who's that? Oh. Connie Wilkinson, ain't it? Oh, my God, you ain't come to keep house for Joe, have you?"

"No, of course not," Connie said feebly.

Angie smiled, showing a row of sparkling porcelain teeth, palpably false, and a wide expanse of pink plastic gum. "I been trying for a month to git a little something stren'thening into them babies' stummocks," she said. "What stuff them fool nurses been feeding them, nor you nor I could live and thrive." She stumped into the nursery carrying the cup and closed the door firmly behind her.

Oh, my heavens! Connie thought in horror. She mustn't be let do that!

Someone responsible must be around, outside, but locked out; there was no time to go looking for anyone now. Connie shoved open the door. "Angie!" she said.

Angie was standing by the window, peering out. "She was hanging out the didies, had a whole basketful still to go," she muttered. "But I don't see her now."

"Angie," Connie said. "Those are beans. Little babies can't digest beans, you know that."

"Jej-jy can." Angie giggled. "And has, several times. You watch."

The front door slammed. Purposeful steps came hustling, and Nellie Overholt's voice clanged through the house. "You git away from them kids, Angie Coons!"

Angie let out a squawk. She tossed the cup, contents and all, straight up into the air and fled. Beans splattered against the ceiling, rained down with a sound like falling buckshot on the floor. Nellie, appearing, made a wrathful grab at Angie as she went by. She missed.

From somewhere in the house Connie heard a door slam as Angie took cover. Nellie, hands on hips, bawled, "You better git in that closet and stay there, you damned old gumboil! You come out here where I can lay my hands on you, I'll take a stick to you. You're lucky I don't come in there after you, see?"

She wasted no more time on Angie. "Did they git any?" she demanded. "Did they take any down? Did you see whether she—because if they did, I've got to get the doctor and a stomach pump quick."

"No," Connie said. "I was here. They didn't get any, Nellie."

"Thank the good God in his infinite mercy," Nellie said.

She collapsed into a chair, mopped her face. "Oh, her!" she moaned. "Her and her damned old beans. I ought to known better, but she was outdoors somewhere when I started to hang out that washing, my God, I can't leave for a minute, but she is in here and—Joe has got to do something, kill her and hang her hide on the barn, I don't care, but get somebody to—Who're you? Did you come to—Oh. For goodness' sakes. Connie Wilkinson. I was in such turmoil, I don't know who I thought you was, never tumbled to it that you was anybody, only one of them teenage babysitters, been answering Joe's ad in the paper and then don't stay because that old punkin-devil scares the bejeezus out of them, and thank the God they don't. You come to take the housekeeping job, because if we don't git somebody can handle Angie, I'll—Well, I am nuts, that's all."

"I should think you might be," Connie said. "But no, I just dropped by to see the babies. I was talking to Joe."

"Uh huh. No such luck," Nellie said. "How's your flu? You look a little peaked still."

"Oh, I'm all right now. It takes a while."

"Well, I'm sure glad you're home. You been down to see Clem?"

"This is the first time I've been out at all, to speak of. Actually I'm headed there next."

"Good," Nellie said. "I must say, it's about time some of you Wilkinsons—what I mean, that one's a handful, let me tell you."

"She always was," Connie said.

"Well, she knuckles under to me, don't think she don't," Nellie said. She spoke a little grimly, but, Connie could see, with a certain amount of relish. "I don't have the time to fool around. She gets a bath, whether she wants it or not."

"A bath? Can't she take it herself?"

"She could," Nellie said. "But she won't. You wait, you'll see. Look, as soon's I get through here and Gert comes, I'm going down there, fix Clem up for the day. Why don't you ride with me? There's probably some things you ought to know."

"Oh, I know. Ma told me," Connie said.

"Well, then, it'll be no surprise. You stick around. I've got to wait for Gert and then go to the drugstore, and a couple errands and then I'm ready." She got up and strode through the door, calling back, "If that Angie comes out, you tell her I'm right in the kitchen."

So there it was. Clementina was sick; senile; what Nellie in her inimitable way would call "a drunk."

And I was running to her, to lean, the way I always have. It seems impossible to have to believe that now I can't; she always seemed so . . . imperishable. But eighty-two is old, and—What was it Lucy had said? "Old age is bad for people." I will have to do what I can.

The three babies slept. They might have stirred during the rumpus, but they had not awakened. Two bassinets, matching except for color— one was blue, one pink—and a crib which did not match at all—an afterthought? They expected twins, not triplets, Connie thought in spite of herself, or why didn't they get all three alike?

In the bassinets the Montgomerys, exact duplicates, sucked on empty bottles, which Connie took away.

At least I know enough to do that, she told herself.

The tiny things didn't look like Montgomerys or anyone else; they looked like babies. How could you say what babies looked like? In the crib was J. J. Randall; no mistaking him. He was big; compared to the others, he was tremendous; his fist, doubled outside the blanket, made their tiny waxen hands look like dolls' hands. He had red hair—

the delicate, fluffy ringlets you might say were Wilkinson red hair, like her own; for the rest of it, he, too, looked like nobody you could mention. Like a baby, that was all.

He had come to the end of his meal; she could hear the slight hiss of air as he pulled at the empty bottle. She reached down to take it away and encountered surprising resistance. J. J. Randall's doubled fists flew up; they opened and grabbed at the bottle. When Connie pulled, he pulled back, stirred, awakened, and let out a bawl like the bull of Bashan.

"Oh, my lord!" Nellie apparently either had not yet left or had just come back to the kitchen. She came pounding in. "I knew it!" She flipped back the blanket, scooped up J. J. "What did you want to wake him up for? I don't know what there is about this"—whack— "baby. Everybody comes in here has got to"—whack—"pick him up. Well, go on, get it up, J. J.!" Whack. "Don't do you a mite of good to hang onto it. Stubborn little—there!"

J. J. Randall had got it up, but apparently there was more where that came from, for over Nellie's shoulder and looking Connie in the face, he smiled.

The smile was one she knew well: wide, innocent, honest; you and I are pals, it said; together, you and I can lick the world. The likeness, for an instant, was extraordinary.

"More?" Nellie said. "Much as a man, I declare!"

She laid the baby back in his crib and turned, her mouth open to say something. There was no one to say it to. "Well, heb'm sake! Where'd she go so quick?"

Connie fled down the steps of Joe's house; at his gate she had to stop.

The tall, white gatepost was solid; at least it didn't shake when you leaned on it. She stood for a moment, holding on to it with both hands.

He isn't dead. He's alive; he's there. He's J. J. Randall.

Oh God, could I be mistaken?

No. There couldn't be that many coincidences. My hair. Ernie's smile. The wise child's story about the doctor and the basket. The mistake was that night aboard the boat, when I thought he . . . died. I must have been sicker than I knew. He was there all the time, maybe they put him in some warm place, like by the stove in the cook's galley. Because he would have been cold . . . and I walked out without even waiting to ask . . . they must have thought I did it on purpose, that I wanted to be rid of him, too. I'm sorry they had to think that, I did what I thought was the best thing.

Whatever had happened, however it turned out, it was done; he was not hers now; he was Joe's.

If I've lost him, I deserve to. But I can bear this better than I could spending the rest of my life knowing I killed him.

Relief, suddenly, was like a flood water pouring down. She held to the gatepost for a moment, feeling it warm and strong, washing over the bewilderment, the uncertainty, the grinding sense of loss. In time, she well knew, it wouldn't be enough; but it was for now.

I was going down to Clementina's. I had better go.

It would be a long walk. Time to think. To think of Ernest Grindle, once dearly loved, whose son, in Joe Randall's house, that surely was. For two and two, put together, made four; and Ernie . . . Ernie . . . Ernie of the clever trick; the fast wangle; the game played with zest and enjoyment for the fun of it, to get ahead of someone, to slide out from under, to win, no matter how, and to feel twice a man's normal size with winning, the underhanded, the dirty tricks discounted, forgotten. Somehow he had managed this; and he was somewhere, going his merry way, without a doubt making a story of it, the story of the eternal drummer and the farmer's daughter, for the greater glory of Anzio Jones and the entertainment of whoever was lucky enough to be listening to him now.

Ernie. How could you be the way you are, and still be someone anybody could love? That I could love, brought up the way I was on honesty is the best policy and wear integrity as a coat of mail; and, God help me, believing it? She hardly noticed the car which slid alongside her and stopped. When Lucy spoke to her, she stared for an instant, uncomprehending, as at a stranger.

Early that morning Amos had gone back to work for the first time since his accident; his hands were still sore and he was unable to drive, but he had had Mack stop by for him in a truck, which left his car free for Lucy. She had taken it for a morning's shopping at the supermarket. On the way back she had spotted Connie, a long way from home, wandering aimlessly along the street and looking, to Lucy's horror, as if she were going to be sick. With restraint—because it was on the street and someone might notice—Lucy flung open the door of the car.

"Connie, dear! For goodness' sake, get in here! What on earth are you thinking of, and you hardly out of your bed!"

"Hi, Ma. I'm glad you came along. I was getting a little tired."

"I should think so. You look as if—Where have you been?"

"At Joe's. I've been getting myself a job."

"A job! In the fish factory?"

The words might have been in a foreign language; Lucy, at least, had obviously never uttered them before.

"Oh, come, Ma. I've got to have some money. Some clothes. Look at me."

"But, Connie! None of the Wilkinson ladies have ever—Why, you can't. You can't possibly. What will people think?"

"What they want to. They'll have to get used to the idea. I'm glad you're here with the car. You can drive me down to Clementina's."

"They'll think your father's having business troubles or something, and it's not fair, he isn't—*Clementina's?*"

"Yes, honey. Clementina's."

Lucy turned pale. "I will not do it. I cannot do it. You can't go there, she drinks, your father—"

"I know how you feel. I'm sorry. If Clementina drinks, she's got a reason, she's sick or lonesome, and my father's as much to blame as anyone for leaving her there neglected for so long."

"She's an awful woman; if it hadn't been for her, for her influence, you'd have stayed home, none of this would have—"

"What you believe is a lot of guff; Pa's pounded it into you until you can't tell black from white."

"Connie, that's not a nice way to speak about your father!"

"No. He and I aren't speaking nicely, remember? Perhaps we aren't to be blamed, I don't know. But I'm sick of blaming and being blamed. Things happen, so you do what you can. What I can do, I've got a job. I'm going to live with Clementina, if she'll have me. If you won't drive me, I'll walk."

"You can't walk, it's too far, you're not able."

"All right. But I'm going there. So—?"

Confronted with a choice between two inevitable evils, Lucy picked what seemed at the moment to be the lesser. She started to drive, but as slowly as possible, down the Shore Road toward the old Wilkinson house.

Connie, out of the corner of her eye, could see her going over in her mind the reasons she could bring up to prevent this insane action. Apparently she thought of one, for she suddenly put on the brake and stopped the car squarely in the middle of the road. A milk truck behind her pulled up in time, but barely, with a blare of horn and a desperate squeal of brakes.

"Ma, for heaven's sake!"

"You haven't got your suitcase," Lucy said.

"Look, Harper was trying to pass. Let him by, before he busts a blood vessel."

"You haven't packed your things. Oh," Lucy said. "What's the matter with Harper, blowing his horn like that? It's impolite."

She pulled over, and Harper Collins, the milkman, went by, yelling something as he went, which Lucy took to be a greeting, for she called back, "Oh, good morning, Harper."

"Oh, Ma," Connie said, choking back laughter. "Are you with it, honey!"

"Yes, dear. But you haven't even a nightgown with you."

"I haven't one, Ma, remember? I've been sleeping in yours."

"Yes, I know, but you can't just walk in on Clementina. Without a suitcase, and coming on a visit, what would she think?"

Suitcase, visit; visit, suitcase. They went together in Lucy's mind, and all the king's horses couldn't have pulled them apart.

Oh, Ma. My suitcase is aboard the *Potluck* still—unless they have thrown it overboard. My nightgown is in a pawn shop in New Bedford. Oh, Ma, you are like . . .

> Lot's wife looking down on chaos,
> Had no saving sense at all;
> So in the midst of this am I
> Striving to be methodical . . .

"What, dear?" Lucy, looking down at her neat, gloved hands on the wheel, glanced over with a little, puzzled frown. "There must be things of yours around the house, I could pack some in that old Kennebecker of Grandfather's, only Clementina might recall that it was your grandfather's and wonder why we didn't buy you a new suitcase, if we couldn't afford to . . ."

"I'm sure you'll think of something," Connie said.

It sounded sarcastic, sounded mean. No, I mustn't . . .

She leaned over suddenly and kissed her mother on the cheek.

The cheek was silky and cool and smelled pleasantly of apple-blossom talcum powder; and Connie drew back hastily, steadying herself to keep the tremble out of her voice. "You always do," she said.

"Mm, I expect I will," Lucy said. Still thinking hard, she drove on, and said no more until another problem, a worse one, loomed before her eyes—the tall gables of the old Wilkinson place in sight above the trees. She stopped the car abruptly. "I can't just appear at the gate, Clementina will wonder why I don't come in, and your father—Oh, Connie, please come home with me, we'll drive on by and—"

"No, Ma. I'll walk the rest of the way, it's only a step. Don't worry, I'll be up to see you soon."

"Well, I don't know that you ought to walk. But of course

Clementina would think . . . Connie! You haven't even kissed me good-bye!"

Connie could see no signs of life as she approached Clementina's house. It had always, within her own memory, looked slightly dilapidated; Clementina had never been one to concern herself over much with scaling paint and sagging porches, her mind being busy with livelier projects. The front walk of cut granite blocks had always had weeds in its crevices, and the lawn grass, cut whenever Clementina remembered to hire someone, had usually been longer than local householders thought was nice. But now the weeds in the walk had thrust up knee-high and the lawn was a jungle. Connie remembered white curtains at the windows; there were none now. The panes were blank and bare. The old house looked as though the creeping rot, incipient for a century in its timbers and sills, had eaten through to the outside as well, and Connie looked at it with misgiving.

Something really has happened to her. Some kind of sickness—a stroke or perhaps just old age. She had her eightieth birthday just before I went away. We had a party, the three of us, she and Ernie and I. She was all right then. Connie remembered the party. Cocktails and candlelight, and one of Clementina's famous meals—she had always been a fabulous cook—and the birthday cake which Ernie insisted on making—oh, he had been wonderful with Clementina, beguiling as only he could be; of course, now, anyone could guess why: he'd known, everybody did, that she had a lot of money. What a time the two of them had had, finding room on top of Ernie's cake for eighty candles, which he had insisted on, too, though Clementina had suggested that fifty or so would be enough to indicate the direction things were taking with her. And because the cake had fallen, the candles went up and down like telephone poles on hillsides and a valley; and Clementina had taken a deep breath and had blown them all out in one puff . . . and said she hoped she'd do as well when there were a hundred. . . .

She felt bad, I knew, because I was going away; but she liked Ernie. She was the one who told me I must go. And we promised to write every week, and I did write, but she never answered any of my letters. Not one. Not even the last one, when I needed help so desperately. Anybody's help. And had to take anybody's help.

But looking at the house—the sagging porch columns, the blank, dark, lonesome windowpanes—Connie felt bitterness and resentment drain away. There had to be reasons. Nobody could change so much if there weren't.

She had started up the walk when she heard a car stopping, somebody beeping lightly on a horn.

Oh Lord, Ma's changed her mind. Now we'll have to go through all the arguments again.

But it wasn't Lucy. It was, she saw, turning, Lura Blandish, who was leaning out the window and beckoning with a bright, cheerful, toothy smile.

"Well, Constance Wilkinson! How nice to see you. What a sight for sore eyes," Lura said. "And how lovely to see you calling on your dear old great-aunt again!"

"Oh. Yes. Mrs. Blandish. Thanks," Connie said.

I sound jerky; but maybe just now I am a little jerky, she thought. What on earth does she want with me?

"I've only a minute, Jones is expecting me," Lura said. "But I did want to tell Clementina—and now I won't have to stop, you can take her the message—the Club would like to have a linen and patchwork quilt exhibition at the parish house before they bring her lovely old things back again. To raise money for the church, you know— so it's in a good cause, tell her, and tell her too that we will give credit where credit is due; we are going to call it The Clementina Wilkinson Exhibition."

"Ah—yes. I'll tell her."

"Oh, thank you, dear, a million, we're all so *grateful*. Tata now, I must be off—" And Lura drove away with a jaunty wave of a hand.

Well, I suppose Clementina knows what that's about, Connie

thought. Has Clementina been selling antiques? I wonder.

She went up the walk and tried the knob of the front door; it didn't turn. The mechanism was stuck, rusted or something. There was no sound from inside the house, and after a moment she walked around the porch to the back.

The space in front of the back door was occupied by a group of long-haired yellow cats; a poodle; a full-grown sheep whose gray, bedraggled wool was stuck full of burdocks. They were waiting to be let in. The cats sat in a disconsolate cluster under the melancholy nose of the sheep, which was pressed to the crack of the door. The poodle sat a little apart, with the air of if there was work to be done, let others do it. He was something new to Connie, but in the rest of the group she recognized old friends. "Mame," she said. "Herbert."

But at the sound of her voice the cluster disintegrated, an explosion which rayed out in six directions. The cats scattered and fled; the sheep ran down the back steps to a lilac bush, into which she plowed headfirst, leaving exposed only a small section of woolly rump. The poodle, more dignified, moved along the porch to a corner, where he sat down back to. And from within the house came the sound of Clementina's remembered voice.

"Nellie! You stop chasing those animals! This is their home, not yours. You are not bound to take after everything with brooms and mop handles."

Connie opened the door and stepped inside. The room seemed, at first sight, much as she remembered it—the old-fashioned wainscoted kitchen, with the wide floorboards of pine worn down around their polished knots, the yellow wallpaper above the wainscot in its pattern of daisy chain. It was untidy, as usual—Clementina had always lived in a kind of inspired disorder of her own and her pets' belongings. She liked her things around her, within reach, and she did not seem to mind if the animals had theirs that way, too—the cats had dishes here and there about the floor, and, Connie noticed with a little surge of amusement, in one corner was an opened bale of hay.

But the room was cold as a tomb. The kitchen range was without a fire and its front covers were off, exposing the rusty intestines of an unlit oil burner. Clementina sat in a rocker in front of it, wrapped from head to foot in a patchwork quilt. She did not turn or move, so that all Connie could see of her was the tight knot of gray hair on top of her head; and this, more than anything else, was a sign of startling change. For Clementina had always worn her hair cut short in a crest, which, within Connie's memory, had changed only in its color—from spectacular reddish gold to grizzled gray and then to pure white; beautiful hair, now dressed like a witch's taglocks, at which Connie stared in anguish.

"Clementina?" she said uncertainly.

"If you want me to hear you, you'll have to speak up," Clementina said. "That is, if you've got anything to say I want to hear. I can't see you, I've mislaid my glasses."

"Clementina," Connie said. "It isn't Nellie. It's me." She slipped her arm around the frail shoulders, startled to find them so frail, bending down so that their two faces were on a level. "It's Connie. I've come home."

The old lady shrugged, shaking away from the encircling arm. "Don't do that. I don't like to be touched," she said. "I've told you times enough—*Who?*"

She caught her breath suddenly and lifted her head, turning toward Connie the same triangularly shaped face that the girl remembered—the gay, high-arched eyebrows and bright, snapping gold-brown eyes. "*Connie!* Is it?"

"Yes," Connie said.

Clementina flung back the quilt. She jumped to her feet, spry as a cricket, bent over the stove and thrust her hand down into the reeking oil burner, poking furiously about.

Horrified, Connie thought, Oh, God help her, she *is* crazy, they're right, after all—

Clementina pulled out of the oil burner her glasses, which she proceeded to clean on her handkerchief. "Why, here you are come home, my own dear love," she said, "and me blind as a godless bat!" She put on the glasses. "Let me look at you!"

Whatever you thought, the first thing would have to be fires in stoves; the old house was like a tomb. Clementina seemed chilled to the bone, and Connie herself was shivering. To light the kitchen range, she found, was out of the question; the firebox was flooded with oil, and oil had dripped down in a pool to the floor. The burners had been turned off and then on again without a flame. Before the stove would be usable again, it would have to be cleaned.

The sitting-room stove, a wood-burning airtight, looked all right; at least, the drafts and damper worked, though the stove was rusty and obviously hadn't had a fire in it for a long time. Whoever had been taking care of Clementina—Nellie, mostly, of course—doubtless considered that the kitchen fire was enough for the old lady. Though there was another reason, which Connie discovered when she hunted in the shed for wood and kindling.

There was wood in plenty, but not in the shed. Whoever had delivered it, apparently from a dump truck, had simply backed into the side yard, upended the truck body, and driven out from under, so that the wood was in a scattered windrow all the way to the gate. It had lain out in the weather and was mostly soggy and damp.

Couldn't be bothered to throw it inside or dump it where she could find it, Connie thought furiously, rooting around in the pile for dry sticks. Oh, I can hear him now—"The old gal's half-blind, she won't know the difference." But I'll bet he made sure he got his money for it.

She made a mental note to have a straight word with Jerry Fulton at the woodyard and stamped back into the house with an armful which looked as if it might burn. There was no kindling anywhere, but she smashed up an old wooden packing box, shoved some of it into the airtight on top of crumpled newspaper, lit it, and stood back, hearing the comforting roll of the fire up the chimney.

A sound behind her made her glance around. Clementina was dragging her rocking chair in from the kitchen, backing through the door. She said not a word while Connie helped her with the chair; then, established in front of the airtight with her feet on the fender, she heaved a sigh of contentment.

"This good old stove," she said. "It always did have a draft that would suck the cat up the chimney. Sets the chimney afire every so often, too, if you don't look out."

Connie gasped and jumped for the damper. She hadn't thought about a chimney fire, though she had seen one or two in this very chimney, she recalled, when she had been a youngster running in and out of the house.

"Let it burn," Clementina said. "I'm so glad to see you, I wouldn't notice if the whole shebang went up in smoke. Where've you been all this long time?"

"Why—" Taken aback, Connie couldn't for a moment think what to say. Since Clementina had never written, nor responded to a desperate call for help, Connie had been prepared for no such joyous welcome. But, she thought, her eyes searching Clementina's face in sorrow and despair, if she's unbalanced, that could account for anything.

The face was changed, thinned down to essential bone, the profile hawklike, the cheeks parchment-colored. But the eyes, she saw with a start, were as vital, as bright, as full of interest and affection as they had ever been; and Clementina, seeing Connie's look of doubt and bewilderment, suddenly smiled.

"I expect you've heard rumors," she said. "There have been some. I'll explain. But first tell me what's gone wrong. I can see something has."

"Clementina—don't you know? Didn't you get my letters?"

For a moment Clementina said nothing. Then, "You did write, didn't you?" she said.

"Of course I wrote! Why wouldn't I? When I first went away, I wrote every week. And then, when you didn't answer, I kept asking Ma in my letters to her what was the matter, were you sick or something, and she never would mention you—"

"I expect your father wouldn't let her," Clementina said crisply.

"Yes. But, Clementina, what happened? Just before I came home, I had to write you for help, for money, I needed it, I—" She burst into tears.

"Stop crying," Clementina said. "You must know that I would

have sent you anything I could lay my hands on if I had known you needed it. Tell me what happened to you, it's time I knew."

Her tone, terse, almost harsh, jolted Connie. It stopped the tears and she found herself able to talk.

Clementina listened in silence. From time to time her fingers crisped slightly on the arms of the chair; when Connie finished, she sat, her head slightly bowed, still saying nothing.

"So I've got this job at Randall's," Connie said. "I'd like to stay here with you, if you'll have me."

Silence was not what you expected ever from Clementina. Uneasy as it grew, and then in beginning anger, Connie burst out, "I'll pay my board. Unless you feel, like the rest of them, that I'm too much of a disgrace to—to the Wilkinson family. I've tried to have as much consideration for them as—"

"Pah!" Clementina said. There were tears on her cheeks, and behind her glasses her eyes blazed with fury. "I would as soon have consideration for a nest of cottonmouth moccasins," she said. "I'm sorry for Lucy. As sorry as a person can be for a complete and utter fool, but—Oh, I'm eighty-two, too old to start out of this house with a gun and a handful of shells, but, so help me, I can and I will if—" Looking at Connie, her tone gentled. "Connie, let it be settled. I would rather have you here than be fifty years younger. I'm sorry about your baby, it would have been nice to have one around the house."

She stopped, thinking, seemed suddenly withdrawn, and absently spread her hands to the warmth of the fire. "The first thing we must do is get my mail from the mailbox in Bishop."

"Bishop?" Connie said.

She thought wearily, She is eighty-two and she's really mixed up. I will have to be the one to help her and I'm too tired to help anyone. Aloud she said, "You mean your mailbox downtown, here, don't you? Yes, of course I'll get the mail—"

"I do not. I mean Bishop. I have had a post-office box in Bishop as well as one here, since before you went away. I wish now I'd told you about it. You could have sent your letters there and I would have got them. The reason I haven't written you, I have never had your address. I telephoned your mother for it, but Lucy did not see fit to give it to me."

"Clementina! What are you talking about? What—"

"You've been told, among other pleasant things, that I'm out of my mind. I can see you wondering. I don't know as I blame you, the way this house is. The way I look." She put up a hand to her hair. "This greenish twist is what Nellie Overholt thinks is suitable for the crazy old," she said. "For weeks I haven't been permitted out of the house for a hair-do. About six months ago I had pneumonia. I was quite sick, and I suppose I lost touch with myself for a while. When I came to, Nellie Overholt had moved in. Now, don't misunderstand me—she and Dr. Garland probably saved my life, and I am grateful; such of it as is left, I plan to enjoy. Nellie's forte, however, is emergency; she is excellent for the sick and the dying, but a cross to bear when you are trying to get better. I have had to take some measure of self-protection."

"Clementina, I didn't know any of this—"

"No. How could you know?"

"What happened to the letters I wrote you?"

"I'd better begin at the beginning." Clementina's voice was dry, harsh again, her hands clenched on the arms of her chair. "I've never in my life said a word to you against your father; I will give him credit now, he's thorough. But so am I, when I have reason to be. In the days when he used to come here, he would always bring my mail. As a favor, he said; but I began to find out I wasn't getting it all, especially letters about money matters. Then there was a spell when my checks didn't come at all."

Connie stared with a face of horror. "Pa took your checks? He couldn't have!"

"Yes. Who would believe it? That respectable man, senior warden of the vestry, in cahoots with the bank and all such stable institutions— who would think anything when he casually picked up my mail at the post office except that he was being kind to his old great-aunt?"

"He's got enough! He wouldn't need to steal. And from you! It doesn't make sense, Clementina!"

"No. It doesn't, does it? Which is why I have never tried to make anyone believe it; at least, not recently. The comment of course would be, 'Who is the crazy one?' You don't really believe it, do you?" Clementina smiled. "Poor lamb, you find me fishing my glasses out of the oil burner, which I flooded to divert Nellie from making me more uncomfortable than I was—you don't know what to think, except old age and hardening of the arteries, I expect I can't blame you. Your father is money-crazy, he has always been so. The ends justify the means. He isn't a thief according to his lights. He would never write my name on the back of my check and cash the check. That truly would be stealing. But he could tear the check up, if that's what he did, whenever he could get his hands on it. Amos is disregardful of women, to him they aren't people. He feels it's his money; Gerald was his grandfather and should have left it to him, to the man of the family. The more of it I'm unable to spend, the more will be left for him when I go. Not that he isn't in for a shock when I do."

She paused, her smile now a little grim. "I have fought him off for too many years not to know how his mind works. About your letters to me, he would consider it his duty as a Christian father to take them. And to read them, too. I expect he knew your whole story before you told him, the night you got home. He seems to have been ready and waiting."

Something nudged at Connie's mind. That night was hard enough to remember, but Amos's face was not. Yes, it had been as if he were ready and waiting. But— "Clementina, he cried that night!"

"I expect he did. Two cold tears. He cried the day Gerald's will was read, too. I'm sorry, Connie. It only meant he was mad enough to kill someone."

The back door opened and closed with a slam. Someone came in, walking with heavy, forthright steps.

For an instant Connie felt her blood turn cold, thinking it might be Amos. If he's come here to make me go home, I won't have strength enough to fight him off . . .

But a voice called, "Yoo hoo! Clem!" and then, deepening to tragic timbre, said, "Oh, my God in Heaven, look what she's done to the stove!" and Nellie Overholt, lowering, appeared in the doorway, her bulky body, clad in nurse's uniform with cape, filling the opening. "You old devil!" she went on. "What kind of works now? I've told you never to touch that oil burner, I've got a good mind to—Oh. You did come here, Connie. You went out of Joe's so fast I never did find out for sure if you really meant to." She stared with menacing intent at Clementina, who said composedly, "Good morning, Nellie."

"Good morning, is it? Well, I'm glad to hear something out of us besides a mumble. What did we do to that oil burner?"

"I flooded it," Connie said firmly. "You'll have to blame me. I've lived in the city far too long."

She was rewarded by a flashing glance from Clementina, which plainly said, And this isn't the first time we've backed each other up against the world, is it? "Yes, she did," Clementina said. "And I told her not to fool with it, too."

"H'm." Nellie glanced from one bland face to the other. "Don't tell me there's two of you here now reaching for butterflies. Because, much more, and I will be reaching for bats. Every day, something new for Nellie. And me with Angie, and the whole grammar school to give polio shots to, which, I must say, I'd rather do than come into this menagerie for one hour!"

She began unfastening the clasp of her cape with gusto. For all her protestations, it could be deduced that Nellie, overworked though she might be, was not unaware of any importance which might attach to her through her job. She had taken over in this house. She would not only give the orders here, she would enjoy it.

M'm, Connie thought. I think I begin to see.

She lifted an eyebrow at Clementina, got an almost imperceptible go-ahead sign in return. I know I begin to see.

She said, "It's all right, Nellie, I'm here now, and I'm going to stay. You're busy, I know. You won't need to come anymore. You mustn't leave those babies alone with Angie, you know."

"Oh, Gert's there. I got hold of her. Going to *stay* here? You?" This was news, a tidbit of the first water, it was easy to see. "Why, honey—" Nellie lowered her voice to a halfwhisper and spoke over Clementina's head, mouthing the words to make the whisper understood. "You can't manage her, dear."

"Indubitably," Clementina said.

"What? What did we say?" Nellie, undeterred, went on, fumbling in the bag she carried and coming up with a cake of soap of a sickly greenish hue. "We're a bad girl, Connie. We hide the soap. But Nellie's two jumps ahead of us. Look at this, Miss Clem! I've brought my own, I don't need to spend time hunting! Not for the soap. Not this morning."

Clementina regarded the soap. She said nothing.

"We're a ba-ad girl, we *like* to be dirty," Nellie said. She shook a finger. "Come on, now. I know we don't like to be washed, but I drove up today, I can't fool around." She ground to a stop. "How long's that oil burner been out?" she demanded. "I'll bet to my life there ain't one scrap of hot water. So that's it! So that's our little present to Nellie for today. Well! We have got a nice fire here in the airtight which will heat a basin of water in jig time. Nellie is still two jumps ahead of us, Miss Clem, ain't she, a-hah?"

I can't stand this, Connie thought. If she doesn't stop, in a minute I am going to throw up.

Clementina, with her cool dignity, who had always been a free soul, independent—talked to, treated like a feebleminded child! This might be one of the prerogatives of old age and sickness; but old age and sickness, it would seem, might for most people be considered enough. . . .

Connie opened her mouth wrathfully to say something of the kind, but before she could say anything, Clementina spoke. The old voice was gentle, slightly amused.

"Nellie," she said. "You have got a single-track mind. They train nurses in hospitals to wash patients every day, so when you come through that door your mind is going tick-tick, wash patient, tick-tick, wash patient. Now, I have always kept my body decent, but I never in my life took a bath every day. I have a sensitive spot between my shoulder blades which has itched for twenty-five years. Soapsuds bring out a rash on it so I can't sleep, and doctors have always told me never to take a bath for the fun of it, only to get clean."

"Sure," Nellie said. "We have been carrying on about that for months. And all I can say is, we have run into a mess of doctors that were liars, that's all!"

"And you will not use plain white soap, which is easier on my spot, you are determined to slather me with that pine-scented stuff the Ladies' Club left here, hoping, as they said, that I would take the hint. You think it is lovely. I do not. I have never cared for cheap-scented things of any kind. Pine in soap has always said 'lavatory' to me, and I never could stand that public smell. So when you go, take it with you. Certainly I hid it. It is in a box in the cupboard behind the chimney."

"Well, for God's sake!" Nellie said in a stunned voice. Her jaw had dropped, and she had to make a real effort to go on. "I don't get it. What's happened to her?"

"We're better," Clementina said modestly. "If we haven't taken the trouble to talk rationally for some time, it is because you have not taken the trouble to listen rationally. I am glad I have at last reached you. If I have."

"Well, I must say, I never see—what is this? You snapped out of it overnight, or something?"

"A lucid interval? Oh, surely you've seen them, Nellie. Everybody has them. Come, now. Right now, I sound more c-o-m-p-o-s than you do."

Nellie's face turned a congested red. She said in a strangled voice, "Connie, I want to talk to you. They's some things you ought to know." She scooped up her cape and bag and stalked ominously into the kitchen.

Coming along behind her, Connie said feebly, "I expect it's seeing me, Nellie. It's done her good, I—" Dear God, help me not to laugh. She clenched her teeth, feeling the jaw muscles tremble.

"You appear to think something is funny," Nellie said. The words came out sizzling. "Well, you can take over and welcome. I'm through busting my gizzards, I'll tell you that. That old hellion's been putting it on with me, three-quarters of the time!"

"Oh, Nellie, I know she appreciates—"

"Appreciates my overgrown continental—Well, she ain't been putting it on that she drinks like a fish, so you go ahead and cope with that, I'd like to see you. Here's the doctor's number, in case the—the *lucid interval* don't last."

Nellie fastened her cape with a jerk.

"Nellie, I'm honestly sorry—"

"Itched for twenty-fi—Nobody has ever itched for twenty-five years!"

"But she has, we've all—I've always known about Clementina's spot. It's fa-famous." Connie's voice shattered; laughter choked helplessly in her throat.

"And *I* have all my life fit filthy old people who didn't want to wash. And heard some excuses, too. Which I ain't swallowed. And *I don't swallow this one!*"

Nellie departed. The windows rattled to the slam of the door.

Oh, my! Connie thought.

Clementina was still sitting quietly where they had left her. She said thoughtfully, "She's gone off mad."

"Yes. Are you ashamed of yourself?"

"I suppose I should be. Granted I had other and sufficient reasons, Nellie has a tough, stuffy leg which it is a temptation to pull."

"What did you mean, the Ladies' Club leaving soap here, suggesting you use it? Incidentally, Lura Blandish waylaid me outside, said to tell you they were using your things in an exhibit at the parish house. To raise money for the church, she said. What did you do, lend them some antiques?"

"Oh, my." Clementina began to chuckle. "A holy show, eh? The Wilkinson exhibit! Well, they did leave a mess of cleaning things here, a whole shelf full. About a month ago they came down in a body, cleaned the house from top to bottom. A Project. They went over the house with a fine-tooth comb. I could hear them upstairs, ooh-ing and ah-ing over Grandmother's things, and the Lord only knows what they got away with. I caught Lura sneaking downstairs with that box of old buttons and I gave them to her. 'You want them bad enough to steal them,' I said, or something of the kind, 'you can have them,' and she said, 'Why, Clem, I only brought them downstairs to show the girls.'"

Her renegade old eye caught Connie's, and Connie found herself suddenly whooping with laughter. "You made that up, Clementina," she gasped, wiping away tears.

"Of course I didn't. 'Tisn't anything new, the Blandishes have been stealing the town blind for years. So when the ladies left, they took along all the quilts and linen to wash. And the curtains. That's where the curtains went, not that I cared much. Things could have done with a good wash."

"But why haven't they brought things back? What do they think they're doing?"

"Oh, you know ladies, when they get their teeth into a Project. I suppose they felt such a dirty place wasn't proper for such nice things, and I agree. The animals do make a mess, and I know I should keep them outside. But at night, especially, they're company. Well. Lura did send a committee down to say that since I wasn't able to take care of myself, how about an old ladies' home. I'm afraid I told them that of course they realized nothing could be done about the antiques in this house until I was out of it for good. So then the minister came, somebody sicked him on, and he tried. I let him talk, it did him good. Poor young man, he's chapped under the chin, got that kind of skin, and the way he wiggles his feet in his shoes, I'm mortally sure he's got chilblains. He was too dignified for me to suggest he take his shoes off, which I could see he was dying to do. He tried out the old ladies' home notion, too; and when that didn't work, he preached a whole sermon on the evils of drink, how it skimped your chances of getting into Heaven, which he went on about until I told him that what he put out about Heaven sounded pleasant, if slightly tiresome to a grown person, and didn't he think the earth could be pleasant, too, if man and God took the same trouble about it. I could see the idea wasn't anything he fancied much. Put him out of a job, I suppose."

"That's outrageous! The whole thing is awful! Going off with your things! I'll have a word to say to Lura Blandish, don't think I won't! She and her antique shop!"

"Now, Connie, those are nice ladies. They haven't really 'gone off' with anything. They have just got things reasoned out according to their lights. People do. Lura has got them all convinced that antiques are a public trust. And what do you think they thought when they came down here and saw that Herbert, an old tomcat, eats his dinner off a Spode plate? Besides, I won't let you spoil their good time. They had a lovely day here, all fuffered up with faith and good works, and there's nothing that sets up a crowd of womenfolks like the sight of somebody else's bad housekeeping. Why, during the War, when Lura went around in a uniform learning how to take an automobile engine apart, she had three children at home and a hungry husband."

"Clementina, why? Were you too sick to hire someone to take over? And regular nurses—you didn't need to have Nellie, did you?"

"I thought I told you. There hasn't been quite enough to live on."

"Oh. I see." That could explain it, certainly. Clementina's money must be, finally, gone. "Well, I've got a job," Connie said. "It isn't much, but we'll have enough."

"Why, God love you!" Clementina flashed her a glance. "It's only a matter of collecting my checks from the mailbox in Bishop. After I got better, I managed to get over there once or twice, so that I've still got some cash in the house. But sneaking off to Bishop by myself was thought to be a part of my irrational actions, so Nellie left word with George at the taxi stand not to send a taxi when I called for one. For my own good, she said. We'll go over this afternoon. There's plenty of money."

"But couldn't somebody have fetched your checks? There must have been someone—"

"There was nobody I could trust, lamb. Nellie talks; she spreads things around. It would have been only a matter of time before it got back to Amos what I wanted in Bishop."

"People can get protection! You could have had him arrested!"

"Who would take my word against his? He is the sane one."

"But, Clementina, why did you let Nellie think you were—were out on Cloud Nine, or something? You must have known it would get back to him. Did you know he—he was trying to have you committed?"

"M'm, I did. I have been three jumps ahead of him all his life, but I will admit it was nip and tuck this time, I'm not so young as I was. But you're here, now, aren't you? We have both got somebody in the house we can depend on. I'm hungry. Let's have some soup. We can heat up a can on the airtight here, and I would prefer tomato."

After lunch Clementina had to rest; she suddenly seemed very tired.

"Clementina, are you sure you ought to go to Bishop?" Connie asked. She said to herself, I wish I knew.

"I'll be fine, I only need a nap. I want to go. You don't know how long it is since I've been out of this house. You call George, tell him to have a taxi here at two. And while you're at it, phone the beauty parlor, make appointments. What we both need more than anything is a hair-do." She lay down on the sitting-room sofa, pulling up her quilt, and fell asleep as quickly and as serenely as a baby.

I'll have to see the doctor, Connie thought, and find out for sure how she is, what she's able to do. She looks so frail. But except for her thinness and matters of appearance such as her hair, she did not seem so very different from the Clementina of two years ago.

The trouble is, she's never been quite like other people. Not a standard edition. Pa's always looked on her as a kind of a nut and talked it around. And people have always thought her stand-offish and strange because she never would join anything—the clubs or the church or the lodge. You couldn't make anyone believe she isn't a snob. But it's only because she's never been interested in what crowds of people do together socially. I've heard her say that she doesn't think most people are either, really; but joining is what everybody does, so they think they ought to do it, too. So Nellie didn't need much persuading—

she's heard all her life that Clementina Wilkinson's more or less wacky. Well, with what seems to have gone on here, it's a wonder she isn't. I don't see any signs around that she drinks, either. Was that a part of the leg-pull? I wonder. But why? Clementina's not stupid. She must have known that sooner or later it would have given Pa his chance.

Things didn't quite make sense; perhaps they would in time.

Whatever's wrong, Connie told herself sturdily, if anything is, with Clementina, I'm here now. Nobody moves in. If Pa tries, he's going to run head on into me. If she's alcoholic, the doctor will have to tell me how to help her. The first thing is to get this place livable.

She suddenly found she felt better than she had in weeks. Something to get my hands on besides my own troubles, she thought, and she started in on the kitchen range.

Since nobody in Amos's house ever called out the service people for anything the womenfolks could be taught to fix, Connie knew how to dismantle the reeking oil burners, sop them out, blot wicks, and put everything back together again. She lighted the fire, set water on to heat for some temporary scrubbing until the big copper watertank behind the stove should produce, and surveyed the kitchen.

On a shelf was ranged a tremendous supply of scouring powder, steel wool pads, cleaning cloths in immaculate wrappers from the A and P—enough for a dozen house-cleanings. What the Ladies' Club had left—but why so much? Yes, of course—it had been a club project, each member had been told to bring something. The things, nearly filling the dusty shelf, had, to Connie, an air of silent criticism. What was it Clementina had said? "Hoping I would take the hint."

It was good-hearted of the ladies to come and clean, you could see that. And to wash the quilts and linen—but what was the idea, not bringing them back?

Lura Blandish, Connie thought, viciously jabbing at a blob of dried cat food on the kitchen counter. She's always rolled over everybody to get her own way, and she's been after Clementina for years about the antiques in this house.

The antiques probably didn't matter quite so much to Clementina as people might think—she had never in her life cared overmuch for things. But the privacy. The independence. To be treated like a child, an old souse with hardening of the arteries. Clementina, who had always kept herself to herself. . . . Didn't she know, for goodness' sake, that she was asking for it, that people will take advantage of old age and sickness?

Somebody knocked at the back door, and Connie jumped. Who? Amos, coming home at lunchtime, would know by now what she had done, that she had left his house for good. Had he come after her?

Don't be a fool. Pa never knocked at a door in his life. He would just come yelling in. Nevertheless, she stood, her heart thumping; then she went over and stealthily peered out of the window.

Nobody was there, but Mame and the cats and poodle had come back. While Connie looked, Mame lifted a polished black hoof and tapped delicately at the door. And waited, with expectancy.

They looked nice, Clementina's animals. The poodle needed clipping, Mame's winter coat was a mess; some of the cats had been into beggar ticks, and one had a very sore paw. They had been neglected, but not through anyone's unkind disregard; they were eager, they were affectionate; they cared whether they got in.

My winter coat, too, is not presentable. And I myself am not . . . I am not eager, nor affectionate, nor do I seem to care, right now, whether I get in anywhere. Still, like them, I run to Clementina. Maybe she has something here, old as she is, seeing what she's seen.

> *I think I could turn and live with animals, they are so*
>   *placid and self-contained . . .*
> *They do not sweat and whine about their condition,*
> *They do not lie awake in the dark and weep for their sins,*
> *They do not make me sick discussing their duty to God,*
> *Not one is dissatisfied, not one is demented with the*
>   *mania of owning things,*
> *Not one kneels to another, nor to his kind that lived*
>   *thousands of years ago,*
> *Not one is respectable or unhappy over the whole earth . . .*

You couldn't have spent half your childhood in Clementina's house without knowing that one. So, all right, don't sweat and whine, then. Feed 'em; they're probably hungry. In the shed, though; we can't all be in the kitchen while I clean.

She wrestled with Mame's bale of hay, managing after a while to upend it through the kitchen door into the entry to the shed, leaving a trail of hay. In the entry, which was small, it stuck and came apart, so that for the rest of the way to a corner of the shed, she carried it in armfuls.

Food for the cats would be no problem, she saw; a shelf in the shed was stacked with canned cat food. She opened the shed door and started opening cans.

How many cans? she thought, doubtfully watching the river of cats flow in. How do you go about feeding such a multitude? Do you dump the stuff in a pan and let them go to? In that case the big ones would get it all. They were all sizes, from Herbert up front to a small, high-pockets, cinnamon-colored job in a corner, who looked as if he never got anything.

What we need is a technique here, she thought a little wildly. Where could I ever find enough pans?

She compromised finally by putting dabs around on the boards of the floor, but stopped when she saw that the majority were merely sniffing disdainfully and not touching.

"What's the matter with you ladies and gentlemen?" she demanded wrathfully. "So you're used to having your meals off of Spode? Well, take it or leave it, there've been changes made!"

Herbert, with the air of someone who has been trifled with over something not worth his time, turned his back on her and jumped to the washbench, where he sat down beside a large white-agate dish pan, into which he glanced once and then back at Connie, with an unwinking, baleful eye. The pan was empty, but, from the look of it, it had once held raw meat. The implication seemed to be that she had eaten it.

"All right," Connie said. "You eat what's dished out, or wait till you're hungry."

It was impossible not to feel the least bit let down.

Quite annoyed, she started for the kitchen and then, pulling up, paused in the entry to giggle at herself.

Miss Christian Charity feeding the needy and starving, she thought, and then mad because nobody's even hungry . . .

She stopped, listening. There was another sound from outside, this time, certainly, footsteps. Someone was coming along toward the shed door, moving carefully as if not wanting to be heard.

Connie froze.

If Amos came down to make her go home, he might use force; he was capable of it. She set her teeth.

If he wants a fight, he can have one, and if he wants to cart me, screaming, through town, he can have that, too.

It wasn't Amos.

She let her breath go with relief as Everard Peterson stuck his whiskery face around the jamb of the door and pulled back out of sight. She heard him grunt and puff, as if lifting a weight; then he came in, carrying a burlap bag, partly full, across the shed floor. She was about to speak to him when he put one foot down on a dab of cat food, slipped, and barely saved himself from going sprawling.

"Well, goddam!" Everard said. "Who around here is laying booby traps for a man?" He stared this way and that, as if he expected whoever it was to come out of the woodwork. "Oh," he went on, peering near-sightedly down. "You cats tooken to going in the shed now, I see. Begun being nasty in the outbuildings. That is one thing I would not put up with from a cat."

He upended the sack and shook it, filling the white-agate dish pan to overflowing with chunked-up meat. "There you are, you old yaller devil," he said. Putting out a hand, he scratched Herbert on the head and up and down the spine, an attention which Herbert, already busy, did not deign to notice.

"All right, then. You eat up and enjoy," Everard said darkly. "Becuz if I strain my laig again in here over your cussed actions, what you will get from old Everard is a nice little surprise."

So that's why they won't touch cat food, Connie thought. They're used to something tastier. And more expensive, I'll say. That looks like fresh stew beef, and if it is—why, there must be four or five dollars' worth. What goes on, with Clementina herself living on soup?

For the second time she was about to make herself known, step out of the entry, when Everard, out of the pocket of his coat, produced a bottle. She watched him hide it on the shelf and then take down a covered tin can, from which he pulled some bills and change. He counted the money, thrust it into his pocket.

"Everard," Connie said. "What on earth are you doing?"

Everard jumped and spun, dropping the sack, which he had started to fold up. "Eh?" he said. "Who hollered at me?"

"I didn't holler," Connie said. "I just want to know what you think you're doing." She stepped into view from the entry.

Everard recoiled. "Who's that?" he said. "I don't recall knowing who you are."

"Of course you know me. I'm Connie Wilkinson. Does Clementina pay you to bring gin here?"

"Why, so 'tis!" Everard said. "Warn't expecting nobody. Thought you was one of them noises in my head."

"Well, I'm likely to be. A loud one. If you don't answer me. Does she, or doesn't she?"

"I don't have no idea in the world what you might be talking about," Everard said. He blinked once, and went on. "Clem pays me to bring meat scraps to the cats. Now, you look-a here, I've gone to trouble. I ain't going to give no money back, now!"

"I should think you had gone to trouble. What did you do—kill somebody's cow?"

"Cow?" Everard stared at her and then took swift umbrage. "I kill a cow? For meat?" Who ever heard of such a thing? "I will have you to know I ain't et a piece of cow beef in forty years, and who are you, I would like to ask, going around accusing people of a state's prison offense like killing people's cows? There's laws to protect a man, let me tell you, Miss Twippet, and you are going to have them on you!

I never killed no cow, this meat is—" He pulled himself up in time. "This is meat-market scraps."

"It certainly doesn't look like scraps to me."

"Well, it is, too. I bring it, Clem pays me. A honest business deal. You got no right to—"

"What about that bottle of gin?"

"What bottle? I put it to you, if I was so lucky as to of had a bottle of gin, would I of give it to Clem?"

"Everard, I saw you."

"You never saw nothing to mention. I heard round town you been sick, acting funny. Something in it, is they?"

It had been a nerve-racking day. Connie's temper let go; she could almost hear a sound when it snapped. She came across the shed floor in a rush and snatched the bottle down from the shelf.

Seeing her face, Everard backed away, turned and scrabbled out the door, rounding the opening just in time. The bottle missed him by inches. Connie heard it smash, outside, against a rock.

"Good God!" somebody said. "Hold everything, whoever you are. It's only me and I'm coming in."

Dr. Garland put his head cautiously around the edge of the door. "Brother!" he said. "Look at that old bayster leg it, I'll bet his blood pressure's up."

Connie stared at him wordlessly. She sat down on one end of the bench, the other end of which was buried in a rosette of cats with their heads in the dish pan.

"Serve him right," Garland said, coming in. "Too bad you hadn't nailed him dead center. Nellie's been trying for weeks to find out who's been sneaking bottles in here. How are you? Over your flu?"

"Yes," Connie said. "But I've just been told I'm crazy."

"By Everard? No doubt he thinks you are. Throwing away good liquor." He grinned. "It's a crazy situation, as near as I can tell. Nellie is put out with it. I thought I had better drop by and—" He looked around for a place to sit down, settled on a nearby keg, and dropped his bag between his feet. "You wouldn't believe it of Nellie, but she is sensitive about this."

"Sensitive!" Connie said. "She's about as sensitive as a road scraper."

"Uh huh, she's a tough customer; in her work she has to be. Sensitive in her inner feelings, I mean. Nobody's ever put anything over on Nellie, her bedside manner's always worked before."

"Yes, I saw some of her bedside manner."

"M'm, she's a dandy nurse, really. It's been her experience that most people like to be bullied, be a good child and Mama will cope. They love it."

"Clementina's an adult."

"Sure. To Nellie, there're only two kinds—some people and sick people. She treats them all alike."

"She rides roughshod over—"

"She's busy as hell. She's tended out here for weeks," Garland said. "The old lady's been on the town's conscience for a long time, seeing your people wouldn't do anything for her. We've all tried. Some of the women've been down to clean, and—" He grinned at her amiably. "What's the matter? Whose responsibility do you figure it is, anyway?"

"Are you trying to tell me I—Look," Connie blazed, "I know whose it is. It's mine. Or would have been if I'd known anything about it. My father took my letters to her out of the post office. She couldn't write me because she didn't have my address. In the past, at times, he's taken her income checks. She's been alone, with nobody she could trust, and not enough money to live on. What do you think it's been like? Your nice ladies and their damn good will, yes, they came down to clean. They also came down to underrun the house. And if you want a fine sample of the town's conscience, regard for a sick old lady, that's the way the woodyard delivers wood here"—she pointed through the open shed door—"all the way from the shed to the street! All the do-gooders, are they cripples? The minister has time to sit and yammer about Heaven, with the wood wet in the back yard and no fire in the sitting-room stove for weeks—and you come down here and tell me I've hurt Nellie Overholt's feelings!"

"Oh, brother!" Garland said. "You've got to allow a little something for old age—typical persecution delusions—" he began.

"I don't know you very well, I don't even know what kind of a doctor you are. But if Clementina is an alcoholic somebody has to help us. Somebody responsible—"

"Yes. Of course. Now that you're here, somebody she trusts, maybe we'll get somewhere. I'll examine her," he said, keeping his voice dry, professional. "We'll make sure exactly what her state is."

"Don't you know?"

"As of the moment? No. I checked"—when had it been? A month ago? Two months?—"but Nellie said things were going along normally, so—Oh, hell!" he burst out. "The trouble with a single doctor in a town this size, there's never time enough. Nobody gets enough medical attention. Everybody gets a little, but—"

"And Clementina's old and no use to anyone," Connie said. "The savages did it better, they carried the old and infirm out of the cave. But we've got progress, we're more subtle. We expose the spirit to that inclement weather, we find it just as deadly."

"Oh, hey, hold up," Garland said, but she had turned her back on him and was facing the cobwebby shed window. From motions she made with her handkerchief, he judged she was crying.

Phew, what a little fire-eater, he thought. Must be the red hair.

He stared thoughtfully at the stiff, resisting back. The last time Constance Wilkinson had been in his mind, he remembered, he'd done considerable speculating about her, and had rejected the notion as improbable. Now, seeing her face to face, he wondered again. His experienced eye chalked up some telltale signs—the look around the eyes, a certain fullness of breast; and, to anyone who had reason to make the connection, the unmistakable resemblance. That hair, he thought; as if she and J. J. Randall flew the same glorious flag.

But, "Carry the old and infirm out of the cave?" Who, knowing what had happened, would dare to say that? Hell, the logical ending to that remark would be, "And chuck the newborn onto the town dump."

I am getting some goddam old mad, wound up in this to the neck. All right, I asked for it, but—

Of course she didn't know. She was no calloused, tough little nut; she was a damned nice girl, or looked to be.

But I'll bet, if I've guessed right, that her father knows. That guy's capable of anything.

Some of it certainly could be so. From the way Amos Wilkinson had ranted around Garland's office trying to get Clementina committed, you knew, all right, where he stood: Carry the old lady out of the cave. Or into an insane asylum, what difference? All one to him. Or let her die at home of loneliness and alcohol, and help her along some, if it was true that the cold-blooded son had been swiping her money. Well, the old, the aged, had it to take; it was nothing more nor less than what was coming up for everybody. Abandoned, not entirely to ill will, but to good will as well—the homes for the aged; the unregarded corner of the son's or the daughter's house. A damned good thing the failing faculties made perception less keen to savor the left-overs, the crumbs falling from the table—a table, maybe, you yourself had bought and, except for hardening of the arteries, might be sitting at the head of now. . . .

Garland shook himself a little impatiently. What am I, he asked himself, a goddam Greek chorus? Of course I should have examined the old girl long before this, should've made time to . . . I might as well admit it.

He stared gloomily at the cats, who were mostly finished with their meal. The big tom, Herbert, had eaten intemperately, he was puffed like a balloon. Some of the others, with their heads in the pan, looked as though they might yet blow up. A cinnamon kitten in the corner apparently had had no share at all; he was nosing distastefully at a dab of cat food, as if making up his mind to eat it; but his whole body yearned toward the pan. As Garland watched, he made a foray, came up against a solid phalanx of furry backs, and retreated with a reluctant hopping step, almost like a ballet dance. A ridiculous object, skinny as a knife; his bones lifted his fur into scraggly humps; his paws, double all around, seemed outsize for such a small construction.

Well, there you had it; it wasn't only the old who were up against the fast operators. The get-in, get-what-there-is, get-out boys, dedicated to making the world a darkling plain where ignorant armies clashed, and not only by night; where the sun rose and shone on the first fast buck and, going down, sparkled merrily on the last one; hell, where was there room on earth for anyone else?

"What's the matter?" Garland said. "Those big hogs got you buffaloed?"

He fished a chunk of meat from the pan, thinking absently, Hey, that's venison, and flipped it toward the corner.

Connie turned to face him. "No, they haven't. And they won't have." She showed no trace of her tears except for a slight redness around the eyelids. She hadn't, as a matter of fact, cried much; the outburst had been mainly stretched nerves and temper not yet quite settled down from the hassle with Everard, though other things entered into it, too. Dr. Garland was the only one who could tell her what she most dearly wished to know; he was here now, at hand. Standing with her back to him, she had been trying desperately to make up her mind, thinking, So much is involved, so many other people; if he doesn't know anything he'll think I'm out of my mind, and . . . and, finally, wait. So Garland was not to know how close he had come to being asked, point-blank, what he could say about J. J. Randall.

"I apologize," she said. "I seem to fall apart easily these days. I'm sorry I said that. Please tell me what to do for Clementina."

"You've already done the important thing," Garland said. "You've caught Everard. We can stop him from lugging any more bottles in here, control it some, taper her off. Of course, she may have a hidden supply. Nellie's hunted, but—you know the house, would you have an idea of where it might be, if any?"

"Yes," Connie said. "You know, I just might." She took three steps across the shed floor.

The hole under the board in the shed had been dug the summer Connie had been nine. She and Clementina had made it as a hiding place for secrets; as with most things Clementina had had a hand in, it had been cleverly done. No one could have told that the board was unnailed or that under it was a compartment lined with brick and waterproof paper, which, in its time, had held many pleasant things—bunches of flowers, notes, playthings, surprises; it had been a great place for surprises. Going there, you looked under the board; almost always there would be something.

It's betraying a confidence. She and I are the only ones who've ever known about it. Connie lifted the board.

The hiding place for secrets was now nearly full—of unopened bottles of gin. Eight or ten bottles, Connie saw at a glance. A secret supply, huddled away where no one could find it. Waiting until she was alone; no one there to say, Stop it, it will kill you . . . Stop, it will make you old and horrible . . .

It was true, then, what they said about Clementina.

Connie dropped the board back into place.

"Well, there it is," Garland said. He put out a hand to help her to her feet. "Now we know. We'll do what we can."

Clementina was not on the sofa; she was not in the chair by the stove.

"Why, I left her here," Connie said. "Clementina? Where are you?"

"What?" Clementina said. She came out of a downstairs bedroom, carrying a broom and a dustpan full of dust kittens, which she carried to the airtight and dumped inside. "I was just getting your room ready," she said. She stopped. "What does he want?" she went on, indicating Garland.

"You're better, Miss Wilkinson," Garland said.

"Yes, I am. Thank you."

"Would you mind if I—" He pulled out his stethoscope.

"Yes, I would mind. I'm sorry, Constance and I are getting ready to go to town."

"It won't take a minute. I just want to listen—"

"Nonsense. I know how I feel."

"All right." Garland coiled up the stethoscope, stuck it back in his pocket. The old lady's color was fine.

"Probably do her good to go," he told Connie.

"I didn't ask you if I could go, young man. I said I was going," Clementina said. "We have shopping to do and a busy afternoon at the hairdresser's. There's nothing fit to eat in the house and no drinking liquor. I can't even offer Constance a decent cocktail before dinner."

"You can't?" Garland said.

Typical alcoholic behavior, he thought. Secretive. Pulling some wool.

"That liquor you have just poked your nose into in my back shed," Clementina said, "is a very nasty brand of cheap, undrinkable gin. My grandnephew, Amos Wilkinson, sends it here, hoping I will go to hell in a handbasket. Up to now I have taken steps to ensure he thinks I am, or he will dream up something worse for me to cope with. I would know Amos is the one who sends it if only by the brand and by the way his mind works. Amos is near; this is costing him. It is for a woman, so rotgut will do."

"I'll be darned," Garland said, looking at her. More woolpulling? Was it?

"I wouldn't touch it with a ten-foot pole," Clementina went on. "And I wouldn't advise you to, Doctor, but you're welcome to all of it if a drink is what you're snooping around my house for at this hour of the day."

The hell you say, Garland said, not aloud.

"And I would not air my family's dirty linen before a stranger, but I can't have Constance thinking I'm an old swill bucket. I will admit Nellie Overholt has smelled liquor here, but not on me; not on my breath. At times she has found opened, half-empty bottles of that stuff left out for her to smash."

"But what did you want to fool her for?" Garland said. "Why?"

"I hoped to," Clementina said with composure. "I will say, it wasn't hard to. Nellie is intemperate about temperance; to her, one swallow makes a bummer. I'm afraid I did aid and abet her notions a little. So that it would get back to Amos his scheme was working. So that he would not dream up something worse, that I might not be able to handle."

"My God," Garland said.

"It got back to him. At least I have been left in peace for a matter of months. He is not easy to cope with, and, alone, I didn't think I could fight my way through another of his shenanigans. Now that I have Constance with me, I can take steps. At the first peep out of him, if he bothers either of us, I am going to have him arrested."

Brother! You know there just possibly could be something to this, Garland thought. By gum, yes, I believe I swallow it. That bastard, getting after an old lady—somebody ought to beat the bejeezus out of him. Maybe somebody did, at that. Whoever it was ought to get a medal.

Clementina said, "As Constance knows, what has always seemed civilized to me is a cocktail before dinner. Or some sherry. I would dearly love some sherry, Connie."

"We'll get some this afternoon," Constance said. She was looking at Clementina, and from her expression, Garland thought, you'd think somebody'd all at once given her a present—something wonderful; something wished for.

"And a steak," Clementina said. "M'm. Cut two inches thick."

"Burnt black on the outside and blood-rare in the middle," Garland said. "Sounds great. Uh—my wife's away."

Clementina gave him a look. "Are you inviting yourself to dinner?" she asked.

"Nothing was further from my mind," Garland said. "I was only thinking that Tony Morelli will cut off a good thick tender sirloin for me, which he won't do unless you stand by and beat him over the head."

Clementina nodded. "Because 'steak,' to Tony, is top of the round, cut thin and fried until it's tougher than the left heel of Lazarus risen," she said. "Talk, talk, talk, that's all you ever do. Sell me a bill of goods." She lifted the cover of the airtight, peered in. "If some nut doesn't stop putting trash into this stove, we'll have a dirty fire tonight and no broiling coals. Well, what a day!" she went on, clapping the cover back on. "I must be crazy. We can have a fire in the fireplace, now, can't we?"

"I would bring butter," Garland said. "And a loaf of French bread, fresh from the bakery. And vinegar and olive oil. Some oregano and blue cheese and garlic."

"And jellies," Clementina said, "I don't doubt, lucent as the creamy curd."

"Uh, sure," Garland said, puzzled. "I guess so, if I can find any."

"And unless you like sherry, you had better bring your own bottle. Nobody drinks any of that rotgut. Not in my house."

Later, around six, Garland came back, his arms laden. From the road, he saw the house lit up as no one had seen it in many months, lamplight streaming from the windows, firelight dancing on the walls. As he brushed through the uncut high weeds on the front walk and stepped up on the porch, he saw, through the window, Clementina, her hair cut short and brushed high in a gleaming white crest. In a black velvet dress and a string of—yes, pearls, she was standing, composed, and as straight as an arrow, looking over a table set with silver and flowered plates, candlesticks and, by gum, wine glasses.

Oh, brother, Garland thought. Let Nellie Overholt once catch me coming into this house with a bottle of Scotch!

And, suddenly, all by himself on the back porch, Garland doubled up, roaring laughing.

Part Four
Christmas, 1959

Winter set in, dark and damp, but not cold. After one big northeast snowstorm, the weather turned mild. A little rain fell, but most days were merely overcast. "Green Christmas," old-timers said, "full graveyard," feeling sad and stiff at the oncoming of the cold, missing it when it did not come.

Christmas, season of the festive Birthday, brightened Main Street. The town tree glittered on the square, wreaths and candles made windows hopefully gay. The competition began, sponsored by the Chamber of Commerce each year, over which householder could put up the most attractive display of colored lights.

The Blandishes usually won it—Lura always went to Bishop for her Christmas lights, ordering the latest, most up-to-date combinations. She had this year a life-sized crèche on the roof of her front porch, complete with Mother and Child, ox, sheep, and ass. It was elaborate and expensive, but somehow not a success. For some reason the scene was embarrassing to most people; not that it should be—it was, of course, the most beautiful and sacred known to man; but somewhere it fell short of intention. Lura had a spotlight on it and had it outlined in blue bulbs, so that it stood out like a lighthouse and could be seen from the top of a hill six miles away. It showed devoutness, all right, and certainly money spent; what was there to criticize? It was hard to say.

It was too real, some said—something about a mother with a newborn baby, life-sized figures, out in the public view; well, after all, such a time in a woman's life ought to be private, hadn't it? For goodness' sake, you knew what a crèche was, and even had one of your own, a little one set back under a corner of the Christmas tree, still . . . it wasn't . . . you come around the corner of Prospect Street, why, that thing took you right in the face, figures like people and just as big. . . . Angie Coons, coming on it unaware, not knowing it was there, took a really bad turn and fled home, crying that she'd seen a ghost. Well, there it was; nobody cared for Lura's crèche; that was all.

The Blandish house was on the west side of Prospect Street, however, so that the open side of the decoration faced east, and the northeast snowstorm, which was a howler, filled the crèche full of snow, crusted so smoothly over the opening that the figures could not even be seen. Lura had to send Harvey Melvin, the Blandishes' hired man, up on the porch roof to shovel it out, and Harvey Melvin was as careful as he could be; but the porch roof sloped and was slippery and Harvey Melvin wasn't as young as he used to be, so that he was nervous of falling. He hurried. After he was through, the figures weren't quite the same; this or that on them looked a little tacky. After someone remarked that it looked as though the Lord didn't care much for Lura's Christmas display, either, things went from bad to worse; someone at Gertie Warren's asked someone else if he'd seen Harve Melvin up on the roof shoveling snow off of Lura Blandish's ass, and this went around the town like wildfire. Tony Morelli won the Christmas-light competition with a spirited homemade rendition of Rudolf the Red-Nosed Reindeer.

Up to the day before Christmas, Amos Wilkinson's house had had no Christmas lights. He had not entered the competition this year, which was unheard of for him; all the church and lodge members always did. This year Amos did not even seem interested. Lucy had put up a few decorations; she had had wreaths for the windows left over from last Christmas and some tinsel of the indestructible variety, but when she had gone to test her strings of lights, she found all the bulbs burned out. Earlier in December, getting ready, she had asked Amos for the usual amount for Christmas light bulbs and had been appalled when he had bawled out, To hell with it, what did she think he was? Rolling?

The way he was now, so worried in his mind and ready to fly out over the slightest thing, she hadn't dared ask him again, though their house, right in the middle of town, without even one string of outside lights, looked very strange indeed. The houses on either side of theirs and up and down the street glittered with lights, and even the poorest people managed something, even if it was only one red bulb over the door.

Lucy was terribly worried—for Amos to be a standout of course meant that he was seriously not himself; but she was terribly embarrassed also, having a bad time whenever she had callers, who would come in and look around and chat and not mention, not one of them, that Lucy didn't have her tree or her lights up yet. It would have been easier to bear if they had, if it didn't mean they were speculating on what was wrong. She couldn't blame anyone for being tactful in a serious matter like no Christmas lights; of course something was wrong, but if only Amos would help, just a little, they could keep it from showing.

Oh dear, Lucy just knew they all thought Amos was having business troubles; when he wasn't, and she knew he wasn't. It had been a mild fall and early winter; the ground hadn't frozen at all; he had two gravel pits working full tilt up to the time of the big snowstorm, and was talking about opening a third—the old Cooney place, he had bought that, and she had heard him say that that seven acres was a gold mine of loam and topsoil. Some of the old Cooneys, years ago, had decided that the best way to get rid of chicken and cow manure was to dump it into the stream that flowed around their place, because they'd had a theory that if you put it on the land, it caused weeds, and to pull weeds, that was work; and why bother when you could get just as good fertilizer out of a sack? So they had filled the entire oxbow of the stream so full that even the spring freshets wouldn't carry the stuff away; one year the stream changed its course after some heavy rains and flowed now down through Cooney's Heath, making the swamp there. Where the oxbow had been, Amos said, was a gold mine if you got at it in a dry season; and this had been a dry season.

Lucy had heard him telling Mack all this, one night in the kitchen. She would have moved out of earshot because she didn't like to hear talk about manure—of course, they wouldn't bother to call it "dressing," as you would do in polite company; men weren't careful; but she was listening with all ears to any of Amos's conversation she could overhear; a wife certainly ought to know what was troubling her husband, making him so strange. She thought, by now, she could guess; but it certainly wasn't business difficulties, she knew that. Among other things, she had peeked into his desk, at his bank balance.

He was badly upset, of course, because Clem was spending all that money on the old Wilkinson house. It was bad enough for Connie to leave home, desert her father and her mother, and go down there to live; but for her to aid and abet Clementina in squandering what rightfully belonged to Amos and should have been kept as a trust—Oh, if Connie weren't your own, you might almost think there was something, well, vindictive about it, because left alone Clem would certainly never—at least she never had. Men hired to cut down the growth on the lawn, grub weeds out of the walk. Carpenters already swarming over the place putting new sills under the house and barn, shingling the roof, mending shutters, replacing old clapboards with new: a major repair job, costing, by the time it was finished, surely into the thousands.

Oh, Clementina was so thoughtless! She always had been. She rode rough-shod, never considering anybody's feelings but her own. All this trouble caused; and even flowerbeds! You had only to drive by to see how they had been spaded into shape again, and loads of dressing hauled to fertilize them for spring planting.

You couldn't deny that Clementina now looked very well. Seen in town as she occasionally was, shopping along Main Street with Connie or at the beauty parlor, she seemed as active as a cricket, nothing out of line that you could lay a finger on. Old, of course, and thin, but her hair stood up in a crest as it had used to do, and her clothes, well, in the same colors, a little too gay, Lucy had always felt, for an elderly person.

She had come face to face with Clementina in the supermarket one day; and Clementina had smiled and spoken as if, for goodness' sake, nothing had ever gone wrong; but Lucy could not bring herself. . . . She had looked straight ahead and gone on by. She would have spoken to Connie, Lucy told herself, if Connie had been there; of course, Amos had forbidden it, and . . . but your own daughter whom you loved and in the same town and not seeing—mother love yearned after Connie, and it was not possible for anyone, not even Amos, to forbid mother love. But Clementina had been alone, and there, parked at the curb outside the market, was that awful jeep that Amos had been so put out about; which had been, for him, just about the straw that broke the camel's back.

You had only to look at it to know that it was special, and expensive, even if you did not know what the Willys dealer had told around town: how Clementina had come in and had sat right down then and there and had written him out a check for it; and the size of the check! And for something not suitable, not even for a . . . a flapper! It was loud; vulgar. Cream-white, with white sidewalls, red trim, and a white nylon top; and seats of bright-red leather.

True, if Connie were going to live down there, she would need transportation. A jeep, perhaps, or something of the kind, where the road was bad, and winter, if normal, would mean deep snow. The driveway to the old house, built in the days of buggies and sleighs, was long; the ridge left by the snowplow along the roadside was two to four feet deep sometimes. And, oh, Connie ought not to wade snow! So perhaps a jeep was justified, but a secondhand one would have done as well. Nothing justified all that expense and ostentation. Clementina, of course, knew how Amos felt; and Connie . . . after I took such care to bring her up to do unto others . . . if she could just see how worried her father is now! Nightmares, and not sleeping, and going out to walk nights, and not caring what people thought— certainly they must think something, no Christmas decorations.

Whenever anyone came in now, Lucy would say at once how hard it was to find a really good-shaped tree, implying that she had hunted for one, which wasn't really a fib so long as she didn't actually say she had.

The neighbor would agree that it certainly was. "Hunt and hunt the woods, they've all got something the matter—either scraggly tops or whopper-jawed on one side."

Of course, there was that little kit you could buy that would stick extra branches on a tree, or a new top on to make it look pretty, but it cost; and times were getting some old tough, weren't they, when you couldn't even find a decent-looking Christmas tree in the woods? And never again would Lucy put off buying Christmas lights until they were all sold out at the five-and-ten, she'd certainly got caught short this year; of course, Aurora Collins, down at the hardware, still had some, but her prices were out of all reason, and the five-and-ten said their shipment was due . . .

"Oh," the neighbor might say, "that shipment's here, Lucy, the five-and-ten had plenty this afternoon." Or, "Why don't you drive out to Frank Saunders's, he's got two carloads of Christmas trees he cut to ship out that never sold, so he's going to have to burn them. He'd sell one cheap, or maybe even give it away."

And Lucy would vow that she'd do that very thing, say how grateful she was to the neighbor for telling her about this good chance. But she did not go. She dithered, wondering what would be the practical thing to do . . . with poor Amos so . . . so touchy.

A few days before Christmas, she rigged up and went out in the back pasture by herself. The snow was melting, but it was still so deep that she couldn't tell whether a small tree was pretty or not, and walking was terribly hard. She finally succeeded in haggling the top off a fir which stuck out of a drift, and managed to get it home and set up in the parlor. Usually they had their tree in the dining room where it was warmer, but the way Amos felt . . . and he didn't go into the parlor much, perhaps he'd be better by the time he saw it. Time, of course, would heal. Time always did. The trouble was, there wasn't much time. She was going to have to trim the tree with last year's things: there were only a few of them, too.

There were no presents to go under the tree, at least, no surprises, but that wasn't anything new. Amos had never been one to bother with Christmas presents. His feeling was that such foolishness was beneath the man of the house, let the women tend to it. So Lucy, in the years when Connie had been growing up, had always bought Amos's presents for Connie and herself and had wrapped them and put them under the tree. The real presents never made very much of a show, though; not only your tree, but what was under it made a great difference, because people always called around to see how yours compared with theirs. Lucy had licked this problem, years ago; there was more than one way of showing the neighbors that the Wilkinsons always got a lot. It might be just a teeny bit deceitful; but she guessed that God in his infinite wisdom would know what her bounden duty was: to keep up appearances for Amos, use her head to have things the way he wanted them. She always saved the Christmas wrapping paper, folded it carefully, laid it away in the closet; then, next year, just before the Day, she would use it to wrap up anything in the house she could lay hands on—a vase or a set of dish towels, or a kitchen utensil that didn't look too used to be passed off as new; or things of Amos's—he had once nearly torn the house down looking for a sprocket wrench he had bought new and left, he was sure, on the windowsill in the kitchen. Fuming, not bothering to tell Lucy what he was looking for, he had decided the wrench was lost and had gone out and bought another. Then, to his fury, the first one was presented to him on Christmas morning as a gift.

Connie, even as a child, had always known that of all that tremendous display of gaily wrapped parcels under the tree, only one or two would amount to anything; the rest would contain what Lucy merrily called, "Some Little Thing."

Lucy was tired after her trip to the pasture, but she spent the afternoon making her preparations for Christmas; after all, it was late, there wasn't much time. She trimmed the tree, carefully stretching out last year's decorations, thinking sadly that no matter how she pulled and covered, the tree looked bare. Oh, if things were only the way they used to be, she could have made it look lovely with strings of cranberries and popcorn; but, my goodness, if you did that now, people would have it all over town in no time that you were ready for Over The Hill To The Poorhouse.

That secondhand wrapping paper looked so tacky, too; she had used it, she thought, over and over for just too many years.

Oh, if Amos were only . . . usually he put up a dreadful fuss if their decorations weren't as good as the ones his lodge brothers had . . . this year, he didn't seem to care at all about his appearances. Poor dear, he just wasn't . . . he was sick, he must be, and never a one to complain about his symptoms . . . if only I just dared to sneak down and consult with Dr. Garland. . . .

She was dispiritedly wrapping up a set of glass tumblers which she had bought last summer from the five-and-ten with money squeezed from the housekeeping and had put away with Christmas in mind—by Christmas time, they would need tumblers; poor Amos broke so many—when a car stopped outside. A truck, it sounded like, but it couldn't be him, home this early. No, it wasn't; whoever it was tried the back door and then pounded briskly; if it had been Amos, he would have let out a yell. Lucy had taken to locking the door lately so that the neighbors, thinking she wasn't home, would go away. So close to Christmas and so ill-equipped, she'd got to feeling that she simply couldn't cope with anybody, though sooner or later, she knew, she'd have to.

She peered cautiously out of the window, moving the curtain ever so little, so that whoever it was wouldn't . . . and the first thing to meet her eye was the red-and-white jeep, backed up to the door, with Connie, pink-cheeked and glowing and in a new coat, pulling out a beautiful, tall green tree.

The first thing she thought—and Lucy told herself, Wasn't it odd how your mind would bounce around?—was *O Tannenbaum. O fir tree bright, O fir tree dear.*

She stood for a moment uncertainly. Her feet, it seemed, all by themselves wanted to walk over to the door and had to be prevented, so that, one after the other, they teetered forward a step and were pulled back. She swayed, with a shuffling motion, in the middle of the floor.

I can't let her in. Oh dear. What shall I do?

Her heart yearned toward Connie. It would be so lovely to see her and talk. It's been so long . . . but Amos has forbidden. . . . To turn my own child away from . . . with a tree for her father and her mother. It's *Christmas*. Just this one time . . . No. I can't go against Amos.

Connie, however, wasn't one to give up. She turned away from the locked door; but instead of going down the steps, she walked across the porch and looked in at the window.

Oh, mercy, right into my face! Lucy thought. She gasped, put both hands to her cheeks, and closed her eyes.

"Ma! I knew you were in there! You let me in! Come on now, stop being foolish. It's Christmas."

Lucy began to cry. She stood for a moment with the tears running helplessly through her fingers; then she thought of a solution. She wiped her cheeks with the palms of her hands, bent down, and wrote busily on the blank back of an old Christmas card, with the pencil she had been using to write hers and Amos's names on the bogus packages. Because it was a card, her hand through years of habit inscribed it as one; it read, when she held it against the windowpane:

> Dear Connie,
> Please go away. Your father says I can't speak to you.
> Love,
> Mother

Connie turned red. She pulled back a doubled fist. "Ma! If you don't let me in, I'll break the window!"

"Oh, mercy, no!" Lucy said.

Connie would, too. She . . . had a terrible temper, too.

Lucy flew to unlock the door.

Connie marched straight across the kitchen floor; she kissed Lucy hard on the cheek. "Merry Christmas, Ma," she said. "I've got the prettiest tree I could find, and your Christmas from Clementina and me," she said. "And in this bundle"—she pulled a small jeweler's box from the pocket of her coat—"is the hatchet. Please bury it, honey."

"Oh," Lucy said. She was so glad to see Connie that it seemed as if the whole sad worldful of worry had turned itself right around and, suddenly, was happy. Connie come home, and, oh, Christmas, and all the good gifts of Christmas, the scattered parts together and whole again! And almost at once, she thought, oh, Amos, and oh, he'll never stand for having her in the house or anything she's brought, I must get her out before he gets home, or . . .

She began to cry again, the tired tears trickling helplessly down.

Connie dropped the package on the table; she put both arms around Lucy and hugged her close; but her eyes over her mother's head were hard as stones.

Damn him! she thought. Damn him and his horrible, cruel, stubborn, peanut mind.

Lucy said, muffled, "Honey, you'll have to go before he comes, he's asked me not to . . ."

"Yes, I know. But it's Christmas. And I had to try, didn't I?"

"Oh, I hoped you would, but I was . . . I'm scared, Connie. Your father's not well . . . not himself. I . . . it's tempting Providence for us to go against him. Against nature."

And what is nature? Connie thought bleakly. This relationship between two people, a man and a woman, without dignity? Because one is a slave and the other can't establish his own identity unless he has slaves around; unless he is the Great Master with all the slaves looking up from under his feet, letting him know he is God. I guess a lot of people feel it's nature. But I don't. It makes me want to vomit. It's the terrible thing that's the matter with people, with humans, why their world is always a mess; somebody thinks he's got to be the boss, tramp everyone else down. It isn't decent or anything anyone could ever build on; it's a child's relationship to the world and the people in it. I . . .

She shook Lucy lightly and smiled into the teary face.

"Never mind, Ma. I'll go. I had to say Merry Christmas and I love you, didn't I?"

"Oh, Connie, how could you?" Lucy sobbed. "Leave us and go down there and get Clem to spend all that money—he'll never forgive you for it, I know he won't, and that money is really his, dear. It's only through the kindness of his heart that Clem has got it at all."

"Yes. I know how he thinks, Ma. I'm sorry."

Poor Ma, you're brainwashed, I can't do anything for you.

"I brought you a whole mess of Christmas decorations, among other things," Connie said. She didn't add that the decorations had been Clementina's idea, who, when she realized that Connie was going to see her mother, had said, "Get her a jeepload of the prettiest stuff you can buy, Connie; for once, give her a *real* Christmas." And, uncomfortable, Connie had known that Clementina was right. New decorations and modern; something money had been spent on, that people could see—it would indeed make Lucy's Christmas.

Connie carried in the tree and the bundles she had brought, which were many—and, she thought, for once with something in them. She kissed Lucy again and quietly went away.

She had put the tree in the usual corner where the family had always had their Christmas—beside the bookcase in the dining room. At first Lucy thought, I will have to drag it out and leave it somewhere. But wherever she put it, Amos would be sure to see it and ask questions. And it's such a pretty tree, one of the nicest-shaped I've ever seen, and Connie went to all the trouble of having a metal standard put on it.

She stood looking at it. Presently she tried under it one of the packages Connie had brought, just to see. . . . It looked lovely.

Oh, I am a traitor, she thought, handling Connie's packages. Worse than Benedict Arnold!

So many . . . so many . . . the child had been extravagant; even some for Amos! All beautifully wrapped and tied. Cute little ribbon bows. Look how she made those; I must remember, for next year. Christmas stickers, that new kind; so expensive, oh, dear . . .

She began pinching the bundles, trying to guess what could be inside each one. But the wrapping had been cleverly done; she couldn't tell a thing.

The bad feelings began to go away from Lucy. There! She should have known they would! But it was when she looked into the big box of new wrapping paper, the best, and Christmas decorations, that sorrow and worry left for good and were replaced by the mood of anticipation and mystery appropriate to the season.

Oh! The lovely things!

An angel with shining nylon wings, encrusted with something that sparkled like true frost, for the very top of the tree. Boxes of tinsel streamers; Christmas balls of assorted sizes to hang from twigs like globes of exotic fruit; synthetic icicles; small objects of all kinds, marvelously shaped to catch light, to reflect, to glitter, to gleam. All the things she had admired for years in the shops at Christmas time and had never dared to buy.

Christmas lights. *Three different kinds*, she thought, in a kind of passion of bliss hanging things on the tree. Oh, who except the Blandishes ever had three kinds; and, as well, a string of bubble lights which, when turned on, produced a procession of pure bubbles, endlessly climbing into candles of colored glass.

She could hardly wait to finish the trimming and turn on the tree. When she did, it looked so beautiful to her that she sat, flat on the floor, just looking. Everybody would think now that she had held back on this glorious display just to surprise people. She felt—why, she felt *holy*, of course she did; it was Christmas, wasn't it, Our Saviour's Birthday, a time for feeling holy, and happy, too.

Connie and Clementina were planning a quiet Christmas Eve, with a tree and presents for each other; but Christmas Day, Clementina said, had no right to be quiet; Christmas was for children. So she had invited Miles Garland and his wife and family for dinner; let there be, for heaven's sakes, some kids around the house—the more racket the better. She was planning wonderful things to do to a Christmas turkey.

Joe Randall, the wound of his loss still raw, was bracing himself to spend the first Christmas without Amy. He went out and bought all kinds of presents for his triplets and for Angie, spending more than he could afford in his hope, unfounded, that even with the kids, Christmas could still be Christmas. He prayed that the day could pass without a ruckus between Angie and the new housekeeper, a stout woman from Bishop, who seemed capable enough and who, so far, had managed, but every day now teetered on the edge of leaving. Joe knew that sooner or later he would have to do something about Angie—send her away to a home for the aged; she was getting worse as time went on. But he couldn't bring himself to take the step; the punishment seemed to him out of proportion to the crime. She had never been easy to get along with, God knew; but could she help it if old age built up in her this torrent of mistaken responsibility? She loved her home and she loved Joe. The responsibility was his. He would put it off, anyway, he told himself, until after Christmas. Angie loved a Christmas tree.

Everard Peterson, it looked as if, unless a miracle happened, would be spending Christmas in jail.

Nellie Overholt had got for each of her girls a new dress and, for Henry, a suit. The clothes were utilitarian; Nellie told herself that on the money she made, they had to be, though she had not actually bought them. She had picked up an oddment here and there, where it would not be missed, from the supplies issued by the Welfare for the needy and the poor. Well, all right—who was needy and who was poor? Beck wanted a catcher's glove, and Kate would mourn if she did not get a new set of oil paints, and Henry had his heart set on a sled; but Nellie was no millionaire. She planned to get out of the house, anyway, on Christmas morning, so as not to have to listen to them. Christmas, anyway, was the day she paid her annual visit to Gert.

Jody Morelli, he told everyone, was going to have a new brother for Christmas. The doctor was bringing it in a basket.

If Anzio Ernest Enoch Grindle the Third Jones had known how he was spending Christmas, he would not have cared for where he was, nor for the situation he was in, which for once he could not run away from or change. He had lain in the sun as long and as lazily as even he could have wished; but he lay, too, in wind and rain, the fine clothes rotting to scraps and tatters, the supple muscles falling away from the long, perfect skeleton. Only the expensive leather jacket and the boots were left to recognize of all his magnificence dumped untidily beside a fallen tree near the hummock in Cooney's Heath. For a while, the swamp's small animals busily had come and gone. Crows had called in, wrangled, and flown away. The northeast snowstorm that wrecked the Blandishes' crèche howled over the swamp for a night and a day, burying him under three feet of soft, unbroken white, so that the moon riding over the trees on Christmas Eve showed not even a mound where the fallen tree was; but the same moon, changing, brought a change in the weather—overcast, puffy clouds, a warm wind that blew for three days and three nights, melting snow, presaging rain.

Night and day the worry ate at Amos Wilkinson, growing worse as time went on.

Nobody goes off the trail in Cooney's Heath; nobody has for years. But what if somebody did? And run acrost that feller where I left him? A night animal—them wild dogs; a bear or a bobcat—could drag some part of him into the trail where it could be found, say anyone happened to go there. Then it would be known there was a dead body somewhere; there'd be a hunt for it. Somebody would go in then, all right.

He couldn't get it out of his thoughts now; his mind seemed automatic. He would try to think of something else; then, before he realized, he would be back, raking over possibilities in spite of himself.

I ought to have put him in deep, when I had the chance to. Out of sight for good and all. I couldn't have dug, the shape I was in; but I could have found a muck hole, shoved him in. His wallet must still be in his pocket telling who he is, and he could be traced to Connie. And back to me.

Lying in bed, awake, at night or while working during the day, he would riddle away at consequences. What might happen. If.

It could be proved easy enough that he hadn't got hurt moving a bulldozer. Mack Jensen, for one, knew he hadn't; Mack was still ribbing Amos, now and again when he thought of it, wagging his big, fat mouth. "That fight you had—down at Gertie's, was it? What did the other fellow look like, for godsake?"

Well, so long as Amos had the upper hand, Mack wouldn't dare to talk that around town. But let Amos get into trouble once, let him be suspected by the law. Mack would be the first one—Amos knew Mack. Whose nose was about as deep into "A. Wilkinson, Contracting," as it could be while he remained an employee. As a matter of fact, he no longer considered himself one because he'd put some money into the business. Not enough, Amos kept telling himself, to carry much weight, but legally enough so that Mack could run the business as part-owner, say Amos had the bad luck to go to jail, or whatever might happen. Mack, moneywise, would be a lot better off if anything happened to Amos.

At first Amos had had it figured that the thing to do would be to get Mack into the family, marry Connie to him. A man's son-in-law would be loyal, couldn't be expected to turn on him. Then one night, lying awake, it came to Amos what a fool he'd been to think so.

I must be crazy. A man's son-in-law would be the logical one to take over. With me gone, he'd be solid. God, it's a good thing I didn't get after Connie harder. Because she'd have done it. She'd have done what I told her in the end, blast her.

He shuddered, feeling cold as ice, thinking how close he'd come to going down there, to Clem's, and snaking Connie home.

Connie—there was another one who knew he hadn't got hurt on Sunday. And Lucy. Lucy knew he'd been in the swamp all day Monday, hadn't got home till near dark. And Lucy was a fool—any officer of the law, questioning her, could get at the truth in five minutes.

No, let once that body be found, identified, it would be all up with Amos Wilkinson. Half-a-dozen men on that boat would know the feller'd left there Monday morning. God, you'd think I'd at least have had the sense to take his wallet, bury it in the mud. Maybe I'd better make a few partridge-hunting trips around the Heath. . . .

But the thought of setting foot in Cooney's Heath filled him with loathing. The thing in there must be horrible by now, nothing a living man ought to have to bring himself to see.

And if squirrels, the goddam things, that ought to be holed up for the winter in hollow trees by now, were still chittering around the gravel pits and in the maples on a man's lawn outside his bedroom window at night, then Cooney's Heath would be full of them.

Damn and blast a mild winter, when nothing was normal or natural, anyway.

And then, suddenly, came a reprieve to worry: the snow that fell just before Christmas. A walloping great northeast snowstorm.

Three feet of it, he told himself, riding home with Mack Jensen in the truck on Christmas Eve. Something, for once, for instead of against. That fall of snow as much as told him in words that he wasn't intended to be found out. It was something solid to hold to, like catching onto a big, reassuring hand.

The steady hand of God, he told himself, recalling a sermon he'd once heard that had appealed to him. What to hell's been the matter with me?

With luck, that snow would stay on all winter, and by spring there couldn't be anything left to identify.

I'm safe enough, anyway. I always was. Nobody's been in there since the Indians.

He and Mack had been down to the pit, checking on the machinery. All work, of course, had stopped because of the snow, but the storm had sneaked in on them—it hadn't even been forecast by the weather bureau; nobody had expected snow, certainly not so much of it, and Amos and Mack had got caught with the heavy equipment out. Normally, Amos would have been roaring mad about this; he would have cursed his luck all the way home. But tonight, as the truck rolled along through the snowy streets, he was chipper as a sparrow. He was able at last to notice how the houses of his neighbors looked, dressed up for Christmas, to think of his own house in comparison.

"Pull up at the five-and-dime, will ya, Mack?" he said. "I got a little last-minute shopping."

Inside, he grumbled because the stock of Christmas lights was low; wasn't much left, everything was picked over. He made his dissatisfaction known to the clerk, who, since it was Christmas Eve and within two minutes of closing time and she out on her feet, snapped back that anybody putting off buying lights till this late date would have to take what there was.

"Well, you tell your boss next time to order enough to go round, not to be so damn cheap," Amos said, and wondered why she looked so put out—good God, these young kids, what was the matter with them, couldn't they take a joke?

Not waiting for his bundle to be wrapped, he went back out and climbed into the truck, wondering if Lucy had had sense enough to get a Christmas tree. Probably not; she wouldn't think of anything unless he got behind her and shoved, so maybe better pick up a tree on the way home, too. He was thinking this, craning his neck at the shops to see who might have a tree left, when Mack said, "Kind of late with your Christmas decorations, ain't you?"

"Yup," Amos said. "Meant to do it yesterday, but I got snarled up, thinking of all that stuff out in the snowstorm. Forgot it."

"Well," Mack said, "the way the weather looks, I guess we won't need to worry about plowing a road out of there with the 'dozers."

Snarled up yesterday! he thought. Hell, the old polecat's been spitting brimstone for weeks, or don't he know he has?

Well, who cared? It was Christmas Eve, and as soon as he got rid of Amos, Mack was headed for a party.

"What are you talking about, we won't have to plow a road?" Amos demanded. "There's three feet of snow in the pit."

"Ain't you noticed the weather? Look at them clouds. And smell it. Going to rain, or I'll miss my guess. Well, that ought to cheer us with a little Christmas cheer. Lay home in bed all day, let the Lord do the plowing."

Mack, who had been humming under his breath a tune that was

running in his head, burst out into cheerful song about his baby, who was some baby and the only one for him, but, reminded by talk of the snow of something he had just heard in the Downtown Diner, broke off to tell Amos, who had his head out the truck window and was staring at the sky.

"Hey, Ame, did you hear about old Ev Peterson trying to diddle the game wardens?"

Everard, up to Christmas week, had been still calling regularly at the post office for Amos's plain envelope, taking the money and buying a fifth of gin; but he wasn't taking the bottles down to Clementina's. The plain truth of the matter was, he told himself, he didn't dare to.

That girl down there was crazy. She belonged to Amos Wilkinson all right, just as soon crown a man with a bottle as look at him. Pretty nigh got him dead center; smashed a whole fifth of nice gin, too. Could have killed him dead; besides, he wasn't going to be a party to lugging good liquor into a place where it would be thrown away. Let old Clem scrange up her own meat scraps; Everard Peterson was not going a-near. As long as Amos wanted to pay for a fifth a week, or every so often, Everard couldn't see a good reason for stopping him. How would Amos know what was done with it, anyway—hold up Everard on the street, maybe, and ask in the full vision of all and Sunday what become of the booze he sent down to his old aunt, so's she'd die of a drunk and he'd have all her money?

The result of this logic was, for Everard, a fine, full-blooming case of the D.T.'s, which came close to killing him. Dr. Garland called the ambulance and had him taken to the hospital, from which, pumped out, rested, fed, and refreshed, he emerged healthier than he had been in years. He felt so well, indeed, that he went straight out into the snowy woods, where, experience informed him, deer would be yarded up, and shot two bucks—one for his food supply and one to keep his hand in, make sure that a stay in the hospital hadn't spoilt his aim any.

His enemies, the game wardens, however, also had known where the deer were yarded. They found the corpses, minus a hind quarter each, and to Everard's astonishment showed themselves capable of following snowshoe tracks through snow. They norated around his house with a search warrant and discovered the two hind quarters of deer meat hanging in the cold room under his barn.

"Them," Everard said with dignity, "is what is left from the buck I tagged last fall. A man is 'lowed one buck, or ain't you fellers got enough to do, so's but what you got to nikkle with the legal deer?"

The thing was, the wardens pointed out, the trout in the milk: tracks in the snow, hind quarters from two different deer.

"Why, ain't no such a thing!" Everard said. "You prove that! Or ain't a man been in the hospital entitled to a peaceful walk by himself in the woods, get his air back? I been talking around town ever since I got that buck over on the hummock in Cooney's Heath last fall, the's ten or a dozen men'll back me up on it, hearn me tell how that feller must've wenched himself or got shot when he was a lamb, so's he was gimpy in one hind laig and that one a lot smaller than the other. Left hind laig, 'twas. Kind of a curiosity, I meant to tell ya about it when I see ya. And, say, when I was over there in the Heath, I found the den where them wild dogs chases the deer that you've been trying to shoot the pack of, holes up during the winter."

This red herring was something, but not enough. The wardens would indeed be glad to know where the wild dogs' den was; but all the same, they had to run Everard in. "Then you'll likely never know where 'tis," Everard said. "I'm a sick man. I go to jail, I'll die there and it'll cost ya for my funeral. Man in my circumstances, I ain't been able to save no money for burying purposes. You fellers is trying to save the deer whilst human beans go hungry, is what you're doing, I s'pose because you wouldn't have no jobs if you didn't. There sure-God ain't no game wardens trying to take care of human beans. I knock down a deer to keep the breath of life in my body when I'm starving to death, and it to God costs more in this State than it would to the deer if he knocked down me. You wait a month, I'll show you where them dogs is. I ain't, o' course, able nor fitten to track the woods now."

The wardens couldn't promise anything; they had already consulted Dr. Garland and found that Everard was indeed rickety—"Which doesn't mean that he'll conk out tonight," Garland had said. "He's had the condition for years and he'll probably live to be a hundred. Or you could find him dead in bed tomorrow. Going to jail won't hurt him, it'll do him good, keep him off the booze for a while."

So Everard, lacking money to pay his fine, got three months in the county jail.

One of the wardens, picking up supper at the Downtown Diner, had told the story to Mack and had let drop casually that he supposed sooner or later something would have to be done about the wild-dog pack that was thinning out the deer on Cooney's Hummock. Such a hunt appealed to Mack; it was this he had to tell Amos about, on the ride home in the truck on Christmas Eve.

"God darn it, if I wouldn't like to go with 'em," Mack said. "From all I hear, them dogs is wilder'n wolves. That female police dog of Matterson's he lost last fall is with them and they's a couple of big mungrils, part mastiff, I heard. A man could have a hell of a lot of fun, hunt like that. What say we find out when the boys are going, Ame, and go along, declare a holiday? Hell, you know your way around the Heath—they'll likely come to you, anyway, get you to help them track. Some hunt, hey—"

Mack had been prattling along, not glancing at Amos.

He was completely unprepared for Amos's reaction.

"No, by God, you don't!" Amos said. "I don't pay you a day's pay for running around a swamp hunting dogs. Or do I?" His voice was a snarl, and Mack glanced over, astonished.

"Hey, hold up," he said, still jovial. "You don't run of an idea that my pay is day by day now, anyway, do you? Or ain't you got it through your thick head that I own a share in the company? Was I just kidding myself that I bought myself a partnership?"

"I let you buy a share, yes," Amos said. "But, goddammit, you can have your few cents back if you think you ain't still working for me."

"Well, for kuh-riced sake!" Mack said. "What's all of a sudden hit you?" He stopped, considering what Amos had said, and, as it penetrated, indignantly sucked a tooth. "Look, that makes me mad!"

he said. "That wasn't the way I understood it when I handed you what you've got the gall to call a few cents."

"Take it or leave it. That's the way it is."

Amos was sitting with his head hunched into his storm-jacket collar. In the light from the dash, he was merely a dark, lumpy presence, out of which issued the hoarse, unpleasant growl which Mack had heard, at times with a good deal of amusement, directed at others, not often at himself. He thought, bewildered and angry, what to hell's the matter with him; what was there about a dog hunt in Cooney's Heath to touch him off?

"Well, is that so!" he burst out. "By God, Ame, I always heard you was a weasel, but if you try any of your quick tricks on me, you'll wish you'd stood in bed. I bought me a partnership, I was led to think so, and if I want to take a day off when we ain't busy, I will, like it or lump it."

The truck was stopping to let Amos off at his house, but he sat for a moment without moving. "The deal was if you married Connie. You didn't. So no deal. If it rains tomorrow, you go down to the pit and fix that stalled truck."

"Oh, yeah?" Mack said. Furious now, he thumped one fist against the steering wheel. By accident, he hit the horn button, which gave off a strangled, choked-out blat. Neither of them heard it. "If that's the way it is," Mack bawled, "by jeezus, we'll take it to court and find out what the hell I did buy from you!"

Talking to the old man like that, he expected an instant showdown, and at the moment would have welcomed it. Up to now the thought had never entered his head that Amos didn't consider him a partner, full-fledged, with a partner's rights. Mack had even told around town that he was. It occurred to him now that if Amos didn't back him up in the matter, he stood to lose considerable face, some might even call him a liar. This had to be fixed up, and soon. Mack leaned across the cab, hollering at Amos; and Amos didn't turn a hair. He didn't answer, even; a thing unheard of, because if there was one thing Amos did, it was talk back. But without a word, he suddenly scrabbled open the cab door, got down out of the truck, and stalked off toward his house.

Hell, what ails the bugger, Mack thought; he must be sick. And then, God darn, he must be! What would he part with two bucks for more Christmas lights for, when his house is lit up like a whore's wedding?

He stared for a moment at Connie's decorations, which, considering the time she'd had, Lucy had made a good deal of; and then, bewildered and red-eyed mad, Mack drove off to his Christmas party.

Lucy had just finished putting up the last of the outside lights and had been standing out on the walk, admiring the effect, when she heard the truck coming. She had flicked inside and was sitting by the table, thinking how surprised he would be. Their house looked as handsome as any house on the street, if she did say so as shouldn't; and, when Amos came in, she looked up, pleased as a child, saying nothing, waiting for him to say so, waiting for the look on his face when he saw the pretty tree.

In the olden days, when Christmas tree decorations were naked candles clipped to the twigs of firs or spruces, a house fire on Christmas Eve hadn't been out of the ordinary; but modern tree-trim had changed all that. The Fire Department, therefore, called out at suppertime to a chimney fire at Amos Wilkinson's house, was inconvenienced and some members were mad, because, after all, Christmas Eve . . . but they had to go. It was an old bowser of a fire, the main chimney on Amos's house standing up like a torch against the night sky, turning the snow pink for rods around. For a while, Jack Riley, the Fire Chief, wasn't sure they could confine it to the chimney, but the night was still, warm as spring, so the hose didn't freeze, and Jack had some newfangled chemical stuff. They finally got the blaze calmed down.

Jack, who had gone down cellar at Amos's the first thing he did, to see what was making such a helmonious fire in the furnace, said he'd never seen anything like that in his life. "Why," he said, "I come up out of there in a state of shock."

He didn't say at the moment why, not being a gossipy man and there being a lot of people around; but later, in the fire house, while they were putting the equipment away, he did confide in the Assistant Fire Chief.

"That guy must be for godsakes crazy," Jack said. "He had his whole Christmas tree, lights, decorations, presents, and all, stuffed in there on top of his furnace fire, what I could see warn't burnt up. What in thunder's with a man, does a thing like that? Well, I'm glad we got a chance to try out that fancy chemical, anyhow. Now we know what we got. Does a real good job, don't it?"

The Assistant Fire Chief agreed that it did; and he was a gossipy man.

Nellie Overholt, riding over to Gert's on Christmas morning, thought she had never smelt such unpleasant weather. It was muggy and warm, like before a summer thunderstorm; the air felt like a horse blanket. The streets were slippery, running rivers of melting snow; she had to be careful driving, careful how she stopped. Nevertheless she did stop, several times, on her way. She stopped whenever she saw another woman on the street.

"Ain't this awful?" she would call from a distance. "Look out, honey, when I put on the brake, the Ford's going to slew!"

She was full of the Amos Wilkinson chimney fire, as everyone else was, only Nellie had something to add to it; she judged the time had come when she would be justified in mentioning what she knew to a safe, chosen few, though the few who were out this morning weren't quite the ones she would have picked.

Foot on the brake, engine running, never once forgetting first to cry out a cheerful, "Merry Christmas!" Nellie would have over with Aurora Collins or Myrtle Wasgatt or whoever it was what she called "the gory deetles"; they were really something, weren't they?

"Well," she would finish, "I wouldn't mention this to no one, not a soul but you, I know you won't let it go no further, but Dr. Garland told me long ago that Amos Wilkinson is a skit-so. I guess it must run in the family, don't it?"

Sometimes she said "skit-so," sometimes she said "paranoid," or maybe "dementia praecox." It had been a long time since Nellie had studied a textbook, but she guessed she remembered the scientific terms. Didn't matter; they all meant crazy as a loon, and you had to explain them, anyway, to most non-medical people.

By the time she was halfway to Gert's, she was feeling a good deal better, almost "Christmasy." She had certainly felt good and put out when she'd left home, after that go-round with the girls. Granted their Christmas wasn't as flashy as some, how could it be? There were plenty around town who got themselves head over heels in debt so's their kids could have all the knickknacks for presents they wanted; Nellie was not one of them. She cut her sails to fit her cloth, and her kids might just as well find out right now that that was the way to do. Henry, for heb'm sake, wasn't old enough to have a sled, or even to miss having one, and if he had gone around all morning hunting, poking under the Christmas tree and in this or that odd corner of the house, it was because that pesky Beck had put the idea into his head.

That Beck, I got my hands on her this morning, I'd of snatched her baldheaded. I will yet, too, when she comes home.

Kate . . . well, even if she hadn't liked her dress, she'd acted like a lady. You never knew with her whether she liked anything or not, she never said. She'd just opened the package and looked and set it down. But Beck—that Beck, I don't know what'll become of her if she keeps on the way she's headed, she's worse than Gert ever was, she gets a little older, I will certainly have to watch her like a hawk—Beck had looked into her package, let out a holler, and turned red in the face.

"I won't wear any crummy old poor-dress from the Welfare," she'd yelled, and she'd kicked the box halfway across the room.

Well, Nellie certainly wasn't going to have that; she made a grab, but Beck dodged and ran out of the house. Where she was now, Nellie hadn't the slightest; but, she told herself grimly, she'll be home when she's hungry.

Driving along up the street in the direction of Shacktown, Nellie noticed from quite a distance away the baby carriage parked in Joe Randall's driveway. It was the three-passenger perambulator that Joe had bought new, not long ago; the new housekeeper must have put the triplets out for some fresh air. Well, it would do them good, it was plenty warm enough today; but why way out there at the end of the driveway, why not up by the garage? Oh, maybe because it could be seen from the kitchen window, in case of Angie. The driveway had been plowed, back in, and lay between two high banks of snow. Nellie was telling herself, with approval, that that was exactly where she herself would have put it when, to her horror, the baby carriage, seemingly all by itself, started to move. It rolled down across the sidewalk into the street and stopped in front of her car.

Nellie slammed her brake on as hard as she could, and had the awful experience, bound to take place with the pavement a glare of ice, of having nothing happen. The car, hind wheels locked, merely kept on going. She hauled the steering wheel to the left as far as it would go, felt the skid begin, and turned around once-and-a-half in the middle of the street, ending up headed in the direction from which she had come.

It had been so awful, so all-to-once, that she hadn't even heard the impact. She set the emergency with a jerk, tore out of the car and around to the back of it, looking wildly this way and that for the smashed carriage, for scattered babies' bodies. There was nothing.

Oh, God, it must be under the car then!

She was bending down to look when she saw the baby carriage sitting tranquilly where it had been, a little farther up, maybe, in Joe's driveway.

"My Lord in the windswept!" Nellie said aloud. "It can't be."

It was. She walked over and touched it. The Randall triplets were indeed in it. They were sound asleep.

I'm going skit-so myself, she thought. My Lord, what's the matter—I swear I saw that! Didn't I?

And then she saw the rope, a section of old clothesline, tied to the rear axle of the baby carriage and leading, out of sight, inside the open garage door. She strode over; there was nobody in the garage. The end of the rope just lay there limply on the floor.

Angie! Why, that old kook! Everybody concerned might have been killed!

But Angie was sitting at the kitchen table with Mrs. Burrage, the new housekeeper. They were quietly doing a jigsaw puzzle and had been for an hour, Mrs. Burrage explained when Nellie, white and raging, burst in at the door with her horrid story. So it couldn't have been Angie.

"Well, somebody shoved that go-cart out into the street and hauled it back with a rope just before I hit it," Nellie said. "Phoo-oo! My heart's thumping so"—she collapsed in a chair with a moan—"it's a wonder I ain't laid out dead in the street with a heart attack. You got any coffee?"

"Help yourself, we've just been having some. But I'd better go out and bring them babies right in!" Mrs. Burrage, appalled, headed for the door. "My soul and body, who would do—who on earth could it have been?"

Who, indeed?

To do Beck justice, she had not meant to cut the timing quite so fine. It had been Jody who hadn't done the pushing fast enough; she might have known. Trust that one to gum up the works, the small-time butterfingers. True, she'd been good and scared for a minute when she saw how close the car was coming to the baby carriage, but what was all the hooting about, she'd pulled the rope in time, hadn't she? Who was hurt? Whose legs were off? All right, then, sharr-ap! That first being scared hadn't been anything to the horror she'd felt when she'd seen that the Ford skidding around in the street was Mama's. Mama was supposed to have gone down to Aunt Gert's this morning. She would have been there, too, and all nicely out of the way if she'd done what she'd said she was going to. Old Mama-Schmama! Probably spent half the day down the street yakking with someone.

It was a good trick; but the next time she and Jody pulled it, she was sure going to take a good look at the car coming, first. Why, seeing Mama, she'd jumped so she'd almost forgot to yank the rope. Even at that, she hadn't been as scared as Jody. He'd peed his pants inside the big chest in Old Joe Randall's garage.

She'd put it up to Jody this morning, when they were walking around the street thinking of something to do. He wanted to play ball with his new catcher's mitt? You had to have two. Each person had to have some kind of a glove, a pitcher's or a fielder's. She was going to have a pitcher's, she told Jody. Who wanted to be catcher when the pitcher was the most important man in the game?

"You ain't a man," Jody pointed out. "You can't be either a pitcher or a catcher not even when you grow up, because when you grow up all you'll be's an old woman."

"I will not," Beck said. "You wait and see."

He was pretty fresh; he had been ever since that business down at the factory. Sometimes, now, he even acted as if he thought he could give her a hard time. Okay, she'd fix that; but later. Now she had plans. A trick. And she had to have Jody, or the trick was no good.

"The people driving the cars will be so glad they didn't hit the baby that they'll give us something," Beck told him. "A dollar. Maybe five dollars, maybe."

"Aw, they'll just be sore at us," Jody said. He wished in a way Beck would go home; if she didn't want to play ball, he knew somebody that did. Other kids along the block had catcher's mitts, and his was new—unwrapped from a Christmas box this morning.

"Oh, we're only kids," Beck said. "They'll think it's just kids playing. If a grown-up done it, they'd put them in jail, but they don't do nothing to kids. You wait. You'll see."

"They put kids in reform school sometimes."

The man whose chicken-house windows he and Beck had busted out had done a lot of yelling about that. Jody hadn't forgotten. He wasn't quite sure what reform school was, but enough had been said for him to suspect that it was a very bad place, like hell, where those went who had done wrong, and he wanted no part of it.

"Oh, poo! If they could have, they would have. Come on. Okay, you're chicken."

Well, Jody wasn't chicken, and it was kind of fun planning the trick. Only the car almost hit the baby carriage, and who in the car turned out to be Beck's mother; and Beck had just dropped everything and gone tearing into the garage and jumped into a big, old pine chest there was there and pulled the cover down, leaving him standing, with old Nellie Overholt right at his heels. So he had just yanked the cover up and tumbled in right on top of her, that was all; and they had stayed there such a long time that—It was *not* being scared that had made him pee his pants; he had *had* to. So Jody was finished; he was through.

When they had finally dared to come out of the chest, he had just picked up his catcher's mitt, which had been lying there in plain sight on the garage floor all this time—somebody might have stolen it— and had walked right out through the front door of the garage and down the drive into the street. He guessed nobody saw him, anyway; nobody hollered at him. But let them; he was good and mad, he didn't care. Old Beck was the one who was chicken; she'd gone sneaking out the garage back window into the snowbanks, and when he'd turned the corner of the street where he could look down across the vacant lots behind the bakery, he'd seen her wading up to her belt, making off. By the time she got out of that deep snow, she'd be as wet as he was, and he was glad of it.

He shoved his cap to the back of his head and went on down the street home. That was the last time in his life he was going to have anything to do with a darn old girl. He went home and got dried off, agreed completely with his mother that he was too big a boy now to have such accidents, and spent the afternoon, after lunch, playing pitch-and-toss with old Strawberry Sudsworth down the block.

The snow in the vacant lots being what it was, Beck was indeed as wet as Jody by the time she came out between the buildings to the street on the far side; but there was method in all this madness. The way she was headed was the shortest cut to Shacktown; to Aunt Gert's. Mama might be there; Aunt Gert might even be busy, she often was. But it didn't matter who or what. Beck guessed that if the plan she had now worked out, Mama or Aunt Gert either wouldn't care about anything, they'd be too busy mopping off the blood.

The thing was, what if Mama'd spotted her in the driveway? Of course, chances were she hadn't, the car had spizzled around too fast in the road. But Beck had had experience with Mama. Too many times, she'd been as sure as could be that Mama didn't know something; and then it'd turned out that the Old Gimlet-Eye had been right on her all the time. You never knew till you got home, and then, Oh, chicken-licken, the sky is falling. So take no chances. If she saw me this time, Beck told herself, it will be in the fan.

But when I am lugged into Aunt Gert's unconscious, she won't do anything. She will only be sorry.

The long and the short of it was, Beck meant to get herself run over. The plan had leaped into her head, full-blown, while she had been hiding in the chest, pondering ways and means. Perhaps it had grown out of the near accident of the car and the baby carriage. Little children run over: a sad and awful sight.

Well, she had got herself drabbled enough, wading the lots. When a car came along that was going slow enough so she would dare to bump herself against it, she guessed she could bite her lip hard enough to make some blood come. She walked along, watching for cars, but the right one just didn't seem to present itself. There were not very many; nearly everybody would be at home this time of day, getting ready for Christmas dinner; and the ones which did pass were going much too fast. You wouldn't want to get awful hurt, only a little hurt.

I wonder if I will get one smidgin of Christmas dinner. I know I won't, not if Mama saw me do that with the baby carnage.

But a poor hurt child would certainly get fed; why, the finest dinner in town!

She was nearly to Aunt Gert's house, almost losing hope, when she saw the very car she was looking for. It was, as a matter of fact, parked in Aunt Gert's driveway. Mama wasn't there; at least her car wasn't, so much the better. But this other car—oh, it was a beauty, a Lincoln Continental, pale green and cream, brand-new; and the man just getting into it to start it up, had on a lovely, dark, rich-looking overcoat and a felt hat.

I'll bet he has got lots of money and if he runs over me he'll give me some.

Oh, it was the very car to get run over by!

The car was backing to turn. Beck began to skip. Just a happy little child, skipping along, not looking where she was going . . . that was how it happened, as anybody knew who had read the signs: Please Drive Slowly. Protect Our Children.

She had forgotten to bite her lip, but, as things turned out, she didn't need to. She had timed herself well, but she didn't even see the patch of glare ice, smooth as glass. Her feet hit it and skidded, throwing her sideways and down; her face smacked hard, nose on, into the car's fender as she fell; and the hind wheel ran over her left foot.

She wasn't knocked out; she knew when the car stopped, and she heard the door slam, and the crunch of the man's feet on the ice and gravel as he ran around, and his swearing as he scooped her up off the ground. Why, the poor man, she thought. He's so scared he's shaking all over!

He was running up the steps with her into the house, and yelling. "Gert! Gert, for godsakes, I've run over a kid out in your driveway! My God, Gert, what'll I do?"

And clackety-clack, high heels coming fast, Aunt Gert, and Aunt Gert's voice, "Oh, Reggie! Oh, no!" And then, "My God, it's Becky!" and a *thunk* as Aunt Gert fell down, fainted dead away.

Seldom had a plan succeeded better; lots of blood and bandages, a mashed nose and a broken leg, and the doctor sent for. Only one thing didn't work out: your mouth and nose were so sore you couldn't eat any Christmas dinner if you'd wanted any, because after a while everything began to hurt. Something awful.

Part Five
January, 1960

T he genesis of the rain took place in the sea a long way off the
coast, with a shifting of ocean currents, cold and warm. The shift
was not much; but a mass of tropical air, which should have come to
its end in fog banks and snow showers off Newfoundland, or gone its
way to warm up the British Isles, found somewhere a loophole—the
icy Northern current off its guard, caught napping, its cold shoulder
for once turned away. Over the snow-covered land, for a week, flowed
dampness, a southern air as warm as spring, but not the same; for,
like an uncouth stranger pushing in where he is unwelcome, who is
out of place and knows it and so has bad manners, this weather made
itself manifest in various unpleasant ways.

Babies, sweating under winter covers, cried in their cribs; mothers
getting up to tend wondered if something had gone wrong with the
furnace—the house was far too hot; fathers, waked to see, came snorting
up-cellar that it was only a warm spell, the weather had turned mild.
They, too, had trouble getting back to sleep; those who had a touch
of arthritis in the joints or old battle wounds—and many had—lay
awake, listening to the drip from the eaves, the masses of snow letting
go and sliding off the roof, *shush* and *plunk*, a sleepy sound, if only
a man could sleep; cursed their prickling aches, and said to the wife
that the damn climate was changing, growing warmer, or the Gulf
Stream was shifting course; recalled old-fashioned winters, when you
got ready for cold and the cold came according to schedule, when, at
night in bed with a hot brick, a feather bed felt good.

The weather even smelt bad; it smelt, Connie Wilkinson thought,
carefully negotiating the jeep along the ruts and slush-filled potholes of
the old Shore Road, like a washing that the soap hadn't been thoroughly
washed out of. Dried in the house and put away damp in a drawer,

she went on, elaborating to herself, trying to say exactly what the mildewed smell was like.

Oh, well, a January thaw, and an odd one. No rain; at least not yet, but rain was surely coming. Each day, puffy rainclouds, swollen, dark; looking as if they might let down torrents at any minute. It was far too warm for a topcoat or the jeep's heater. The snow had gone so fast that you wouldn't believe it; the road was running rivers, and the wide brook which flowed through a culvert under the road, was purling along as it did in April or May.

Connie was going to work at the plant. She had been working since before Christmas, as bookkeeper; for Sarah Jerdan's boyfriend, emerging at last from the Marines, had whisked her away overnight and married her on Christmas Eve. Her going had been a relief to all concerned; at least, Joe Randall said it was to him, and Connie, privately, had thanked God; for Sarah in the days before she had left had made things hard. She was that most touchy of all touchy individuals, the veteran office-worker who has worn a groove so deep that any suggested change is a personal attack, a wound in flesh. She had kept the plant's books for seventeen years; her way was the only way. Modern training was for the birds; she defied anyone, no matter whom, to function properly in her own particular field. She had let this unmistakably be known; and Connie, in the beginning, had been too dispirited to fight back.

She had felt all right, at least no longer shaky and ill; in the three or four days before she had started work, Clementina had made her rest and had produced a lot of excellent food. This had helped; but Connie couldn't seem to rest. The moment she lay down, her mind would take over, automatically going through the whole series of events which proved the case, setting each one out to look at, to find a flaw; and there was no flaw. Her baby was in Joe Randall's house. She was grateful for whatever crazy connivance had put it there; what mattered was that it was alive. At first the simple fact that it was had seemed to be enough—and then, suddenly, it wasn't.

You'd think, she would tell herself—lying in the afternoon on

Clementina's ancient, hard horsehair sofa, her face turned carefully to the wall so that the old lady would think she was asleep; or wide-eyed, in the night, staring tensely into darkness as the hours ticked toward morning—you'd think I'd been given reprieve enough to last a lifetime. He's alive. He isn't dead and thrown in the sea; he isn't dead because I was a stupid fool and killed him. I was sentenced for murder, to live with it the rest of my life; and he's alive. Isn't that enough? What more do I want?

It was simple, what she wanted.

She would tell herself sturdily that things were best as they were. J. J. Randall was Joe's now, and Joe loved him. For his own sake, the way things were, he had better stay Joe's, with Joe's name. To take him away, even if you were willing to do that to Joe after what he had had to take, would be cruelty you couldn't face. How could you live with yourself if you did that? And even if you could, how prove your claim? Only by telling your own story, parading it out in the open; the scandal would tear the town apart. The Randall triplets were famous in town; people were always calling in to see them, or stopping to peek into the perambulator when Joe's current housekeeper or Nellie Overholt wheeled them out. They were already becoming an institution; their pictures had been in the Bishop paper, and people were as proud of them as if they had been the town's achievement, not just Joe and Amy Randall's. Oh, if you stopped to think, there was no end to the harm you would do. Miles Garland, for instance, he must have been in on it, he must have known. If such a story came out, it might ruin him. And you liked Miles.

No.

But tell yourself how you would that you had lost title, there was more to it than thinking, than cold logic, could handle. There was an ache in the night, especially in the night, not to be borne; you couldn't sleep; things went over and over in your head until morning.

The baby was yours; you wanted him.

Thus it was not to be wondered at that, in the beginning, Connie had been no match for an old battle-ax like Sarah Jerdan. She had finished her first day in the office staggering with weariness, wondering how on earth she could have dreamed that what brain she had left was worth wages from anybody. On Friday night, when Sarah's clang had finally stopped for the weekend and she had gone home, Connie had stayed for a while, alone at the desk, hopelessly turning the pages of the plant's books. A C.P.A. might have figured out Sarah's system; so far as Connie was concerned, the sheets of beautiful figures might as well have been written in Sanskrit. They didn't mean a thing.

I'd better tell Joe I'm no darn good to him. And quit. It'd only be honest . . . but I can't come unstuck. Lord, I need this job . . .

A loose sheet of paper fell from between the pages of the ledger and fluttered to the floor.

One of Sarah's "signposts," she thought, leaning to pick it up. Sarah had them everywhere—loose pages, notes, reminders to Connie; if they were "signposts" they pointed in fifty different directions.

However, this was not one of them, she saw; it was a note to Sarah, succinct and dry, written in a forthright up-and-down hand:

> Sarah, I admire your head, it is full of rocks and
> beauty. What I want to see is a SIMPLE TRIAL BALANCE.
> So, for the sweet Pete's sake, hop to it and draw one.
>
> A.

Amy Randall, it seemed, had got to a stage where she was taking no more nonsense from Sarah.

It was comforting; just the look of the strong, sensible handwriting was like a steadying hand on the shoulder.

"That's the way to talk to the old bat," it said. "Give her as good as she sends. I always did. Bring her up with a good round turn."

Connie sat for a moment holding the note in her hand. This was not the first trace she had found around the office of Amy Randall, who apparently had been a power there, listened to; a balance wheel. Somebody you would have liked, whom you would have been glad to know; who, you dearly wished, could be here now.

Poor Joe. To have had this and lost it. No wonder he couldn't care a whole lot what went on around him now. And, here in the plant, he's stuck halfway between those two prima donnas, Sarah on one side and Marvin Coles on the other.

Why on earth did he feel he had to put up with them? Old employees, yes; but one or the other of them was at him about something from day's beginning to end—enough to drive a man crazy.

The office door behind her clicked open and shut and she glanced up, startled, to see Joe himself come in. She'd thought he had gone home long ago.

Joe blinked a little, apparently as startled as she was.

"Judas priest," he said. "You still here, Connie? I thought everybody'd gone home."

"Well, I had a few things . . . I was just leaving," Connie said.

"Shoot, you don't need to take Sarah that hard," Joe said. "She'll have you making up your bed down here, if you don't look—" He saw the note which she was still holding in her hand, and stopped short, as if he had suddenly run head-on into something hard and cold and unyielding; like a wall. You couldn't mistake that handwriting and Joe hadn't; he had recognized it from halfway across the room, and had been caught unprepared, his guard down. In the moment before he set it up again and before she glanced quickly away, Connie saw the grinding misery in his undefended face and realized, appalled, that he was fighting to keep back tears.

Then he walked quickly past her desk to his own and began turning over the papers there. "That Johnson folder," he said in his normal, quiet voice. "You know where it is, or has Sarah got it stuck away somewhere?"

And this is the trouble I have been scheming how to make worse, Connie thought. Lying awake nights, thinking how to do it.

She slid Amy's note back between the pages of the ledger, found the missing folder for him, said good night, and went home.

The problem was settled once and for all. You could not add to grief like that, not and live with yourself afterward, not in a million years; and that night, having made up her mind, she slept soundly for the first time in weeks.

By the middle of Monday morning, Sarah Jerdan was good and mad. She was padding around the office, opening file drawers and slamming them to, and muttering under her breath about "twippets" and "know-it-alls." At noon on that day, she had grabbed up her bag and swept off, dripping icicles, to the restroom.

Joe, who had been sitting unobtrusively at his desk all morning while the battle raged over his head, glanced over at Connie, deadpan. He said, "It's the seventeen years her boyfriend's stayed in the Marines."

Now, in January, Sarah was long gone, somewhere on her honeymoon. Left alone, Connie had found she could figure out the wonderful accounting system, though sometimes she made heavy weather. Sarah, apparently because she had been fascinated by figures and what could be done with them, had many times gone around Robin Hood's barn and back, doubled on her tracks, then crisscrossed from front door to entry and at last gone out a window to achieve, sometimes, a simple result. Following her was like tracing out the maze puzzles that from time to time occur in local newspapers: the pencil mark goes down a good many blind alleys and back to the beginning before it finds the clear way through. Connie was finding the clear way through; but she had not needed to go far to discover that the Randall Packing Company was on its last legs.

It was a small company, competing in a big field. If you wanted to know what was the matter, you had only to listen to Marvin Coles, the other prima donna.

Marvin had not given up trying to argue with Joe about the business; but with Joe stubbornly going ahead and not listening to him, Marvin needed an audience. He took to coming in when Joe wasn't there and roosting on the corner of Connie's desk, putting the matter in a nutshell to "the girl." A large nutshell.

"You can go to the supermarket and buy a can of fishballs cheaper'n Joe can sell one wholesale," Marvin snorted. "And the stubborn bas—

son-of-a-gun won't quit."

"He must have his reasons, don't you think?" Connie said.

She wished Marvin wouldn't. Somehow it didn't seem quite the thing to discuss Joe's business behind his back with another employee. Besides, she was busy.

"Reasons?" Marvin said. "The trouble with that boy is that he's got goldarn radical ideas. Too radical for this one-hoss town, I tell ya."

"Is he a Socialist?" Connie asked absently.

She had been trying to add up a column of figures and had just arrived at the third different total. However, hearing Marvin's breathing start to get heavy, she glanced up, and judged from his expression that she had used a dirty word.

"I ain't ever heard he's gone that fur," Marvin said icily. "For the godsakes, ain't being a registered Democrat bad enough? We ain't ever recovered from the Welfare State shoved onto us by old Franklin D., and it'll take the country years to recover, if you ask me, when a good boy like Joe swallered him and his criminal practices down hook, line, and sinker and ain't never got over it, even with that old dogtrot dead fifteen years and more. I was glad when he died, I danced a jig, but, by gumpty, I'm sorry now he ain't alive to see how his poison notions has ruint the country."

Marvin himself had never recovered from the PWA, from which, during the Great Depression, he had had to accept a job or see his family go hungry. Winters now, when Joe by either hook or crook couldn't keep the factory going, Marvin without protest accepted the unemployment checks that enabled him, along with others, to sit all winter listening to Westerns; but that was different. Somewhere back along, a corrupt old politician had personally forced him, Marvin Coles, free and independent citizen of the U.S.A., to take a charity job from the State, a crime which his pride had never forgiven or forgotten.

"Look," he went on. "Joe says to me, people has jobs, they buy; they buy, he sells. So what does he think—one piddling little shedful of fishballs is going to selvage the country? That growed good for nigh onto two hundred years, and that it took Fuh-ranklin D. Roosevelt just twenty to knock into the bilges? I warn't never *for* him, by the god, I was for the rich, and I am today. When the rich is rich, the country's prosperous and I got a job, is all it amounts to, and when the rich ain't rich, but is snowed under by gov'ment rules and reglations, and anything they make over'n above expenses took for taxes, then the country's poor and nobody's got a job, and it's preposterous to think different."

Having arrived at this climax, Marvin would remember to pound his fist on the desk. If the racket did not bring any interruption, such as Joe coming in, he would go on.

"Fishballs? He can't sell 'em. Market's tied up. And even if 'twasn't, who wants the damn things anyway? Anybody ever et one, knows that a fishball is a sometime thing."

By that time he would be needed somewhere in the plant and would stump away, leaving Connie fascinated by his analysis.

Today she arrived at the office to find Marvin confronting Joe across Joe's desk. Pay day had come around again, and Joe was apparently down early to fix up the envelopes, for they lay neatly arranged on the blotter in front of him. As Connie came through the door, Marvin was yelling, slapping his fist into the palm of his hand, to emphasize each word.

"I . . . don't . . . care . . . if . . . you . . . are," he said. "Me and the boys ain't taking money this week."

"I can't see any of you affording to work for nothing," Joe said. "What to hell's this all about?"

Marvin's face went deadpan. He shoved both hands into his pockets. He might have been going to announce that it was a nice day, or raining, though relish was evident in the note of triumph which he was unable to keep out of his voice.

He said, "We figure the time's come for us to eat our own codfish cakes."

Joe turned red. "Don't you kid me," he said. "I ain't in the mood. By God, Marvin, this is a poor time for second-rate jokes."

"I ain't kidding," Marvin said.

His envelope, containing his pay, which, for foreman, was a substantial sum, was lying on top of the heap; he reached a blackened, grease-encrusted hand, picked it up and shook the contents out onto the desk. "I'll take, say, five bucks for beer," he said. "I got to eat them goddam things, I got to have something to wash 'em down with."

"You serious? You know as well as I do that one payroll ain't a drop in the bucket," Joe said.

"Ain't I been telling ya." Marvin stalked away, pocketing his five-dollar bill.

Joe sat looking after him. His face was still red and his underjaw was thrust out. He said under his breath, "Why, the damned old son!" His eyes met Connie's. "That old coot's schnozzle is so deep in my business," he said loudly, "that I don't know why I don't just walk out of here and let him do the closing down."

"Why don't you fire him?" Connie asked.

She had been listening, growing more and more indignant. She knew from the books that, while the plant's trouble had been bad before Amy's death, it was since then that emergencies had been piling up on Joe, and she couldn't help knowing that some of them existed because he had been too dispirited to deal with them.

"Huh?" Joe blinked. "Fire Marvin? Oh, good glory, I can't do that. He's been here since—" Joe shook his head wearily, not wanting even to make the effort to say how long Marvin had been there.

"He's obstructionist," Connie said. "He tries to clobber everything you do."

"I guess he does."

Joe made some aimless doodles on the blotter with his pencil, four curlicues ending with a big round number in five figures, to which he added a dollar sign and then, after a moment, a period.

"I've pounded my brains out thinking," he said. "The only reasonable answer to it is a deep-freeze plant; and that ain't reasonable because I can't swing it. And even if I could, there's just about enough frozen-food products on the market, anyway, to keep prices high. So I have to sit here and take charity from my own workmen, which is what that emulsified old windbag has dreamed up to prove to me what a fool I am."

"Well, this is a rotten time for him to take advantage of you, Joe.

"Yeah. Marvin wants his own way. So he gets it. Oh, you wait. You'll see. He'll have the whole work force lined up, he saw to that before he came in here and made his talk."

Marvin had. Before the day was over, it became evident that he had lined up not only the factory, but the entire town. Word had been passed around. People from all over came in and bought codfish cakes. Some bought them by the case. Most of the work force, however, took their pay envelopes—men with families had to; but they used their grocery money to buy what codfish cakes had stacked up, so far, in the storage shed.

Marvin was in his element. He spent his day at the storage shed, selling; he set the price, took charge of the money, and only once came in to the office. Then it was not to consult Joe, but to whack down on his desk three cans of codfish cakes. Marvin said, "For supper," and stumped back out again. Satisfaction stuck out all over him.

Joe said nothing. He sat at his desk all day, sometimes doodling, sometimes figuring. At five o'clock he got up, picked up his hat, began stuffing the cans into his pocket. He had had no lunch and he looked strained and tired. "I'm going home," he said.

"Are you going to eat those things for supper?" Connie asked.

Joe stared at the last can on the desk as if it had been a snake. "I guess so. Looks like everyone else is."

Connie got up from her own desk. "No, you are not!" she said. "You are not going to have them crammed down your throat plus everything else, today. For heaven's sake, Joe! You need a decent meal."

She stopped, steadying her voice, which she realized was shaking with rage, and Joe glanced at her, for the first time that day at anything with interest.

"You sound mad," he said.

"I am mad! I'm burnt up. You're coming home with me. We're going to have hot roast-beef sandwiches, and that sounds like left-overs, but you don't know what Clementina can do to a hot roast-beef sandwich."

"Roast beef?" Joe said. He stood for a minute looking a little stunned, before the light of hope dawned in his face. He grinned. "Why, God love the living girl, where? You don't know what I could do to a hot roast-beef sandwich."

"Why, Joe," Clementina said. "How nice of you, you even remembered my cats!"

Circling around the kitchen, helping Connie clear the table after supper, Clementina had spied the cans of fishcakes, which Joe, for comfort's sake, had removed from his jacket pocket and stacked on the table.

"My cats love these, I buy them all the time," she went on, spryly opening cans on the mechanical opener screwed to the cupboard door. "Of course, you can't give animals too much fish, it's bad for them, and uncooked fish is dreadful—worms, you know." She sniffed appreciatively at an opened can. "But these are so good, and they make a nice change. I've often thought that if you could make a nice pet food, Joe, like that man—what's his name?—Hill, you would make a million. Here, Herbert. Here, Ginger. Suppertime!"

Only two cats came at the call, Herbert and a smaller one, cinnamon-colored, who followed tentatively at his heels. The cinnamon-colored job was fatter than he had been, but he was still respectful of his elders.

Due largely to Connie and Dr. Garland, the cat population was now within bounds; there were still many, now fed outside, but not twenty-three. The S.P.C.A. shelter in Bishop had been useful in finding homes; Garland, in his visits around outlying towns, often ran across people who would welcome a nice cat. Clementina had not minded, she said, so long as she could be sure the poor, friendless things would be taken care of; human beings were likely to be disregardful of cats sometimes.

"Those kittens the summer people leave behind to fend for

themselves," she told Connie. "I'm afraid I'll always take them in when they come to my door missing their people. But, of course, what you are doing is better."

Mame, also, had had some changes made; she now had a comfortable pen in the shed and seemed not to mind much living there instead of in the kitchen, though she came in when she was invited, which was fairly often.

Joe blinked a little at the sight of only two cats; he had expected more. From the talk around town, he hadn't known quite what to expect from Clementina's establishment, though he hadn't thought much about it until now, being immersed in his troubles.

A lot of talk and jabber goes around, he told himself, and stretched his legs comfortably to the fireplace.

This place was wonderful. Quiet and candlelight; a good, ample fireplace fire; a soft chair, built to hit a man in all the right places— with a belt of Clementina's Scotch and her dinner inside him, Joe felt better than he had for days. God knew what she had put into the hot roast-beef sandwiches to make them taste like that, but he had eaten three. Not small ones, either.

He winced a little, though, seeing the cats tear into the mound of fishcakes. They had eaten right through and were coming out on the other side, still going strong. "Something seems to like the cussed things," he said moodily.

"Why, don't be silly," Clementina said. "What could be nicer than good fishballs? You should try some, sometime, with my barbecue sauce."

"Yes, you should," Connie said. "They're out of this world. We're very good customers of yours, Joe."

"You are? Well, what I need is a couple million customers like that," Joe said, nodding at the cats. "Maybe I ought to can cat food."

"Well, why don't you?" Clementina said. "People all over the country buy it by the ton."

"Sure. The supermarket shelves are piled with it. Big companies, with their name brands. I couldn't compete, unless I had some kind of a gimmick. Something unusual, it would have to be."

"Maybe you could find one," Clementina said. "Why don't you go to see the laboratory people over in Bishop?"

"Yes," Connie said. "They're always experimenting with animal foods. They use a lot of it, too—when I worked over there, it was about sixty thousand pounds a month. And they've grown since; so probably it's more now."

"A swell market, all right," Joe said. "Oh, brother!" He laughed, and his laughter sounded a bitter note in the room.

"Look, wait," Connie said. "I had a letter, Joe. Let me show you— it's in my room. I'll get it."

While she poked around among her things, hunting the letter, in the bedroom off the living room, she could hear Joe. The idea apparently had made him mad.

"That would be the pay-off! The real, honest-to-god, shot-in-the-arm pay-off! I grew up in the Depression. When people didn't have enough to eat. When pretty nigh the whole town lived on surplus food, sent in by the Government. I thought I learned something in those times. I guess I didn't. I guess I'm simple-minded. I thought if there was a lot of food around, it'd be cheap, people could afford to buy it. Well, there is now. There's so much food around that I ain't got a market for a good, honest, well-made product; and the cost of living's so high that after a man buys his week's groceries, he has to get anything else he needs on tick. Hell, I live on tick myself."

Blowing off, Connie thought. Well, it's about time.

Surprising, the effect Clementina had on people. She poked them in the prejudices of a lifetime until they were shocked and appalled and boiling mad and went off saying she was crazy; or they ended up her friends forever, telling her their life history. Whatever, it was never neutral. In a minute, if Joe lets drop that feeding animals isn't as important as feeding people, the fur is going to fly.

She found the letter, which was from the chemist in whose laboratory she had worked in Boston, and went back into the living room.

Joe had got up out of his comfortable chair. He was standing, straddled, on the hearth, his hands shoved into his pockets, his chest out, glaring belligerently down at Clementina, who sat looking up at him serenely, with wide, innocent, tawny eyes.

"So my business goes on the rocks, and my workmen hand me back their week's pay, or try to; and the townspeople flock in to buy my surplus, to help out poor old Joe. So he can eat. Maybe meet this month's payments. And the only answer that comes up, is that I quit making food for humans and can cat food! By God, that grizzles me!"

"Why, Joe!" Clementina said. "Is that what happened—people came in and bought? . . . Why, I think that's wonderful. It should show you what the town thinks of you."

"Yeah. That I'm a booby. Traveling on two lame legs and with holes in my head."

"Granted, you might be," Clementina said. "But I don't see it that way at all. You must know that there're many people, like me, who have been watching you for years and who know well enough what you've been trying to do. There isn't a man living who has done as much for the town as you have."

"I hear you talking," Joe said.

"Keeping your factory going, paying wages winters, when it's taken as much out of you as it has? What do you think would have happened if it had still been old Montgomery's factory, or even your father's? Marvin Coles's? Would the townspeople have moved in, done what they could, the only thing they could think of, to help? You know perfectly well what they would have said: 'Serve the old weasel right!' "

There was no doubt that she was making an impression. Joe was still mad, but he was listening. He took his fists out of his pockets, undoubled them, and sat down.

"And they would say: 'He's made money out of us, all these years, now let him see what skin-poor feels like.' But they don't say that about you, do they?"

"You keep on," Joe said. "I might swallow some of that." He snorted. "If I could see up over being sore at Marvin."

"Marvin Coles? A small matter. H'm," Clementina said. "We have left from primitive times, dug in tooth and claw and hanging on, the cockroach, the horseshoe crab, and people like Marvin Coles. He is a troglodyte."

"A trog—a what?" Joe said, staring at her.

"A troglodyte. A prehistoric caveman, a hermit who lives to himself, doesn't know what's going on outside his cave. We have many of them still."

Joe grinned. The grin grew to a chuckle; to a roar. He put back his head and laughed till the tears rolled down his cheeks. "Oh, wait," he gasped when he could. "Wait till I call him that and hand him a dictionary!"

"Good enough," Clementina said. "I'm in favor of that. I will buy the dictionary. Look at Connie's letter now, see what you make of it. It is from a chemist, who seems to have perfected a formula for a quite revolutionary pet food. He is going to market it, he says, and he wants Connie to come back and work for him."

"Oh Lord!" Joe said. He spun on Connie. "You going? Because that's all I need, by God, to break my back."

"No." Connie shook her head. "I don't want to, Joe. It might turn out to be a pretty good job, though. But read what he says, Joe. It's interesting."

Joe read the letter through. "He sure wants you to come back," he said glumly. "Gone to considerable trouble to balance up a meal for a lot of useless critters, seems like."

"My dear Joe! Don't be a numbskull!" Clementina said. "If you can't beat the troglodytes, don't join them! Granted that they have tried, since they began, to rid the world of animals, I doubt if even they would agree that animals are useless, certainly not since a dog, I believe, was first in orbit. If you can rid your mind of the bias that feeding animals is a worthless occupation, I suggest you go for information to the Bishop Laboratory, where research in the causes of human disease could not exist without mice."

She glared at Joe with such ferocity that he recoiled, speechless. His bias, in the first place, had not been against animals, but only against the man who, whatever he was doing, wanted to remove Connie. Since she had been in the factory office, she had not only unscrambled Sarah Jerdan's books, but her company had been the only brightening he had been able to see of his black loneliness. The kids—J. J. Randall— had helped, of course; but they weren't anyone you could talk to. Joe could argue with Marvin; he could listen to, and put up with, Angie's foolishness; he could pass the time of day with the trawler skippers. But a man needed someone he could lay out his ideas to and have them, whether they were good ideas or not, sensibly considered. Connie at least understood what he was trying to do at the plant, and she was for it. Contemplating what the office would be like without her, he dropped the letter on the table as if it were hot and glanced over at her. She shook her head at him, almost imperceptibly, and smiled. Well, what did she mean by that? That she wasn't going?

"Well, skip it, Joe, if you aren't interested," she said. "It was just a notion I had, when you said you needed a gimmick."

"I suppose I could get used to the idea," Joe said. "But—"

"Animals aren't good enough, is that it?" Clementina said. "They are a lower form of life? Nonsense. They're your blood relatives. Mame, my sheep, will do what other sheep do, by instinct. She is a silly creature if there ever was one. But what about the ladies who got themselves into the New Look and looked like perfect fools and most uncomfortable? Or tapered slacks, my heavens? What living organism in its right mind would ever willingly put those on if everybody wasn't doing it? And the men are worse; only sillier, and more dangerous, because they run things. They have to get dressed up to kill. Put on a costume and go around wiping out. Every fall I'm treated to the insane spectacle of them in fluorescent coats and caps of many colors, running around my back pasture passionately shooting deer. I suppose one reason is dark wool suits. Poor things, dull as dishwater for eleven months of the year, when history blazes with shining armor, ruffs, lace, silks, and satins! Why, what a sight, humph! when all it proves, at least all it proves to me, is that man is the only living animal who is browbeaten into a helpless pulp by his self-esteem!"

"Oh, honey," Connie said. "Poor old Joe! He just isn't a nut about animals, the way we are. He doesn't rate such a talking-to."

"Sure, I do," Joe said with some spirit. "I put a deer into my freezer every fall, if I'm lucky enough to get one. I enjoy hunting him, too." He had started out by being a little touched up, but he suddenly grinned. "I do wear an old red-and-black checked shirt, but only so some hotshot won't plug me in the—"

"Who said anything about a little decent hunting for food?" Clementina demanded. "I certainly didn't. I'm talking about the instinct to kill so-called inferior forms of life because it pumps up the ego. A curb has got to be put on that, which might as well start with the animals, because so far as I can see, it only leads to bigger wipings out of anything which differs, including other men; and that could end in the dolphins, who have large brains, taking over. Or if there weren't any of them left, there are lots of well-protected chickens. What if it should be chickens? What then? My bedtime," she said briskly, getting up. "I find myself old and incompetent if I don't get my rest. Don't go, Joe, stay and talk to Connie. If you think her chemist friend has got a business proposition there, I would like to invest. If you were handling it, that is."

Joe got up, looking at her with a stunned expression. "I thought you were sore," he said. "To hear you talk, a man would think so."

"Oh, mercy, no, not at you. Once in a while one of you breaks loose and gives me hope. You do; and there was a man somewhere in eighteenth-century literature who caught a fly in his study and let it go out the window. I don't think I would have done that; I'm more likely to swat flies. But he made a speech when he did it, very short, a sort of poor man's Sermon on the Mount. He said, 'Surely there is room in the world for me and thee.' Good night, Joe. Come again."

She went off, closing the bedroom door behind her.

"I'll be darned," Joe said. "What's the idea, Lura Blandish and them putting out that that old lady's crazy? She makes a damn sight more sense than I do."

He lingered. He talked and talked. He helped Connie finish the dishes, sat down again in front of the fire and went on talking. The wall he had built around himself, high and thick, with all the loopholes plugged, came down. From behind it, Joe's backed-up problems rattled out—things which, since Amy's death, he hadn't been able to discuss with anyone: the day-in-day-out hassle with Marvin Coles, which was like kicking a pillow; the plant and Joe's hopes for it; money; even Amy.

"Holy smoke!" he said suddenly, looking at his watch. "It's one o'clock! How'd it get to be so doggoned late? I've got to go. No telling what shenanigan Angie's thought of by this time. I'm sorry, Connie. I've had my troubles scurrying around here like mice."

He got up to go. His reserve, now that he remembered it, started to build up again.

Well, that's all right, Connie thought. But I doubt if he's able to reassemble the whole structure. She said aloud, "I've enjoyed it, Joe. Clementina did, too. She sounds off"—Connie smiled—"and it clears the air. At least it does for me. It always has."

"Something seems to have cleared it for me," Joe said, half under his breath. He glanced at her and seemed about to say more; then he paused, standing on the back doorstep, as she let him out. "Look at the darned weather, will you?" he said. "Just like spring."

It was; and yet not like spring because there was on the air no smell of green, of freshness, of anything growing, only a heavy malodor, musty as the inside of an abandoned house. Over the town, the moon rode high in the sky, not clear and not overcast, but slurred, as if seen through a window screen. There were a few dim stars; and the tropical wind blew with intent, clashing bare branches together, rattling shutters, flattening out tufts of long, uncut grass, visible now because the snow was nearly gone.

"Ain't that a funny wind, though?" Joe said. "Makes your overcoat feel like the wrapper on a Tootsie Roll at a Fourth of July picnic. Look, Connie, I've got that letter in my pocket, you mind? I want to mull it over some. I might, like a fool, just go over to see the lab people in

Bishop tomorrow. If I'm not at the factory, that's where I'll be. Don't tell Marvin. If I come up with something, I'll surprise him myself."

Connie had not been in the office five minutes, the next morning, before Marvin came in. He was cock-of-the-walk today. His well-padded chest stuck out, and he was carrying a canvas moneybag, which, Connie judged, held yesterday's take from his selling operation. He walked with a strut, making a parade out of bringing the money in. His divided stare, circling the office, passed over Connie—someone of no importance—and came to rest with disappointment on Joe's empty chair. Only then did he condescend to notice that anyone was in the room. He did not say good morning. He barked, "Where's Joe?"

"Isn't he around the plant somewhere?" Connie said innocently.

"No, he ain't around the plant! What's he think, he can lay home abed whilst the rest of us does the work?"

"Well, he's the boss. I expect it's his privilege," Connie said.

Oh, you old windbag, she thought. Wouldn't I just love to slow you down! If only there was some way—

Marvin obviously did not care to be reminded at this time that somebody else was the boss. He drew down the corners of his mouth and stared at Connie, going over in his mind what would be most appropriate, right now, for the foreman to chew out "the girl" about.

There was a way. Clementina had pointed it out last night. Connie thought of it now and she smiled—a nice, friendly, sincere smile—right in the face of Marvin's beginning yap.

"Marvin," she said, "I wanted to tell you, I didn't get a chance to last night, but I think that was the most wonderful thing you did yesterday for Joe."

"Huh?" Marvin said.

"Why, I can't tell you what it did for him. Here he was, discouraged and down, and just about ready to quit; half out of his mind with losing Amy and with bad business troubles on top of that—if there ever was a time when a man needed a friend . . . Why, Marvin, I was proud of you. You certainly came through."

Marvin stared. He wasn't sure, in spite of the friendly smile, whether she was being sarcastic. By gum, if she was, the twippet, taking Joe's side, mixing into something that warn't none of her business, she was going to hear tell! He opened his mouth, but Connie went smoothly on.

"Of course, you've known him a long time, longer than any of us, so you knew just what to do to set him up again. Why, when he realized that you and the men and the whole town were behind him one hundred percent in what he's been trying to do—"

Marvin found his voice, which, at first, came out in a raspy squawk. "What to hell you talking about—behind him one hundred per—"

"What else could he think? You turned in your pay, the men did what they could, the town turned to, spent their grocery money to buy up his surplus. Why, when Joe left last night, he was a new man. Now you mention it, I do recall where he might be this morning. He said something about going over to Bishop. You don't suppose he was headed for the bank, do you, to see about some more financing so that he could keep the plant open?"

Marvin lifted the canvas bag high and crashed it down on the desk. The string with which it was tied broke and the money came bulging out. A fifty-cent piece flew through the air past Connie's head. Reaching, she fielded it neatly and held it out to him, still smiling.

She said, "Why, Marvin, you've busted your string."

Talk and talk to Gert, Nellie Overholt told herself. Kick a pillow. That one! Agree with every word you said, then go her way as if you'd never said it. Many times Nellie had given up on Gert. "I've told you to straighten out and you can't see it. At least you might have a little respect for Mama's mem'ry, if not for me. So You Go Your Way And I'll Go Mine."

Gert would nod. She would say, "Yes, I expect that's best."

For all the difference it ever made. If I appeared to her in a cod's head and spoke with the tongue of a crocodile, she would never

Straighten Out. At least not so long as that Frances stayed there, in Mama's house, egging Gert on.

Frances was from somewhere away. The god in his heaven ever knew where Gert had picked her up, but there she was, lug and luggage, prepared to stay forever. Whatever she did, Gert did, led around by the nose; without Frances, Gert would never have gone the way she had.

Nellie had long spells of having nothing to do with Gert. She would stay away. "I Will Never Speak To You Again." But then in her travels around town she would get word of something new going on down there; changes being made. You seen Gert's new coat; or they tell me Gert and Frances had the kitchen done over. So Blood Would Turn Out To Be Thicker Than Water again, and Nellie would go. She guessed that even if she had sold her share of the house to Gert—got her pay for it, too, she'd certainly seen to *that*—she had a right to set foot in her old home if she wanted to, particularly if Gert was going to make changes In Mama's house.

Whenever she went, things started up all over again. In the first place, she couldn't stand Frances, and she let it be known. And from all she could make out, Frances couldn't stand her. On one occasion, the time Nellie had gone down there and found a whole new electric kitchen, even to garbage disposal—chew up even the bones, at least it said—and she hadn't been able to keep from speaking her mind—when you thought!—Frances had taken it upon herself to order Nellie out of the house; and she would never know how near it come, that time, to blows.

Nellie had said, "Gert, for heaven's sake, you haven't got no respect for nothing, have you? Hnf, I guess you girls have got it made."

That, she told herself, put it in a nutshell.

Frances—sitting there doing her fingernails as if she thought she had any kind of a say in Nellie's old home—said, "Yes. We're about the only people in town aren't living on tick."

Well, of all the— That touched Nellie up; it certainly did. She gave Frances a good glare.

Frances gave it right back.

A tough little nut, if there ever was one. Not worth my or anyone's else's time; and Nellie turned her back right on her.

"All I can say is," she said to Gert, "and I never thought I'd catch myself saying it, I'm glad poor Mama's dead."

Gert said, "Yes, I guess it's a good thing," in that kind of all-gone voice that let you know she wasn't hearing you, she was somewhere out on Cloud Nine.

"She never had nothing but a plain, old black-iron sink, if you recall," Nellie said. "When I think of how she would have loved this one . . . But she would of carted the whole works straight to the dump, garbage disposal and all, if she would of known what kind of money it was bought with."

Gert said, "I guess she would."

She was beginning to look, Nellie was pleased to see, good and nervous. Well, there ought to be something that would get to her. Mama's mem'ry, if nothing else.

"*My* wages don't run to no fancy gadgets to chouse up orts with," Nellie said. "My God, I ain't even got a garbage can, not with a cover, but I would slap that to the dump so fast it would land there red-hot if I would of had to buy it the way you— Tch! Oh, when I think of What you've turned Mama's old home into, I—"

"Look," Frances said. She had got the polish onto her fingernails. "Let Gert alone, why don't you?" And she spread her fingers out to dry, like claws, in the air.

"I am talking," Nellie said, "to My Sister! I don't need nobody with green fingernail polish to tell me what I can say and can't say."

"Well, talk to somebody that talks back. Take somebody your size. Poor old Gert can't fight and you know it. Fight with me. I'd welcome it. But if I were you, I'd just go home."

"You ordering me out of this house?" Nellie demanded. She could feel herself beginning to breathe heavy and she looked Frances up and down. Little pint pot, just about half her size, claws or no claws; so if she thought she could—

"I wouldn't put it quite that strong," Frances said. "I was just making it known that any time you went, it would be all right with me."

"This is My Old Home, I'll have you know!"

"Sure. It may have been once, but now it's Gert's and mine, and paid for. We fix it up how we like to, and where our money comes from is no skin off your transom. For all you know, we found a gold brick under the doorstep." She spied a little place on one thumbnail that wasn't covered with polish, and she began to fix it out of the bottle with the brush.

"Well, you *better* pull your claws in," Nellie said. "I don't take that kind of chat from nobody, let alone a two-dollar—"

"Oh, phooey!" Frances burst out laughing. "Takes more than two dollars to buy garbage disposals, honey!"

"I don't doubt it took several two-dollar *occasions*," Nellie said. "If you ask me, they were probably *countless*. I—"

"Well, anyway, we never stole it from the Welfare. Look, if you want a knock-down-drag-out, I'll oblige, but I promise you it'll be a fight that the neighborhood'll hear."

"I'll say it will!"

Nellie got right up. Twit me, will she, when all I ever took from the Welfare was a few things the kids needed, never be missed, and I certainly earnt them, if anybody ever did! On my wages.

There was no knowing where things might have ended if Gert hadn't all to once begun to holler. She had as fine an old case of the slapping hy-strikes as was ever seen on land or sea. It took the both of them to pull her out of it, and by that time they had cooled off. Nellie went home. They had kept an armed truce ever since, and that had been two years ago.

Nowadays when she went to Gert's, Nellie took care to phone ahead. Frances would be upstairs or in the next room, but they seldom saw each other. Nellie didn't go often, only when she had reason to, and there was the annual visit, Family Feelings, on Christmas Day. To see the Old Home (what had been done to it now) and, of course, Blood Was Always Thicker Than Water on Christmas.

On this Christmas, she'd been delayed. This and that; and almost running down that baby carriage had taken it out of her, so that she'd had to sit with Angie and Mrs. Burrage, drinking black coffee until her legs would hold her up again; so that when she got to Gert's finally it was to find Beck there, run over, and Dr. Garland and Gert and Frances flying around like fools, and the place covered with blood; and some man with a bald head and a pod in front crying his head off into a whole box of pink Kleenex. She thought at first he was a part of their trade; but he turned out to be the one who'd run over Beck, and he was going to pay for it, too, Nellie told him. She guessed he could, all right, if that big new Lincoln Continental setting out there was what he'd done it with and *if* it belonged to him; and all of a sudden, to her utter surprise, Gert turned on her Like A Tiger.

"You let Reggie alone," she said. "He feels bad enough as it is," and she went right over and kissed the poor fool right on top of his bald head, and he bawling like a baby into the front of her blood-stained dress.

Nellie thought, well, she never, it was as if the world's rabbit had gone up and kissed the Ugly Duckling; and then Dr. Garland took over, and they fixed Beck up and found she wasn't too bad hurt, but enough—a mashed nose and a broken leg—so that she had better not be moved around for a day or so; stay right where she was, in Gert's bed, and It Was No Place For Her; and Dr. Garland said it was right now, till he saw. There was no need right now, but maybe tomorrow he would take her to the hospital, if that was where Nellie wanted her to go.

Well, the hospital would be expensive; no doubt, that bald-headed man's insurance would take care of that, but with these characters that traipsed in and out of Gert's, you never knew; it might turn out that he didn't have that kind of insurance at all, or if he did it might not be enough to cover, and Nellie get stuck.

No, the thing to do, of course, was, Gert would have to move over to Nellie's house and take care of Beck while Nellie had to work; take no chances.

And Gert dug her heels right in and said no. She would not.

"Well, why, for heaven's sake?" Nellie demanded. "What's the matter with you—it's your place to help out the family when needed. Have you got to be *paid?*"

"Coming at any other time but now," Gert said, "I would. But as it is, I can't and I won't, and I have my reasons. I'll take care of her here."

"I won't have her here now any more than I ever would. And you know why."

"Nothing is going on here now," Gert said, "That a child shouldn't see."

"I'll just bet there isn't!"

"Not to hurt her, there isn't," Gert said. She did not think it necessary to tell Nellie that Beck had visited at her house off and on for years, to be read to out of Aunt Gert's magazines and to have treats she didn't get at home; but never, never, had she seen anything Out Of The Way; Gert had taken special care of it. She loved Beck dearly; anyone ought to know she wouldn't do a thing to alarm her. She would take care of Beck gladly and enjoy it, even though, right at this moment, it meant a sacrifice. But it would have to be here.

"I am not going to leave home now," Gert said. "You'll just have to take it or leave it, Nellie."

Nellie took it. What else could she do? Pay for help at home, extra? Pauline, the babysitter, wouldn't nurse; she'd made it plain, often enough, she was a babysitter, pure and simple. Take a chance on getting stuck with bills from the hospital?

"All right," she said. "But I'm going to keep tabs, don't think I ain't. The first thing Beck tells me out of line, I'll snatch you bald-headed, Gert."

So what was the matter with the slimpsy thing—dug in, heels first, for the first time in her life and you couldn't move her with dynamite?

It was lovely at Aunt Gert's, even lying in bed with your leg up and hurting. All you had to do was say something hurt and Aunt Gert and Aunt Frances would fly around, telephone the doctor, give you an aspirin or, if whatever it was hurt really bad, a big capsule, what Aunt Frances called a Red Bullet. And wonderful things to eat on trays all fussed up with lace doilies, and somebody to talk or to read to you—something interesting going on every minute of the day. And above all, Uncle Reggie.

Uncle Reggie came every evening, sometimes in the daytime. He felt so bad that he had run over Beck that he always brought an armful of things. Why, Aunt Gert had had to clear off a whole shelf in the room, just to put the things Uncle Reggie brought. First it was something foolish, like a doll.

Beck thought, hnf, he is one of the Santa-Claus-for-little children people. One of those. Thinks you ought to like dolls. Little-girl; so-likes-dolls. But then she got to looking at the doll. It was nice; lovely clothes and would walk. Aunt Gert liked it most of all the things Uncle Reggie brought. She and the doll would walk around the room hand-in-hand, carrying on fit to kill; one day, she just happened to press a little button on the doll and they found out that the doll could talk, so then they would walk and talk together, like two people, and if Aunt Gert liked it that much, Beck knew it was all right.

But what if, next, Uncle Reggie didn't turn up with a whole mess of clothes, beautiful dresses and underclothes of all kinds, and one dress to exactly match the doll's! Honestly, he was enough to kill you.

"Mother-and-daughter set," he said. "For my little bird with the broken wing."

He came walking through the bedroom door with the bundles piled so high in his arms that all Beck could see over them was his big, old bald head and his nose hooked into the top bundle to hold it from sliding off. Aunt Gert and Aunt Frances came in, feather-white, to see what. All four of them excited as could be, while Beck opened and opened and opened—dress upon dress, all brand-new; socks and shoes and sandals; a pair of red rubber boots and a raincoat; sets of underclothes to match the dresses.

Nylon briefs, Beck said to herself. Blue, yellow, aqua, and pink, like the paper napkins on the TV. Only these are *nylon*. Oo, I'll bet they cost him!

Aunt Frances said, "*Look* at this yellow dress! How could a mere man ever pick out such lovely things!"

Uncle Reggie looked at Aunt Gert. "I guess we know," he said, "what little lady helped me. And to get the right sizes, too!" He picked up a blue beret and put it on his bald head. "How do you think this looks on me? Terrible, huh?"

It did; and he made funny bows to everyone, until Beck had to stop laughing so, it hurt her sore face.

The thing about Uncle Reggie, he *liked* everybody so much. It was nice to have somebody around who liked you and showed it. Of course, Aunt Gert did and Aunt Frances, too; but Uncle Reggie was a stranger; so many strangers acted as if they didn't like anybody. Of course, he was kind of homely; big in front, and bald, and a great nose, and Beck guessed she could tell false teeth when she saw them. But who cared when he was so nice?

Aunt Gert said he lived in New York and Traveled In Lipsticks. He only came to Bishop four times a year; and then, she said, he was her Prince Charming.

Beck said she didn't see how anybody could stay Prince Charming so far away and only four times a year, and Aunt Gert said she couldn't explain, exactly, how that could come about; but maybe if you lived and learned, that might be the best kind of a Prince Charming because for nine-tenths of the time he was Something To Dream About; and Aunt Frances looked at her and said, Well, after all, it was what there was, wasn't it, honey?

On that night, the night of the clothes, Beck went to sleep thinking Prince Charming and nylon briefs; she woke up in the morning, thinking nylon briefs, blue, yellow, aqua, and pink. There were eggs for breakfast, and then that old Dr. Garland.

He came in with his little black bag and set it down on the floor beside the bed. Beck couldn't help herself; at the sight of it, she gave him one good ugly old scowl.

He said, "You don't like me any better today, do you?"

Beck said, "No."

"Why? When I've fixed your nose so it won't look like a fried egg?"

"You know why."

He did, too. He looked where she was looking, at the little black bag, and he said, kind of grunting, "Single-track mind. You still harping on that? Shoot, you know where babies come from, your mother told you. Here." He poked his old, cold funny-tasting thermomenter into her mouth. "No, don't talk. Keep your fat lip shut on it."

He didn't say it mean, but all the same she thought, I'd like to bite the end off, so's he'd have to buy a new one. Cost him. Of course I know where babies come from. But he don't.

He had his hand on her wrist, counting. "Strong as a mule," he said. "Not even sick."

Hnf, my leg's broke. I guess that's sick.

Beck sniffed, watching him while he poked around in his bag. Bottles and pills. That was all there was room for.

"Brother!" he said. He'd laid out a couple of little bottles and was looking around the room. All the dresses were hung out on hangers, so she could keep seeing them. "Look at the new duds!" He grinned at her. "I guess it paid off, getting run over, didn't it?"

Beck couldn't help it; she turned as red as a beet. She opened her mouth to say she hadn't got run over on purpose, but not a word would come, and the thermomenter dropped right out on the sheet. He picked it up and looked at it.

How had he known? Mean, stinking old snooper! She said out loud, in a kind of wail, "You sneaked and watched me, you old—"

He was busy, looking at the thermomenter. He said, as if he wasn't quite paying attention, "Tit for tat! Who's sneaked and watched me, time after— What!"

For a minute, he didn't say another word; then one of his eyebrows started to move, it crept up, almost into his hair.

So he did know. He must've seen. And he'd tell. She said, before she could stop it coming out, "You going to tell Mama?"

Because if he did, Aunt Gert would know and Aunt Frances. And Uncle Reggie. How could you bear it if Uncle Reggie knew what you'd done?

Tears came into Beck's eyes and began to roll down her cheeks.

"Hey, hold it," Garland said.

He was appalled and practically speechless himself. He hadn't actually known anything; coming in, he'd been tickled to death to see all the new clothes hanging around, because Gert and Frances had told him, both sputtering with indignation, about Nellie's Christmas presents for her kids. His remark had been casual, smack off the top of his mind. What it had produced had shocked him as deeply as he had ever been shocked in his life.

Goddammit, the poor little devil, what people do to their kids. Serves Nellie right. Brother, this one took matters into her own hands with a vengeance.

"Certainly I'm not going to tell anyone anything," he said. "Why would I?"

What was the use? Beck asked herself. Good things never lasted anyway. You grabbed what you could of it. You had to if you ever wanted anything.

"You will so tell," she said. "You all tell each other. And I told on you. You fibbed worse'n I did, too."

She began to wail, not loudly but with a sustained despair that curdled Garland's breakfast in his stomach.

"All right," he said. He snapped a couple of Kleenexes out of the box on the bedside table and dropped them on her hands. "Mop up now. And listen."

Listen to what? What was there to say? Garland cleared his throat twice. According to her standards, I'm as bad as she is, and I'm grown up, so nobody's after me. All right.

What was there to listen to? Beck thought. Disaster, as usual. A pep talk. Don't do what you done.

"Look," Garland said. "People have got to trust each other. Some can't; but some can. I'll trust you if you'll trust me. I'll shut up if you will."

"I already told."

"All right, don't keep on telling. Quit yakking about it. Is it a deal?"

Beck said nothing.

Goddammit, this was a hell of a thing to—

"Look," he said desperately. "What would you do if you found a lost baby?"

That did something. Beck stared at him, bleary-eyed but fascinated. "A luh-lost baby?"

"That's what I said. A little baby, just born, lost in the world, with no one to take care of him? What would you do?"

"I'd—I'd *keep* him!"

Oh, dammit! Blast it!

"What if you couldn't keep him? Would you chuck him away? Or find a place for him? Take him somewhere in a basket. Look here, you know what an orphan is?"

"Sure." Beck stared at him still, her eyes electric. "They live in—in *buildings*. They got no papa and no mama."

"And no whiskey soda," Garland grunted under his breath. My God, I'm crazy.

"If anyone finds a baby like that, he has to send it away to be with the orphans."

"Why does he?"

"Because if he doesn't, it's against the law. If a doctor didn't, he could be put in jail."

"I think that's a mean law."

"All right, I didn't make it. Now listen. I don't say I did anything, or what I did. But that could be one way the baby got into the basket, and if you figure out that there's a way, you could, for the love of Pete, quit being so mixed up, couldn't you? Also, yakking around, you could cause a lot of harm. The baby could be taken away from the people who love it and stuck with the orphans."

"Oh, yes. Yes, it could. I'll never, never breathe one word about it again. It was right, what you done. It was the right thing to do."

"Well, let's not say that. Let's say it seemed like the right thing to do at the time. Sometimes anybody doesn't know. Like you had your reasons for getting yourself run over. Seemed right then. And—"

Garland glanced around at the dresses, of which, at the moment, there seemed to be a roomful.

Dammit, what am I saying? Do it again, the first chance you get? Crime pays? Oh, hell, yes, it does, but—

"Look, I won't do it again if you won't. I won't tell on you if you won't tell on me. Okay?"

He held out his hand, which Beck solemnly shook.

"Not that we both oughtn't to have a good licking for it," she said. "Hadn't we?"

Safe in his car, Garland pulled out his handkerchief and mopped his brow.

The ring-tailed devil, floating a foot or so in the air in front of him, said, What an unmoral son-of-a-gun some folks turned out to be!

Look, you repair damage you've done if you can; I did some to that kid that day, Garland said.

She has got you over a barrel, buddy boy. She will probably go yapping to Aunt Gert and Frances the minute your back is turned.

I am getting so, Garland said, I don't care who has got whom over a barrel. Unmoral? Maybe. Hell, it all depends on what you think doesn't rate getting found out. Good God, the poor kid has got to be able to trust somebody. So to heck with you, if you get what I mean.

Outside Joe Randall's office a bunch of his workmen were lined up on the edge of the loading platform, just sitting. They looked a little glassy-eyed and bloated, and made frequent trips to the water cooler; some stomachs kept rumbling in a windy way. Nobody made much of this—it was a discomfort common to all. If you spend the week's grocery money on fishballs, you've got to eat them, there's nothing left over for anything else.

The factory was shut down today. Joe was in his office, not talking to anybody, apparently figuring. He had been to Bishop and had come back and closed down the plant, some said for good, some said temporarily; nobody knew. The work force was waiting on Joe. Nobody had anything to do but sit on the loading platform and shoot the breeze.

"Them fishballs," someone said meditatively; and someone else: "Yeah. I hear a couple wells in town been drunk dry. Folks starting to haul water."

There was a silence; then a third voice took up the theme: "Not to speak of other liquid refreshment."

And: "Godfrey mighty, yes, the Coke and Pepsi salesmen's had a field day."

Two oil trucks, belonging to different companies, went by, one after the other, barreling off down the road like bird dogs on a hunt.

Someone said, "Well, anyway. You got time now to read what's printed on the sides of the oil trucks."

"Yeah. Which would you rather be? 'Flammable' or 'Inflammable'?"

"Well, I d'no. That's a moot question."

Inside the office Joe grinned. A wry grin. The situation in a nutshell. Couldn't have been put neater.

The commentary said all there was to say about next spring's oil bills; you could stretch it, if you wanted to pursue disaster, to include the monthly payments on this and that, and the money that would be due for Christmas presents; if you went really whole hog, you could put in the world of plenty, full of goods and services, all high-priced and gilt-edged, and the pressure put on a man to buy, whether he had any money or not. So, would he rather be flammable or inflammable? Be caught going? Or coming?

A moot question.

Joe took a long breath and called through the office door. "Come in here, will ya, boys? I've got something to talk over."

Might as well get it over with. It was a real newfangled notion this time. Marvin was really going to tune up over this one, but Joe was through listening to Marvin. He hadn't as a matter of fact seen

Marvin today; the old coot was staying away from the office, holed up somewhere in the machinery. Sore about something. Waiting for Joe to come to him. He had been, however, Joe saw with some amusement, keeping an ear to the ground, because after the men had come in from the loading platform, Marvin eased himself sideways through the door.

Joe said, "Well, boys, we're quitting for good on fishballs."

Marvin wasn't so mad that he could help putting in his two cents. He said, "Good godfrey, no! What in chrise-name'll the town eat this winter?"

The sarcasm in his voice was pretty nasty. Joe paid no attention to it. He said, "I've got a different idea."

"Joe's got an idea, boys," Marvin said. "Another one. Well, I heard tell of an outfit down the coast going on to Irish sea moss for junket. Ain't enough Irish sea moss in this area, though, to fill a bucket, is there? Or are you going to can a bucketful, Joe, and hope to find more?"

Joe looked him in the eye. "Not exactly. What would you say to clearing a patch of ground this fall, having it plowed and fitted, and next spring planting it to beans?"

There was a silence.

Somebody said in a breaking voice, "Beans?"

And somebody else: "Good God, Joe! If this town was to put beans down on top of all them fishballs, we could go back to sailing ships with no trouble or expense."

"Look," Joe said. He spread out some sheets closely covered with figures. "This is the best bean-raising land in the country—"

Marvin, so far, had added nothing to his initial remarks. He had been standing by the door, his fists shoved into his pockets, his lower lip thrust out. "I take it," he interrupted portentously, "you think you can shove this town backwards a hundred years, that it? Well, my grandfather—"

"You shut up, Marvin," Joe said. "I know all about your grandfather. The last crop he raised 'he got ten cents a ton.' I bet we could double the price and still make a profit."

"Hanh?" Marvin said, puzzled.

"What we're going to need is a lot of cheap beans. I can get them this winter, shipped in; but what we could do next year, if we wanted to, is raise our own, save on shipping charges, spend our money in town."

Marvin blew out his lips with a snorting sound. "Who, for godsakes, in this town remembers how to grow beans? Ain't no farmers here no more. Nobody's done any farming to amount to anything for years, except once in a while a man's wife hounds him to spade her up a cucumber bed."

"Look, I'm trying to tell you what we could do if we wanted to. Use what we've got. Why don't you listen and—"

"Because it's the goddamnedest foolishness I ever heard, that's why!" Marvin's face slowly turned purple. "Who wants to go to all that trouble, do all that work for next to nothing? I can get a package of dried beans all ready to bake, don't even need to be washed, from the A and P for half what it would—If you think you can make a day's pay out of canned beans—"

"I don't plan to—" Joe began.

"And where do you think you're going to find any farmland that Ame Wilkinson ain't turned into a gravel pit?"

Joe sat back in his chair. "All right, hurry up, get it off your chest. When you're through, I'll talk."

"You ain't got anything to say I want to hear. Like I say, a mess of radical, damn-fool—"

"If you want to spend the winter sitting around listening to Westerns," Joe said, "it's all right with me. You can pick up your Social Security tomorrow and live like a king, compared to the rest of us, and maybe you'd better. If you don't want to listen to what I've got to say."

This certainly was something new, from Joe. The work force listened, deadpan but fascinated, their heads swiveling, as at a tennis match, from Joe to Marvin. You could not have told from their faces what anyone was thinking, whose side anyone was on. Polite interest was the keynote—your fight; nothing-to-do-with-me.

Marvin didn't turn a hair. He thrust out his hands, palms up, and let them drop. "Oh, take over," he said. "Let's all hear what there is of interest now."

"I've been talking to the lab over in Bishop," Joe said. "About canning animal food. There's a chemist who's come up with a new formula for making it liquid out of stuff like dried beans, fish, seaweed—"

Marvin said, muffled, "Oh, my God!"

Joe set his jaw. He went on. "All local products for us, nothing we'd need to ship in. That is, if I can drum up a little interest in growing some beans. Ought not to be too hard. We grew a lot of beans around here once. We would now if there was any market. Well, the plant can offer a market, maybe a pretty decent price, when we get going. The Bishop Laboratory uses around sixty thousand pounds of animal food a month; if we make it under their supervision, they'll use it. What's more, they'll give us an approval stamp, let us use their name on our can, so that other big laboratories—" He stared around him at the faces, on which so far no light of understanding was beginning to break.

"That's a hell of a sales gimmick, that lab's world famous. A market made to order. And we're in on the ground floor if we want to be. I got this chemist on the phone and talked to him; he's all ready to come and supervise making his formula—"

That got Marvin where he lived. He rose right up.

"You're getting a—a damned egghead in here to—to—" He choked. "Hell, you never needed nothing like that canning fishballs for humans."

"That's right," Joe said. "But it seems you can't be too careful what you feed a million pedigreed mice. One reason we ought to grow our own beans is that we can't risk getting a shipment that's been doused with insecticide. Humans, it seems, 'll put up with that. Mice won't, it kills 'em. Okay, Marvin, let me finish, then you can sound off all you want to. Raw material, other stuff besides beans, is a dime a dozen around here. Rockweed, the Lord knows, there's plenty of that around for the picking up, and fish—what about the culls the draggers throw away? We could get them for little or nothing."

Be darned, he thought. That rang a bell. Something they understand, know about personally. Not a man there who couldn't see in his mind's eye the fleets of trawlers and draggers headed in from sea, with the tons of dead fish, culls too small for market, bobbing in their wakes. Waste, pure and simple, thrown to the gulls, that any fisherman would be glad of a market for. Not a man there who hadn't had his say time and again about that.

"Well, there it is," Joe said. "It looks like a watertight proposition to me. We can use some of our old chowder machinery, and for what else we need, I—"

"Well, I was wondering about that," Marvin said in a voice curdled with sarcasm. "What you planned to use for money, I mean."

Joe had been planning to go into that next, to say that with the laboratory's backing he could set that up at the bank; but he had held his temper too long.

He said, "Anybody else got a word to put in? Anybody besides Marvin?"

Nobody had. After the one slight flicker, the faces had gone back to blank.

Joe stared at them. He guessed he could tell what they were thinking.

Joe. Old Joe. A helluva good guy, but inclined to be chancy. Look at the way he'd run a good business into the ground. It was all very well for him to take risks on his own; when it came to involving them, their time, work and investment—because clearing fields, plowing, all that, would cost. Hadn't he thought of that? Who had a plow? It was something that had to be thought over; and they would. But nobody was going to commit himself right now.

Somebody in the background said under his breath, "Raise beans? Oh Jeezus!"

Joe heard, and his voice rose to a bawl. "All right! Look at us! Look at this town!"

"What's the matter with it?" Marvin said. "Good enough town, for godsake. It's the town now, is it, it ain't you."

"Yes, by God, it is the town," Joe said. "We ain't amounted to popcorn since the last sailing ship sunk in the mud in 1911. We've let our land go till it's all gravel pits or burnt-out slash or puckerbrush, till the whole works looks like a bomb crater in an old battlefield."

"So what? Who can do anything about that?"

"It ain't going to be anybody but us. Nobody's going to come in here and fix things up so we won't be shoving last year's debts ahead of us like a pissamire up a cornstalk. Hell, people used to like to farm, got some fun out of it. Didn't need a sledgehammer to pound it into their thick heads either, that that was a way to make a living."

"Well, you ain't going to pound it into my thick head," Marvin said. "I'll be doggoned if I'll go backwards. I'm a modern-minded man, by the god. I'm living now, not a hundred years ago."

"Yes, you are," Joe said levelly. "You're as modern-minded a man as I ever saw. So you go ahead and live all winter on your unemployment checks, or your Social Security, or any other handout you can wangle. Me, I personally don't like the idea of rocking-chair money if there's anything else I can do. Them government handouts is a damn good thing, I'm for 'em, but I kind of run of an idea they're for them that can't find work, not for them that don't want to. I'm opening up, canning pet food. Anybody wants a job can have it. Anybody that don't, I'll give him his time and welcome."

"All right, I quit!" Marvin bawled. He waited, looking around as if to say to all there, he can't run without me and he knows it.

"Okay," Joe said. "I'll write you out a check."

Marvin spun around and slammed out the door.

Joe gazed after him. Well, that was that. He was sorry.

He thought, he's an old man, and I was damned tough on him. Maybe I ought to go after him. He's been here a long time . . .

But something in his mind shrugged a little . . . You could be a lot sorrier for a long association's ending if you were sure it was. Marvin had stated his opinion, gone out on his limb, before. He had always been against; but he had always come back.

Joe looked around at the faces. Marvin's opinion carried weight in the town. To his surprise everybody looked relieved, and some, unmistakably joyful.

He said, "Anybody else?"

Somebody said, "I been thinking."

And somebody else: "What about?"

"My back meadow."

"Oh, yeah? What about your back meadow? Full of puckerbrush, ain't it?"

"Uh huh. I got the best crop in town. Lays all over yours."

"Well, I wouldn't say that. Not exactly. I got more kinds than you have. I got good blackberry bushes and alders thick's a bull's hind laig."

The meeting began to break up, the men sauntering out of the office to the loading platform, headed home.

A voice carried back: "Might taste better than fishballs at that. Liquid, he said, go down easier, anyway. And, hell, a man could lace it with rum—"

Not sarcastic; friendly; interested, anyway.

Okay, Joe said to himself, and he grinned.

Some would; some wouldn't. Like anywhere, you always had a few.

Day after day the damp wind blew, as if on special assignment to melt away the snow. Whatever its warm breath touched grew moist and dripped; asphalt highways steamed; mist crept between the panes of storm sash and windows, blinding them, so that if a man wanted to see out, he had to open a door. Wherever he went around town, people talked about the weather.

Amos Wilkinson watched it; lying in bed, awake, at night, he listened to it. Blinds rattled, tree branches clashed together, anything loose banged; drainpipes and gutters, in the beginning gurgling full, clanged empty in the wind now because the snow on the roof was gone. No man, mentioning the weather once to Amos, wished to do so again.

"Well, for goodness' sake, what ails *him*?" Aurora Collins said.

"Seems as though the weather's one thing you could comment on, without getting your arm bit off at the wrist."

Aurora, clerk at the hardware store, was having lunch at the Downtown Diner; the matter had come up because the waitresses, between servings, were going over to the back window to peek out at Amos, who was sitting hunched down in his car in the Diner parking lot.

"Not doing nothing; just sitting. With a face like a meat ax," they reported.

"Well, he's hanging round town for something," Aurora said. "Gives me the creeps, if you want to know. Every time I glance out the store window, seems I see *him* going by."

Not that it was strange for a man to hang around the street; with Randall's temporarily closed for reconversion, many were; it was only strange for Amos Wilkinson to do it. His gravel pit was working night and day; he had been driving his crew, snatching at the mild weather, digging in on the "gold mine" at the old Cooney place. "Driving everybody's tail off," Mack Jensen had reported. "In case two cents gets away from him before the ground freezes."

"Well," one of the waitresses said, "he's acting some old peculiar, if you ask me."

"Maybe," Aurora said, "it runs in the family. I heard Nellie say she wouldn't be surprised if it was something like that."

Clementina, of course, was off her rocker; and nobody in town had forgotten Amos's Christmas tree.

Mack Jensen, confronted with a small crisis at the pit, which he could have handled with a word if he had had Amos's go-ahead, went looking for him in town and finally spotted him in his car in the parking lot back of the Diner. Biding his time, in case matters ever came up in court, Mack would do nothing now on his own; he was building up a stack of witnesses to the fact that the old man wouldn't so much as let him tighten a nut on a crankshaft without looking over his shoulder. He pulled up alongside Amos's car.

"What to hell's with you—you in love with one of them waitresses?"

he asked. Matters were still strained between them; Mack didn't give a damn if they were. He went on, "You favoring us with your presence out at the pit today?"

Amos said, "What's the trouble now?" He looked about as usual, his old felt hat jammed down to his eyebrows above the hard blue glare; the long, leathery cheeks clean-shaven; his work clothes, washed and ironed by Lucy, clean, though, where usually at this time of day they were covered with muck and engine grease.

"We run into boulders under that layer of surfacing gravel," Mack said laconically. "I told ya we would."

"Yeah, you knew a lot about it, at the time. Well, what do you want me to do? Come and pick 'em out with my teeth?"

"I don't doubt you could, if you took a notion to. What'll I do?"

"You just go ahead. The way you would if I was there."

Amos was well aware of what Mack had in mind about a court case; it wasn't anything, he told himself, that he couldn't stop in its tracks when he got around to it. One way or another. The feller was going to need some tending to, later on, when Amos had time. He went on, "You make a mistake, I'll come out tomorrow and change didies. Today I got business here in town."

"Okay." Mack clashed the truck into gear and drove away.

Amos sat on.

He was waiting for the game wardens, who might drive into town any day, now that the snow was gone, to start the wild-dog hunt in Cooney's Heath. To get there, they would have to go through town; usually they stopped to eat at the Downtown Diner, which was where, if they came, Amos meant to drop in, casually speak to them, pass the time of day. The matter of the hunt was sure to come up. Amos meant to advise them. They were both young fellows, know-it-alls, but from another part of the state. They'd take advice from an authority on local conditions. If they'd had any training at all, they must know that that swamp wasn't one you just went into, not knowing anything about it.

Still deep snow in there in the underbrush, he would tell them. The time to go would be when just enough was left to do a little tracking, but not enough to hamper a man, and when the water from the meltage had had more time to drain away. Better still, wait for a freeze. Water on that deer trail into the Hummock would probably be halfway to their belts.

That'd stop them. In the old days young fellows wouldn't have cared two hoots if they got a dose of swamp water. Take him, for instance; spent night after night sleeping wet-arsed on the ground or, in zero weather, with a campfire built between the brush lean-to and a snowbank. But the boys were sure careful nowadays how they got their pants cuffs wet. Of course, they might go pig-headed on him, decide that, now they'd come this far, they'd give it a try; you never knew. In that case he'd go with them. He guessed he could set a track that they could follow; it wouldn't be anywheres near a fallen tree off the trail, where there was something lying that he couldn't afford to have anybody see.

If they postponed the hunt or if they didn't come today at all—and maybe they wouldn't—then he would have to go into the swamp tonight. It was still too soon; there'd be some snow left to leave tracks in, but with this warm wind blowing, they wouldn't last. Maybe even now, with all that meltage water flowing around in there, he'd find enough bare spots so he wouldn't have to leave any sign at all. A man could always cover up a few tracks.

But it would have to be tonight: he had cut it fine, too fine; he didn't dare put it off any longer. People were beginning to wonder why he was hanging around like this; you could tell. Mack was, and them waitresses peeking out the back window of the Diner. So better not any more after today. Go in tonight; do the job; get rid of everything, once and for all.

Now that he'd made up his mind, he was suddenly furious at all the senseless reasons why he, Amos Wilkinson, should have to be pushed around like this, and not by anything he could get his hands on or fight back. Cooney's Heath, a piddling little swamp compared to some he'd seen, and crossed, in the North Woods, in places where his own foot was the only one that ever made tracks there; and here he was, waiting on it, lying awake nights, figuring how much snow would be left in there, how much water from the thaw over that branch trail, how to get in there in the daytime and not be seen by some nosy jackass—Ev Peterson, kids hunting rabbits in the woods this side of the Heath—who'd want to know what Ame Wilkinson was doing over there, lugging a spade. A hell of a job to have to do by moon and flashlight and make sure you left no sign.

This thaw; who could have foreseen it? This time of year it didn't make any sense; aimed right at Amos Wilkinson. Not the first time, either, that the reasonless works and ways of weather, nature, whatever you wanted to call the goddam thing, put into the world for no purpose but to hinder a man, destroy his plans, interfere with his rights, had been aimed at him . . . What fool sets foot in melting snow over a shaking bog, black muck who knew how deep? Well, he would have to. At night.

He stiffened suddenly in his seat, spun around, thrusting his face toward the open car window. In the maple trees, somewhere, over there on the edge of the parking lot . . . oh, the goddam thing . . . where? No. It wasn't. The senseless rattle, the tinny clatter, blown toward him on the wind from somewhere far off; hell, it was two fellows with a compressor and an air drill, opening up the sidewalk in front of the bank. He had seen them when he came by. Been hearing that off and on all the afternoon, for godsake. Must've noticed it now because it had just stopped. Sure, quitting time; no use hanging around here any longer, the wardens wouldn't be likely to show up this late. Nevertheless, he listened a moment longer, his head bent sideways, concentrating. There was nothing now but the wind. The warm wind, thawing the snow.

It swung the creaking signs—HARDWARE and DRUGSTORE and COCA-COLA and POST OFFICE; it blew the wrappers of civilization— gum-candy-bar-crackerjack-ice-cream-lollipop, printed or plain, wax-paper-cellophane-tinfoil-polyethylene-brown-paper-bag—in a witch's dance across the parking lot; Aprilwarm, smelling of fungus, of rot, of dead-leaved decay, it blew against Amos's face the insult with the i's dotted and the t's crossed and the period added at the end: that no man, no top dog set by God over the heap of lesser creatures, to own, to rule, to work his will, could do a goddam thing about the wind if it wanted to blow.

The game wardens, busy in another part of the county, did not come that night, or any night. Nothing was further from their minds than a wild-dog hunt in Cooney's Heath. True, in the Diner that day with Mack, they had mentioned the dogs, but only in telling, making a good story out of, that smart old cooky, Everard Peterson. The hunt actually had been Mack's idea, and they had agreed that sometime it would have to be done—"But not till spring. You couldn't get in there now."

The wardens, having had reason to at the time, knew a great deal more about conditions in the Heath than Amos Wilkinson did.

Lucy, waiting supper, saw the lights of Amos's car turn into the driveway and go past the house to the barn. She always had supper ready by dark, which, of course, came early now: short days, long nights. Amos was generally home by four o'clock and he wanted his supper the moment he got there. Sometimes he was late—he was, tonight.

So thank goodness, nothing's spoiled, she thought.

Amos was going to like his supper, which was ham hocks boiled with cabbage and potatoes, one of his favorite meals. Lucy hummed a little song to herself as she hustled the dishes onto the table. And then, with everything getting cold, Amos didn't come in.

She called tentatively from the back door, "Amos, dear, supper's on," but he couldn't have heard her; at least, he didn't answer.

I had better run out and see where he is, she thought.

Perhaps he's doing something I can help him with.

The barn was old-fashioned and big. It had once housed a herd of cattle from which the previous owner had made his living running a dairy farm, but now did double duty as garage and storage space for Amos's earth-moving machines. Except for a dim light at the back, where Lucy could hear him moving around, the barn was dark, full of shapes and shadows which she couldn't see around. She peered fearfully past the blunt nose of a power shovel, wondering what on earth was keeping him so long with supper waiting, if he would mind her telling him that things were getting cold, or if she turned on the overhead light.

She never could tell these days what would upset him; he still seemed to be put out with her all the time. Over the Christmas things it must still be, because she herself wasn't over that yet. It still made her shake to think how dreadful it had all been. The way he had come into the house and stood there looking, so that at first she'd thought he'd been rendered speechless by the beautiful tree; and then she'd turned around and had seen he was in one of his awful rages, about what, she didn't know, except he must've found out that Connie had been . . . and although she knew she mustn't ever, ever talk to him when he was . . . like that . . . she'd burst out before she could stop herself, "Oh, Amos, dear, not on our Saviour's Birthday!"

For a moment she'd thought he was going to . . . hurt her . . . the way he looked, coming at her that way with both of his hands out in front of him as if he were going to . . . clutch; but it was only the Christmas things he grabbed and tore. Oh, it wasn't right for him to hate Connie so. His own flesh and—oh dear, *flesh*, such a horrid word, I must think not to use it—and Lucy had been unable to watch, but had sat with both hands over her face while he ripped everything down and up . . . all those pretty . . . and the tree chopped in the cellar; and the presents—She would never know now what to put in her thank-you notes to Connie and Clementina, because she didn't know what had been in the packages, of course you couldn't ask them, you couldn't say, I don't know what it was because Amos burnt . . . you couldn't let that get around, even to your own—oh, dear, not *flesh* again—blood—that was better—your own blood relatives, let them think he was crazy. Amos might know, he had torn the bundles apart; but you couldn't ask him, mercy, no, not with him feeling . . . and besides, he'd forbid. He'd said not to speak to Connie, but he hadn't said not to send a thank-you . . . but how could you send a thank-you if you didn't know what to say thank you for?

She had sat in horror, hearing the fire growling in the chimney getting louder and louder—oh, he must know that chimney, with that one he ought to be careful—once trying to call out, Amos, dear, the chimney's afire, but not able to make her voice come out, until he had stamped yelling up the stairs . . . with his face . . . and calling those dreadful names because she hadn't told him; and the Fire Department, thank goodness . . . she did hope it had all been burned before Jack Riley saw; and since then Amos had been . . . oh, dear. But he would come around; he always had. Things would be better, of course; they always were.

It was awfully dark in the barn; that lightbulb back there was behind something. She couldn't see Amos or anything but the black bulk of the machines.

She said, "Amos, dear, supper's on," put out her hand to the switch beside the door and turned on the overhead light. Amos was half in and half out of an old storage cupboard; all she could see was his end. As the light came on, he backed out and turned around to face her. He said, "Where's my five-celled flashlight?"

"Why, in the house, dear. You brought it in, remember? You told me to get new batteries—"

"Oh God," Amos said. "And you didn't."

"Well, I was going to, but—"

Oh dear, what had happened, he hadn't given her the money. If she'd taken it out of the housekeeping money, she couldn't have put by that teentsy bit each week for emergencies. So she'd waited. She was sure he knew she had the teentsy bit somewhere, and that he expected her to use that; but then she'd forgotten all about the flashlight.

To her surprise he didn't yell at all. He got out his wallet and handed her a bill.

"Get in the car and go down to the hardware. Get me ten batteries.

Get a hustle on, before the store closes."

"But, Amos, supper's—"

He didn't say any more; he merely started the car, backed it out, and turned it around. "Now you won't be any goddam half an hour doing that," he said. "Go on. Get a move on, will you?"

Oh, mercy. It must be some terrible emergency with his work . . . if he wasn't taking time to yell. Supper would be cold, and he would yell about that but . . . Lucy flew.

She made it to the hardware just as Aurora Collins was locking the door.

"Lucy, I'm closed!" Aurora said. "I've got to get home and get supper for Harper and the kids, and I'm late as 'tis."

"Oh Rora, I know," Lucy said breathlessly. "I did hurry and I'm sorry to be so late and such a nuisance, but Amos has an emergency for these flashlight batteries, he has got to have them."

Aurora grumbled, but she opened the store and got the batteries. "Ten!" she said, staring. "What's he, for goodness' sake, going out jacking deer?"

Lucy drew herself up. "Amos," she said, "is not one to break the law, you know that, Rora."

"Hnf," Aurora said.

Later, at the supper table, she told Harper about it.

"An emergency!" she said. "I should think 'twas! Ten batteries, and him with all those spotlights on his trucks. If people need stuff that bad, they could take the trouble to get to the store before closing time. She wouldn't hardly wait for me to put them in a bag. Tore out of there and into her car and off she went, slap against the red light, stopped the whole line of traffic coming in on Route Sixteen."

"Where to heck was Willie Saxton?" Harper said.

He was the same Harper Collins who drove the milk truck; in his rounds he had more than once coped on the highway with Lucy Wilkinson driving a car.

"Oh, Willie, you know him!" Aurora said. "Traffic or no traffic, suppertime, home he goes, to eat. But if he'd been on duty at the time, Miss Lucy'd have got herself a ticket and a good, fat fine, I can tell you that."

"Hadn't ought to be allowed to set foot into a car," Harper said morosely. "You meet her, you have to stop, back up, or go round."

"And either one you do," Aurora said, "up she'll start and try to pass you whilst you're doing it."

"What was she in such a hurry for?"

"Oh, Amos. Something in the gravel pit, I guess. She didn't say. What's the matter with him, Harper, setting in the parking lot back of the Diner all the afternoon?"

Amos was still in the barn. He had got together some things—his rifle was leaning against the wall next to a long-handled spade, and he had put on his hunting coat and the hip rubber boots he used on fishing trips. He grabbed the paper bag out of Lucy's hand and began poking batteries into the big, empty flashlight, not saying a word until he had clicked it on and seen that it was working.

Then he said, "Go on in the house. I got some work down at the pit. Won't be back till late."

"Amos, your supper!"

"You go eat it. And then you lock up the house and go to bed."

"But . . . oh, well, I've got a new magazine. I'll read it and wait up for you."

"You turn out the lights. You leave them on, you'll get callers to open your big mouth to about me not being home, and I'll—oh, for godsake, git!"

He turned, picked up his rifle and spade, and strode past her out of the barn. She heard his heavy steps go past outside, headed for the back.

Towards the woodlot, she thought. Now, what could he be going there for? Surely he isn't going to walk down through the woods to the gravel pit, when he could just as well use the truck.

And taking his rifle, what was that for? And that spade? A rifle was to hunt with . . . to kill with. Oh, certainly not jacking deer, he would never . . . he was so against things like that. But why the rifle, just down working at the pit?

A nameless worry nudged at Lucy's mind; something in the back of it, put away, forgotten because it was not nice to remember . . . what? Oh, yes. he' d come out of the woodlot last fall, when she'd thought . . . but he hadn't . . . of course he hadn't. Oh, it had been so dreadful when, for a while, she'd thought he might have . . . Oh dear. Was it something to do with those men on the trawler, something to do with . . . *that*?

Why, what ailed him—he'd made all that fuss about ten batteries and then gone off leaving five of them in the paper bag, there on the barn shelf!

She grabbed the bag and ran out waving it and calling, "Yoo hoo, Amos!" but he was either already gone or he didn't bother to answer.

Amos went down into the swamp. He followed the path through his own woodlot, noting with relief as he went that, even in the undergrowth, the snow was nearly gone. It was soft underfoot, puddles in places; he was, he told himself, probably going to get wet out on that branch path where the fallen tree was; wouldn't be anything he couldn't handle. Last summer and early fall had been dry; the rains in November hadn't amounted to much. Of course there'd be snow water; but with so much snow already melted, a lot of that would be drained away. The swamp had a fine, unclogged outlet brook which always took down high water fast. He guessed he'd figured things about right, after all. The only difficulty would be to find the exact fallen tree at night; there were a lot of fallen trees. The feller had run every which way; but it was the main deer track and the branch paths he'd got back to; in that swamp, it had had to be. But there'd have been a lot of wild-animal tracks around there, bound to be. Even with the thaw, there'd be traces left; and later on, there'd be a piece of a moon.

Darned cumbersome, having to carry the spade and the rifle in one hand, so he could use the flashlight with the other. For two cents, he'd stash the rifle here, somewhere, under a tree. He'd brought it only in case of the wild-dog pack. The story was, they'd tackle a man as soon as they would a deer. Amos figured he knew better; they were only domestic dogs gone wild, and normally they wouldn't pay any attention to a human except maybe to duck out of sight when they saw one. But one of them was a German shepherd, a treacherous breed even when tame, so Amos had heard all his life and was convinced of; so take no chances with that damn thing. With deep snow in the woods for a while, small game holed up and no deer scent to follow, dogs might have fared slim in the woods, anyway, and a hungry pack might turn out to be a different matter from a fed one. The rifle was a nuisance; but better be with it than without it, just in case.

And, by God, it was going to be a satisfaction if he got a chance, just once, to take a crack at a squirrel. Blasted things ought to be holed up in hollow trees for the winter this time of year. They weren't; they were all over town—in the trees around the gravel pit, the maples around his house. Probably this warm weather bringing them out. Well, let them come, tonight, out of their hollow trees and sound off in unison, he guessed he could tell, tonight, which was real and which was part of a nightmare; now that he was doing something at last, taking the action that would end all the trouble. He had it figured, anyway, now, what was giving him that bad dream. A man who'd grown up in the church and belonged to the lodge would have to believe in the Ten Commandments, God's Word, direct from God. He felt he had lived his life pretty much in accordance with them, insofar, of course, as a man could. During his lifetime, he'd shaved it thin, maybe, but who didn't? He guessed he'd committed adultery a few times, but what was that—a common occurrence with a number of men—and only by stretching a point could you call some of his business deals stealing. A still commoner occurrence, and only what any man had to do to keep his head above water.

But killing had turned out to be a different matter, with him. Once done, there it was; a finished thing; something he couldn't undo;

stayed heavy in his mind. Until he had sense enough to reason it out; the way he had now.

A destructive kid like that—a kid who'd give a woman the kind of a deal that bastard had given Connie—had the seeds in him of doing something a damn sight worse; he was better out of the world where he couldn't do the living any more harm. Amos wouldn't have just gone out and killed him, the way anybody'd be justified in doing—the way you'd put a harmful animal out of the way; but he'd had to. It was self-defense. And what it was, if you followed it through from the beginning, and all it was, you'd been a tool in the hand of a just God.

And if the world looked on that as any kind of a crime, then the world was in small business.

The trouble was, the world did. You couldn't get found out; people would get the wrong idea, being the way they were and mostly damn fools. You broke the law, they were after you like hounds. He guessed that, all in all, it was the idea of that that had been giving him bad dreams. Well, not anymore. Now that he had it figured, he felt better out of all reason. After tonight's job of work he could put it behind him and forget it.

He trotted easily along the deer trail on the near side of the Heath, finding the going even better than he had expected as the land dipped down. Muddy in spots, the trail was bare of snow except for a few grainy traces here and there, which he had no trouble going around or jumping. Not that he needed to bother about leaving tracks, the way the weather looked now.

The swamp was alive with wind. Puffy, ragged clouds blew fast across the sky. The damn wind, having blown forever and made everyone miserable out of all reason, had finally decided to make something of it. Rain. Rain before morning; and all to the good. By that time Amos would be home, warm in bed; the feller'd be sunk good and deep out of sight in swamp muck where nobody'd ever get a sight of him again; and his wallet, surely the only thing that by now could let be known who he'd been, burned up in Amos's furnace. Take no chances with that damn thing; burn it. Only thing to do to make sure. He in bed and rain falling over the swamp, washing away any tracks or traces; that would be the end of it. Once and for all.

As for being in the woods alone at night, what was that? A woods at night looked dark and lonesome; in daylight, at times, it might scare the tripes out of somebody wasn't used to it. Still, after all, what was it? Trees. Underbrush. Water. A swamp—what you got your feet wet in. Something he himself would've had the sense to leave out if he'd made the world. If there was ever anything that made a man doubt his religion, wonder if God really knew it all, it was stuff like a damn swamp; and if Amos Wilkinson had had any say, in the beginning, there'd have been some changes made.

Trotting along, he pulled up suddenly as his boots splashed ankle-deep into water.

Now what? The deer track was fairly high here, hadn't ought to be this much water. Expect some farther on, maybe; not here.

Peering ahead, he could make out through the swamp growth a kind of milky radiance. Water, sure enough. Where to hell did so much of it come from?

There certainly couldn't be a lot; not according to his calculations. He'd figured it; it had to be right. Hell, a little water, up to a man's ankles, what was that to bother about?

He stepped into it, going along, going in deeper. Up to his knees; then down; then bare ground again. Humph, just as he'd thought. Low place on the trail there, full of snow water; temporary pond. Then, without warning, he was into it again, to his thighs.

That was the way of it and, by God, it made him mad. Spend your life learning what there was to know about something; get to be an expert, an authority, the known best in your field. Learn the sign, learn how to foretell the way things were going to be in a given place, like in this place here; and along would come some piddling circumstance not foreseen to knock your calculations galley west, so you had to go back and start again from the beginning.

Well, he could have stood it once in a while, but it had happened too many times for him not to know what their intent was. They aimed it, personally and straight as a rifle barrel, right at Amos Wilkinson. Any other man come in here tonight, he'd have found the water down where it ought to be.

Amos did not stop. He went on. Up to his boot tops, up to his waist. He only half-felt the trickle of the icy water as his waders filled and as it soaked through the woolen layers around his middle; he was too hot with the blast of his fury. Whatever they were—the Devil or Tom Walker—Whoever took over, times, and ran it, there'd never been a One of Them yet able to stop Amos Wilkinson. And there wasn't going to be now.

The "they," in this case, was a colony of beavers, which had migrated to the outlet stream of Cooney's Heath early in the fall, after game wardens, farther upstate, had had to dynamite their dam. The colony in the beginning had had the bad fortune to choose a stream which was excellent for beavers, but bad for farmland and apple orchards along its banks when backed up into a pond behind a beaver dam. The beavers had put up with dynamite on three successive occasions. Each time they had patiently rebuilt their dam; then, disgusted, they had gone away from there—a long ways away, traveling down country, looking for a wild place where humans, the pest of the world, wouldn't fool around with a practical beaver's plans for a peaceful winter. They had settled on Cooney's Heath, where, it might seem, humans would have no reason to come. Working frantically against time and the coming of cold weather and aided immensely by the mild fall, they had thrown their dam across the mild, meandering stream that drained the swamp. They were snug behind it now with a winter's food supply. Over them, a fine, secure pond had backed up the trickles of swamp water and snow meltage for miles back into the Heath, and was still rising.

The game wardens had known about the beaver pond for some time, and had decided to let it alone. Beavers certainly couldn't do any harm in Cooney's Heath and, if they were driven out, they might go somewhere else where they would. This was the "they" whose actions had postponed the wild-dog hunt; the "they" whose works and ways

Amos had not foreseen. Not an Ultimate Power in the Universe, but only the result of the normal living conditions of a pack of overgrown rodents.

Amos plowed along, holding his rifle over his head to keep it from getting wet. He had had to put the flashlight into his pocket to free his left hand for the spade; the path was not hard to see—a white, watery line threading the undergrowth—and God damn them, he would show that he could follow it. The late moon was beginning to come up, anyway, lightening the eastern sky; he caught an occasional glimpse of it, ducking in and out of the hustling clouds. He concentrated on where he set his feet, feeling the slip and give of the muddy path. Get down off the trail . . . or fall down . . . get the gun wet . . .

The ground after a time began to slope upwards; the water fell away from his chest and thighs. Presently he was in swamp muck and then on bare ground. To his astonishment the moonlight showed tall trees towering against the sky.

For godsake. Hadn't come that far, had he? Those looked like the big pines on the hummock in the middle of the Heath. Couldn't be.

But they were. He had come halfway across the swamp, completely forgetting what he was there for. Must have plowed right past the entrance to the branch path he needed to find; which, of course, he ought to have been on the watch for, because it would have been under water, too.

What to hell ails me? Coming along by there too fast? Ought to have had the sense to use the flash; at least, I could've held it up so it wouldn't get wet, I'll bet it's drowneded out now.

He'd forgotten that, too. But maybe the rubber-lined pocket of his hunting coat had kept it dry.

No. The pocket was bulged out like a bladder and gushing streams. Leaked full.

Amos jabbed the spade upright into the mud at the margin of the hummock, hauled out the light, and flashed it on. Seemed to be all right; its powerful beam jerked out through the ranked boles of the pines, creating enormous shadows. The big trees of Cooney's Heath, at which Amos now stared with his underlip out.

He flashed his light from mighty bole to bole.

There they stood, the big ones, the virgin growth, three, five feet thick at the butt, trunks going up into solid blackness.

Damn them, a good many of their kind he'd whacked down, or knocked down, in his time, and enjoyed it.

"Kuh-riced! What I could do in here with a bunch of the boys and some bulldozers!" he said aloud. But, hell, this stand, here in the swamp, like this, nobody could—

The sound of his voice was echoed by a similar sound coming from a few feet away. It was almost as if the trees had snarled back at him.

Amos spun around, his blood curdling in his chest; it took him an instant to realize that some animal, a big one, was close by; and another to swing the light, low, around, and catch the eyes, red-hot, ruby-colored, which vanished instantly, but not before he caught a glimpse of the critter. A police dog. Looked to be all of five feet long.

Amos flung the rifle to his shoulder, but the flashlight, before he dropped it, hampered him. His shot plowed up the mud a few feet in front of his boots.

Them dogs. That pack of wild ones.

Maybe you'd had it in your mind that they wouldn't tackle a man, but that was when you were thinking about the possibilities. Now you had them here, right in front of you. How would any man know for sure what they might do? Nothing so bad, nothing so treacherous, the old-timers always said. A domestic dog gone wild was worse than a lucifee, worse than a cougar or a wolf. Real wild animals wouldn't go after you; but a wild dog would, as if, they said, once belonging to humans made him more dangerous than if he'd been born in the woods.

Maybe you didn't put no stock in it, but—well, they know what a gun is. They wouldn't dare to run up on a gun, but I'd better not turn my back.

He backed slowly down the slope of the hummock, felt mud suck at his boots and heard the splash and tinkle as he entered the water. Then he remembered the flashlight.

The light. He was going to need that. Now, by the time he found what he was looking for, the moon would have set, likely. Or even if it hadn't, in that thick undergrowth . . . Where was the blasted thing? It had fallen into the undergrowth where he'd been standing.

Slowly, step by step, holding the rifle cocked and ready, he went back, cautiously bending down, groping with one hand among dead wet sticks, moss, rotten fungus; thinking, with a cold stir at the back of his neck, how easy it would be for the damned things to jump a stooped-over man; scrabbling, swearing . . . until there it was, the round, cold metal cylinder, not near where he'd thought it must be, but sideways, where it had bounced to. He grabbed it, jumping upright and snapping on the button, almost with one movement; but the flashlight was dead. Either the water had at last soaked in, or the bulb was gone.

Well, try the other batteries, anyhow . . . and then, feeling in his pocket, he realized he'd left the other batteries behind in the barn. . . .

He hauled back and threw the flashlight as hard as he could into the trees; heard it land with a metallic thud and tinkle of broken glass against a tree trunk; and stood listening, the rifle at his shoulder, ready to let go at the first thing that moved in front of him.

There was nothing; nothing moving but the wind. And the only sound of anything living nearby was the squelch his own foot made, pulling out of the mud.

Scairt the buggers, he thought. Well, sure. Ain't one of them don't recall the business end of a gun; and from somewhere nearby a squirrel let go, the tinny drill, the maniac chitter exploding not like a sound but like a flash of light in his head. He dropped the rifle, spun around and ran headlong, stumbling, splashing, falling, vanishing under water as he fell. His head and shoulders emerged where the water deepened, like the forepart of some animal, half-land, half-water; a swamp beast, wild and hunted, surging toward safety in its secret lair, away from the ultimate destruction known to its kind.

The water drops of that desperate passage splashed on the twigs of flooded bushes, hung in the moonlight, sparkling for a moment before they lengthened and dripped down, falling with soft plat sounds into the water; a few translucent small waves curled up the margin of the hummock, their edges tipped with a shine, silver-colored but colder than silver and more pure; the roiled muck settled slowly. The trees, the big ones that got away, stood as they would stand until they rotted or the gale brought them down, with a soft sound among them of wind in their needled boughs, and on them cloud shadows and moving moonlight. The swamp went back to waiting for whatever it was waiting for; and presently the dog pack came down to the margin of the hummock, where Amos's spade still stuck upright in the mud.

They seemed an ordinary pack of dogs such as anyone might see around town on any day, sniffing at automobile wheels, lifting legs at hydrants, sitting sunning outside the post office or on the village green. They were a collie, a boxer, a German shepherd, and two black-and-tan mongrels related to a hound. They were neither lean nor starving; their winter coats were glossy and their sides sleek from living on the deer population of the hummock. Unexcited by the squirrel, because there had been none that any ear but Amos's could hear, they hunkered down around the spade, sniffed of it and then went back and sniffed again, as if they found something companionable in the smell of the homely thing.

Lucy had tried to do as Amos had said: eat supper, turn out the lights, go to bed. She followed the letter of the law, but she could not make herself follow the spirit of it. She lay awake, turning and tossing. She was nervous, the bed was damp, it was this muggy weather in wintertime; the wind blew. Sheep after sheep after sheep jumping over a gate: it was no use, she couldn't sleep.

It was not the first time, of course, that Amos had been out late at night; he often had meetings, lodge or vestry, or business, he would tell her, perhaps with Mack. But never before had he told her to put the lights out. It was such a luxury to read in bed; she loved to; and she never got a chance unless he was out, he wouldn't allow it. All she could do now was think of things.

She thought of poor Amos working down in the gravel pit in the dark night; she only wished she dared take him down some coffee. When she was young, before marriage, dreaming of husbands, she had always thought of hers, the one she would have, as being someone she could comfort, take coffee to, as you could take coffee to, say, Gary Cooper, and he be so gentle; but no—the car couldn't get into the gravel pit, anyway, and walking up that hill, carrying coffee in the dark . . . besides Amos had said.

At ten o'clock, she thought of the change from the bill he had given her to buy the batteries with . . . he hadn't remembered to ask for it back, it was still in her pocketbook. Why! She got up; without thinking, she switched on the bed light. (My, it was comforting, a light when you couldn't sleep and the wind blew.) She went downstairs, snapping on all the lights as she went (you had to see your way), found her pocketbook, counted the change.

What a lovely lots! It could go in a cup on the shelf, where she could produce it at once if he asked for it; but driven up the way he was right now, he might forget; and then it could go into her little hoard, a nice little tiddlebit to add. For—well, for what? Oh, for whatever came up. You never knew.

Mercy, if he got home right now and saw the house lit up like a . . . No. Not like a Christmas tree. She was certainly not going to think about Christmas trees tonight, with the lights off. She hurried back upstairs, turning them off as she went, forgetting the one in the kitchen. When it came to the bed light, she hesitated.

It was too late for callers, of course; no one would try to be social this time of night. Amos would understand that; that was all he'd meant—keep the lights off as long as there was reason to.

Lucy went back downstairs, turning everything on again. Why, for goodness' sake, it was a good thing she'd come down; if she hadn't forgotten that one in the kitchen! She found her new magazine, checked all the lights carefully, made sure they were out, and went back to read in bed. She read until she was sleepy—such nice stories!—and then she slept.

Thus she did not hear, at one o'clock, the wind stop as if someone had turned it off, nor, on the roof, the first thunderous crash of the rain.

How long he ran, wading, smashing through undergrowth—toward the last of it, swimming—Amos did not know, nor in what direction he had gone. He suddenly knew he had got into water in places over his head, and deepening; some lingering instinct of self-preservation, or perhaps it was suddenly finding no bottom under his feet, warned him; he had better get out of this fast. He was freezing to death; his soaked heavy clothes, the filled waders, were pulling him down. He managed to get out of the hunting coat, left it floating; the waders, of course, he could not budge.

He clung to the leafless top of a shadbush which thrust out of the water, feeling it give and bend—not enough to hold a man up—and stared around him. The moon had gone under, as if someone had dunked it in a bucket; the sky was black with clouds. No way to tell direction, even if knowing it would do any good. He had no idea where he was, which way was out. The only thing was to keep going. How in hell had he got into this? The whole thing was crazy beyond calculation. There wasn't any water in the Heath as deep as this; never had been, not in his lifetime. He could see ahead of him the white, slick shine—bushes, undergrowth, sticking out of it—water, all right; something hellish wrong had flooded the swamp out of all reason. Peering ahead, trying to plot a straight line—a man could go round and round in a circle here and drown if the cold didn't get him first—spotting the next bush to pull to, Amos suddenly realized what was here. A round, solid outline thrust out of the water; that was no bush. He wallowed toward it. His hands caught and clung to the rough, bristling mass of mud-plastered sticks. A beaver house. And not far away, in the little light left from the drowned moon, he could make out the straight black margin of their dam.

"Beavers!" he said aloud. "A goddam mess of chrisless beavers!"

And whatever it was that all his life had tried to rock back Amos Wilkinson, tear him down to the animals, had put it there. By the god, they weren't going to get away with that.

Two tears, cold as snail trails on wet leaves, rolled down his cheeks. In a black flood of fury he began tearing with his hands at the soaked mass of sticks.

"Oh, Mack, dear, I just don't know where he could be," Lucy said. "But he took his big flashlight. He said he was going to work down in the gravel pit."

On the other end of the phone Mack Jensen did a double take, gathered his wits, and boomed heartily, "Well now, he may be doing just that. We did leave a truck stalled down there. Now don't you worry, Lucy, you know he wouldn't give up till he had it fixed . . ." He grinned to himself. The runicky old devil! Probably had a woman somewhere, must've got stuck on the way home. This was some rain. But no gentleman could tell Lucy that.

"But, Mack! All night, in the rain? It's raining," Lucy said and, automatically, finished it, "cats and dogs. And what would he need his rifle for, or a spade? And his high waders?"

"Rifle and a spade?" Mack said. What to hell? He went on, realizing it sounded foolish, "Uh—maybe he heard the forecast, thought he might need his boots."

"Oh, Mack, I'm so worried. I didn't dream that when I woke up this morning he wouldn't be here. What will I do?"

"Oh, he's down on the job, all right. Take it easy, Lucy. I'll fetch him down some coffee."

Rifle? he thought, hanging up. Spade and waders? The flashlight sounded as though the old coot had gone out jacking deer. But hell, Amos wouldn't break the law, not with anything he could be caught at. Where would he need waders? In the woods around, where a man would be likely to go this time of year, a pair of leather-tops were enough to keep his feet dry . . . Of course, there was Cooney's Heath, but what crazy man would go in there at night? With a spade, too.

Well, Ame had been acting pretty funny lately, the whole town'd noticed it. Maybe he had gone off his rocker. If you thought it through, it sounded as though he'd gone to dig up or bury something down in the Heath.

And, by gum, come to think of it, the first time he blew his top with me was when I was talking about Cooney's Heath and them wild dogs. If that was where he went, he sure would take a gun, be a fool not to, in case he run afoul of that pack. Been acting pretty damn peculiar if you ask me. Well, I'll have to take a circle down around the job, just in case, I s'pose.

No work today. Not in this rain. Mack had promised himself a good blowout over in Bishop; take the day off. Show Amos he could if he wanted to without consulting the boss. It was about time matters were brought to a head. Dammit, if he hadn't been so lazy, overslept, Lucy's phone call wouldn't have caught him. Half an hour more, and he'd have been gone. He got into his foul-weather gear, backed his truck out.

It was sure one old rauncher of a rainstorm. Coming down in parallel streams straight as strings; no wind; making such a racket on the cab of the truck that he couldn't hear the engine. If the old bayster was down in the Heath, he was sure getting his tail feathers wet. And that bulldozed road in to the old Cooney Place, that slope, wasn't going to be any cinch to drive, either.

The road, a mere gash through undergrowth, bulldozed free of old stumps, boulders, and bushes and leveled only enough so that Amos could roll his heavy equipment in to the old Cooney Place, was now a running river of orange-tan water. The truck slithered and slid, but she was a good one, built for rough going—a power wagon with four-wheel drive. Mack made it, all right, in to the pit. He pulled up at the entrance just in time, and sat staring, astonished, unable to believe his eyes.

The pit was flooded, with water lapping at the edges of the raw hole in the ground, beginning to overflow and run down the road. This was the orange-tan stream he had met coming up. Across from where he sat, a stream fifteen feet wide had breached the wall of the pit and was pouring in, not with foam or rapids as a shallow brook runs, but slick and fast, with a down-suck of muddy water, smooth as silk.

My God, that's a baby river, he thought. Where'd it come from?

All the trees, puckerbrush, and mess of broken, rotten wood, the boards from Charley Cooney's old outhouses, bulldozed down and pushed back to make way for a good, clean operation, had washed back into the pit; a big old apple tree, turf still clinging to its roots, lay across the cab of the power shovel. The rest of the debris floated in the swirling water, from which the heavy raindrops, thundering down, bounced back a mist.

Hol-ee Moses, what a mess! Mack thought. It must be that old deadwater the Cooneys shoved full of dung, cut its way out through there. But how? It ain't flowed a pint of water for years.

It hadn't, indeed; but it was now. Close to eight inches of rain had fallen in the night with nowhere to go but down. From the cut-over, slash-burnt-out hills and slopes, with nothing to hold it back, brook and runnel had gathered into a torrent and flung it down into Cooney's Stream; and the stream, with a water memory for ancient channels, was hunting its oxbow. Not Mack himself riding the biggest bulldozer could have smashed a more businesslike passage through the clogged, manure-filled trench, where Rupert Cornier's womenfolk once grew cress and the red-winged blackbirds sang. It made no difference that the trench was a gravel pit now, containing three pieces of expensive equipment. The oxbow was found, and it was full to the brim of homesick water.

Only the bright-red cab of the power shovel, the thrustup top of its crane; the roof of the truck; the long, dripping snout of the gravel screen, like a prehistoric monster drowning, showed above the flood.

Mack swore, staring out past the clicking windshield wipers.

All that stuff there to clean up, get going again. Water in the engines, cost a mint to fix. The whole pit to strip again, shove muck and mess out of the way. . . . Well, Amos certainly wasn't down here anywhere.

Mack hadn't really thought he would be. Not with the rig-out he'd gone off with; nothing to do here with a rifle and a spade. But it was where he'd said he was going, so you had to check, for the looks of it.

His eyes narrowed a little, looking speculatively down on the drowned equipment.

If the old bayster's gone, if he's dug himself down into a rabbit hole and never comes out, that stuff down there belongs to me. Partly, anyway. Mostly, maybe, because if he's come to grief somewhere, I ain't got nothing to contend with but a couple of women.

Hell, what's it to me where he is? Sneaking off that way, with that kind of gear, he wouldn't want anyone to know about it, he'll only be sore if I hunt him up. Whatever it is, couldn't have happened to a nicer guy. And his fix ain't my mix, anyway.

He grinned slightly.

Quite a poet. Don't know it and can't show it. His fix ain't my mix. I've checked and he ain't here. I'm going over to Bishop, find myself a nice, warm, dry bar and tie one on. Them that wants me can come after me.

He turned the truck around with some difficulty—the water, he realized, even in this short time, had risen under the wheels.

Nothing to do here, anyway, till the rain lets up.

Lucy waited until noon for word from Mack. When none came, she finally called his rooming house again.

"Why, he was here early this morning," his landlady said. "Went out somewhere early and come back about eight. Got all dressed up and said he was going to Bishop. Said not to wait supper."

Well, there, Lucy thought. With relief, she hung up the phone. Mack isn't worried, so he probably knows where Amos is and forgot to call me.

Oh, but I wish he had! Still, maybe Amos is on the way home now.

But by midafternoon, with early winter dusk beginning to come out of the dark sky, and no letup in the rain, she was nearly frantic. No word with anyone since morning; she could stand it no longer.

Amos had said to stay in the house, not see anyone until he got back; but something had happened to him and something had to be done. True, it wasn't the first time he had left her alone to worry, with no word of him for a long time; but last night had been so . . . so strange.

She put on her raincoat, tied a plastic scarf over her head, and started for the barn, where the car was. To her astonishment, she found she had to wade—the yard was flooded. Water two inches deep on the driveway; it had even crept partway up the ramp to the barn door.

It was indeed raining cats and dogs; it was raining floods, torrents, and had been since one o'clock in the morning.

Connie, inside Randall's all day, had been too busy to take much note of the rain, except to hear, with half an ear, an occasional comment about it. She had remarked when she had driven to work that morning that it was a terrible downpour, but her mind was full of the plant and what was going on there. Sarah Jerdan's wonderful accounting system was long gone; Joe, marveling, said the books looked now as if they kept themselves—even he could understand them. The small office was humming with preparation; Joe was going ahead full tilt, and he was a different man.

No one would have recognized him for the limp, beaten, indifferent fellow he had been. Even his hair seemed to snap with energy. Connie was beginning to recognize the cracking sound that Joe's heels made on the concrete walkways outside the office. She would catch herself, from time to time, hoping that he was coming in; but he spent little time in the office these days. She could hear his voice out on the floor, giving orders; he had taken over the foreman's job himself. Marvin Coles had not been near the place since his ultimatum; as was his custom, in the fall, whenever he had been able to persuade Joe to close down for the winter, he had signed up for his rocking-chair money and settled down at home to loaf till spring.

"He'll be back," Joe said. "Ready to take over again when the time comes. First thing he'll want to do is throw the science boys out, and I can sure hear him carrying on about all this newfangled sterilization."

Frank Wilson, the chemist and Joe's new partner, had arrived and was established in a small storage room next to the office, which had been turned into a laboratory for him. Two scientists from the Bishop Laboratory were spending a good deal of time at the plant, checking and supervising. They were being careful because they had to be; they couldn't take chances. Some of the strains in their genetics research had been traced through many generations of animals; any disease caused by faulty feeding would be disaster. Joe's plant had always been clean, highly rated by government inspectors; now it was not only going to be clean, it was going to be sterile.

"Can't you hear Marvin?" Joe grinned. "Insulted down to his boot tops because 'they' are calling us dirty?"

Joe himself was fascinated. The factory, the pride and joy of his life, was at last going to serve a useful purpose, going to mean something after all the years of moribund plugging along; Joe wasn't taking chances either. Anybody who didn't follow specifications and directions was going to get blasted; a couple of workmen already had. Connie had heard the uproar outside the office door; Marvin Coles in his heyday had never made such a noise. A racket like that from Joe, after what had gone on with him, was a heartening thing. Connie smiled a little to herself, hearing what was going to happen to any workman who didn't toe the exact line laid down by the experts.

The plant was not going to open quite as soon as Joe had planned; there was too much to do first. He had most of his material for the finished formula lined up: he had got in touch by telegram with Walt Sheridan and had asked him to pass word around among the dragger skippers that Randall's would buy culls; he had a fleet of small boats, manned by local men, lined up to rake seaweed. The main difficulty, he could see, was going to be with the supply of dried beans. There were plenty of beans which could be ordered and shipped, but no grower could guarantee any which were insecticide-free. They all said the poison had been removed, at least so that it wouldn't kill human beings, but the laboratory was very tender about feeding it to their mice. Joe finally ran across a group of organic farmers in the Middle West who not only did not use poison sprays but who seemed to have an emotional set against them. He was able to order a supply of dried beans from them; "But," he told his workmen, "all the more reason for us to raise our own. Look at the freight bill."

There were some, of course, in town willing to go along with the experiment; but the majority were waiting to see what happened. The main result was, there was no more abandoned farmland for sale at a low price. People were hanging on to their loose acres, just in case they might turn out to be worth something after all. And there was, of course, one difficulty that nobody had foreseen. Nobody in town owned a plow.

A farmer in a neighboring village had a plow, but, it seemed, he had to live, too; his price for a day's work with it, plus tractor, was, people said, out of all reason. Many contended that to root alders and puckerbrush out of the fields would take a bulldozer. Who had a bulldozer? Amos Wilkinson. And he charged eighty-four dollars for an eight-hour day. So it looked as though nobody in town could afford to have a piece of ground fitted.

"All right," Joe said. "I can buy beans. Meantime, you fellows mull."

Connie sputtered, "If they could see firsthand what their great-great-grandfathers cleared out of those fields with nothing but axes and grub hoes, they'd all drop dead!"

"Yup," Joe said. "A man's pretty scared of a day's work now unless he's got some kind of a machine to do it for him. But the old-timers weren't plagued to death thinking how much quicker a bulldozer could do it."

"Maybe the plant ought to buy a plow."

"I'll be darned if I will!" Joe said. "Let 'em figure it. If they want to, they will, and if they don't want to, you could present them with a field plowed and fitted and with a ripe crop on it, and there'd still be some excuse why they couldn't pick beans."

"Not everybody, Joe."

"Nope. Jack Malden's yanking alders out of his back meadow with an old Chevy. At least he was, up to this rain."

Joe had been in the office this morning when Connie had arrived, and had lingered, talking. Not a great deal was going on in the plant today; half the work force hadn't showed up on account of the rain.

"Not that I blame them," Joe said. "You know, Connie, this is a corker. I don't know but we'd better shut up shop and all go home.

You better, maybe. The Lord knows what shape that Shore Road'll be in by five o'clock. Someone was saying a while ago that even little old Walker's Brook is over its banks."

"Walker's Brook? Who ever knew that to run more than two trickles?"

"Nobody. Well, yeah, I've heard my father say it used to be a nice little stream down through town when he was a boy. But after they cut the trees back in there, it stopped running. Water table went down some, I guess, and then, of course, they left the channel clogged with slash. You could go in there now and not be able to see where it was. Couple of mud holes, that's all." He went over and stood by the window, peering out through the drumming rain. "But, by golly, she's finding a way out through there now, all right. Come look, Connie. Darned if she ain't started to run over the road."

He moved sideways a little so that she could see past him.

The dead brook in years past had been lively enough to cut itself three-foot banks, which early settlers, building the town road, had had to span with a bridge. A grandson of this bridge, in asphalt and concrete, now crossed the gully, which within Connie's memory had always been dry. Walker's Brook now was no roaring torrent since its channel had grown up to bushes; but these bushes were already half submerged in a pond which had backed up behind the bridge and was spreading. Water was running under the bridge, but some was coming over the top of it, too.

"You know, that ought to be snow," Connie said. "My goodness, Joe, what ails the weather?"

"Darned if I know. Reminds me of them tropical storms we used to have in the Pacific. Something's out of kilter. Everybody's got a theory," he went on, grinning. "I heard today out on the plant floor that radioactivity fallout has got between the Labrador Current and the Gulf Stream and caused friction. Well, that guess is as good as mine."

He went off out, and she could hear him for a while in the next room, talking to Frank Wilson.

Joe did close down around midafternoon. Even so early, it was beginning to get dark; the rain was still thundering down, and people were jittery. Some of them had a long way to drive.

Connie was nearly ready to go, tying a scarf over her head, when Joe came in. He said tersely, "I'm going to drive down behind you, make sure you get home all right."

"Why, Joe? What's wrong? I'll be all right. That jeep'll go anywhere."

"Sure, but she'll drownd out like any other car if she has reason to," Joe said. He was already struggling into his rubber coat. "If Walker's Brook's coming up like this, that big one down on the Shore Road'll be raging, and the Lord knows what shape that culvert's in."

"Well, I could tell you," Connie said. "I clank over it twice a day."

Of the three brooks on the Shore Road, two were small, in normal weather imperceptible except for a few rushes and cattails to show there was dampness there, and the asphalt-covered cylinders of the culverts humped up the width of the road. Peering out through the puddled section of glass which the jeep's windshield wiper couldn't begin to keep clear, Connie could hardly believe her eyes at the sight of the first brook she passed. The water was up to the road, though not yet over; it had backed up a pond. She caught a glimpse, as the jeep hit the culvert with a bone-shaking thump, of cattails sucked flat and trailing on the surface as the current poured through the culvert and shot out on the other side like a stream out of a fire hose. The shoulders of the road on both sides were gone, washed out; and she thought, Oh dear, I wish Joe hadn't insisted on coming, he may have to walk back.

He was coming along, at a safe distance behind; the jeep's rear-view mirror, outside the cab, was so clotted with rain that she couldn't see his car at all, only his parking lights.

What a nice guy he is, she thought; and suddenly she was glad he was there, that the two pinpoints of light were following so steadily. Because, much more of this and I might get panicky. It's not a nice rain.

No. It was not a nice rain. She found out, all at once, that she was, a little, panicky.

Get home, she thought. Under cover. Under a roof. I could go faster, maybe.

But when she did, Joe beeped his horn for her to slow down.

Well, he was right. It was hard to see.

She caught a glimpse of the second brook as the bump from its thrust-up culvert reminded her that here it was. It was no worse than the first one, but no better; she wondered with a little clutch of dread what Carter's Brook was going to be like. Carter's was the big one; if these pale little trickles were torrents like this, Carter's would—

Even though she was thinking this and watching out, she might not have been able to stop in time if Joe hadn't suddenly let go with a tremendous blast on his horn. The afternoon was closing in, the light dim, the rain on the windshield like a layer of something viscous and thick—glycerine, maybe—distorting vision. Connie stopped the jeep, set the brake, and sat shaking, looking at the gaping hole where the water had cut the road away. The naked culvert showed in glimpses through racing tan water, gray, rounded, half-hidden under ragged asphalt chunks.

Joe pulled up behind her. She heard his car door slam, and he came tearing. He yanked open the door of the jeep, and she saw that his face under its tan was sallow white.

"My God, Connie, somebody's gone into it," he panted. "Here, shove over . . . no knowing how far back the road's undercut . . ."

He moved fast, his dripping raincoat slapping against her as he pushed under the wheel, backed the jeep away from the hole, and set the brake.

"Take my car," he said. "There's a turn-around about forty feet back, watch it when you turn. Get back to town and send the wrecker down and all the help you can find . . . Hustle!"

And he was gone, his figure in the black raincoat scrambling down the sloping side of the road toward the torrent below, to the long, flat object, which now she saw, with the rounds at its four corners, indistinct in the streams of rain and incomprehensible at first because it was the part of a familiar object not meant to be and seldom seen; but suddenly, unmistakable and indecent, an automobile upside down, over whose undersides the water poured and from whose wheels tailed out strings of yellow foam.

Oh, who? Connie thought, and, sickened, Nobody could tell who, not from that . . . from that . . .

And driving back to town, she thought, Who?

Some one of her neighbors. Which one? As long as I don't know, that person is living, in my mind is, like me, alive; but as soon as I find out he will be dead . . . Who?

Perhaps he was able to get out, she told herself, under her breath, pushing Joe's big Cadillac as fast as she dared through the streaming dusk, toward town.

Lucy had not seen the hole in the road. Already panic-stricken, she had been further demoralized by the weather. Hurrying to the only place she could think of, now, for help, to Connie and to Clementina, she had started to pray. When you prayed, you closed your eyes; but not, of course, driving a car; and she hadn't, not, anyway, for a while. She had been knocked unconscious when, plunging into the washout, the car had turned turtle; mercifully; because, among other things, here at last was reality that would never change for better; here, for always, a corner she could not brighten.

Amos Wilkinson had disappeared; the hunt for him went on for a week in the woods adjoining the town, before the delayed winter weather set in. Then temperature dropped overnight to twelve below zero and hovered there for four days. Ponds, marshes, swamps froze deep. For a few days a man could have walked anywhere in Cooney's Heath, even over the boiling springs from which the swamp had its being and which had never frozen within the memory of man; and over the shaking bogs, which had been known to freeze, but treacherously, with breathing holes hard to tell from solid ice. But spring and bog were frozen deep now under the frozen beaver pond. Many men went through the Heath—wardens and state troopers and search parties made up of Amos's neighbors. Mack Jensen had a hunch, he said, that Amos had gone there. "Had something down in there on his mind," Mack told people. "That's for sure. Didn't say what, but said enough so I know he did."

Mack didn't say anything to anyone about Lucy's phone call to him on the morning of the big rain. He figured that the less said about that, the better. His not doing much about it when she called him hadn't done any harm, he guessed, but it wouldn't look good if people found out he hadn't; so he kept mum.

A crew of Amos's men, headed by Mack, crossed the Heath on the ice and went all over the high ground of the hummock, carrying rifles, with which, Mack said, they might clobber two-three of them wild hound-dogs, if they run acrost any, kill two birds with one stone.

They found none of the dogs, who, on the first night that ice had frozen deep enough to bear their weight, had left the hummock and all gone home, where they now slept in warm kitchens, played with children, and were fed canned dog food from plates. The hunt did, however, turn up traces of Amos. A spade stuck in the ice at the margin of the hummock bore his name, neatly burned into the handle, and it was reasonable to suppose that the smashed flashlight found among the trees belonged to him. But there was nothing else.

"Kuh-riced," Mack said at the end of the hunt, as the party left to go home. "Look at them trees. I'll bet they're worth twenty dollars apiece."

"All of that," someone said, "to the poor devil that had to cut 'em. The dealer that sold the finished lumber'd probably git a hundred. No sense worrying your head, Mack, nobody could get at these ones."

"I dunno about that," Mack said. "Give this bog a couple weeks of zero weather, man could run trucks acrost the ice." He narrowed his eyes, speculating. "Who owns this hummock, anyway?"

"Never heard anyone did. Who'd ever be fool enough to pay money for it? Part of the old Cooney place, I guess." The man glanced back uneasily at the stand of big pines. In his opinion Mack had got pretty far off the track of what they'd come here for. "I got the confoundedest feeling," he said, "that old Ame is around here, somewhere."

"Never found him, though, did we?" Mack said cheerfully. "Doubt if we ever will."

He realized that the fellow was looking at him in a puzzled way, and hastened to fix his face and make a comment more suitable to tragedy. "He warn't right, Ame warn't," he said lugubriously. "What I think, the poor old bugger committed suicide."

He shook his head in gloom and sorrow, lowering his voice to a note which he hoped sounded reverent. "We'll never see hide nor hair of him again, you wait and see."

That was enough, that took care of that. After a moment he said under his breath, "Jeezus, what I wouldn't give to be able to git them trees."

On both points, the trees and Amos, Mack turned out to be mistaken.

The winter, as a winter, was a dead loss. Cold weather did not last; after a wet snowstorm, it grew mild again and rained. While, from time to time, the temperature dropped to below freezing, it did not again make ice in the swamp thick enough to risk trucks on, and never did because, in the spring, the wardens dynamited the beaver dam.

They had planned at first to leave it alone, seeing no reason not to; at least, they had one colony of beavers staying put in Cooney's Heath, where they weren't damming up some brook that would flood out cellars and destroy orchards somewhere else. But the tropical rainstorm, in which upwards of twelve inches of rain was dumped in a night and a day, had caused over a million dollars' worth of damage. Not only around Hillville, but in many other towns and villages along the coast, dead brooks whose existence had been forgotten for a century, had roared into life in a night, cutting highways; ripping out culverts not designed to carry run-off such as no one within the memory of man living had ever seen; washing away hundreds of yards of road shoulders; taking out bridges; coming up over the outlets of cellar drains so that water rose in basements and flowed merrily through the delicate mechanisms of electric furnaces and pressure pumps and deep-freezes, not designed for that either: a flash flood, someone said who had been West and had seen one, like in the desert, which snapped its tail over the land for a night and a day and dropped back to normal so fast that in twenty-four hours, if it had not been for massed debris, road washouts, and disarranged culverts, nobody would have been able to tell where the brooks had been any more than they had before the rain.

Thus public opinion was sensitive about anything which might have contributed to the raising of the water. Around Hillville, the consensus was that it was a bad storm, yes; but if those cussed beavers hadn't put up the water in Cooney's Heath, made that old dead waterway change channels till it filled up Ame Wilkinson's gravel pit to overflow like a dish and run down the bulldozed road, not half that water would have got into the town.

Undeniably there was a measure of truth in this reasoning. The beavers, without a doubt, had cooperated with the rain and with the slopes, eroded and bare, where once a forest of trees, now destroyed, had hindered disasters of water running down. Deserts had floods, of course, and they had them in China, didn't they? But not here; nothing like this had ever been known in this place. It must have been caused by something unusual, and everybody took comfort in having something to throw the blame on. Those damned beavers. The State had better get busy. Those beavers had got to go.

After the dynamiting, when the water from the beaver pond had drained away, the wardens found what was left of Amos on the up side of the dam. Unwilling to compromise and unable to beat them, he had joined them.

PART SIX
Spring, 1960

Town meeting, on the first Monday in March, stirred Marvin Coles out of his winter sleep. He ran for First Selectman and was elected, mostly on his campaign promises to rebuild the old Shore Road that ran past Clementina Wilkinson's house. That road, most people felt, had been a disgrace for years, and it was a shame that nothing had been done to it before someone got killed down there. Of course, you couldn't blame town officials for anything that happened in that storm, and everyone knew how Lucy Wilkinson drove a car. The road had been patched temporarily and was as passable as it ever had been; still, word somehow seeped around town that Marvin Coles, if elected, was going to rebuild it if he had to mortgage the Town Hall. This pointed out with a certain amount of delicacy and a nice sense of timing that, while, of course, the present incumbents might have had some difficulties in raising money for the job, and no one was calling them negligent, still, the thing wasn't impossible, and who knew what might have been accomplished—or prevented—if they had extended themselves a little. This logic got around, and Marvin's ticket was elected by a handsome majority.

Tax assessing kept him busy through most of April, but at the time when he normally did, he got out his cleaned and faded coveralls, with RANDALL'S stitched across the shoulders and FOREMAN on the chest pocket, and prepared to go back to his job to resume his habits of half a century. He laid the coveralls on the front seat of his car, weighted them down with his lunchbox, got in, and drove down the side road, on which his house was, toward town. As he turned into the highway and accelerated, an old-fashioned privy walked across the road in front of him.

Marvin let out a yell, yanked at the wheel, and jammed his brake to the floor. His rear wheels spun on the sandy shoulder, skidded sideways; he missed hitting the telephone pole head-on, but his fenders scraped against it the full length of the car with a noise like a falling washboiler full of flatirons.

Marv in was shaken up, but not hurt; he sat there, paralyzed, for only a moment.

For godsakes, that was a backhouse! One them old-time, high one-holers. Walked acrost . . . what's the matter with me, am I crazy?

His reddened, choleric eye caught sight of a stir in the bushes by the roadside; he was out of the car and over there, bow-legged, in an instant, just in time to see a kid, a girl, scrabbling like a rabbit to get out of sight in the underbrush. On the ground, apparently where she had just crawled out of it, lay a tall shipping carton which had once held an outsize refrigerator.

That one! That hellion of Nellie Overholt's. Walked acrost the road inside of that thing—just the size and shape of a one-holer, no wonder I . . . Damn near killed me.

As Marvin realized what, almost, had been carelessly done to him, he put back his head and opened his mouth; his outrage, offered freely to heaven, made the empurpled welkin ring.

By the blistered this-and-that, he told himself, as he stamped back to his car, too much hell was being raised in this town by kids, and by that uncircumferated little devil in particular. Keep on, she *would* kill somebody, and it was time the law put a stop to it. As First Selectman, by gumpty, he guessed he could put a stop to it, too. He needed an issue, anyway, something that people could get their teeth into, to take their minds off of repairing that cussed Shore Road; and, you count up, there was plenty to add up to the reform school. There was the windows in Wickham's henhouse; there was them copper cents into the factory machinery; enough other shenanigans, and witnesses for 'em, too, all over town. Might mean tangling with Nellie Overholt, but what of it? He guessed that flapping the law in her face would slow her down. Them Overholts and Warrens was a weedy combination, anyway; look at Nellie's husband, that Billy, and Gert Warren. And this one, unto the third generation. It was about time for a clean-up; a good morals issue—nothing like it to turn a town upside down. Hoe out that house, get rid of them undesirable elements, and straighten out some of the young hellions that was headed hell-a-hooting right down the same path. Too much was enough. And too much was too much, he added, glaring, enflamed all over again, at the paint and fenders on the First Selectman's car.

He didn't get down to the factory that day.

No real hurry, he told himself; time enough when the town business slacked off a little.

Beck was caught this time, well and truly caught. She had set out sincerely that morning with Kate for school; halfway there, she had suddenly ducked into the bushes and run, paying no attention to Kate's frantic yawp that they'd be late.

It was too nice a day to go to the old-fool school; anyway, Mama wanted her to. Go to school, get your education, Mama said. That was what *she* wanted; so . . . that was what Beck wasn't going to do. Chicken-licken, the sky is falling—who cared. It hurt ten minutes and then was over. Meantime you'd had your whole day.

If old Mama-Schmama wanted Beck to do anything, then she had better let Beck do some of the things Beck wanted, not be so poison. Let her go back to see Aunt Gert once in a while; let her have some of the things Uncle Reggie brought. After all, they were Beck's things, they weren't Mama's. Mama had had them all, somewhere. The airplane suitcase, Just the right size for a child, the doll, the dresses, the nylon briefs, and Uncle Reggie's going-away present, the little transistor radio, made too big a bundle to be hidden anywhere in the house; they weren't there, Beck was sure; there wasn't any place she hadn't looked. They certainly weren't around now. Mama said Kate and Henry didn't have any such nice things, so it wasn't fair; and then she said she'd considered the source; and that was all she would say, but Beck was beginning to guess what. Old Strawberry Sudsworth, the one Jody tracked around with now, had a transistor radio now;

he said his father had bought it at the secondhand store in Bishop; and it was hers, she knew, because it still had her initials, R. O., that Uncle Reggie had had put on in gold leaf. You could see where old Strawberry had tried to scratch them off and then stopped because it made too deep a mark in the paint. So the secondhand store was probably where the rest of the stuff had gone, too.

All right. What you were waiting for now was just to grow up. Just to get big enough.

Beck's leg was healed—not quite so limber as it would be, Dr. Garland said; but all right now. She'd limped on it good and hard for a week, a lot longer than she'd needed to, hoping Mama'd let her stay some longer with Aunt Gert. But it was no use. In the end she'd had to go home. Now she couldn't go back at all. Even Aunt Gert said, "Honey, you mustn't, not if Mama says no, it'll only make bad trouble. Wait a while, and we'll see." Well, Mama was watching like a hawk, knowing she'd go if she got a chance. Even Uncle Reggie was gone—back to New York. He'd come again, Aunt Gert had said. So far, he hadn't.

So nowhere to go except old-fool school; nothing to do. Nobody to play with—even with Jody she was all fouled up. He'd taken up with Strawberry Sudsworth whilst Beck had been sick and they ganged up on her now if she tried to horn in; so she guessed she knew when she wasn't wanted. The only thing she had on Jody, his little brother had come, the doctor had finally brought it in his little black bag; she guessed she could snicker over that, but only to herself, she couldn't tell anyone, because Dr. Garland trusted her and she trusted him; she guessed he was about the only one left she could trust now.

She schlurked around through the bushes and came up on the back lots behind the business section, and had almost decided that it might be worthwhile to get run over again, when she spotted the old refrigerator carton in the rear of the electrical shop. It was just lying there, not doing anything, so she crawled inside it. It was nice and private in there, but nothing to do; so presently she took her jackknife and made handholds in two sides of it and eye slits so she could see out on all four. At first she just stood it up alongside the highway and, from inside it, secretly cased the cars going by, Sally Spittleoffsky, the Russian Refrigerator Spy; then she got the idea. When she saw a car coming, she would lift the carton by the handholds just high enough so its bottom edges wouldn't scrape, but not high enough to show her feet, and walk it, upright, across the road. It was wonderful to watch what the car drivers would do; some of them were a living sketch, screeched their brakes, wabbled all over the road. That old Marvin Coles wouldn't of run into a telephone pole if he hadn't been so decrippit he couldn't stop his car, anyway; and he never would of caught her if her darn leg had been as limber as it was going to be.

But that old Marvin Coles had sent the Constable to see Mama. Mama said they were going to serve papers. There was going to be a hearing. A school for de-something children, she said it would probably be; but Beck guessed that was only a nicey-nicey way of saying the reform school.

Well, if none of them, Aunt Gert or Uncle Reggie or Aunt Frances or Mama, cared a hoot, neither did she. At least it would be something different. Mama had gone on about it something fierce; she said Beck ought to have thought; she said what with Beck's cussed actions, there wasn't one single, solitary thing that Mama could do.

"I've told her," Nellie said, "that there ain't one single, solitary thing I can do. I've talked with that old turkey buzzard and he won't listen, in spite of his car insurance will take care of the damage, all except his fifty-dollar deductible, which I've offered to pay. Out of what little I make, three kids and barely able to keep my head above water. I don't know as I take it kindly, Gert, you getting yourself all dressed up to the nines and walking in here as if you was welcome."

The rumpus was all over town; Marvin had seen to that and that people knew the First Selectman was taking action against the undesirable elements. Gert had heard about Beck right away; and in spite of the fact that she had plenty of troubles of her own, and Frances said they had better lay low for a while till that old rutabaga cooled off, Gert had come right over to Nellie's.

She had worn her baum-marten cape, which, she now realized, had been a mistake, it did look a little too rich a diet inside Nellie's, but too late to remedy it now. She said, "Maybe you are willing to set by, Nellie, and see that little kiddy sent away. But I and Reggie and Frances are not."

"I would like to know what you and that ragtag and bobtail can do," Nellie said, "that Beck's own mother can not. The way you're carrying on, Gert, anybody'd think you thought you'd got some rights in it, but—"

"No," Gert said. "I only wisht I did."

"I s'pose you think you could have done better. I will tell you, nobody could, not with that young one, who I don't know where she come from, who she takes after. Not after Billy, that limp shrimp, and the god knows, she don't take after me. I swear, Gert, you might as well be her mother, she's more like you'n she is like anyone, I never could handle you no more'n I can her. But I must say, if someone'd took you and shoved you into the reform school, in time, something would of had to give; and if Beck ain't stopped in her tracks now, the Lord knows where she'll end up. And you have got a gall to come in here and tell me you think you could have done better!"

"I," Gert said, "would've done some things different, yes, Nellie."

"Mm-hm. And what, kindly tell me, would they of been? God knows, I've licked her. It don't do no good."

"Oh, I would never of licked her, never!" Gert said. "I would not of give her a Christmas present from the Welfare, Nellie. And I would not of took the things Reggie give her to the secondhand store. Her having them, where was the harm?"·

"What I do with my own child, bringing her up, is none of your cotton-picking business," Nellie said. She had turned bright red, not having planned to have the secondhand-store deal known. "I don't know what snoop had her nose into that to find it out, prob'ly that Frances. But—"

"Oh, no. Not Frances," Gert said. "But it's known, Nellie."

"I can't say I give a Christian damn if it is. A woman with her head hardly above water, three mouths to feed, makes it where she can and what she can, if she sees a way to extry. And I would not have my child, a child of mine, owning expensive stuff from one of your—Well, I consider the source, that's all."

"Those things b'longed to Beck, that Reggie give her. Reggie is a very nice man. A prince. And he is not poison. I have been on the phone to him. I was on the phone to him last night for an hour."

"Well, all I can say is, you'll have a phone bill to scare the sandman."

"Collect," Gert said. "Reggie has always said that if I ever needed anything, to make it collect. So he is coming. He is coming now instead of waiting until June."

"That'll be a help to you, I'm sure."

"Well, it will. To get married," Gert said patiently. "Now, instead of a June wedding."

Nellie's jaw sagged. "Get married? To you?"

"Yes. To me. We would of before, only his wife only died last March. We was waiting a reverent Time—for time to pass to make it seem reverent, that is."

"Oh, my God! What would any—What on earth would he want to marry you for?"

"For what reason you may suppose," Gert said. "He likes me. Now, Nellie. All this is neither here nor there. Reggie says if you will let us have Beck, we will take her to New York to live with us. He dearly loves children, not being able to have any of his own, from getting hurt down there during the war."

"Well, for the god's simple sake!" Nellie said. "You and your fancy man run of an idea, between you, that I'd let one of *My Girls* go off with—"

"Better with us than be sent away," Gert said. "Now, Nellie, you have always had to live me down. If Beck has to go to the reform school, you will have her to live down, too. Any more people going to be lived down, Nellie, everybody will think something surely is the matter." She fingered the clasp of her alligator bag, pulling the bag around to the front in her lap. "So you could listen, couldn't you, to the rest of what Reggie told me to say."

"No, I couldn't . . . To what?"

"I am not going to put it on the basis of Beck. You let me have her, go with me; you can have the old home back."

"That palace in Shacktown? I wouldn't live there if—" Nellie's eyes narrowed a little as her mind took in what had been said. Property. It was property. It could be sold, realized on. She said, staring at Gert, "So what about that Frances? According to her, she's got a say."

"Oh, Frances is willing. We are both going. She says that to stay here—uh—now, would be small business."

"Hnf, what was it ever but? You willing to put that in writing?"

"I already did." Gert opened her bag. "A warranty deed, not just a quit claim. I got it in Bishop this morning, and this other paper that says you let Reggie and me adopt Beck, legal."

"Well, it looks like you thought of everything."

"I did," Gert said. "Except nothing is signed, it has got to be done before witnesses. Reggie says we will all sign when he comes, he will see about the witnesses."

"What about the stuff in the house?"

"I make no mistake about you, Nellie, I knew you would hold out for what you could get. It says here, lock, stock, and barrel. What would I want anyway, a deep-freeze, a garbage disposal, pack them all to Scarsdale, New York, when I have got Reggie?"

"Well," Nellie said. "I guess you know what you've got. H'm, it ain't that I can avoid seeing certain advantages . . ."

A respectable woman with a job to keep . . . a sister with Gert's reputation and a young one headed straight for reform school—both of them out of town and well away; the old home, Gert's things—the garbage disposal; one less mouth to feed . . .

"How's he going to feel?" she demanded. "When he finds you ain't got nothing—that you've deeded it all over to me?"

"Reggie? Oh, it was his idea, what did you think? He has *got* Plenty. A good job and a ranch-type house in Scarsdale, New York, and a

Lincoln Continental, and, to boot, He Is All I Have Ever Wanted In A Man. He don't need houses and garbage disposals from me."

Nellie was suddenly furious. Savage. "You don't rate it, Gert! A good man with money, and the rest of us with our heads not half above water! You ain't got it coming, and it ain't no use you to think you have!"

Gert nodded. "I never made no plans on what I got coming, I just made plans on what there was."

"What is that man—a plain fool? He must know what you are."

"Oh, yes, he does. I told you. He likes me. He says I'm The Prostitute With The Heart Of Gold and, I tell you, his ain't made of no pewter. Oh, Nellie, leave off talking! I never could tell you nothing, not how it was, nor why I done what I done, not nothing, no more'n I could pound it into an ox with an ax. All there is to say is do I get Beck or don't I, and so good-bye."

"All right," Nellie said. "You can have her."

I can't do nothing with her nohow, Gert might's well have a try. It's that or the reform school, and Blood Is Thicker Than Water. What more was there to say, anyway? So good-bye.

Gert's establishment vanished overnight from Hillville. Marvin Coles, going there for the second time to rant and threaten with the law unless, found the house locked and empty.

H'm, he guessed he knew what was being tried on—them loose women hid in there, lying low, so's they wouldn't have to talk to him. Well, they'd find out what it was to be outside the law.

He banged on the front door, went around and banged on the back, and, finally, broke a pane in one of the lights beside the door, reached through and turned the key. He went all over the house, searched the rooms.

By the gumpty, if they warn't gone. Ought to have known it when he come in from the empty smell in the house. Left everything, too. Well, it had been a nice house. Too bad he'd had to close it up, the town was going to miss it. But if he knew the town, it wouldn't be long before another one started up somewhere, and probably worse, so that to close it up would be a bigger feather in his cap when he needed one. In case he did.

He was coming down the front stairs when he saw Nellie Overholt, head-on and breathing fire and brimstone.

She said, "Let me see your search warrant, Marvin Coles."

Marvin sputtered. He guessed she had him there. He drew himself up. "I am in the pursuit of my duties as the First Selectman of this—" he began.

"And I am in the Welfare," Nellie said. "Going around to people's houses. And I know that the President of the You-nited States, which you are far from, could not go into anybody's house without a search warrant or invited by the owner. That is in the statues of the State Code of Law and I can show you the page in the book and the paragraph. What you have done, you have broke and entered, and there is a page in the book about that, too."

"Well, a town official can—" A town official couldn't, and Marvin knew it. He finished, somewhat ineffectively, "—do what he thinks is the right, without a lot of—of damn foolishness . . ." It was, too. What did she think? He broke into a bawl. "This ain't your property! You can't order me around in it, you ain't got a word to—"

"I have got here a warranty deed to this place that is as legal as the cupolow on the Statehouse roof," Nellie said. "I could have the hell arrested out of you so fast that people wouldn't see your heels vanishing over the treetops. You ain't one mite better than anybody you have preferred charges over or drove out of town, everybody knows you come here with the best of them. So you let me hear one word about one member of my family further, I will get out a Warrant, and it won't be no search warrant, neither. Now you make tracks. Heels towards this house!"

Marvin guessed he better. Never heard such talk out of a woman in his life. She even went so far as to bawl out the door after him, for the whole neighborhood to hear, "And you can send somebody to fix that windowpane you broke, if you don't want to hear further from me!"

Well, there! It had been some old satisfactory to tell off that pompous coot. Nellie guessed she wouldn't hear any more about his hounding Beck into the reform school, not that he could now anyway. Gert hadn't left any address—better that way, her man Reggie'd said—and Nellie couldn't even remember the name of the town, so if what Marvin's idea of the law was ever caught up with Beck, it wouldn't be because of anything Nellie could tell them. The god ever knew how Beck would end up, but that man, that Reggie, seemed to be real nice in spite of what you knew about him; and money, too—he had given Nellie a nice fat check, said it was from Gert, for letting her have that wonderful little kid to keep, and not to worry, he'd see she got a nice education. Well, maybe he would; it was hard to say.

The thing that was hard to take, of it all, Nellie thought as she poked around through the house seeing what there was, what Gert had left here, Beck seemed to think the world of them, even that Frances; she couldn't wait to go, had hardly even kissed her mother good-bye. Well, that was the way of it, bring up kids, slave your life out, and no gratitude, leave you without looking at you. When you'd done your best. I wasn't that way with Mama. Gert was; but I wasn't. I looked after her as long as she needed it; and I buried her, too, paid the expenses out of my own pocket. Well, Beck takes after Gert, I guess, and it ain't as if I didn't have two more of my own.

There certainly was a lot of stuff abandoned here in this house. That electric kitchen, alone . . . washing machine, stove, icebox, even a drier. If this place wasn't in Shacktown, I'd move in here myself, but there, I doubt if I could even swing the taxes on it. No. Better sell it, take the money, but it certainly would simplify my housework. H' m, a whole shelf of canned groceries, though, which I certainly can take home.

Before she left, she went over to the sink, turned on the garbage disposal, listened to it hum.

Mack Jensen, a week or so after Amos's body was found, made Connie an offer for her father's house and business.

"For his share of it, that is," Mack said. "Being as I was a kind of a silent partner."

He was getting married, settling down, he told her, with an air of deadpan relish she couldn't miss—in other words, she needn't think she was the only pebble on the beach; she'd had her chance and now it was too late, he was spoken for. He produced estimates of the worth of the business—the number and condition of the earth-moving machines— the bulldozers, backhoes, power shovels, trucks—saying that he was the logical one to do this since he alone now knew the value of things. He pointed out that three of the machines had taken an awful racking in the flood, so weren't worth much; and he asked that she'd make up her mind as soon as possible because, with the season starting, he'd like to get things settled—he had a lot of work lined up.

The estimates seemed businesslike enough at first glance. Connie found one or two mistakes in addition, in Mack's favor, which might, of course, have been honest mistakes. She corrected these and then realized that, so far as she was concerned, the rest of the data might as well have been in Greek. She took the estimates to Joe. Not wanting to take up his time at the plant, since everybody there was working at top speed these days, she dropped by his house one evening after supper.

She found Joe stretched out in his armchair with his feet on a footstool and his lap full of babies. The babies were asleep and Joe was nodding; all four faces had a look of milky contentment so much the same that Connie had to smile, in spite of the fact that her heart contracted at the sight of J. J. Randall.

Oh, how you've grown, she said silently to him, as Mrs. Burrage, Joe's housekeeper, ushered her in. He had, too, and so had Cary and Gary, who were fine and fat now, though still with a delicacy of structure, a transparency of skin, that made them what Nellie Overholt called "touch-and-go" babies. But not J. J.—nothing transparent about him. He was tremendous, solid as a railroad car. And you're almost six months old, now, Connie said to him. Aloud, she said, "Oh, Mrs.

Burrage, it seems a shame to wake anybody up. Joe's probably all in; I know he's had a day. Why don't I come back some other time?"

She didn't, she realized, want J. J. Randall waked up, because, asleep, without that heart-twisting, wide smile, he didn't look at all like Ernie Grindle. He looked a little like the Wilkinsons, it was true, the slight resemblance was unmistakable, but mostly like a baby.

"I'm awake," Joe said. "I'm just paralyzed under all this tonnage, that's all. Some of you women folks haul it off somewhere, so I can move, I'll come to."

"Don't make out it's a hardship," Mrs. Burrage said. "You'd think, to hear him talk, that we hogtied him every night and piled him up with babies. But there ain't a one of the four of them that wouldn't squall the house down if they didn't have that snooze together after supper. Here," she said to Connie, "you take this one and I'll get the one in the middle, and I guess Joe can manage Gary." She scooped up J. J. Randall and thrust him into Connie's arms and went off into the bedroom with Cary.

Connie held him; he was easy to hold. She felt a strange sensation in her arms of lightness and heaviness at the same time; and, He's heavy, she thought, but my strength doubles to hold him; he's mine. She couldn't help it; she bent her head and laid her cheek against J. J. Randall's velvety one; it was warm and smooth, and he had a rich, powdery, vaguely sour-milk smell.

"Pss-t," Joe said in a whisper. He was scrabbling awkwardly out of his chair, with Gary balanced on one arm as delicately as an egg. "Don't wake him up, Connie, or this act of mine'll all have to be gone through with again."

She followed Joe into the nursery and laid J. J. down in his crib, tucking his blanket over him. The crib blanket had safety pins in its corners; there were tapes on the crib slats to fasten them to. Connie fastened them.

So you won't kick out in the night, she told him. And catch cold.

Back in the living room, she handed over Mack Jensen's estimates to Joe. "I'm sorry to take your time, Joe. But I think I need some help with this. I've an idea Mack's treating me like a woman, but I don't know enough to see where."

She was surprised to find her voice casual and steady.

"Well, you are. You sure are. Thank God," Joe said, his eyes crinkling slightly with amusement. "Here, le'me see." He took the estimate sheets to the table and sat down, shuffling them apart. "Where's a pencil? You ain't got a pencil on you, have you?"

"Yes," Connie said. "In my bag."

She fumbled in her bag, found the pencil, held it out to him.

"My godfrey mighty," Joe said, taking it. He glanced at the point, pulled out his jackknife and proceeded to sharpen it into his ashtray. "Anybody's only got to look at a woman's pencil to know that it don't belong to a man," he said. He glanced at her above the small, curling shavings. "It beats me," he said, "how two people ain't related can look so much alike as you and Jay do. I see you, there, with your faces together, it took a real jump out of me. Why, he could be yours, Connie, and not a question asked."

"Yes," Connie said. "I guess he really could, couldn't he?"

She almost told him. She almost told him then and there. To have someone know; to have Joe know; to ease the ache . . . the homesickness . . .

He is Joe's, she told herself steadily. I have lost title. He's Joe's and Joe loves him. I can't tell him and I won't. He mustn't know.

She watched him while he figured—the stub of pencil in the square, brown capable hand, setting down notes, check marks, with quick little jabs; the lined, sensible, absorbed face, with its steady dark eyes and confident chin; the wide, strong shoulders. Joe.

A man, she thought. Why do there have to be so few of them?

If you had had what was here. If you had had it before the flawed years twisted the course, muddied the springs of the love your childhood had, that your young womanhood looked forward to; the love that was in you when you began. Because it was, she thought. It is in any girl when she starts out, so much of it that she can't think of anything else; over everything—school, work, career—is a screen on which the young men move like a flowing river; their hands, their eyes, their hair, the deep sound of their different voices; and "Which one?" sounds through her waking life like a theme in music. If that could be used in trust, not wasted in conflict, beginning with the nastiness of your mother telling you, and going on through the wrestling match in the back seat of a car, and the wet mouth smelling of gin of somebody you hardly knew and who hardly knew you, while you thought, scared and sickened, is this what it is, is this what you have to do? And, fighting the damp, clutching hands away from your thighs and breasts; before you were ready, before you knew how to handle it; in terror, remembering the gentle, informing voice, "Now that this happens every month, you'll have to be careful, dear, or you'll have a baby"; a girl, not dry herself behind the ears, getting broken in, firsthand; to what would end in Ernie Grindle; in Amos and Lucy; in the life with King Kong . . .

Joe laid down the pencil.

He said softly, "Wow!" and grinned. "Mack tell you he'd like to close this deal quick on account of, oh, this and that?" he asked.

Connie nodded. "Mm-hm. He says he wants a free hand to start work."

"Well, give it to him," Joe said. "If that's what he wants, give it to him, by all means. Of course, he can't take title till the probate gets around to settling your father's estate, but if he has it in writing that you'll sell to him, why, that'll be okay, too. Because with any kind of an outside audit, some things'll likely come out, like, for instance, he's got two bulldozers listed here, one in good shape and the other one damaged by water. Well, I happen to know your father had three, because I've been dickering to buy the third one. And with a sand-and-gravel business this size, there ought to be a lot more movable tools—shovels and stuff—that I don't find listed here; if I know Mack, they're stashed away somewhere and wouldn't show up on any estimate. He thinks you're a fool, Connie, honey."

"Yes, I know he does. Well, I would be, wouldn't I, if I promised to sell to him on his say-so, without an outside audit?"

"Nope. You'd be a fool if you didn't. Here's why. If I had even a pie-shaped slice of a gravel business in this town, right now, I'd unload it so fast you couldn't see me for smoke. Nobody's going to sell farmland for gravel pits, not in this town, not now. There's quite a number of old fields being cleared out to plant this spring, and there'll be more when the idea's had time to sink in. Seems a lot of people got tired of looking at puckerbrush, don't want to see it grow any higher. You don't find surfacing gravel just anywhere; it's mostly under the places that grow the best beans, if you know what I mean. Fields like that in time to come ain't going to be bought cheap, which is the basis of that business. So you get his offer down in writing and signed. And fast."

"So he isn't cheating me after all," Connie said thoughtfully.

"Well, he thinks he is, and he's so busy getting himself a deal that he hasn't bothered to look ahead. But he's offered you just about a fair price, and if I was you, I'd take it."

Mack Jensen, Connie thought. Taking over where my father left off. With the same elephant-hide indifference about other people's rights, and no misgivings as to his own. She had never felt sorrow for Amos. For a while, in her grief over Lucy, she had even hated him, telling herself that Lucy was what she was because of him, an identity trampled and shapeless, an appendage to selfishness, and no more; but now, with a little time to think, she had come to see that, as Clementina had said, many things had gone to make up Lucy, not all of them Amos; and that many people who did manage to grow up by the time they were middle-aged, did not live longer because of that. You couldn't assign blame; it was useless to try. So Connie did not hate Amos now. If he had been insane, she told herself, she ought to feel pity; but Amos sick had not been enough different from Amos well—it had been only a matter of degree. She could not remember a time when he had not stamped over anything in his way, no matter whom, no matter what, his privileges twisted with a sick logic out of his religion and, according to him, God-given: man is the master of creation, top dog of the heap; what he wants, he takes, and is justified because he can.

You would think when the old men died, with their mistakes log-piled behind them, the young men might profit from folly obvious to fools; but if Amos were insane, then you had to wonder how much of the world was, too; there seemed to be no end to that insanity. The troglodytes circling a vicious circle; around and around and around. Amos Wilkinson giving place to Mack Jensen, his spiritual son. Get-in, get-what-there-is, get-out. And the devil take the hindmost.

A warm brown hand came down over hers and she jumped a little, startled. Joe had got up from his chair behind the desk and was standing there.

"It ain't that bad, Connie," he said. "Godsakes, nothing could be," and she looked at him, seeing the kind, steady, concerned face close to hers start to blur and waver through her tears, the rough material of his shirt dissolving to a patch of misty blue.

"Oh, Joe," she choked, and finished nothing, but leaned her head against the blue patch, feeling him there, strong as a stone, the solid rib cage under her cheek shaken with his caught breath, and the sudden hammering of his heart.

"We both had it, Connie," his voice said over her head. "Both of us, too rough to take." Held close, she heard the deep vibrations of his voice; or it was as if her body heard it, echoed it, and answered. "But time goes," he said. "It has to. We'll make it go, together."

On a bright morning of May, almost June, when the new leaves were unfolding on the trees like babies' fingers; when the grass was greening and the whitethroats sang like flutes from every bush, and the nights were warm enough for a man, even an old one, to camp out without freezing to death, Everard Peterson took off for the stay he had long promised himself in Cooney's Heath.

A man spent the winter in jail, account of the crocodiles in human form not believing his given word, had to norate around awhile till he got back his leg muscles. Everard had been out for a month, around town, walking, hunting along the fringes of the woods. He guessed he still might not be quite up to such a long trip, but he had looked people between the eyes and into their teeth too long; he was sick of the sight. He wasn't going to stand for them no longer. He could take it easy if he had to; but bad legs or no bad legs, he was going up over the hill and down into the Heath, and he was going to stay a week. Shoot them ducks, or a nice pa'tridge or two; have a roast on a stick over a fire. Them duck aigs, too, if they hadn't been sot on too long by this time, and he guessed maybe he could find some late ones that hadn't, would go almighty good. His mouth watered at the thought.

Blanket roll on back, rifle, plenty of shells, Everard set out. For the first part of the way he followed an old woods road, so grown up with alders and hardhack that it was barely a trace. God, it was a passion the way the bushes grew nowadays. Why, he remembered when this road was swamped out, between tall trees; come down here with a team and a loaded wood sled, many's the time. For years it had been a good, passable road, part corduroy; then, all of a sudden it seemed, the alders took a-holt, and the corduroy was so rotten now that you had to go out around it, fall through you'd break a leg, sure'n God. Well, it was a hard scrabble; if you went this way, you had this road and you had to climb the hill; but downslope a ways, you could hit that old branch coon trail and save two miles. Besides, in jail all winter, he'd been looking forward to seeing the top of that hill. It was nice there.

He made it to the top, breathing hard. It was as he remembered, one of the few places didn't change. Big gray-granite ledges stuck out, warm in the sun; there was one in particular that made a seat with a back, comfortable as an armchair; plumb on the tiptop; you could set there and look off over the countryside in all directions whilst you got your breath. The seat was there; warn't nothing, no reason for the spoilers to smash that up; one thing. Everard leaned his gun against the stone, took off his cap to cool the sweat on his forehead, and sat down.

That was more of a climb than it used to be to a man, by God.

Now that was country that used to be country, once; in the old days. Slash and puckerbrush now; but off north there once had been the woods, miles of wilderness, rising and falling to the shape of the land. Black spruce and pine; hardwoods like spots of yaller-green mist this time of year, where the leaves was opening out, with patches of blue here and there in the glades to show where lakes and streams were. That was the old wild in there, in them days, the real old wild; and gorry, some old good place to go hunting in. Shoot ten deer in a night if you wanted to; once he had, just for the hell of it, shot thirteen. Shoot all you want to and leave lay what you don't want. Them was the good, old free days. Not like now. Spit now, and you hit a game warden.

Off south was the ocean, covered the whole horizon from southeast to southwest, so white with the glare of morning sun that you could hardly see the offshore islands. Hard on the eyes, that glare was; who wanted to look at salt water, anyways? Pretty, if you liked it; but the idea of working on it, fishing, made him want to cry. He had; had had to; times. But it wasn't no life for a man. He turned his back on the ocean and on the roofs of Hillville, which he could see if he looked down, west. Let that go, too; wasn't nobody there he cared to think about. Them people; taking in each other's washing for a dime a throw, as if that made them better than a man, even if they thought so. Let 'em think so; it was one thing they had to keep alive on, thinking they were better than someone else.

As for him, as for Everard Peterson, Cooney's Heath, down below there, running off miles to the east, was what he had come to see. That was a sight on a spring morning to make a man feel like a king and this rock he sat on a kind of a throne.

Come to think of it, he *was* a king down in that Heath; wasn't a thing in it he wasn't smarter than and the master of. Why, hell, when a king walked around his kingdom, all the people fell down, bumped their heads on the sidewalks; and when Everard Peterson went through that swamp, by God, every living thing in it fell still—the frogs, the birds, the rabbits, the deer; just as you walked, you could hear the stillness start to grow. A bullfrog would cut off in the middle. "Ker-chunk!" he would say. "Ker-" and then stop; a bird would cut off in the middle of his song. Like they said, "Shush up, boys, the old king's coming, old Everard's coming," and sat, not a rustle, waiting to see who was going to get the little surprise.

A king? Why, hell, I *am* one. And by God, I got a pretty kingdom.

In that swamp down there, must be four miles of that pink lambkill in blossom this time of year, it was like looking into a big pink bowl. Shadbush in bloom, too, and wild cherry. A goddam flower garden, and all mine.

Not much water, looked like; be muddy, but not too, on that branch trail. He could make it all right to his old camp in on the hummock. Be damp sleeping, but he could make him a nice bed of spruce boughs. The squirrels had probably chewed up that box of oatmeal he'd left when he was in here last time; but, well. Squirrels was good eating; old Everard'd likely get his own back.

"Yah, yah, yah," said a crow from the top of a tree.

Everard didn't look around, but he grinned slightly to himself. Same crow, he didn't have a doubt.

"Well, you fly around awhile," he said under his breath. "I kind of run of an idea this'n is going to be your day."

Well, huddle up, boys, here comes the king; and he picked up his gun and went on down the hill.

In the thickets at the foot of the slope, he found he had to stop for breath again; harder coming downhill, almost, than going up; got a man right behind the knees. Pouf and phew!

The branch trail was as he remembered it; growed up some, but not too bad; not too muddy. Had to part the bushes here and there.

What in hell was that, over there, like somebody left a pile of old rags under a tree?

He moved closer, saw what it was.

A body, by the gumpty; someone's body? Now, who in creeping tarnation could that be? Whoever 'tis, he ain't a pretty sight. Been there all winter. Took a helluva jump out of me, too.

Everard looked around for a place to sit down; his heart, he realized, was pounding.

Must be one of them out-of-state deer hunters, got lost in here, died, like. Never heard about one of them missing last fall, but the way they flock the woods, hunting season, could very well one of them dropped out and nobody missed him. Tall feller. Them's about the longest thigh bones I ever see on a man.

If I'd got here last fall, I might've had me a nice leather jacket, but that ain't no good now. Wonder if he had any money on him? Well, if he did have, it can stay there, all of me. I ain't going a-poking round in that mess.

Most of folks would go high-arsed back to town, couldn't wait to get told what they found in the woods. A body, a body, a body. Gab, gab, gab. Not old Everard. Not the king. I ain't going to miss my trip for nothing. This feller's waited a long time, he won't go nowhere whilst I'm in on the Heath. Maybe he can stay right here, let somebody else find him, if anybody does. Any way I look at it, I go tell it, all I'm going to get is mixed up with cops and gawpers. Whole town'd be in here, tearing up the woods. Wouldn't be any hunting in here for months on end. And, anyway, all 'tis to me is them spoilers couldn't find nothing else in here to destroy, so they've started in on destroying each other. To hell with it.

Everard went on, into the Heath.

It was tough going, tougher than he remembered. By the time he got to his old camp on the hummock, he was wet and muddy and beat out. His camp was just about eaten out—walls fallen down, next to nothing left a man could use. But he had got him two nesting ducks, and he built a good hot fire to roast them and to dry out by; he braced up the old camp, cut himself a spruce-bough bed. But by the time the ducks were ready, he was too tired, almost, to eat. Didn't seem to feel hungry, not the way he used to. Maybe it was because it was earlier than he was used to eating supper; couldn't be only but about three o'clock; but he ought to be hungry, hadn't et since breakfast. By God, come this far . . . He ate the ducks, every morsel, forcing down the rich, gamy-tasting meat and sucking the bones. There! Show that, whatever it was, bothering him. Now for a nap till dusk, deer-hunting time, and he'd wake up fit to live with himself again. He lay down on his newly made bed, covered himself with his blanket, and went to sleep.

Later he woke up with a jump.

Now, what was that? Come wide awake, all to once, as if there was something, some noise around the camp woke him up.

He listened; there wasn't a stir. Wasn't dark yet; about five o'clock, he should judge; sun way over in the west, beginning to heave down to set. The fire was out, not even smoking; he was chilled to the bone, dead cold. There weren't even any ordinary noises to hear; the swamp was as still as the inside of an egg, the yolk. Better get up, build on a fire; no sense catching pneumonia out here, that'd be a fool thing to do. That duck meat was bothering him; shouldn't of et so much this early in the spring; after a winter, and him in jail to boot, a man needed spring tonic first, maybe a nice mess of dandelion greens.

Everard sat up. The world tilted and swung. A light exploded behind his eyes, started a bright pinwheel spinning. He fell sideways, choking, his hands trying to tear away from his throat the heavy swelling, the lump, growing, pressing, so he couldn't get a breath.

What had waked him, what it was, that had sneaked up on him while he slept, made itself known. It should not have seemed unfamiliar, not to him, who all his life had seen it, many times held it in his hands—the new-dead duck, the bleeding squirrel, the beaver, the heron, the turtle; the thrush blown to shreds in the middle of its song. It was only that it was new to him; a little surprise, just for Everard.

"Yah, yah, yah," said the crow from the top of a nearby tree.

Epilogue

On the margins of the pond Amos Wilkinson made out of swamp land which had once been the oxbow of a running stream and had ceased to be when the Cooney boys decided that the way to get rid of manure was to dump it in the creek—Hell, you put it on the land, you get weeds, and weeds have to be pulled and that's work, and why bother when you can get just as good fertilizer out of a bag for half the trouble; the cussed stuff would float off somewhere in the spring freshet and be out of the way (only after a few years it didn't, it clogged the channel and the swamp plants grew in it like crazy)— on the margins of Amos's pond the miraculous process, interrupted, now resumed.

Shards and ashes of the burned farmhouse, bulldozed over, settled into earth, washed by rain, disturbed by frost, shone on by the sun. Fireweed took root there, in bombed-out cities called the "weed of sorrow"; it throve, thrust out a mass of purple blooms pleasant to bees and butterflies. Among char and burnt timber ends, and the rotting boles of smashed orchard trees, beetles lived, drilling secret tunnels, going peaceful ways; and under a flat, gray plank, which had once been a doorstep, a colony of ants made an anthill.

About the Author

Born and raised in the Maine fishing village of Gotts Island, Ruth Moore (1903–1989) emerged as one of the most important Maine authors of the twentieth century, best known for her authentic portrayals of Maine people and her evocative descriptions of the state. In her time, she was favorably compared to Faulkner, Steinbeck, Caldwell and O'Connor. She graduated from Albany State Teacher's College and worked at a variety of jobs in New York, Washington, D.C., and California, including as personal secretary to Mary White Ovington, a founder of the NAACP, and at *Reader's Digest*. Her debut novel in 1943, *The Weir* was hailed by critics and established Moore as novelist, but her second novel, *Spoonhandle* reached great success, spending fourteen weeks on *The New York Times* bestseller list and was made into the movie, *Deep Waters*. The success of *Spoonhandle* provided her with the financial security to build a house in Bass Harbor and spend the rest of her life writing novels in her home state. Ultimately, she wrote 14 novels. Moore and her partner, Eleanor Mayo, travelled extensively, but never again lived outside of Maine. Moore died in Bar Harbor in 1989.